Praise for Michael Bishop's
A FUNERAL FOR THE EYES OF FIRE

"Originally framed decades ago in a period when new writers were bringing the insights of the softer sciences of anthropology, sociology, psychology and the like to bear on the SF tropes of adventure in outer space, *A Funeral for the Eyes of Fire* reads as startlingly modern. It's sobering to realize how well the story fits our own age of economic crosscurrents and population upheavals, ideological resistance and fanaticism, and the venomous battles of evolving gender politics."
    —Suzy McKee Charnas, author of *The Vampire Tapestry*

"Michael Bishop is one of my favorite storytellers, and this edition of *A Funeral for the Eyes of a Fire* is his wholesale revision of his youthful first novel. So buy this book, take the battery out of the phone, curl up in your favorite chair, and spend a few hours in the company of a master."
    —David Gerrold, author of *The War Against the Chtorr*

"Eloquent . . . Michael Bishop brings to his work a poet's love of language and a profound understanding, wedding those gifts to an imagination that knows no bounds."
    —George R. R. Martin, author of *A Game of Thrones*

"Michael Bishop is a spectacular writer."
    —Vonda McIntyre, author *The Moon and the Sun*

"Being handed *A Funeral for the Eyes of Fire* after all these years is like receiving an old photograph and falling immediately into reverie. Could that captured moment possibly be as good as you remember? The answer, of course, is a resounding yes. Michael Bishop's debut novel shines bright in this Twenty-First Century edition from Fairwood Press."
    —Jack Skillingstead, author of *Are You There*

"Fine and rare . . . an impressive, fully realized achievement."
    —Norman Spinrad, author of *The Iron Dream*

"His best work to date . . . The world Trope and its people are etched on my mind in a series of vividly alien images. . . . the story fascinated me."
    —Joan D. Vinge, author of *The Snow Queen*

"*A Funeral for the Eyes of Fire* is Bishop's seventh novel, a brilliant rewriting of his first novel—not in any ordinary sense of 'rewriting,' but in the sense of composing a whole new symphony based on his original themes and motifs, augmented by fresh ones. And now, in a remodeled hall, so to speak, that symphony sounds again, with sharper melodies and subtler grace notes, for Bishop is the exotic, cunningly metaphysical anthropologist of SF, the sublime his destination. Which is another way of saying: Listen, Word Wizard at Work!"
    —Ian Watson, author of *The Flies of Memory*

"Michael Bishop's *A Funeral for the Eyes of Fire* dares to go where few novels do: straight into the heart of what it means to be human. Ostensibly a clash-of-cultures story in the tradition of the best anthropological fiction, *Funeral* conveys a sense of human possibilities through characters who are differently human, transhuman, barely human, and all-too human."
    —David Zindell, author of *Splendor*

Other Fairwood Press /
Kudzu Planet Productions novels
by Michael Bishop

Brittle Innings

Ancient of Days

Who Made Stevie Crye?

Count Geiger's Blues

A
FUNERAL
FOR THE
EYES OF
FIRE

A
FUNERAL
FOR THE
EYES OF
FIRE

MICHAEL BISHOP

KUDZU PLANET
· PRODUCTIONS ·
BONNEY LAKE WA

A FUNERAL FOR THE EYES OF FIRE

A Fairwood Press/Kudzu Planet Productions Book
May 2015

Copyright © 1975 by Michael Bishop
Afterword "First Novel, Seventh Novel" © 1989 by Michael Bishop,
but revised for this May 2015 edition
Introduction "A Phoenix Arises from the Funeral Fires" © 2015 by Paul Di Filippo

All Rights Reserved

No part of this book may be reproduced or transmitted in any form or
by any means, electronic or mechanical, including photocopying, recording,
or by any information storage and retrieval system, without
permission in writing from the publisher.

Fairwood Press
21528 104th Street Court East
Bonney Lake, WA   98391
www.fairwoodpress.com

First published 1975 by Ballantine Books
Published 1980 as *Eyes of Fire* by Pocket Books
First hardcover edition published 1989 by Kerosina Books

Cover & design by
Patrick Swenson

Book design by
Patrick Swenson

Kudzu Planet Productions
an imprint of Fairwood Press

ISBN13: 978-1-933846-49-1
First Fairwood/Kudzu Planet Productions Edition: May 2015
Printed in the United States of America

This edition is in memory of my mother,
Maxine Elaine Willis *(1920-2013).*
*

It is also for **Klaus Krause,**
proofreader par excellence *and long a faithful friend.*

A PHOENIX RISES
FROM THE FUNERAL FIRES:
An Introduction to Michael Bishop's Revised First Novel
by **Paul Di Filippo**

Well do I recall receiving the October-November 1970 issue of *Galaxy* magazine in the mail. I had only discovered SF prozines a couple of years earlier, with a gift subscription from my parents to *F&SF*. And so each issue of the two magazines impacted with fresh explosive power as it rocketed into my mailbox.

Of course, that issue of *Galaxy* contained "Piñon Fall," the tenderly astonishing debut by one Michael Bishop. It registered keenly, imprinting his byline firmly in mind, and I took much enjoyment in his short-story output over the next several years, particularly a run of great tales in *F&SF*. Around this same time, Mike also became a part of Don D'Ammassa's legendary fanzine *Mythologies*, in whose pages I also appeared, and so we had an extra-literary connection and friendship as well.

Then in 1975 appeared something wonderful and much anticipated: a Ballantine Books paperback original, Michael's first novel, *A Funeral for the Eyes of Fire*. As an impecunious college student, my budget for books was extremely limited, but I made sure to scrape together the $1.50 necessary to snatch it off the bookstore shelves, with its gorgeously lurid cover by Gene Szafran. (That volume is still in my collection today, natch.)

I recall reading the book in a gulp and enjoying it immensely, even discussing it with local fans. But now, forty years on (can that incredible interval be veridical!?!), I find I retained little of the specifics of the story, other than the potent image of its jewel-eyed aliens. And so when I was offered the chance to get reacquainted with this book and share some thoughts on its new edition, I leapt at the opportunity to meet up again with an old friend from distant times.

But the exercise was not one entirely or even mostly composed of nostalgia. I am happy to report that I found a novel which, were it to be issued as the debut book by a hot young writer in 2015—and please recall that Novice Michael Bishop was all of thirty years old in 1975—would be hailed as utterly hip and state-of-the-art SF, wrought with immense skill and compassion and wit. (As Mike reveals in his generous and fascinating "Afterword," the text we see today has been majorly modified from that first printing, but not, I believe, so drastically as to utterly erase or even minimize the inspired words of his youthful avatar.)

What are some of the salient, particularly stefnal attractions of this novel? Let's start with the brilliant setup. Our protagonist, Seth Latimer, is the clone of a dead man, one of two such clones in fact, and relegated to almost servant status in the uncanny familial menagerie. Right away we have a potent character, one who operates from the fascinating outsider underbelly of society and status. His perceptions are bound to be piercingly skewed. Then, to add to the allure of the scenario, he's trapped on an alien planet, Gla Taus, a world whose strange culture is detailed at entrancing length by Bishop, in the "thick anthropology" manner he became famous for, replete with alien myths and history, in a mode derived in part from the lessons taught by the novels of Le Guin.

Next, Seth is promised his freedom and return passage to Earth if only he undertakes a diplomatic mission to a second alien world, Trope, which proves to be even more bizarre in its denizens and their beliefs and ways than Gla Taus. Now, I put it to you that most fledgling writers would have been content trying to capture only one invented world, a place inhabited by an Everyman protagonist of lesser oddity, in deference to the famously conservative C. S. Lewis quote about "strange world plus strange hero amounting to one strangeness too many." And in fact Gardner Dozois's comparable first solo novel from this same period, *Strangers* (1978), took just such a strategy. But Bishop, in a high-wire act so essential to the best SF, boldly piles on the weirdness and skillfully manages to make us savor every tasty morsel in his banquet of strange flavors, without indigestion.

Having arranged this elaborate setup, Bishop goes on to deliver a story rich in ethical, political, religious and psychosexual conundrums, a gripping tale whose outcome is never predictable and whose emotional and intellectual ripples continue to spread beyond the final indeterminately unfixed page. The book succeeds in mapping its many exotic happenings onto our contemporary world—or vice versa—without being ham-handed or preachy. That's the essence of fine science fiction, by my lights. And right out of the gate for its author, despite subsequent modifications!

Mike cites many influences from the period of the book's composition: Ballard, Ellison, Delany, Zelazny. I'd add two more: Jack Vance and Robert Silverberg. Bishop's word portraits of his aliens and their geographical venues bring to my mind such classics as Vance's "The Moon Moth" or *The*

Last Castle. And Seth's immersion in the Tropiard *Weltanschauung* harks to Silverberg's classic *Downward to the Earth.*

As far as casting its influence forward, I think that this book occupies a seminal place in the canon. Without its model, I doubt the novels of C. J. Cherryh, Octavia Butler, or Joan Slonczewski would read quite as they do. Michael Bishop truly showed us how to inhabit alien cultures both from the inside out and the outside in. Anyone dealing with such themes today owes him a debt, even if they have received his influence only through a chain of other writers.

Having this polychromatic, stunning, shocking, and absorbing tale back in print today is a major victory for readers and scholars alike. The passage of forty years has not dimmed these eyes of fire.

—November 2014
Providence, Rhode Island

Paul Di Filippo published his first story in 1977. Since then, he has produced over two-hundred more. Collected, many of his stories, along with his stand-alone novels and novellas, constitute a published canon of some thirty books. These include, among others, *The Steampunk Trilogy* (1995); *Ribofunk* (1996); *Fractal Paisleys and Cyphers* (both 1997); *Lost Pages* (1998); *Joe's Liver* (2000); *Little Doors, A Mouthful of Tongues, Babylon Sisters,* and *A Year in the Linear City* (all 2002); *Fuzzy Dice* (2003); *Neutrino Drag* (2004); *The Emperor of Gondwanaland* (2005); *Shuteye for the Timebroker* (2006); *Roadside Bodhisattva* (2010); *After the Collapse* (2011); and *WikiWorld* (2013). Despite all actuarial stats, he hopes he is at the midpoint of his career. He lives in Providence, Rhode Island, with Deborah Newton and the ghost of H. P. Lovecraft.

CHARACTERS

Humans

Abel Latimer, isoget of Günter Latimer, lately slain
Seth Latimer, his isohet
K/R Caranicas, pilot of the *Dharmakaya*, an Ommundi Trade Company
    light-tripper

Jauddeb

Lady Turshebsel, Liege Mistress of Kier on Gla Taus
Porchaddos Pors, Point Marcher of Feln, Kier's Winter Capital
Narthaimnar Chappouib, aisautseb, or patriot-priest, advisor to Lady
    Turshebsel
Clefrabbes Douin, advisor to Lady Turshebsel and Kieri man-of-letters
An aisautseb (patriot-priest), assigned by Lady Turshebsel to the
    Dharmakaya

Various Kieri shopkeepers, **aisautseb** (patriot-priests), soldiers, servants,
taussanaur (orbital guards), etc.

Gosfi

Ulgraji Vrai, Sixth Magistrate of Trope, political heir of Seitaba Mwezahbe,
    founder of the state of Trope
Ehte Emahpre, his Administrative Deputy
Commander Swodi, leader of the Palija Kadi surveillance force
Captain Yithuju, driver of the lead vehicle of the evacuation convoy

The Pledgechild, sh'gosfi heir of the departed Holy One, Duagahvi Gaidu
Lijadu, her heir, fleshchild of Ifragsli, recently deceased
Huspre, attendant of and advisor to the Pledgechild; a midwife
Tantai, attendant of the Pledgechild
Omwhol, a child, recently appointed keeper of the gocodre

Various j'gosfi guides, administrative workers, surveillance-force personnel,
etc., along with various sh'gosfi elders (midwives), laborers, children, etc.

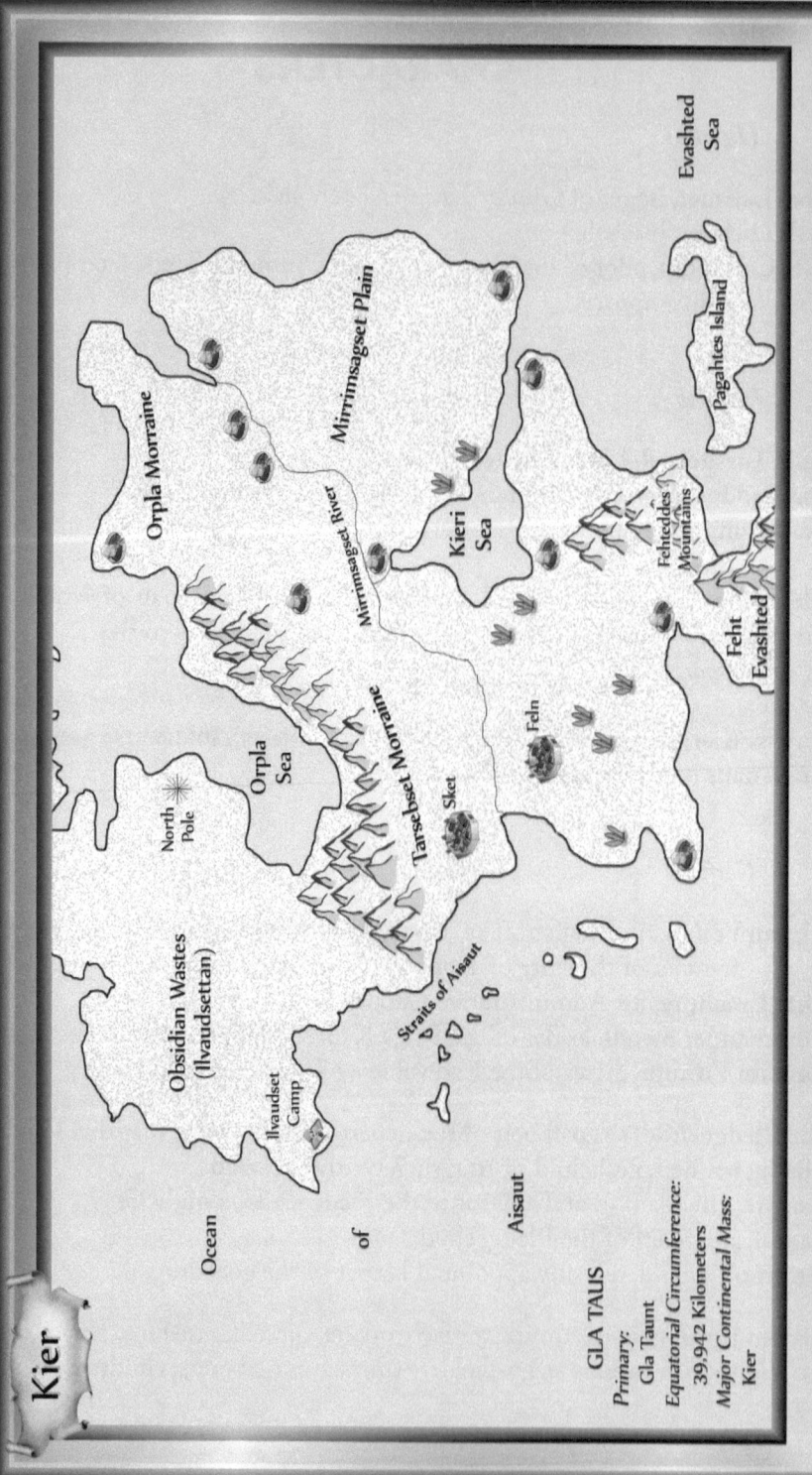

Kier

Ocean

of

Aisaut

North Pole

Obsidian Wastes
(Ilvaudsettan)

Ilvaudset Camp

Orpla Sea

Orpla Morraine

Mirrimsagset Plain

Mirrimsagset River

Tarsebset Morraine

Straits of Aisaut

Sket

Feln

Kieri Sea

Fehteddes Mountains

Feht Evashted

Pagahtes Island

Evashted Sea

GLA TAUS
Primary:
Gla Taunt
Equatorial Circumference:
39,942 Kilometers
Major Continental Mass:
Kier

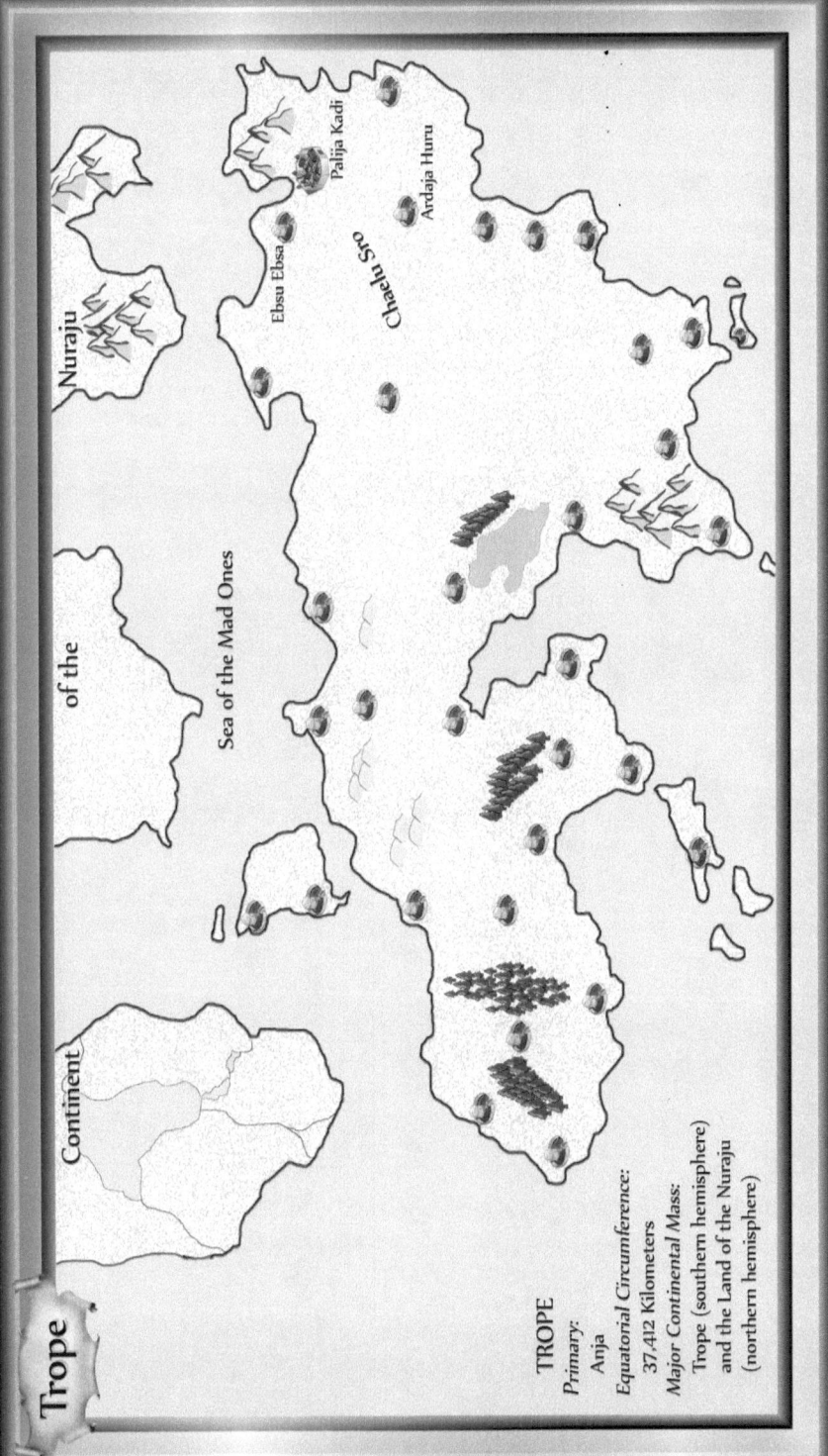

Trope

Nuraju

of the

Continent

Sea of the Mad Ones

Ebsu Ebsa

Palija Kadi

Chaelu Sro

Ardaja Huru

TROPE
Primary: Anja
Equatorial Circumference: 37,412 Kilometers
Major Continental Mass: Trope (southern hemisphere) and the Land of the Nuraju (northern hemisphere)

A
FUNERAL
FOR THE
EYES OF
FIRE

PROLOGUE

Long ago there was a jongleur-thief in Kier, before Kier was yet a nation, and the name of the jongleur-thief was Jaud. Gla Taus, The World, was new in those days, only lately formed from the primordial slag, and in every situation in this new world Jaud acted out of the selfish center of himself. This was not unusual, for in the beginning the world was without law and the people had no word for conscience.

Jaud's disposition was merry and cruel at once, and he chose to live by stealing. After each theft he whirled before his victim and deftly juggled the items he had stolen: rings, bracelets, coins, seashells, beads, digging tools, and even weapons. Often his victims applauded these performances. Only rarely did the aggrieved Gla Tausian try to recover his belongings, for Jaud was impatient of those who interfered with his juggling, and throughout the land his deadliness with knife and hand ax was well known.

In the infancy of Gla Taus, Jaud honored only Jaud and a few fellow thieves who served as his disciples and retainers, having recognized in him a sorcerer of chicanery and bloodthirstiness. For untold years, the Thieves of Jaud preyed upon the people of Kier before Kier was a nation. They made themselves a bastion in the Orpla Mountains, from which they undertook forays of theft, jugglery, and slaughter.

But as time passed, people drew together against the indifference of Gla Taus and the cruelty of Jaud. From these first feeble bands tribes arose, and from the tribes chiefdoms, and from the chiefdoms primitive states, and from the primitive states a nation that called itself Kier. Kier exercised dominion through the authority of the first Prime Liege, whom everyone knew as Shobbes or Law. Only Jaud and his fellow jongleur-thieves failed to acknowledge the preeminence of Law, for they were free spirits obeying no statutes but those written in the runes of their blood. How could they know that the superstitious taboos of the first bands had become the inhibitory customs of the tribes? That the customs had become ordinances, and that finally Shobbes had had these ordinances codified in writing?

In truth, Jaud and his family of cutpurses, clowns, and cutthroats did not know. Not until a contingent of Kieri soldiers captured one of their number after the fellow had robbed and slain an innocent citizen of a village on the Mirrimsagset Plain. For instead of ordering the beheading of the outlaw, Shobbes sent him back to the Orpla Mountains with this message: "Jaud, Shobbes has told me to say that at last the taboos, the customs, the rules, and the ordinances have become the Commandments of Law. And Law declares that no Kieri may steal from another or commit murder. Not even Jaud stands outside these Commandments. Shobbes demands that your thieving, juggling, and killing instantly cease." The messenger bowed low before his lord, and Jaud struck off his head.

"It is not in the blood for us to follow Law!" Jaud raged. "Therefore, I ordain—not with my own voice, but with that of our singing marrow—that we shall continue to thieve, juggle, and slay! So be it always!" Shortly after Jaud delivered this impassioned speech, he journeyed alone out of the Orpla Mountains and down the Tarsebset Moraine to Sket, the summer capital of Kier.

Full of bravado and curiosity, he had determined to breach the fortifications of the Summer Palace and behold the upstart Prime Liege whose name and word were equally law. By stealth and cunning Jaud got past the outer wall of Sket and into the buttressed chamber of the sovereign's throne room. Soon he would meet Shobbes face to face.

A noise halted Jaud dead still. A host of helmeted guards set upon him. Although he struggled like ten Kieri and slew one of his attackers, Jaud was eventually overcome and delivered to Shobbes in halt-chains and wrist-irons.

Shobbes, Law, was an aged gentlewoman wearing starched black skirts and a black overtunic. Her mien was gracious and refined, her voice pedantic and precise. Never before in his life had Jaud seen or heard anyone like her. "You are banished to the Obsidian Wastes," Shobbes told Jaud with no-nonsense authority. "You may not return until you find Aisaut, Conscience, in his dwelling there and bow before him in sincere obeisance as his vassal. Only then may you know again the company of civil, scruple-inhibited beings."

Northward along the Kieri coast, in High Summer, an ice barge carried Jaud into exile. At Ilvaudset Camp he was put ashore and abandoned to his sentence. Facing inland toward the pole, Jaud saw beneath the half-frozen ground cover irregular veins of the extrusive black glass that gave the Obsidian Wastes their name. How would he survive the decree of Law and find amid such desolation the hidden dwelling of Conscience? The bigness of his task both appalled and invigorated him, and he departed Ilvaudset Camp and its small garrison of Kieri soldiers in an odd humor of elation and self-doubt.

For seventy days and seventy nights Jaud trekked into the hardening wilderness of the Wastes. He did not eat, drink, or sleep. At the end of the seventieth night he came upon the Escarpments of Aisaut, a maze of towering obsidian walls and interconnecting canyons of glass which none but the innocent or the penitential could traverse with ease. Jaud was neither, but he entered the daunting labyrinth and for seven more days and nights wandered through it in search of Conscience. On the morning of the seventy-eighth day he approached a wall of dizzying height and perdurable finality and could go no farther. Looking back, he saw not one opening into this compartment of the labyrinth but seven, and he could not find the one by which he had come to his destination. How would he ever return to Kier and the Orpla Mountains? Jaud gazed again upon the final wall, thinking that now, after all the merriment and bloodshed he had known, it would perhaps be sweet to die.

But a voice called out, "Jaud, you may not die until you have confronted me and sworn your allegiance!"

Although these words had the ring and tenor of authority, the voice conveying them sounded thin and distant. Jaud, both perplexed and irritated, looked for the invisible crier.

"Approach me, Jaud! Come toward me!"

"Where?" Jaud shouted.

"Here in my prison of glass, child!"

Jaud did not like being called child, but he approached the towering cliff face and peered into it like one looking for flaws in a jewel. "Who are you?" he asked the thing moving sluggishly within the glass. "What do you want of me?" He pressed his face and hands against the obsidian. The piercing light of three high morning stars revealed that the crier in the rock was none other than a second Jaud.

But this Jaud was dressed in starched black skirts and a seamless black overtunic embroidered with threads of a darker black, and Jaud was amazed to see that his double had no hands, only stumps that he moved back and forth through the channels he had worn in the glass.

"I am not your second self," the creature said. "I am the half you denied. Shobbes has sent you to reclaim that half by bending before me and asking pardon for your crimes."

"You are Aisaut, then?"

"Yes, I am Conscience, Jaud, and you must let me rule."

"But you are not the half I have denied, Aisaut. I've denied no half at all. I am whole without you and always have been."

"Shobbes decrees you outlaw, and unfulfilled. We were born when Gla Taus took shape from the matter of creation, but the lava flows of that anarchic time captured me in their searing floods and swept me into this great prison of obsidian. You—more fortunate than I—awoke in the Orpla Mountains, faulb blossoms dancing red and orange upon the hillsides and a paean of self-celebration coursing in your veins.

"All that has kept the Kieri from destroying themselves during my imprisonment here and your mad profligacy in the world is the fact that I took a precaution. Before the lava entrapped me, Jaud, I bit off my hands and summoned a pair of hawks to carry them southward into Kier. These brave birds dropped a bleeding finger at every place where people might have a chance to thrive, and my fingers pushed up through the earth in the shapes of great-boled mirrim trees. By every tree a village also grew, and when the villages merged each with each in the Mirrimsagset Alliance, Shobbes at last had a nation over which she might beneficially rule. She called it Kier. So I am cofounder of your country."

"Over the Thieves of Jaud neither Shobbes nor Aisaut rules," Jaud scoffed. "Law has sent me here, but she owns neither my followers nor my heart."

"That's because my absence is felt," Conscience replied. "The nation of ten villages has grown beyond the ken of Shobbes, and, to your own and the Kieri's coming sorrow, you have ignored her suzerainty from the beginning."

"What would you have me do?"

"Release me from the rock. Let me lead you home."

Jaud laughed. "Aisaut, you are wrong. I have never felt your absence. And by sacrificing your hands to found the state, you became less complete than I."

"Law demands that you release me."

"Where is Law, Conscience?" said Jaud, turning about. "I do not see her here. Nor any of her vassals, either."

"The Obsidian Wastes are still untamed," the creature in the wall admitted. "But one day the Kieri will come to subdue them. Already there is a garrison at Ilvaudset Camp. With these soldiers and pioneers will come the Commandments of Law, in full and magnificent panoply."

"Why, then, must I let you go?"

"You must do me homage if you wish to see Kier again."

"My mind brims with memories of the Orpla Mountains, which may be enough. Perhaps I no longer desire to return."

The thing in the wall shifted uneasily.

"Further, Conscience, I am far older than you, for the Kieri recall in legends the upheavals that shaped the Obsidian Wastes. Of my birth, however, they have no record of any kind."

Aisaut protested, "I am as old as you."

"Not so," Jaud told his despairing image. "But lacking hands and trapped in this wall, you are more helpless than I."

"What will you do, then?"

"Await the arrival of those who come to tame the Obsidian Wastes. As in the old days out of Orpla, I will fall upon them as a thief. Any who resist I will murder before your eyes, even as you cry 'Stay!' and impotently behold my deeds."

"Law prohibits these enormities, Jaud!"

Jaud glanced showily about. "Where is Law, Conscience?"

"She will come! Mind you, she will come!"

But Jaud turned his back on the creature, and Conscience knew that Jaud's true name was something else. The jongleur-thief had fallen into Shobbes's hands too late to alter his nature, and Aisaut could gain no hold on his heart or his intellect. The future, at least in the Obsidian Wastes, would unfold exactly as Jaud had prophesied: Conscience, crying out "Stay!" as he struggled to free himself, would witness both the banditry and the bloodshed.

And would weep because he could not intervene.

—*A Cultural Sourcebook: Myths, Legends, and Folk Tales of the Kieri*
Retold in Vox by Clefrabbes Douin, Minister-at-Feln, 6209 G

BOOK ONE

BOOK ONE

ONE

"Why, you callow couchling, wake up! Seth, wake up!"

Seth roused slowly, recasting his brother Abel's idiomatic Kieri first into Vox, the established galactic tongue, and then into their native Langlish, which they had avoided speaking together for several Gla Tausian months. But, in Seth's grogginess, every word drifted athwart his understanding, and sleep held him like a womb.

Abel's hand tugged his forelock. "Damn it, Seth, it's three hours to sunfall! Get up! The Liege Mistress of Kier, and thus of all Gla Taus, wishes to see you!"

To awake is to be reborn. Seth felt like an infant hoisted into the air by its heels and slapped loudly on the bum. Such a sensation defied memory, for it lay outside Seth's experience. The little parturitions of ten thousand earlier awakenings, however, had given him a vivid, if numbing, analogue of the shock attendant upon live birth, and a galvanizing dread told him that it was to chaos and uncertainty that Abel was delivering him. Bolting upright, Seth struck aside his elder isohet's hand.

"Damnation, Seth!" Abel histrionically shook his wounded hand. "What's the matter with you?"

Seth regarded Abel with the same fear and grudging admiration that had marked his relationship with Günter Latimer, the slain Ommundi mercantile representative to Gla Taus. Latimer, although two weeks dead, was preserved genetically in the persons of his "sons." Seth and Abel were isohets—as clones of disparate age were called both on the Earth of the Ommundi Trade Company and elsewhere throughout the range of Interstel where Vox

was spoken—and Günter Latimer, a man of towering commercial ambi-
tion, spotty charisma, and a convincing humility in the presence of "quasi-
humans," had been their common biological template, their isosire—if not,
in fact, their "father." In any case, Latimer's genes lived in the persons of his
isohet Doppelgangers stranded in Feln, the winter capital of Kier. Abel had
been twenty-eight years the dead man's junior, and Seth, at twenty-one, was
fourteen Earth-standard years younger than Abel.

"I'm not responsible for what I do in the first full minute of awakening,"
Seth managed. "That's a period of legal insanity." He was disoriented. His
head hurt.

Abel, portly at thirty-five, continued trying to shake the smart out of his
hand. He seemed a blowsy distortion of their isosire, Günter Latimer.

What a hideous end the old man had come to. A host of angry aisautseb,
or patriot-priests, had caught Latimer outside Feln's Winter Palace, stripped
him naked, and hauled him by the heel up the southern face of the Kieri
Obelisk in Mirrimsagset Square. Palace security had not intervened, and by
the time the turreted copperclads from Pedgor Garrison arrived to disperse
the crowd, Latimer's body was spiculed with glass darts from the rioters' ceramic blowguns, weapons they wore like necklaces and whose ancient Kieri
name meant "demon killer." But even violated to this degree in death, old
Latimer had retained an aura of dignity alien to Abel. Abel could not mus-
ter a comparable presence even in parade-dress attire and formal mourning
cap—the attire, Seth recalled, that his isohet and he had worn to the long
state funeral directed by Master Douin, their host. Jauddeb, like human beings, appreciated ritual.

"While you lie sleeping," Abel said, "I plan our future, consulting with
Kieri high and intermediate. And when I come to report that my work has
secured us an audience with the Liege Mistress, you greet me thus? *Damnation*, Seth!"

Seth ignored Abel's wheedling tone, for he could be an unpredictable,
sometimes even treacherous man. In his lumbering way, before Latimer's
death, Abel had proved an effective stand-in negotiator with the Kieri. Seth,
on the other hand, had remained by his isosire's and his isohet's joint decree
in the background, a son to the one and alternately a little brother and a
sexual object to the other. Toddler and concubine, Seth resented the suppression of his innate talents and despised himself in the person of Abel,
that grotesque caricature of his own face and figure. Simultaneously, Seth

feared being cut adrift from the only human being who had ever made, or been forced to make, a long-term commitment to him. Günter Latimer had merely called Seth into existence; Abel had raised him like a natural parent.

"The question is whether we'll live as exiles in Kier or as freegoers among the nations of the Ommundi Company on Earth," said Abel, shifting into Langlish for the first time that winter. "Do you want to spend your whole life on Gla Taus, shuttling back and forth between Feln and Sket with the monkeys of the Kieri court? Or would you like to see Lausanne again and live among real human beings?"

"The Kieri seem as human as you or I," Seth said in Langlish.

"Because they're born? Polecats and ratlings descend through a uterus. Birth is a negligible criterion for the assignment of humanity, Seth. The Kieri are jauddeb, not human. Just because—"

"All right. All right."

Abel continued his assault: "Take your pick, Seth. Remain on Gla Taus or return with me to Earth."

"The latter, of course."

"That demands that we cooperate with Lady Turshebsel, the Liege Mistress. Also with her uppity Point Marcher and the well-meaning Master Douin. I've bent myself to that end ever since Günter's murder. We have no ship. We're at the mercy of the quaz."

"Why do you use that shabby epithet?"

"Quaz?" said Abel. "No one here understands Langlish. No need to worry. And what better term for our isosire's assassins? The memory sickens me."

Several successive nights since the aisautseb attack, Abel had awakened sweating ice water and trembling. Only after vomiting in the stone urinal in the lavalet of Master Douin's Ilsotsa Era home could Abel return to sleep. And, clutching Seth to him atop their sour-smelling quilts, he slept fitfully. These had been the only times in the past year, not counting perfunctory bouts of "love making," that Seth had felt even remotely necessary to his isohet. He was grateful to Abel for his vulnerability—which, however, was not a sentiment he could voice aloud.

Instead, he asked, "Will the Kieri let us go home aboard the *Dharmakaya*?"

"That depends on you."

"Nothing depends on me, Abel."

"This does. We have an audience with Lady Turshebsel in half an hour. If you give a good accounting of yourself, we may yet get home."

"A good accounting? What do you want me to do?"

"Answer her questions."

"Is that all?"

"And the questions of both Porchaddos Pors, her Point Marcher, and Clefrabbes Douin, who is kindly disposed toward you."

"Questions about what?"

"About the mission we'll undertake to earn our passage home, even if we must earn it aboard a vessel already ours. Be yourself, Seth. That will bring us through."

The *Dharmakaya*, whose Mahayana Buddhist monicker derived from Günter Latimer's only wife's fascination with Eastern mysticism, was the ship by which all three men had come to Gla Taus. It was a light-tripper, a vessel of more than five hundred Earth-bound metric tons, and it belonged to the Langlish Division of the Ommundi Trade Company. At this very moment, it hovered in synchronous orbit six hundred kilometers above Feln, the winter capital. Two days after Latimer's murder, the Liege Mistress, urged on by the increasingly vocal aisautseb, had revoked the formal trade agreement with Ommundi and seized the *Dharmakaya* for the Kieri state. Its seizure, Master Douin had apologetically told Abel and Seth, was in recompense for the violence done Gla Tausian spirituality by the elder Latimer's desire to open up to cultivation and animal husbandry the forbidden territories in the evil southern ocean. That Lady Turshebsel herself had championed this project until the aisautseb uprising merely demonstrated the mutability of Kieri politics.

Seth swung his feet to the floor, knocking to the carpeted flagstones the reader with which he had fallen asleep. Abel picked it up and examined its casing.

"What were you reading?"

"Myths, Legends, and Folk Tales of the Kieri," Seth replied. "Master Douin gave me the download this morning."

"And how did you find these little jauddeb histories?"

"The story of Aisaut's release from the Ilvaudsettan labyrinths put me to sleep."

Abel laughed. "I can see that it did."

"That and the motion of the draperies," Seth hurried to add. "And the comfort of this couch. And my own fatigue and distraction."

"You protest too much. Come on, then. The author of this soporific masterwork awaits us without."

*

Clefrabbes Douin—advisor, diplomat, man of letters—sat on a stone bench in his ancient house's *laulset,* or pool court, staring into the roiling, reddish water. Most of the power generated for home and industrial use in Kier was geothermal, and the households of powerful or wealthy citizens were often distinguished by the laulset. The central feature of the pool court was a natural hot spring circled by colorful ceramic tiles and equipped with hand rails and submerged stone steps to facilitate bathing.

During the long winter just past, Günter Latimer and his isohets had bathed often with the Clefrabbes *geffide,* which consisted of Master Douin, his two wives, an elderly female parent, and five young children. Seth had come to conclude, on anatomical as well as metaphysical and sociological evidence, that the jauddeb were *approximately* human. Moreover, he liked Master Douin's geffide, as a unit and as individuals. How could Abel call them quaz?

Douin rose to greet his guests when they entered the laulset, and Abel asked about conditions in the streets—whether they could safely venture out again.

"There's been no danger in Feln since Lady Turshebsel claimed your ship," Douin said in Kieri. "Did you feel unsafe during your earlier outing to the palace, Master Abel?"

"Not in the palace itself, but in the streets—"

"You were perfectly fine, despite your fears. That's another reason we seized the *Dharmakaya:* a sop to the aisautseb. It's imperative to placate so powerful a force with the people."

Douin turned to Seth. "Good afternoon. Come, Master Seth. We'll be late for our audience with the Liege Mistress." He led them toward a door opening on Mirrimsagset Square.

The Clefrabbes geffide—the term implied the physical structure of the house as well as the family within it—stood on the southeast corner of this great square; and, from a window in Douin's third-story library, Seth and Abel had witnessed the last act of their isosire's martyrdom and the cutting down of his body from the obelisk. Seth had not been outside the geffide since the state funeral, and until this morning Abel had hazarded trips to the Winter Palace only after sunfall or in the dim hours before the dawn songs of the patriot-priests. Now Abel was venturing forth for the second time that day, again in sunlight, and Seth was undergoing a kind of baptism of his own. His heart fluttered in his breast like a trapped bird.

Pedalshaws and motorized carts cruised through the immaculate square, but most of Feln's citizenry went afoot.

Near the obelisk, an aisautseb sold tinfoil prayer-and-proclamation balloons. These he inflated with lighter-than-air gas from a tank on wheels. He then decorated the balloons in elegant Kieri script with religious or patriotic squibs. The stylus he used looked vaguely like a weapon, and his patrons were adults rather than children. Instead of walking merrily off with their purchases, these people found shop railings or bench backs or pedalshaws to which to tie their balloons—so that their prayers or proclamations might soar aloft on whatever they had been able to afford. Sunlight ricocheted off the tinfoil balloons, whose messages revolved against a backdrop of unceasing mercantile activity. High above the square, tethered to the Kieri Obelisk itself, drifted a huge hot-air balloon whose message was patched against its off-white bulk in velvety black letters as tall as any adult jauddeb.

"What does that one say?" Seth asked Douin. Although Abel and he could speak Kieri, they still could not read its fluid written characters.

Douin replied, "*God is the foremost patriot, for the land is holy.*"

"It's a veiled allusion to the presence of offworlders on Gla Taus," Abel told Seth as they strolled northward toward the pool of the Shobbes Geyser and the stone-and-ceramic façade of the Winter Palace.

"Nothing of the kind," said Douin, without rancor. "It's an expression of belief—pure, if not altogether simple."

"But it wasn't there before the murder," Abel said.

"Then let's simply note that the proposals of Ommundi Company have led to a resurgence of religio-patriotic fervor in Feln. Even so, Master Abel, the proclamation on the obelisk balloon is a traditional one."

"And those on the smaller balloons?" Seth asked.

"Prayers, market slogans, warnings, even witticisms. The sale of the balloons is an aisautseb monopoly, and their customers, by buying the balloons, are exercising their rights to creative expression and free speech."

"Do the customers make up the slogans, then?"

"Many do, yes. Of course, Master Seth, the aisautseb may veto any message he doesn't care for and refuse to sell the balloon. It's customary, though, to pay him before announcing the slogan you wish written."

"Ha," said Abel, pointedly.

"Translate that one," Seth said, pointing to a balloon jiggling from the awning of a nearby bakery.

Douin halted, cocked his head to one side, and read, *"Beware such demons as would drag us back to Hell."*

"Meaning us?" said Abel.

"Yes, I'd suppose so," admitted Douin. "But let me comfort you by pointing out that this is also a ritual warning of some antiquity. Its pertinence to you, if any, may be accidental."

"I doubt that," Abel said.

"As do I," said the affable Kieri.

When they resumed walking, shouldering through a crowd devoid of deference for Douin's ministerial skirts and leather cap, Seth noticed that almost everyone in the streets was wearing a "demon killer" about his or her neck. Some of these lethal ceramic flutes hung straight down, while others lay crosswise like tubular gorgets. *Dairauddes,* the Kieri called them. And the small glass darts that these instruments propelled the people wore on combs in their hair, or as pins in their clothing, or even as ornaments on bracelets and boot tassels. Since everyone was armed, including the patriot-priest near the obelisk, Seth took scant comfort from his knowledge that a single *thet,* or glass dart, was seldom sufficient to kill. Too, Seth had gradually become aware of the attention that Abel and he were attracting: long, sneering stares and snatches of angry talk in bistro and market-stall doorways.

As they edged past one shop, a woman weighing a handful of tubers in a scale shouted, "Go back to Hell!"

To show that Abel and Seth were under his protection, Douin passed an arm over the isohets' heads; and the woman, thus rebuked, turned mute and mottle-faced back into the fusty darkness of her produce cove. But she had spoken her mind where others had held their tongues.

Hell, Seth knew, was all of Gla Taus south of Kier, which was country, continent, and world. Hell constituted especially those equatorial and sub-equatorial regions—the Evashsteddan—where for ages a terrible volcanism had held sway in the great hemispherical ocean called the Evashsted Sea. The islands scattered throughout this sea the Kieri regarded, quite literally, as stepping stones to damnation. In the mythical prehistoric past of Gla Taus, according to accepted aisautseb lore, God had deserted the Evash-steddan, and anyone who left Kier to explore the southern ocean and its smoldering archipelagoes thereby forfeited his soul.

This belief, Günter Latimer had told his isohets, appeared to stem from a strange complex of causes: an ancient war or natural upheaval that had displaced early Gla Tausian peoples towards the north, the continuing volcanism in the Evashsteddan, the eerie variety of sea- and island-going life forms in the south, and the inability of present-day Kieri to tolerate temperatures much above 17°C. This last was one crucial respect in which jauddeb differed fundamentally from human beings; and when Lady Turshebsel had made known that she and Günter Latimer had concluded a long-in-the-formulation agreement whereby Ommundi representatives would exploit the untapped resources of the Evashsteddan, the patriot-priests had called upon believers to make their outrage known. Few in Kier were not believers, and the principal mistake of the Liege Mistress's advisors—Porchaddos Pors and Clefrabbes Douin among them—lay in their failing to foresee the likely reaction of the Kieri to such a public announcement. The aisautseb, sluggishly complacent through nearly four decades of Lady Turshebsel's rule, had leaped awake, and the citizenry had leaped after.

For these reasons, then, Günter Latimer had died.

He was a demon, and his spawn were demons, and religious patriotism was the order of the day.

Seth watched a shopkeeper finger his dairauddes.

How disturbing that the people of Kier regarded Abel and him as something far worse than quaz, as soulless beings who sullied the holiness of their country. Although Seth half expected Douin to rebuke this ugly jauddeb, as he had done the woman at the scales, Douin fixed his eyes on the Winter Palace and led Abel and Seth upward from the square as if escorting them to a gallows.

TWO

At the palace's outer gate a pair of sentries from Pedgor Garrison halted the three men and took their names, even though Clefrabbes Douin was far from a nonentity in Feln, even though Abel and Seth were recognizable as living if imperfect mirrors of the dead Latimer.

Seth stared past the guards.

Beyond the gateway: a pool outlined by tiles and pinched about its circumference with immersion nooks. In these nooks, pilgrims could give themselves to the waters of Shobbes. Today, however, the inner court was empty, and the tiled façade of the palace reflected the face of the pool as the pool reflected that of the palace.

"You must wait for Shobbes to admit you," said one of the guards. He and his companion wore leather pants and vests. Carrying mech-rifles, they radiated a hostility that seemed to encompass even Douin.

"It was like this this morning, too," Abel told Seth. "Before the aisautseb uprising, you could walk in whenever you wished, so long as you had an invitation. But now, as in the old days, you must wait for the blessing of Shobbes."

The geyser in the pool, Seth knew, had a regular interval, but he had forgotten what it was. How long would they have to stand in the shadow of the stone-and-ceramic palace before certification came? The guards blocking their way and the Kieri in the teeming square below them made Seth equally nervous. He was caught, with his isohet, between Scylla and Charybdis.

At last Shobbes Geyser blew. The eruption was presaged by a churning in the pool and then an audible bubbling—whereupon the surface seemed to peel back and a pillar of reddish water shot upward, fanning out like a peacock's tail as it climbed. Although the continuous plashing of the geyser made talk impossible, its eruption lasted scarcely a minute and soon a guard was able to say:

"Now you may pass."

Seth was startled by the *warmth* of the drops that had misted down on him. The eruption had been too well foretokened to surprise him. But as Douin led them through the gate, Seth could still see—in his mind's eye—the central plume dancing eighteen or twenty meters in the air.

It was a long way—over the wet mosaics surrounding the pool, then across an apron of enormous flagstones—to the palace entrance, and only when they were well beyond the hearing of the guards did Douin speak:

"Master Seth, did you see Aisaut in the geyser?"

"Aisaut?"

"A man of conscience should see the image of Aisaut projected against the palace through the geyser's dancing. I was wondering if you saw such a thing. I know better than to ask your isohet."

"I saw only water," Seth said. He looked at Abel. The expression on Abel's face was quick with apprehension and disgust. It seemed to say, *Haven't you the sense to give your host the answer he wants to hear?*

"Nothing else?"

"No, sir. Only water and sunlight and tiles."

Douin's eyes were cryptically merry. "That's all I ever see," he said. "In twenty-three years, that's all I've ever seen." He led the isohets up a final set of steps and into the Winter Palace.

Despite its ancient façade—the building supposedly dated to the early days of the legendary Inhodlef Era—the palace was luxuriously appointed within and almost shamefully comfortable. As in Master Douin's geffide, the interior flagstone flooring was carpeted with a synthetic fabric both durable and eye-pleasing. Here, however, the carpet's nap was iridescent, dyed cobalt and crimson in an immense cartographic pattern representing the world.

Seth, who had stood in this anteroom once before, waiting for Latimer to return from an audience with the Liege Mistress, distinctly remembered that on that occasion the pattern in the carpet had depicted stylized figures thieving and juggling—a portrait of people rather than a graph of the globe.

"Lady Turshebsel has changed the decor," Seth whispered. For Douin's benefit, he nodded meaningfully at the carpet.

Douin was briefly puzzled, then finally comprehending. "Oh, no," he said. "It's the same carpet, Master Seth, but a different alignment of its nap. It has four separate designs, this carpet, depending on the direction in which its fibers are brushed. Master Günter was very interested in the process."

Abel said, "I prefer walking across it to talking about it."

"Very good," Douin replied. He indicated a tilework archway farther on and led them toward it. There was a sound of gently lapping water from the higher chamber just ahead.

Seth had never set eyes on Lady Turshebsel, Liege Mistress of Kier. He knew that her people considered her the rightful inheritor of the geffide that was their nation, even though she had won her place not through descent from any previous ruler but instead from the happenstance of a lottery conducted by the aisautseb on the death of her predecessor. She was Liege Mistress, then, not through primogeniture but rather through the influence of patriotic prayer. Only young jauddeb females who obtained menarche on the death day of the last Liege Mistress, and who were residents of the city in which she had died, were eligible for selection. To ensure that no geffide sought to feign a daughter's eligibility by misrepresenting the advent of her womanhood, the Kieri had long since evolved joyous first-blood festivities encouraging the geffide to proclaim a daughter's time and to celebrate it before the world. Kieri girls, therefore, were quick to tell their parents of their arrival at menarche so that the news could be spread. A tardy report was almost unheard of, for girls were considerably more likely to err on the impulsive side. Further, to prevent the adults of a geffide from conspiring to place one of their daughters on the Kieri throne, tradition demanded that the family of the new Liege Mistress suffer the confiscation of all its goods and exile to a remote and overwarm area of the continent, usually to Feht Evashsted, a coastal area near the great southern ocean. For many, particularly the aged, this was a virtual death sentence. That, too, was why the passing of each Liege Mistress was customarily made public three full days *after* its occurrence, when an official of the court could verify, with little fear of either error or deception, all the first-blood registrations of the regal lady's death day. After that, the aisautseb selected her successor from among the available candidates by a lottery that Seth did not wholly understand. Latimer had said that it involved the immersion of the bleeding girls in either the pool of the Shobbes Geyser (if the Liege Mistress had died in Feln) or in the sulfur baths of Shobbes in the forbidden moraine territories west of the Summer

Capital (if the Liege Mistress had died in Sket). Purity and endurance were important criteria, and the famous pinkish cast of the waters of Kier was said to derive not from ferric oxides but from the pure, enduring tincture of the royal menses.

Although Seth had often heard Abel describe the Liege Mistress as an unprepossessing woman with a squat body and a full-moon face, he now began conjuring images of a dragoness or Gorgon—only to step into her laulset and find Abel vindicated.

Lady Turshebsel stood beside a small but exquisitely proportioned bathing pool shaped like the central cluster of a meadowland flower; each of its nine semicircular petals was an immersion nook. The tiles here were a dazzling burgundy, and to keep from slipping on them, the Liege Mistress wore a pair of thongs with adhesive soles and carried a rubber-tipped metal staff. In a row of tilework chairs growing out of the floor behind her sat Lady Turshebsel's advisors, attendants, and sycophants: the members of her palace geffide. Not counting the Kieri over whom she ruled, Seth reflected, they were all the family the Liege Mistress would ever have. As an avatar of Shobbes, she was betrothed forever to the state, virgin to her death day.

Beyond that, old Latimer had said, she was an enlightened woman who quite early in her reign had renounced all but the most trivial ritual authority of the aisautseb. She had forced them out of the palace by command, securing their obedience because they themselves had chosen her and could disobey her only by openly conceding their own fallibility. Until two weeks ago, Lady Turshebsel had been able to survive—in fact, to prosper—without the aisautseb, largely because Gla Taus had remained for so long outside the range of Interstel's benign meddlesomeness, and because the patriot-priests of Kier had found no cause to dispute the wisdom of her rule. Then, after sending an emissary to the court in Sket, Interstel had given the Ommundi Trade Company permission to seek mercantile rights on the planet, and the Latimers had come to Gla Taus to negotiate these rights with the Lady.

One of those sitting in a tilework chair, Seth noticed, was a priest. Engulfed in robes, his legs drawn up beneath him on the ceramic seat, his unblinking eyes like silver nail heads, he sat in a chair reserved for a prominent advisor. Two weeks ago, that chair had belonged to another, but to appease the aisautseb after their uprising, Lady Turshebsel had not only declared the *Dharmakaya* Kieri property but had reestablished a patriot-priest advisorship. This man was the first to hold that position in thirty-seven Gla Tausian years.

"Welcome, Master Seth," Lady Turshebsel said from across the laulset. "Please join me in the waters."

A woman advanced from another doorway, took the Liege Mistress's staff, and removed her starched skirts and jacket. Then, wearing only her awkward-looking thongs, Lady Turshebsel descended into the pool. Her squat, naked body, like that of other Kieri, was lightly haired over its entire surface (excepting only the face), the hair deepening in color rather than in thickness at the pubic region: an unremarkable body, really, at least here on Gla Taus.

Once Lady Turshebsel had positioned herself in her immersion nook, her smile seemed that of a little girl who has tasted a forbidden confection. If she was indeed past middle age for a jauddeb, she bore her years well.

"Come," she said. "All others may attend this conference from vantages of their own choosing, but Master Seth must join me in the waters."

Kieri garments were made to don or doff without lifting the arms or raising the feet, and before Seth could protest or demur, an attendant had unstrung his jacket and split and peeled back the resealable leg seams of his pantaloons. Soon he stood before the mighty of the land in gooseflesh and breechclout, and that the Lady also wore no clothes was paltry consolation.

Half panicked, Seth looked to his isohet for aid.

"I suffered through the same thing this morning," Abel said in Langlish. "Off with your breechclout, too. She wishes to take your measure."

But Clefrabbes Douin took Seth's wrist and led him toward the nook opposite Lady Turshebsel's. "Perhaps he'd be more comfortable, Lady, if only those immediately concerned with this matter take part in our talks."

Lady Turshebsel looked to right and to left, nodding each time, and, in a moment, there remained in the laulset only Seth, Abel, Douin, the silver-eyed patriot-priest, and a tall, ugly Kieri dressed in blue pants and a long, rope-hooked coat.

This man Seth knew as Porchaddos Pors, Point Marcher of Feln. It was his function to formulate and implement local policy. Although one of the highest-ranking courtiers in the Liege Mistress's service, Pors was hierarchically subordinate to the Point Marcher of Sket, who, possessing his title through a more ancient lineage, exercised a greater authority nationwide. Pors was of the Kieri nobility, whereas Douin was a career civil servant who had won his position and his house through the sometimes uncertain preferment of scholarship and ability.

Seth did not like Porchaddos Pors because of his aggressive temperament and the animalish cast of his features. Although grateful to Douin and Lady Turshebsel for emptying the hall of extraneous onlookers, he still did not like to remove his breechclout before this man. The stare of the aisautseb, enveloped in his stiff, white robes, was also disconcerting. Why must he disrobe in front of strangers?

Abel and Douin flanked him, and Abel, nudging him in the side, muttered in faint Langlish, "Remove it and get in. The priests believe that a naked jauddeb speaks the truth; naked humans, too, apparently."

Bathing with the Clefrabbes geffide had seemed a natural thing, a strengthening of the bond between host and guest—but this, despite the kindness in Lady Turshebsel's eyes, seemed designed either to humble or to test; both, maybe. And because Abel had earlier said that getting back to Earth depended on how he conducted himself here, Seth tasted fear. What was he being tested on? What did they want of him?

He unknotted the breechclout and dropped it to the floor. His scrotum contracted, and his legs threatened to give way. But he kept his teeth clenched and entered the warm water, settling into the immersion nook and relaxing a little the moment his body was covered.

Water moved around him, and Porchaddos Pors came to the pool's edge to stand behind the Liege Mistress. Half visible in the glare of light behind and to the left of Pors, the unblinking priest kept watch.

"Your isohet says you wish to return to Earth, Master Seth," Lady Turshebsel began. "In the *Dharmakaya*."

"Yes, Lady."

"The ship you came in, formerly the property of the Ommundi Company, now belongs to us. The aisautseb, however, agree that you may regain it if you, your isohet, and the pilot who now lies aboard it in cold sleep agree to undertake a mission on behalf of the Kieri state. Master Abel has already agreed. The pilot, he tells us, will obey him, for Master Abel is now the Ommundi representative on Gla Taus with legal authority. But because you're your isohet's equal in all but age, Master Seth, we wish to acquire your consent, too."

"I agree to whatever Abel has agreed," Seth said, still not understanding what they wanted. He had the uneasy apprehension that he was being played like a fish with a hook in its gill, and yet . . . and yet Lady Turshebsel's voice and manner were kindly. Her pale round face, framed with blue-black ringlets, bobbed lightly above the waters flowing between them, and he found no deception in her.

Accompanied by the sucking of his thongs, Pors neared Seth by stalking around the pool. "Have you no questions about what we require? No curiosity about the task? No doubt that you may be able to accomplish what we wish you to accomplish?" He halted halfway around and stared at Seth impatiently, meanwhile towering against the backdrop of a farther portal.

"If Abel believes we can do what you want—"

"Not Master Abel and you together," Douin broke in, "but you alone, with Lord Pors and me as minor accomplices."

"You're at the very center of our plan," said Pors.

"But why?"

"Because of your innocence," Lady Turshebsel said. "A quality that everyone else in this laulset long ago forfeited. Your innocence, Master Seth, is your principal asset and an essential factor in our calculations. Let me be frank: We wish to use you. You lack many of the preconceptions and biases that could thwart Lord Pors, Master Douin, and your own capable isohet. You are clean and unspoiled."

Seth was not flattered. *We wish to use you.* Along with Günter Latimer, dating from his sixteenth year, he had visited four solar systems, mastering Scansh and Kieri (in addition to Vox, Langlish, and two other human tongues), and he had heard of or actually witnessed cruelties that many persons far older than he would never have credited. His brief experience of the universe had early on apprised him, in fact, of the ubiquity and multiformity of Evil. To be termed an innocent, he felt, was to contradict the whole thrust of this experience. *We wish to use you.* He could still see his isosire's body hanging like a butchered carcass from the Kieri Obelisk. . . .

"You don't care for my candor?" Lady Turshebsel asked.

Seth had no answer.

"All right. You've lived among us better than a year. Do you regard the people of Gla Taus, us jauddeb, as"—the Liege Mistress shaped the alien word with humorous distaste—"what your isohet sometimes disdainfully calls, well, *quaz*?"

"Oh, no," Seth blurted, reddening. At his back, he heard Abel shifting from one foot to another in acute embarrassment.

"This word implies a lower order of development and intelligence, does it not?" said the Lady, pressing her advantage. But Seth's reply was apparent in his flustered silence, and she continued: "We too have ugly epithets for foreigners and offworlders, Master Seth. But I believe you when you say that *you* don't regard us as . . . quaz. Your isohet's opinion I cannot discern, however, for the word first fell from his lips."

"Lady Turshebsel—" Abel began.

"Quiet!" Porchaddos Pors snapped.

"My question now," the Liege Mistress resumed, "is if your openness to the humanity of other intelligent alien species is broad enough to include the inhabitants of Trope?"

"Trope, Lady?"

"The world that circles Anja, seven lights from our star, Gla Taunt. Do you know that world, Master Seth?"

"It's a technologically advanced planet that holds itself aloof from Interstel, I believe. It has light-trippers and communicates with passing vessels by using Vox, but it refuses either consular contact or trade. Interstel is biding its time, as it did with Gla Taus until granting Ommundi permission to attempt a mercantile alliance."

Pors said defensively, "We wished to develop certain aspects of our technology without aping the methods and paraphernalia of Interstel. Now we have orbiters of our own, if not light-trippers, and we did it by techniques and designs of Kieri origin."

Lady Turshebsel ignored the Point Marcher's chauvinistic outburst. "But what do you know about the gosfi themselves, the people of Trope?" she asked Seth.

"Their eyes—"

"Yes?"

"Their eyes are strange. But they are shaped in their bodies just as you and I are shaped."

"That's what *we* suppose," Lady Turshebsel conceded. "But Master Günter told me that Interstel recently induced the greatest Tropish nation to become a provisional signatory of its charter. By your own official classification system, then, the Tropiards are *jauddebseb*."

By this word, Seth realized, Turshebsel meant "humanlike" or "humanoid"—but the silver-eyed priest made disapproving wheezing noises at her mentions of both Latimer and the Tropiards, and it was clear that in his view only Kieri were without question jauddebseb.

Lady Turshebsel continued her argument: "Knowing these things to be true, and knowing that we on Gla Taus have been in contact for some months with the Magistrate of Trope by means of the communication system aboard the *Dharmakaya*, would you regard the Tropiards as quaz if you had to deal with them?"

"No, Lady."

"You'd deal with them"—the Liege Mistress surprised Seth by saying her next three words in Langlish—"*human to human?*"

"Yes, Lady," he said, disguising his astonishment. Latimer must have taught her a great deal before his murder.

"Good. Because at this moment, Master Seth, I appoint you my personal envoy to the Magistrate of Trope. His name is Ulgraji Vrai, and his nation is called by the name of his world."

"But what am I to do?" Seth craned his neck to look at Abel. There arose within him a panic occasioned by his own inadequacy.

"As you're told," Abel said curtly.

"Lord Pors," said Lady Turshebsel, "while Master Seth soaks in the waters, please detail his mission to Trope. Leave out nothing, but be succinct."

Pors stalked about the laulset's pool, his thongs crepitating rudely, and in fifteen minutes he outlined the economic basis of the Kieri plan and the nature of the protracted cultural conflict on Trope that seemed to make his strategy feasible: nothing but benefits for all concerned. But as Pors spoke, Seth glanced often into the ceramic glare nimbusing the white-robed priest.

Clearly, Lady Turshebsel's plan had grown out of priestly resistance to her trade agreement with Ommundi Company. The aisautseb wanted no one to exploit the very real resources of the Evashsteddan, but to acquire the basics of an interstellar technology Kieri scientists and industrialists were even now venturing into the Obsidian Wastes from Old Ilvaudset, the first such explorers in several centuries. They were looking for rare ores, insulating materials, natural conductors, and any other serendipitous loot the Wastes might contain. The aisautseb did not object to this expansion because it was northward, but because the Wastes could support neither crops nor livestock, the Liege Mistress was counting on Ommundi Company to establish food-producing strongholds in the islands of the Evashsteddan and a reliable supply line to Kier and the pioneers pushing poleward in the Ilvaudsettan. That hope had died with Günter Latimer. This stratagem involving

Trope—which Pors was now explaining—was a contingency plan, and its chief virtue seemed to be that it was acceptable, if only barely, to the aisautseb.

"What do you think?" Lady Turshebsel asked when Pors had finished.

"I don't like it much, Lady," Seth replied.

"Why?"

"It works hardships on us all, even if Gla Taus and Trope do ultimately stand to benefit."

"The Latimer isohets also benefit," Lady Turshebsel said. "If you succeed, Master Seth, you return to your home world. If you decline my appointment, the *Dharmakaya* stays in orbit and you and Master Abel remain our guests. Narthaimnar Chappouib and his fellow priests have approved this mission as well as the reward attendant upon your coming home to Gla Taus." She nodded to suggest that Narthaimnar Chappouib was her silver-eyed advisor, confirming Seth's suspicions about the man's influence.

"Gla Taus isn't our home," he said, "and the *Dharmakaya* is already ours."

"He agrees," Abel interjected. "He accepts your appointment as envoy to the nation-cum-world called Trope."

"He accepted before he'd heard the whole proposal," Lady Turshebsel rejoined. "I'd like to hear his opinion now."

Lacking certainty that he could do what they wished, Seth hesitated.

"Tell her!" Abel whispered.

"I accept your appointment," Seth heard himself say.

"Then go to Aisaut Chappouib for a blessing. You'll depart Gla Taus tomorrow—whereas I will remove to Sket until your return." She lifted her arms and clapped her hands. A woman entered the laulset, helped Lady Turshebsel from the water, and draped her cloak over her shoulders. Wet, the fine black hair covering the Liege Mistress's body lay along her limbs and flanks like a delicate fur.

When the two women were gone, Clefrabbes Douin assisted Seth from the pool and pointed him toward the unblinking priest.

"My garments?"

"Not yet," Douin said. "Go to the aisautseb."

Seth walked naked past Lord Pors and halted before the priest's tiled throne.

"Kneel," said Narthaimnar Chappouib.

Seth lowered himself to the cold tiles, knees aching with the hardness under them, his flesh crawling with a variety of unnamable chills. He was kneeling, naked, before one of those who had helped slay his isosire. As Latimer had gone naked up the side of the tower in Mirrimsagset Square. . . .

"You will carry a gift to the ruler to whom Lady Turshebsel sends you as envoy," the priest said. "This will be my blessing, for you have no belief in aisautseb prayers. In any case, your nature is such that they would have no meaning." Chappouib looked about for someone to command. "Master Douin, would you assist me?"

Douin came forward and freed from the inside of the aisautseb's collar a chain on which was strung a dairauddes, a tube of black ceramic as long as Seth's hand from wrist to middle fingertip.

"Give it to me," Chappouib said.

Douin held the dairauddes out to the priest; and Seth was taken aback because when Chappouib reached to take it, lifting his great sleeves so that they fell to his elbows, he accepted the dairauddes with a pair of raw-looking stumps. This aisautseb, like the mythical namesake of all Kieri priests, had no hands.

The dairauddes dangled between his stumps, threatening to slip away and shatter on the floor. Even so, Chappouib wished to put it around Seth's neck, and Seth, despite not wanting the thing to touch him, inclined his head to make the transfer easier. He felt instinctively that the ritual had sexual overtones, and these confused and frightened him. Was he being honored by the priest's gift, or was the transfer a contemptuous mockery of his manhood?

At last Clefrabbes Douin took the dairauddes from Chappouib and bestowed it on Seth. Now he was wearing a "demon killer," and to many Kieri—this thought chilled—Seth himself qualified as a demon.

"Your dairauddes," Chappouib said, shaking down his sleeves and covering his stumps again, "once belonged to Lady Turshebsel. She forfeited it when she drove the aisautseb from her service. I brought it back. Now she bids me give it to you to bestow on Magistrate Vrai of Trope."

Seth waited, bemused.

"You may depart his presence," Douin told Seth.

Seth hurried to do so, retreating toward a young Kieri attendant who had come back into the laulset with his clothes. Dressing, he watched as Abel, Douin, and Pors went forward to receive Chappouib's blessing—even Abel, who supposedly could not benefit from the recitation of an aisautseb prayer. Afterward, the silver-eyed priest spoke softly to Pors and Douin, excluding

Abel and punctuating his advice with vigorous nods and shakings of the head. At last, quite audibly, he cried, "You are my hawks, the hawks of Aisaut. Go forth with truth and courage.

"Aye, my hawks, go forth!"

"He had no hands," Seth said as Douin led Abel and him back down the steps of the palace toward the teeming square. Sunfall was imminent, and Gla Taunt—perversely, it still seemed to Seth—oozed down the eastern sky like an egg yolk sliding through its white.

"A traditional aisautseb practice," Douin said. "The holy one who keeps a place at Kieri court sacrifices his hands for the honor. He becomes the conscience of the nation. His handlessness signifies that he neither gives nor takes, for his domain is spiritual rather than worldly."

"He gave me the dairauddes."

"A spiritual gift, Master Seth, itself to be passed on to another."

"When did Chappouib lose his hands?" Abel asked.

"The day Lady Turshebsel officially restored the aisautseb advisorship abolished thirty-seven years ago. Chappouib was chosen by his fellows, and gladly relinquished his hands to the sword."

"Barbaric," Abel said. "Barbaric superstition."

Douin halted at the entrance to the square, his dark eyes flashing. "I agree." His tone suggested that some doubt still plagued him. "It's the sort of thing Lady Turshebsel fought successfully until the arrival of Interstel, Ommundi, and your isosire."

This veiled accusation was as close to rudeness as Clefrabbes Douin had ever come in his dealings with the Latimer isohets, but Seth sympathized with their host's point of view. Their presence on the planet had been an irritant and a provocation, and now they were preparing to travel somewhere else, on a mission for which Seth could summon little enthusiasm.

"Barbaric," Abel repeated.

Now Douin held his tongue.

And Seth, looking toward their host's stately geffide, saw a marketplace filled with bobbing tinfoil balloons. Even in the gathering twilight, the lofty dagger shaft on which Latimer had died, the Kieri Obelisk, pierced him to the heart. As for the dairauddes about his neck, it mocked him: Seth was sure of it.

THREE

The cabin's blackness was riven by a scream. Although Seth had been having a nightmare (a succession of blurred images underlain by an impalpable distress), the cry was not his.

"Dear God!" Abel was pleading. "Dear God, *don't let them put their hands on me!*" The plea soared into a bloodcurdling falsetto that seemed incisive enough to split the hull of their light-tripper and let the void spill in.

Seth pressed a button. Their cabin was filled with a soft, Earthlike twilight. His isohet, clad only in a pair of nylon sleep trousers, had scooted across his bunk so that his naked back met the bulkhead and pressed insistently against it. His pupils were fat, black suns.

"I'm here," Seth said, lowering himself onto the foot of Abel's bunk. "I'm here. We're aboard the *Dharmakaya*, five days out from Gla Taus on our way to the Anja system."

Abel's pupils collapsed spectacularly, drinking in the reality of the cabin. Seth reached out and gripped his isohet's ankle. He saw that Abel was finally focusing on him—but his flaccid torso ran with sweat, and his hair was plastered to his face as if he had just returned from a shower.

"Again?" Seth asked.

"They were preparing me for the obelisk," Abel responded. "A rope hung down from its highest grate, and the aisautseb were moving in, moving in to . . . to disrobe me."

"They didn't get you tonight, then?"

Abel fixed Seth with an outraged, uncomprehending stare. "He was our isosire, Seth, and I'm your *brother*. How do you remain immune to what happened to him, immune to my suffering of what he suffered?"

Seth removed his hand from his isohet's ankle.

"It happened to you, too!" Abel informed him for the umpteenth time. "You and I went up that tower with Günter Latimer, but the truth of that still escapes you. For you, Seth, it was an external rather than an inward occurrence. That's not the way it's supposed to be!"

"I'm supposed to have nightmares in living, bloody color?"

"Yes!"

"And wake up screaming?"

"Yes!"

"And go stumbling into the lavalet to heave up my panic and my compassion?" This was a hit, Seth knew, because now that Abel had recovered from the psychic pummeling of his nightmare, his body would begin to react. His face had already blanched, and his breathing was quickening again. Fresh diamonds of sweat were popping out on his already sweat-lacquered jowls and forehead.

Abel controlled his temper with difficulty. "My *self*-compassion, you're trying to imply, aren't you? Well, that's all right, that's fine. The word of Interstel is that we're all imperfect isohets of the same perfect progenitor."

"You don't even pretend to believe that, Abel."

"Compassion begins at home."

Seth winced at both the hypocrisy and the banality of this bromide. "That, perhaps, you believe."

"You don't *feel* anything!" Abel countered. But the trauma of the nightmare was belatedly catching up with him, and he swung his feet to the floor and headed for the lavalet, replete with the sanctity of his suffering and so close to being caught short that the argument was effectively over. Having no desire either to confront or comfort Abel on his return, Seth pulled on a pair of coveralls and let himself into the corridor outside their cabin.

The *Dharmakaya* was immense. Its living, sleeping, and study quarters occupied a pair of windowless nacelles positioned below and aft of the triangular conning module. Up there, the pilot—K/R Caranicas, an indentured Ommundi triune—was installed in cybernetic linkage with the astrogational and life-support capacities of the vessel. Caranicas, who possessed a single left cerebral hemisphere interwired with twin right cerebral hemispheres, had remained in cold sleep during the Latimers' entire stay on Gla Taus, the equivalent of nearly ten Earth-standard months, and so had known nothing of the murder of Seth and Abel's isosire or of the coopting of shipboard communication systems by the Kieri.

Not until revived by Seth had the triune understood that the ship's body had been violated by forcible entry and its voice stolen by agents of Lady Turshebsel's taussanaur, or orbital guard. Now, as if indifferent to its new masters, Caranicas was transporting five of the *Dharmakaya*'s captors—Clefrabbes Douin, Porchaddos Pors, two officers of the taussanaur, and a minion of Narthaimnar Chappouib—through subdimensional idspace toward the world called Trope.

Caranicas was neither male nor female, neither isohet nor natural child, and Seth mentally referred to the triune as "it" because no other pronoun seemed to work. What gender did you consider a being whose body lacked sexual differentiation and whose fundamental *raison d'être* was conning five hundred tons of vanadium and vitricite through a nonexistent medium that Interstel wags had long ago dubbed The Sublime? Moreover, except through the computer in the conning module, Caranicas couldn't speak.

An inability to speak struck Seth as the perfect recommendation for a companion. After composing himself against the shock of standing upright again, he set off through the corridor toward the step-shaft leading to the command unit. On the way he passed the adjacent cabins that Douin and Pors were occupying, and recollected that one of these jauddeb was probably already aloft. Their sleep cycles aboard the *Dharmakaya* seldom overlapped, and he hoped that if one of the Kieri had chosen to visit their pilot, Douin would be the one.

Seth's argument with Abel still rankled inside him. Isohets—just as the members of any tupletry of clones—supposedly shared a heightened empathic sense, a bond of deep dimensionality. No such bond existed between Abel and Seth. Although Abel had raised him—except for Seth's first eight years at the Ommundi Paedoschol in Lausanne—he had never felt a real psychic communion with his isohet. Gratitude for Abel's love Seth had often known, and affection, and a terrible fear that without Abel he would never achieve a viable identity. But Abel and he had never shared any of those telepathic insights, swift and accurate, that isohets were supposed to experience. He could read Abel's feelings only in the usual ways, by direct observation and a merely human sensitivity to nuance and mood. Abel's mind he could not read at all.

Never, Seth reflected as he climbed, had he known anyone so prone to vomiting as Abel. Günter Latimer had never quelled his anxiety attacks—if, indeed, he had ever *had* anxiety attacks—by retching up his guts. And Seth got that shamefully sick only when he had eaten or drunk too much. Most people, he knew, were not so susceptible to nausea and vomiting; and yet if anyone should share Abel's unenviable combination of body chemistry and hypersensitive mind, why not he? He was a duplicate of Abel, for Abel was a duplicate of Günter, and Günter Latimer was the die from which they had both been struck:

If A=G, and if S=G, then S=A.

In which case, of course, it was pretty surprising that their minds seldom strained along the same cable toward a common anxiety, and that Seth was not also a vomiting fool. Must he feel guilty for having escaped the harsh confessional of the lavalet?

"No," Seth said aloud, climbing through the step-shaft. But speaking the denial aloud didn't alter the fact that his guilt was even now pursuing him through the corridors of the *Dharmakaya*.

His guilt was Abel's revenge for his own unfeeling innocence.

Pors rather than Douin had preceded him to the conning module. It seemed to Seth that every card dealt him bore a black spot.

At the auxiliary astrogational console, he eased into a lounger next to the one occupied by Pors, then studied the Kieri's concave profile. The man's nose, eyes, and mouth all seemed to be set inside a dish of bone—but, in spite of that somewhat apish facial arrangement, he appeared both alert and cunning.

We are all imperfect isohets of the same perfect progenitor, Abel had said. A ludicrous declaration. Abel's belief in deity ascended little higher than had Günter Latimer.

"Good morning, Master Seth," Pors said without taking his eyes from the astrogational screen. He spoke in Vox, which all the Kieri but the aisautseb had agreed would be their official tongue for the duration of their mission.

"Is it morning?" Seth asked, amused.

"For me it is. Master Douin awakened me only a brief while ago."

Douin and Pors took turns babysitting the *Dharmakaya*'s pilot to en-sure that Caranicas didn't craftily maneuver the vessel off true toward some reasonably obtainable Interstel world. Considering that the triune's programmed mission kept it course-correcting for the whole of any subdimensional voyage, this was an unlikely possibility. An override required either Abel's own feed-in or an apprehension of disaster on the part of the triune itself. A passenger would quickly notice any major change of course because of subfield resistance and the resultant shipboard discomfort: heat, oscillation, and noise. A wholesale shift from The Sublime to the more predictable ridiculousness of normal Space-Time would be even more wrenching. But the two Kieri took their self-assigned work seriously and monitored the astrogation consoles round the clock. Seth had taught Douin the basics of this monitoring, and Abel had taught Pors.

Both were already well versed in the operation of the ship's communication system: Shortly after the Latimers' arrival on Gla Taus, Günter had conducted a tour of the *Dharmakaya* for several high government officials and a contingent of Lady Turshebsel's taussanaur (literally, "world circlers"). One of the high points of this tour, at least for the Kieri, had been Latimer's demonstration of the sublimission radio/receiver, with which he had rather showily contacted Ommundi Station on Sabik II and an Interstel facility on a colony world circling Acamar. These brief exchanges with jauddebseb beings hundreds of lights away, along with the vivid sublimission images hovering like ghosts in the radio's receptor well, had immensely impressed one of the taussanaur—who had asked permission to put through a call to Trope, picking that world because of its relative proximity to Gla Taus.

Latimer had graciously instructed the jauddeb in the use of the unit, and even though the Tropiards were not full-fledged signatories of the Interstel Charter, the guard had easily raised a response from a tracking outpost in the Tropish hinterland called Chaelu Sro. Latimer had translated the guard's Kieri into Vox, and the Vox of the anonymous Tropiard back into Kieri; and then, in order not to lose face before the delighted taussanaur, Porchaddos Pors and Master Douin had each politely demanded a turn at the console, speaking Vox to impress the others with their erudition. That this entire exchange had proceeded without any visual input from Trope had dulled the excitement of the touring Kieri scarcely a whit.

In fact, the episode had seemed such a triumph of public relations that Seth had inwardly approved his isosire's spontaneous suggestion to Pors that a pair of orbital guards remain aboard the *Dharmakaya* to monitor the radio and study first-hand the electronic and mechanical intricacies of a bona fide light-tripper. Trust was the order of the day, and no one had then suspected the possibility of an aisautseb uprising, the seizure of the ship, or the need to negotiate with the Tropiards an alternative to the doomed Ommundi trade proposal. Who could have foreseen that the taussanaur aboard at Latimer's invitation would turn pirate because of the archaic belief system of a priestly order that had exerted little real clout for almost four Gla Tausian decades? Neither Abel nor Seth had advised Latimer of the foolishness of his trust, and K/R Caranicas, who might have had a weird opinion in the matter, had been deep in cold sleep. . . .

"How long must we share subdimensional nonexistence with that creature who pilots us?" Pors asked, nodding forward.

Seth glanced at the gyroscopically mounted chair in which Caranicas, blinkered and belted, could move vertically or horizontally past the various astrogational computers and both in and out of the cystlike conning turrets set about the nose of the module. The triune itself was scarcely visible in this chair. Its arms and legs were wired, and at the back of its head was the cranial prosthetic housing the additional right lobe cloned from an embryonic extraction of brain tissue before Caranicas's "birth." The housing was pure platinum, and the appearance of this artificial cap always put Seth in mind of an enormous silver goiter that had rotated unaccountably around to the nape. Caranicas was not pretty, not by any means, and Seth could easily understand how Pors could call the triune a "creature."

"Can't you tell from the console display?" he asked the impatient noble.

"The figures beside the miniature vessel say"—Pors shut his eyes, working to deduce the Kieri equivalent of the Arabic numerals he had painstakingly learned months ago— "twenty-three, I think: twenty-three more days."

"If the texture and consistency of the subdimensional field we're generating doesn't change in the meanwhile. Then, yes, twenty-three days."

"Earth reckoning," Pors stipulated.

"That's nearly thirty of your own," Seth replied.

"If conditions in The Sublime don't alter and so delay us."

"They're just as likely to alter in our favor, Lord Pors. The Sublime is highly mutable. That's why a light-tripper must have a pilot who reads the subdimensional fields quickly and expertly, and who's able to compensate almost intuitively for the changes. Interstel and most of the trade companies develop their pilots from birth. In truth, the selection is prenatal, and one such as Caranicas is destined for no other occupation. This triune has spent almost sixty years in the service of Ommundi, although much of that has been in cold sleep."

"Of what . . . species . . . is your pilot?" Pors asked.

"Caranicas is human." The fact that in Vox the pronoun "it" had three forms—one for animals and plants, one for inanimate objects, and one for abstract concepts—momentarily stymied Seth. After sifting among his choices, he settled almost at sheer random upon the feminine pronoun. "Despite her appearance, she's human—of the basic stock from which Latimer, Abel, and I derived. The differences are genetic, surgical, and cybernetic.

"The platinum lobe on the back of her neck augments her ability to create a cognitive map of The Sublime. It gives her a heightened awareness of spatial relationships. She has good depth perception, good orientation in nonlinear environments. She's capable of rapidly synthesizing all this simultaneous intake for navigational purposes. The third lobe was cloned and developed especially for subdimensional flight, Lord Pors, and Caranicas uses it almost exclusively when she's jockeying back and forth among the conning turrets. The computers handle many of the analytical functions involved in piloting, but she feeds the information gleaned from her observations to the machines by way of the keyboard at her left hand. Her own right hemisphere—the one she was born with—processes a musical code through the keyboard in order to file the information."

"She?" Pors asked.

"Or he," Seth admitted. "Caranicas is without sex, although a chromosome study would probably reveal her original *in vitro* gender."

"She doesn't speak?"

"Only through the keyboard, to both her consoles and to us—when, that is, she has anything to say. We talk to her through the computer, which converts our speech to her musical code. It's an eerie, triple-layered twelve-tone system, if you amplify it, with some difficult phonetic correspondences."

The triune emerged from an overhead turret, whirled in its chair, and spun along its gyroscope tightrope to a bank of equipment directly in front of the two men. In many ways, Seth suddenly realized, Caranicas seemed even more alien than the Kieri lord whose manner and appearance he had grown to dislike so. Pors was at least a personality, whereas their pilot seemed merely an inarticulate complex of tropisms and linkages that defied anthropomorphic cataloging. Did anything but spatial calculations and solid geometry happen inside Caranicas's head? Of what value was his/her/

its humanity? Latimer had never said, and Seth had never inquired.

We are all imperfect isohets of the same perfect progenitor.

Pors looked at Seth with an expression full of complicated loathing. "I wouldn't be your triune for all the wealth of Ommundi," Pors said.

Seth attempted to change the subject. "Have you been in contact with Magistrate Vrai's people?"

"You've cut away her spirit," Pors persisted.

"No," said Seth. "This is all Caranicas has ever known. Her existence is piloting. Piloting is therefore her happiness." He was amazed to find himself on the defensive, particularly since it was the brutish and insensitive Pors who had put him there.

As Seth understood it, Pors, like the male children of all Kieri nobles, had been raised in a camp in the Orpla Mountains northwest of Sket and trained to a life of aggressive self-reliance. The products of this system were seldom well attuned to the feelings of others, although they did emerge competent and independent. You recognized a courtier on Gla Taus by his swagger and his latent hostility toward the lowborn rather than by his mastery of the social graces, which were largely the province of appointed officials like Clefrabbes Douin. But here was Pors expressing an angry sympathy for Caranicas and holding Seth responsible for the triune's denatured spirituality.

"I want to talk to her," Pors declared.

"But what for? Talk is a distraction from her piloting. She can handle it, of course, but it imposes a low-level strain she'd probably be better off without."

"Doesn't she eat, eliminate, sleep?"

"She slept while we were on Gla Taus. She feeds and eliminates through the hookups on her chair. She may also rest by switching back and forth between her original right hemisphere and the cloned one. She shuts completely down, though, only in cold sleep."

"Does she pray?" Pors asked.

Seth's exasperation mounted—first the argument with Abel and now this inane discussion about Caranicas. "I don't imagine she has the time," he said, hiding his impatience. "Nor would I imagine she's had much opportunity to think about it."

"Ask her."

"Ask Caranicas if she prays?"

Pors irritably gestured his assent, and Seth removed the microphone from the astrogation console, switched it on, and said, "K/R Caranicas, a visitor aboard the *Dharmakaya* wishes to know if you pray." Nothing more. He felt infinitely silly framing the statement. Even before he had finished speaking, the computer had begun coding his words into the three-layered dodecaphonic language by which the triune communicated with its shipboard colleagues. The weird music of the translation ran through the pilothouse like a bevy of electronic mice.

"I may have to define that term for her," Seth told Pors, averting the microphone. "I hope you have a definition ready to hand."

But when the triune's chair whirled away from the equipment bank in front of them, threaded noseward, and dropped into an underslung turret at the module's apex, Seth began to fear that—in spite of the eerie music from the computer—his message had not coded through at all. He was about to repeat the message when a second series of indecipherable notes began toodling in cryptic response to the first. An instant later the translation sounded from a console speaker:

"*My piloting is a prayer.*"

Seth felt vindicated. He had not expected this answer, but because it seemed to turn the tables on Pors, he inwardly congratulated the triune on its cleverness. If the life of the *Dharmakaya*'s pilot was a prayer, how could Caranicas be spiritually bereft? As for Pors, skeptically watching the triune scoot and spin along its gyroscopic tracks, he made no more demands on Seth to have it speak. Its first response had killed rather than piqued Pors's interest.

"Have you been in touch with Trope?" Seth asked him again.

"Master Douin informs me that the Tropiards prefer to wait until our arrival to begin full-blown discussion. They keep their radio contacts brief and send no visuals."

Seth had hoped to see a Tropiard by way of a sublimission image. Here on the *Dharmakaya* he had reviewed all the library tapes devoted to the Anja system and its one inhabited planet. The available information was scant and sometimes self-contradictory. Interstel had never established a secure foothold on Trope, and because its level of technology rivaled or surpassed that of the most advanced members of Interstel, no one could pretend that coercing Trope's full partnership would lift that world out of the dark ages. Therefore, only an ambiguous partnership—if any—obtained. The result was ignorance about both the planet and its people. That the Tropiards had long ago adopted Vox for their dealings with Interstel ships and agents seemed highly promising of a comprehensive accord, but no one could guess when that accord might come. Seth realized that it would be a rather humbling irony if Porchaddos Pors, Point Marcher of Feln, proved instrumental in bringing Trope into full alliance with Interstel. Gla Taus, after all, was a somewhat backward newcomer to the partnership.

For now, though, the principal thing Seth knew about the Tropiards was that their eyes were hard and gemlike. The text accompanying a solitary photograph in the library tapes described their eyes as "an organic variety of crystal"; the photograph itself, meticulously enlarged, revealed a more or less human face studded with a pair of water-green jewels where its organs of sight should have been. Seth had a good deal of trouble crediting the legitimacy of the photograph.

We are all imperfect isohets of the same perfect progenitor.

Maybe that was true, each humanoid species either a small or a grotesque distortion of some hidden Platonic Norm of Ideal Humanity. One theory held that aeons ago a common ancestor had seeded as many of the galaxy's inhabitable planets as it possibly could, before succumbing to extinction on its own dying world. Another hypothesis assumed, against countless subtly or grossly dissimilar planetary backdrops, parallel evolution. A third pointed to the instrumentality of God. The first theory, Seth knew, ran headlong into the unsupportive archaeological records of Earth and other Interstel worlds; the second was statistically unlikely; and the third seemed to ascribe to God a shabby paucity of imagination. You didn't win with any of them. Nor, apparently, were you supposed to.

"Where's the dairauddes Chappouib gave you?" Pors suddenly asked.

"In my cabin," Seth said, surprised.

"You should be wearing it."

"Even when I sleep?"

"It's your gift to the Magistrate, which once belonged to Lady Tursheb-sel. You should have it on you until you present it."

"A demon killer?"

Pors studied the display screen, feigning or perhaps actually experiencing deep interest in the movement of the *Dharmakaya* through The Sublime.

"I didn't believe you were a follower of the aisautseb," Seth challenged Pors. "I thought you a courtier and a progressive."

The Point Marcher turned on him angrily. "You should have it on your person," he said. "When awake, have it on your person!"

*

In the corridor outside his cabin, Seth encountered the priest whom Chappouib, with Lady Turshebsel's grudging executive consent, had assigned to them for the voyage. This man was young but dutiful. He seemed to sleep only for brief periods. Now he was wearing garrison pants rather than robes, and his head was uncovered. He was obviously on his way to the conning module, either to relieve Pors or to engage him in conversation. A true aisautseb, he spoke no Vox, and made no attempt to learn.

"Good morning," he said in Kieri: his standard greeting, regardless of the hour.

"Our triune's piloting is a prayer," Seth told him in Vox.

"Sir?" the priest said.

Seth repeated his words, knowing them to be unintelligible to the aisautseb but taking a perverse delight in the fact.

The priest's expression darkened, and he brushed past Seth with cold dignity, lengthening his stride at every step. Seth suffered a pang of remorse for his pettiness, but couldn't bring himself to call politely after the jauddeb in Kieri.

Instead, he went in to Abel, who lay on his bunk again, somewhat recovered from his bout of nausea but still pasty-faced and glassy-eyed in the cabin's artificial twilight.

"You're a bastard to leave me in this shape, Seth. You're a bastard to escape my nightmares."

"Neither one of us quite qualifies as a bastard." Seth smiled to show his isohet that he was joking, but it didn't take.

Abel pulled himself to a sitting position to renew the attack: "They were going to hoist me up that tower! They were—!"

"If it'll make you feel any better, Abel, I was on the verge of a nightmare of my own when you woke me up."

"But you couldn't quite get tuned in, could you?"

Seth gestured at the cabin's door. "This nacelle has nineteen other cabins. Why don't I take another one?" He proposed this as means of making peace, not as a threat—but, again, his intended meaning failed to register.

"No," Abel said, frankly conciliatory. "I'd appreciate it if you stayed. Give me a moment, just a moment, and I'll be out of this again." He pointed to the foot of his bunk. "Sit down, please. Please sit down."

Seth lowered himself to Abel's bunk and stared across its linen into a face that was a bloated and admonitory likeness of his own. That—not Abel's nightmares—was what he couldn't escape.

BOOK TWO

FOUR

Twenty-three days later, the hangar doors of the *Dharmakaya* parted like the lids of a great eye, revealing the green-gold mists of Trope's atmosphere. A transcraft floated free of the hangar bay, dropped languidly toward those mists, then turned to align itself with its programmed path of entry.

Seth Latimer was piloting. His passengers were Clefrabbes Douin and Porchaddos Pors, neither of whom spoke as he maneuvered the transcraft out of the cold shadow of the mother ship. Looking up, Seth saw the fanciful bulk of the *Dharmakaya* retreating against a backdrop of strange stars and wondered if he'd made a mistake letting himself be isolated in this way with the two Gla Tausians. His gut ached, and his hands—even within a pair of lightweight, vented gloves—were clammy with sweat. On the afternoon of his visit to the Winter Palace, Seth recalled, Abel had said, "*Monkeys are born. Polecats and ratlings descend through a uterus.*" Now, falling from his isohet's companionship and guidance, he felt he was being thrust from the great Ommundi light-tripper along with two decidedly inhuman litter mates.

The transcraft plunged, its heat shields already incandescent.

As Seth monitored the controls and watched the horizon of Trope roll giddily upward, his nervousness abated. At least he was effecting his own delivery. After glancing at his grim Kieri passengers, he realized that for the moment their lives were in his hands, and that they were apprehensively aware of their dependence on him. By their looks, they'd found it far easier to trust K/R Caranicas, whatever the triune's spiritual state. But in his passengers' uncertainty Seth found a partial antidote for his own, and he determined to outface them and set them down uncracked.

Underlying the mists of Trope were wide, yellow-orange plains crimped with ridges of beige and umber. They looked as if they'd been applied to the planet with a palette knife. Greens and blue-greens were rare; the world had very few seas or inland waters, and its forests, judging from the evidence of an aerial overview, must consist predominantly of flame- or earth-colored foliage.

Seth banked the transcraft, and Anja, Trope's faintly blue sun, blinded him with a long stab of light. Abel had advised him to wear tinted goggles on the surface, but in the transcraft Seth let these collapsible plastic eye coverings hang unused inside his collar. Outside his collar, strung horizontally on a thin silver chain, was the ebony dairauddes that Narthaimnar Chappouib had given him, as a gift from Lady Turshebsel to the Magistrate of Trope. It swayed whenever Seth moved. The sooner he could transfer it into the keeping of the Tropish administrator, the happier he'd be.

Soon the transcraft had an escort. Two remotes swept up beside them on either flank, to accompany them into the southern hemisphere. They looked like delicate metal mosquitoes, spike-nosed and spindly-limbed, but their tensile strength was obviously every bit as staunch as the transcraft's, for they sailed with plucky, economical grace. Seth momentarily feared that the mosquitoes were near enough to provoke a collision, but an attempt to drop out of their embrace proved that they were locked in formation at precise intervals impossible to close. No danger of either collision or escape. Meanwhile, deserts of yellow-red parchment fled by at speed, rising inexorably. From what he'd seen of Trope so far, Seth would have judged the planet an uninhabited desert. The pilotless mosquitoes seemed its only native life form.

A voice crackled over the transcraft's radio in confident Vox:

"Permit our remotes to lead you in. Don't attempt to shake or outrun them."

"As you say," Seth replied.

Then, with the same gap between their wings, the mosquitoes shot forward fifteen or twenty meters, and Seth pursued, adjusting and readjusting to keep from falling farther behind. A clockwork city flashed into view beneath them. It lay in the lee of a tablerock, or plateau, upon which showed a complex pattern of rust-colored edifices and bone-white walkways. The mosquitoes peeled away on either side, and both the clockwork city and the acropolis on the tablerock disappeared behind the transcraft before Seth could adjust to the fact of their existence. At almost three-quarters the speed of sound, the transcraft kept skimming southward.

"You've overflown Ardaja Huru, our capital, and Huru J'beij, the tablerock on which we have our administrative facilities," said the melodious Tropish voice over the radio. "Make a circuit and land atop the butte, please."

"Where, exactly?" Seth asked.

"Do you require a landing strip?"

"No," Seth answered. "Our vehicle's capable of both hover and vertical descent."

"Then put down on the landing terrace in front of the J'beij—the great building running the western length of Huru J'beij."

The radio cut off, and Seth banked the transcraft into a stiff southerly wind to return to Ardaja Huru and its sheltering tablerock. Douin and Pors were rubbernecking like tourists—which, indeed, they were. For his own benefit as well as theirs, Seth slowed and swung wide, bringing them in so that they could get a leisurely panoramic vista of both the city and the government complex.

Ardaja Huru—as much mechanism as living entity—shone in the desert like the intricate, perfect bones of an extinct land leviathan. It was clockwork and skeletal at once, ordered but spare, so pruned of excess and ornament that the wind might have scoured it into this shape. The metals comprising its structures were the color of red-clay bricks. The pedestrian wheels clicking through its heart-hub and the transport cars circumnavigating both its oval perimeter and its many interlocking circular courts might very well have been sophisticatedly wind-driven. The trees lining the city's thoroughfares and standing like sentinels on its terrace levels burned in the sun like torches. Ardaja Huru seemed to be alive principally by virtue of the movement of its parts rather than by that of its population, for its people were mostly invisible—indoors, underground, somewhere out of sight.

More than this, Seth and the Kieri envoys had no time to deduce.

Huru J'beij, the butte behind the city, filled the transcraft's windscreens, and Seth was suddenly busy shifting into virtual hover and easing the vehicle across a magnificent expanse of blood-red rock toward the government buildings on the plateau. These had more substance than the structures of the city, as if they'd been hewn rather than delicately carved—but even they seemed outgrowths of the land. Unnatural outgrowths of the land. Unnatural outgrowths, like tumors or lepromata, but physical extensions of the planet, nonetheless. The landing terrace, which Seth now saw, was a circle of whitened stone in the midst of all this encompassing red.

Seth put the transcraft down within that circle, shot the turret back, and unstrapped in the stingingly cold air. A surprise, this coldness—even though, intellectually, he had known that Trope's desert uplands were chilly and that the atmospheric mix would sustain all three of them. Had he waited to throw the turret back, doubt might have intervened. He knew himself just well enough to understand that hesitation rather than conscience frequently made a coward of him.

"A prayer for all of us," said Porchaddos Pors. "I thank God that this place is blessed with a proper coldness."

"And I, too," acknowledged Clefrabbes Douin.

They descended to the terrace and stood in the canting shadow of the J'beij, a monolith of rust-red stone and metal. Ten fluted columns fronted the great building, buttressing the long winglike awning of rock capping its portico. The J'beij was almost as large as the *Dharmakaya*, and behind their transcraft, for a distance of perhaps a kilometer, stretched flat tablerock lined with bone-white walkways, intermittent buildings, and an occasional structure resembling a gazebo of stone. Far to the east Seth thought he could see a flotilla of mosquitoes—remotes—glinting in the afternoon sun on the plateau's landing field.

A pair of Tropiards stood in the portico of the J'beij. Tall figures in cloaks, they neither approached nor retreated.

Seth was disappointed to find that he could still tell nothing about their eyes, for their garments hooded them, putting half of each man's face in shadow. They might call their planet Trope and their humanoid species gosfi—an ugly, ugly word in Seth's estimation—but at this distance they were more aesthetically pleasing replicas of Earth-born humanity than either Douin or Pors. (This, Seth knew, was an ethnocentric bias, but he was powerless against it, at least after long incarceration in The Sublime with the Kieri.) The clay-colored cloaks of the Tropiards seemed to betoken . . . Seth's imagination galloped off higgledy-piggledy, and his hands began to sweat again. Above, the sky flowed like thin blue lava.

One of the Tropiards beckoned to them, after which he and his companion turned and retreated toward a hidden doorway. Wordlessly, exchanging uncertain glances, Seth and the two Kieri envoys followed these monkish figures beneath the portico and between a series of tall metal stelae depicting what Seth supposed to be episodes from the heroic Tropish past.

There were seven of these stelae on each side of the aisleway, staggered rather than directly opposite one another—but they were not especially informative about the facial features of the gosfi because the figures in each panel almost invariably had their heads averted or their eyes shielded. One figure recurred from panel to panel, but in every case it was depicted without eyes. The engraver had simply—and purposely, no doubt—failed to include its organs of sight.

A door of buff stone and red-gold metal admitted the three offworlders into the vast interior of the J'beij.

White predominated here, accented on the walls and vitricite partitions with hanging tapestries. Seth took a deep breath. The ceiling was a good four stories from the floor, and the tapestries—whose designs resembled wiring diagrams, or the convolutions of a human brain, or maybe even the intricate layout of Ardaja Huru—hung at various heights all the way to the ceiling. Individual floors did not exist as such. Instead, arranged at different levels above the main floor were transparent scaffolds to which you could ascend by lifts or narrow, helical stairways. The Tropiards employed on these scaffolds seemed to hang dreamily in the air.

Despite the enormousness of the J'beij, and the number of platforms distributed like pieces of kaleidoscopic glass throughout its interior, its gosfi occupants were few. The cabinets and consoles on the various levels were probably self-sustaining types of equipment, for information storage or arcane telemetric tasks.

Light flooded the J'beij, emanating from everywhere at once. But when one of the Tropiards turned to urge Seth's party on, letting his hood fall aside, it was still hard to see what kind of eyes he had. He wore a pair of slitted eye coverings. Tropiards elsewhere in the J'beij were similarly outfitted. Everyone seemed costumed and masked.

Grabbing Seth's arm, Pors spoke in his own tongue: "You represent not just you, Master Seth, but Lady Turshebsel and the Kieri state. Have a care about your presentation. Don't speak until the Magistrate has spoken to you. Remember, too, that—"

Seth shook off Pors's hand and glared at him angrily.

"A reminder," Douin said placatingly. "Nothing more, Master Seth."

The three companions followed their guides to the center rear of the J'beij, where the Tropiards halted beneath a scaffold unlike all the others. Its floor was carpeted with a material of luxuriant plum. Where all the other platforms were open but for safety rails and discontinuous banks of silent equipment, this one had opaque, papery walls. Indeed, Seth realized, it formed the base of a genuine *room*. One of their guides climbed a set of clear steps and disappeared into the boxlike structure. The other guide, still hooded, faced about and stared at them appraisingly.

"Lord Pors and I have complete trust in you," Douin said. "For that reason, we won't go with you into the Magistrate's presence. We'll wait for you here or wherever else our hosts are kind enough to permit us to rest."

Seth swung about on Douin in perplexity and terror. No one had said anything about his confronting the Magistrate alone.

"Wait! I don't want to usurp your own involvement. What will the Magistrate think if you and Lord Pors don't present your credentials?"

"Master Abel informed his people by radio that you—an Ommundi Company representative empowered by Lady Turshebsel to act as her agent—would be our sole intermediary in this matter."

"Why would Abel do such a thing?" Seth whispered urgently.

"He told the Tropish deputy magistrate that it's the custom of Ommundi Company negotiators to deal with government representatives on a one-to-one basis. With our blessing, Master Abel also said that Lord Pors and I were merely your onworld seconds."

"Neither of those things is true!"

"They are indeed," Pors contradicted Seth. "Here on Trope—as little as I care to acknowledge it—you command as well as speak for us. This has been our intention from the beginning."

"You never said I was to meet with the Magistrate alone!"

"What difference does that make?" Douin asked. "You knew you were to be our envoy, that you were to do the speaking."

"But not that you'd abandon me on the Magistrate's doorstep!"

"Give him the dairauddes," Lord Pors said, ignoring Seth's accusation. "Begin with that."

"Yes," Douin interjected. "That may calm you down."

"If I command as well as speak for you," Seth reasoned desperately, "then I command you to accompany me to this audience."

"Your command authority doesn't extend so far as that," Pors countered. "Do well, Master Seth. I think they're ready for you."

At the top of the helical stairway, the cloaked escort gestured to Seth. Then he disappeared into the room again.

"What's this about?" Seth demanded. *"What are you doing?"*

"You know your mission already," Douin replied, purposely misunderstanding his first question, ignoring the second. "You have our prayers."

"The dairauddes," Pors added. "Don't forget it."

When the Gla Tausians withdrew from Seth, he went hesitantly forward because there was nothing else to do. Why had Abel isolated him with Lord Pors and Master Douin? And why, now that they had all set foot on Trope, were the Kieri—both experienced administrators and envoys—isolating him still further by prodding him into this important meeting alone? Seth's heart thudded, his hands clenched and unclenched at his sides, and a sense of inadequacy climbed his constricted throat like an ill-digested meal, its taste at once brackish and insipid.

At the base of the stairway waited the Tropiard who had not unhooded. As Seth passed him, he noticed the alien's impersonal stare—an impersonality heightened by his slitted goggles—and his impossibly smooth, coffee-colored flesh. Also, he was tall, taller by a head than Seth, as perfect and as unreal as a mannequin.

"The Magistrate expects you," the Tropiard said in Vox. His mouth—a thin, smile-shaped scar—scarcely parted to speak these words.

Neither acknowledging this greeting nor looking back to determine the whereabouts of his companions, Seth climbed to the Magistrate's chamber. At the top of the stairs he pivoted and entered the sanctuary of the highest official of the most advanced nation on all of Trope. Günter Latimer dead and Abel inaccessible in the *Dharmakaya,* Seth crossed the threshold and faced a being of stunning appearance and power. . . .

FIVE

On the wall behind the Magistrate of Trope, a white banner. In the banner's center, a large blue circle. Separating Seth and the Magistrate, a wine-colored table made of stone and featuring on its surface a number of inset panels. Sheets of bronze plastic, these panels rippled in the light like tiny lakes. A similar substance capped the elevated chamber, concealing it from the eyes of any in the J'beij employed on still higher platforms.

Neither Seth nor the Magistrate spoke. As they faced each other, the alien by the doorway silently departed.

The Magistrate wore an immaculate white jumpsuit. About his neck was a silver chain from which hung a soft brown amulet. Beholding it, Seth put his hand to the dairauddes he'd brought from Gla Taus. The Magistrate duplicated this gesture, tenderly caressing the leather amulet. Immediately, Seth felt that the man—a gosfi—was trying to put him at his ease, settle his nerves, establish a bond.

But like all the other Tropiards Seth had seen, the Magistrate wore a pair of slitted eye coverings that interposed a disconcerting barrier. They concealed and excluded, giving him the spooky aura of a thief or an executioner. Seth was forced to concentrate on the features he could clearly see: dark skin, smiling lips, a head with the softly polished look of worn stone. Also, considering the height of the Tropiards who had guided them in from the landing terrace, Seth was surprised to find that the Magistrate was not quite as tall as he. Although not a small man, neither was the Magistrate a primeval giant.

"I am Ulgraji Vrai," he said in perfect Vox.

Seth dropped to one knee before the Magistrate, as Latimer had taught him to do before an important head of state on a planet in the Menkent system, and obediently recited his brief genealogy.

"Isoget of Günter Latimer," the Magistrate repeated. "And younger iso-het of a pair separated by fourteen E-years. Is that correct?"

"Yes, Magistrate."

"Please rise, Seth Latimer." Seth stood. "Now, explain for me the significance of such terms as isohet and isosire."

Seth concisely explained them.

"Then you have but a single birth-parent, and that birth-parent in your case was perpetually *j'gosfi*?"

"I don't understand," Seth replied.

"*J'gosfi*. You would say male. I think. A more precise translation might be sapient male: *j'gosfi*."

"Yes, then. My isosire—my birth-parent, as you would have it—was perpetually male. He was perpetually sapient, too. At least until he permitted the priests in Feln to—" Seth stopped.

"To what, Seth Latimer?"

"His death might have been prevented, I meant to say."

Seth glanced nervously behind him, his thoughts turning to the Kieri ministers who had just deserted him.

"A difficulty, Kahl Latimer?"

The Tropish honorific sounded strange to Seth. "My—" He could scarcely get the word out. "My seconds await me below, Magistrate, and I fear—"

"You fear they're uncomfortable. Very well. I'm now dispatching the men who guided you here to see to their comfort. One of them speaks exemplary Vox. He'll show your seconds about Huru J'beij before escorting them to a dormitory for visitors. You and I, meanwhile, are alone to conduct our business, Kahl Latimer."

Seth waited for Magistrate Vrai to call aloud, to push buttons, to clap his hands, to do anything that would indicate he was "dispatching" a guide to Pors and Douin. But nothing like that happened.

—Shall we get on with that business, then?

The Magistrate studied Seth with the expression of a praying mantis. He hadn't spoken aloud. His lips had not moved. Instead, the words that Seth had just "heard" had opened inside his brain like tiny fire roses.

"You registered my message?" the Magistrate said aloud. Seth neither moved nor spoke. Something wonderful and terrifying had occurred.

"As the guardian of the Mwezahbe Legacy, Kahl Latimer, I'm a rational being. But even before you set foot in the J'beij, I'd had the irrational certainty that I would find you a creature after my own mind. Isn't that a presumptuous clairvoyance? After all, we're quite literally from two different worlds." Magistrate Vrai began rapidly snapping the long middle finger of his left hand against his palm, a reflexive mechanism that Seth supposed was the gosfi equivalent of human laughter. "And yet . . . and yet I believe I've just established the complete reliability of that clairvoyance, no matter how irrational it may strike you."

"What did you do?" Seth asked.

—*What did I do?*

There it was again, a kind of lovely violation. A windfall of microscopic seeds penetrating Seth's gray matter and instantly germinating. His own startled consciousness briefly evaporated in order to let this other burst through.

"Please," Seth said. "What are you doing?"

"Testing a hypothesis," the Magistrate said aloud. "You're an offworlder, but one descended from a solitary male birth-parent. We have this last in common, Kahl Latimer. Also, despite your otherworldly origins, you're able to receive my . . . *cerebrations*, let's call them. That further testifies to the bond between us. Somehow I don't believe your Gla Tausian friends will experience a like receptiveness."

Seth wobbled in the knees. The air in his lungs was thin and metallic tasting. This capacity of the Magistrate to plant messages in his brain frightened him. It implied other capabilities: insight, knowledge, power. Guilt welled up in Seth, but why? What was reprehensible in being fearful in the presence of the unknown?

—*Being men of one mind, we shouldn't have to deprive the Kieri too long of your company.*

This was torture. Although the phenomenon did not in the least hurt, it bewildered and disorientated.

—*Being men of one mind, we should obtain agreement quickly.*

"You flatter me," Seth managed, his voice raw in the otherwise silent chamber: raw and intrusive.

Taking pity, the Magistrate told Seth aloud, "Kahl Latimer, it's exactly as I've said. I believe we have many things in common. Despite our physical differences, despite the differences in our backgrounds, I believe we're creatures of like motive. Don't you feel this, too?"

"No," Seth said.

The Magistrate's long middle finger began to snap against his palm. "Am I too esoteric for you? Have I embarrassed you?"

"No. Neither."

"What, then? You're exceedingly nervous."

"I'm exceedingly nervous," Seth agreed.

"Why?"

"You were thinking with my mind. Can you see into it? Do you know my thoughts, the range of my fears?"

"No," Magistrate Vrai said. "I've spoken in a manner you would call telepathic, yes, but I don't blithely pull information from your head, if that's your fear."

"Momentarily it was."

"Then put it aside. I've thought a good deal about a telepathic community, Kahl Latimer, and my belief is that it would most likely create either a thoroughly paranoiac or a thoroughly homogeneous unit of individuals. Complete suspicion and hostility in the one instance, total harmony and concord in the other. I don't care too much for either alternative."

There it was: Seth's excuse to broach something of his purpose in coming to Trope.

"But isn't it true," he began, "that you have a telepathic group of the second type here in the very nation you rule? A body of people in total concord?"

"You mean the Sh'gaidu, do you not?"

"Yes, Magistrate."

Magistrate Vrai lowered himself into a chair of a pale-gray, glassy substance and then swiveled about to face the banner hanging on his wall. "With regard to their state government, Kahl Latimer, the Sh'gaidu have adopted the first attitude, that of suspicion and hostility. Perhaps, in the past, we've given them cause." Face averted from Seth, he tilted his elegant head back. "You come quickly to the point."

"Not so soon as I might have, Magistrate." These words, spoken, sounded like a rebuke, but Seth had intended them . . . innocently.

His thoughts flew back to Gla Taus. On the morning that he'd entered the laulset pool with Lady Turshebsel, Lord Pors had explained a little of the complicated case of Trope and its troublesome Sh'gaidu subculture. Later, aboard the *Dharmakaya*, Seth had tried to learn still more about the Sh'gaidu from both the Point Marcher and the various library tapes. The truth, however, was that information about Trope was scant, and information about the Sh'gaidu dissidents almost nonexistent.

Basically, the Sh'gaidu were an embarrassment because their entire orientation as a culture was shamanistic and mystical, not rational and technophilic. For innumerable revolutions of Trope they had stymied their government's best efforts to bring them to heel, drawing upon formidable spiritual resources to resist state domination. As a consequence, small as the sect apparently was, its vitality was an affront to Tropish ideals and a dangerous beacon to young or disillusioned Tropiards who had failed to lay to heart the statutes of the Mwezahbe Legacy, the rational code by which the Tropish state professed to operate and into whose rigorous teachings it scrupulously initiated its children. The Sh'gaidu, as Seth understood the matter, represented an unacceptable challenge to this code. Moreover, the state feared the Sh'gaidu because in their insistence on the mystical unity of all gosfi they had developed full interencephalic communication among their own number: an exclusive sort of telepathy.

Magistrate Vrai swiveled about in his chair—it resembled a glass tulip, a truncated corona for a seat—and beckoned Seth toward him. "Here," he said, rising and moving along the other edge of the table. "Please sit. Ordinarily my own advisors stand, but you've traversed many lights and I want you to be comfortable."

Seth assumed the Magistrate's chair, easing himself down.

"I'll walk about, Kahl Latimer, as you outline your proposal."

Still uncertain, Seth scrutinized his gloved hands. The proposal he intended to make was already known in part to the Magistrate because of earlier sublimission exchanges between Trope and various taussanaur officials aboard the *Dharmakaya*. How he acquitted himself in the voicing of this proposal, however, would determine whether the Magistrate accepted or rejected its terms. Prospects for success seemed good, else the Tropiards would never have permitted them to come. Although little comforted by this fact, Seth decided to speak bluntly.

"We wish to remove the telepathic Sh'gaidu from your planet to Gla Taus in order to—"

"No, wait a moment!" The Magistrate, who had been strolling toward the banks of white communication consoles at the other end of the room, turned and let his hands play distractedly with his amulet. "The Sh'gaidu, Kahl Latimer, are no more telepathic than any of us here in the J'beij. What they have is a shared intuitive ability. Because they follow the spurious *Path of Duagahvi Gaidu,* they're like so many interwired robots. They share one another's preprogrammed world view. That, not telepathy, is the secret of their community. Sometimes, in fact, I think them a peculiar clan of spiritually leveled individuals."

This phrasing recalled to Seth the attitude of Lord Pors toward the pilot of their light-tripper. Caranicas, the Kieri had implied, was little more than a robot interwired with the astrogational components of its ship.

Seth shook off the incongruous recollection. "How many Sh'gaidu exist on your planet, Magistrate?"

"Perhaps a few more than three hundred."

So few! Seth was astonished to think that a tribe no bigger than that could so disastrously tie up the machinery of the state. Was it Pure Reason that had prohibited the Tropiards from annihilating the Sh'gaidu?

"I think I understand your surprise," the Magistrate told Seth. "In the past, the Sh'gaidu numbered considerably more, perhaps into the modest thousands, and the state instituted both vicious and subtle pogroms against them. I'm the first of five magistrates since Seitaba Mwezahbe to resist a policy of harassment against dissenters. In the case of the Sh'gaidu, who arose fairly recently in our history, I have actively sought a kinder solution to the problem, often against the bellicose counsel of my administrative deputy and the leaders of Trope's Thirty-three Cities. It's my *duty*, Kahl Latimer, to find a humane solution."

The Magistrate strolled away from Seth again, trailing his fingers along the edge of the wine-colored table. "We Tropiards—we gosfi, to be more accurate—are not a prolific species. We live long lives, bear few young, and evolve only by preserving individuals—even individuals who would thwart the evolutionary goals of the Mwezahbe Legacy and the Tropish state. Three hundred lives have real meaning here, Kahl Latimer. And now it's my understanding that you wish to take our exasperating three hundred Sh'gaidu back to Gla Taus with you. Why? How can this profit you?"

Seth picked up a thread he had dropped earlier. "The government of Kier wants to open up an uninhabited territory called the Ilvaudsettan, or the Obsidian Wastes, in the northern polar region of their world. The pioneers and technicians in this territory require supplies that Kier itself seems incapable of yielding. Outside of Feln and Sket, its two major cities, life is often at the subsistence level. This need has caused the Kieri government to look to Trope, Magistrate. Isn't it true that the Sh'gaidu economy is based on a self-contained agricultural system?"

"Quite true. They eat only what they grow."

"Well, then, Lady Turshebsel, Liege Mistress of Kier, wishes to deed to the Sh'gaidu—forever—a large area of land in a subtropical region along the southernmost margin of Kier. This territory is called the Feht Evashsted. The land here, generously manured with volcanic ash, is very fertile. The volcanism, however, is a thing of the past and poses no current danger."

"Why does she wish to give the Sh'gaidu such desirable holdings? Why don't the Gla Tausians open up *this* area—rather than the inhospitable polar region where supplies are scarce?"

As Seth explained the Kieri susceptibility to heat and the fanatical aisautseb prejudice against colonizing any area south of the Feht Evashsted, Magistrate Vrai came back to his chair, pushed a console key, and summoned a bronze plastic panel in front of Seth out of its inset well.

This panel rose from the surface of the table and opened like a book before the two men, revealing what appeared to be an animated satellite image of Gla Taus. The Magistrate pushed another key and the planet grew larger in the dim bronze screen. Light illuminated the image from behind, and the entire northern hemisphere was revealed, almost as if in three dimensions.

After the Magistrate had frozen this image, Seth pointed out the Feht Evashsted, the Obsidian Wastes, and the waterways by which Ommundi shipping could transport agricultural products from the proposed Sh'gaidu commune to the pioneers working their way northward from Old Ilvaudset.

"You see, Magistrate, Kieri priests forbid the development of the Evashsted Sea and its islands because they regard these places as Gla Taus hell. Only demons would wish to go there, and only the vilest would use its products. My isosire was murdered for proposing the development of the area to Lady Turshebsel, a progressive ruler who regrets the opportunities being squandered because of the backwardness and superstition of the aisautseb. Opening the Feht Evashsted to the Sh'gaidu is only an interim solution to a much larger problem, but the aisautseb have grudgingly approved this plan because they regard this coastal region as only an antechamber to Hell rather than as Hell itself, and because no Kieri will be required to go there. At present, only misfits and exiles live in the Feht Evashsted."

The Magistrate peered past Seth at the image of Gla Taus on the rippling panel. "For which reason you believe the Sh'gaidu will be at home there, too?"

"Oh, no, Magistrate; not because they're misfits. Lord Pors tells me that the Sh'gaidu thrive in an environment similar to the Feht Evashsted's."

"The land they hold," said the Magistrate, standing erect, "lies about a thousand kilometers northeast of Ardaja Huru. At one time it was considered worthless, though the protogosfi of Trope's prehistoric past may have found the basin hospitable. There's some evidence to support this conjecture. No matter. Seitaba Mwezahbe didn't approve the basin as a site for one of the Thirty-three Cities of the Tropish state, and the Sh'gaidu inherited it by default."

"The land is no longer considered worthless?"

"The Sh'gaidu made it otherwise. In doing so, they've earned the envy as well as the disapproval of many Tropiards."

Seth's nervousness fled. The Magistrate's words had rekindled his enthusiasm: "Magistrate, all would benefit by the removal of the Sh'gaidu to Gla Taus. The Kieri find new allies in their assault on the Obsidian Wastes, Trope is disencumbered of an embarrassment, and the Sh'gaidu escape the persecution of their fellow Tropiards."

Magistrate Vrai—Seth noticed to his chagrin—winced at the world persecution, but did not rebuke him for using it.

"What of the Latimer isohets, Seth and Abel?" he asked instead. "How do they benefit?"

"We earn our passage home by succeeding in our mission to you. At present, you see, the *Dharmakaya* is effectively in Kieri hands."

"You gain nothing in the way of material wealth?"

Seth was startled. "No, Magistrate."

—*You gain nothing in the way of material wealth?*

Again, the gentle, uncanny mind rape that simultaneously warmed him and made him feel petty.

"No," Seth said again. "I get to go home. Nothing more than that, Magistrate, but it's everything."

The Magistrate absentmindedly played his console keyboard—whereupon the bronze panel in front of Seth closed like a book, collapsed upon itself, and settled back into the table's surface. Then Vrai walked to the far end of the room, his fine dark hands clasped at his back.

"What material would you require, Kahl Latimer? Assuming, of course, that the Sh'gaidu accept our offer."

Seth stood. "*Our* offer," the Magistrate had just said. That meant that he, the younger of Günter's two isohets, had singlehandedly carried the first phase of their mission to Trope to a successful conclusion! His nervousness returned. His gloves were wringing wet.

"For the initial evacuation from their basin—" Seth stumbled, thinking through what Pors and Douin had drilled into him were their likely needs.

"They call it Palija Kadi," the Magistrate said, misinterpreting his hesitation. "It means the Great Wall. Nonetheless, Palija Kadi is what they also call the basin itself."

"For the evacuation of the basin," Seth said, virtually ignoring this, "we'll need trucks or vans and drivers to operate them. The *Dharmakaya* is large enough to transport all three hundred Sh'gaidu to Gla Taus. Once there, the Kieri government will provide them with everything necessary to become self-sufficient in Feht Evashsted."

"Trucks. Drivers. That can be arranged. We also have transcraft to convey the evacuees to your light-tripper."

"Good," said Seth, elated.

The Magistrate crossed his office's plum carpet and paused at the head of the stairs. "Come. Let's see what arrangements have been made for your friends."

Together Seth and Magistrate Vrai descended into the vast cathedral of the J'beij, where the young isohet marveled again at the clear hanging scaffolds, the ornamental tapestries and banners, and the strange radionic cabinets and equipment banks manned by silent Tropiards.

SIX

Somewhere amid the crossing pathways of the government building, Magistrate Vrai introduced Seth to another Tropiard who spoke Vox. This person was attired in a jumpsuit the color of day-old cream and a pair of glinting white goggles. He stood at least a quarter of a meter shorter than Seth, and although his body appeared a weak and breakable thing, his movements had the punishing rigor of an ineptly handled marionette. He bowed, nodded, and gestured as if too tautly strung.

"Seth Latimer, this is my administrative deputy, Ehte Emahpre."

A jerky, birdlike nod.

Deputy Emahpre was wearing an amulet similar to the Magistrate's: a pouch of dark brown embellished by a tiny amber gem. Seeing another amulet, Seth was reminded that he had not yet given the Magistrate the dairauddes that Pors had repeatedly told him to present *at once*. This realization stung and befuddled. His answering nod to the Deputy was awkward, without follow-through, and his attention to the little man disintegrated into the fragments of his broken pledge to Pors. Still, this was not the right time to remove the ceramic weapon and hand it to his host. . . .

"Deputy Emahpre," the Magistrate was saying, "is the most incorruptible and self-confident of my advisors."

This testimony failed to focus Seth's concentration. He wanted to be free of the moment, but hoped, too, that Pors and Douin would not appear before he could hand over their bothersome gift. Günter Latimer had understood the mechanisms of such trifling protocol. So, perhaps, did Abel. But, for him, the demand on his patience was a minor horror. Hadn't he accomplished the first phase of their mission without any such meaningless formality?

"The most annoying thing about our relationship," the Magistrate was saying, snapping his fingers, "is that Deputy Emahpre's incorruptible thinking almost inevitably leads him to conclusions different from my own."

Emahpre politely demurred. "Not inevitably, Magistrate."

"But often. Quite often."

Although the Magistrate continued snapping his fingers banteringly, Seth slowly awoke to the fact that conflict as well as respect bound the two administrators. Wasn't it true that Abel often laughed as he filtered a relationship of grudges? Apparently gosfi psychology permitted a similar tack among Tropiards.

Seth was alert again. He wished to survive.

He listened as the Magistrate explained to Deputy Emahpre what had just occurred between Seth and him. He listened as the Magistrate declared his intention to accompany Seth and the two Kieri envoys to Palija Kadi to speak with Duagahvi Gaidu's Pledgechild about the proposed removal. And he listened as Emahpre, taken aback by this declaration, began expostulating with Vrai in their native tongue.

"For our visitor's sake," the Magistrate interrupted his deputy, "I would prefer you to speak in Vox."

The Deputy glanced at Seth, as if surprised to find him still there, and then obeyed the Magistrate: "You needn't go to Palija Kadi yourself," he said more composedly. "The decision of the Pledgechild may be secured through me or some other intermediary, Magistrate. The danger to you is such that—"

"I've decided to go, Deputy Emahpre."

"Why?" Emahpre asked.

"It's my word that determines in which direction Trope moves, and the Sh'gaidu are Tropiards—even if they sometimes seem to disown us, and we them."

"Sometimes!" Emahpre said. "They reject both union with us and repatriation as enfranchised citizens."

"My responsibility requires that I go to them directly with this proposal, Deputy Emahpre. My *position* requires it."

Seth watched Emahpre strut away along a bank of consoles as if to regroup his wits. Even if he walked like a marionette, he was obviously far from being the Magistrate's puppet.

Jerking about and jabbing a finger at Vrai, he said, "Your word need not arrive in the Sh'gaidu basin in your own person in order to be implemented. If you're killed there—"

"I won't be killed."

"If you're killed there, Magistrate, you will have sacrificed yourself—the leader of Trope—not to state ends, but to private ones I'm totally unable to fathom."

Seth asked, "Are the Sh'gaidu prone to violence, then?"

"Precisely the opposite," Vrai said.

"Precisely what they're prone to is a matter of conjecture," the Deputy rejoined. "Which is precisely why they remain under state surveillance."

The Magistrate approached his deputy with his hands spread, but halted an arm's length away and dropped them to his sides. "Alone among our magistrates, I've dealt humanely with these people. Why should they wish to kill me? I don't fear them, Deputy Emahpre, and I intend to go."

"Why?"

To Seth the question had the ring of insubordination. The Magistrate, he saw, reacted almost as if he had been slapped, turning his face and then walking a step or two aside.

Still, Vrai did not resort to Tropish: "I've come to my position"—a strange, gravid pause—"honestly, Deputy Emahpre, and I intend to fulfill its responsibilities to their most exacting letter. Tomorrow morning, I accompany our visitors to Palija Kadi. No more about this, please."

"Very well," said Ehte Emahpre crisply. "But it's *my* intention to go with you. Until the morning, then, Kahl Latimer."

He performed a bobbing bow and stuttered off into the open labyrinth of the J'beij.

Outside, it was far colder than Seth recalled. The sky was a dolorous purple behind the massive red-brown planes of the buildings, and a wind came careering along the plateau from the northwest. Seth saw that their transcraft was no longer on the landing terrace. His heart misgave him, and he grasped the Magistrate's sleeve.

"We'll go to Palija Kadi in a Tropish aircraft!" the Magistrate shouted in response to his unspoken query. "Yours has been towed away to clear the landing terrace for other vehicles!" He pointed to the east.

Among the silver-strutted remotes on a distant landing field Seth saw the *Dharmakaya*'s transcraft. It was too big for the playmates it was grouped with, even though it looked alien-seeming and tiny because of the distance.

Relieved, Seth shouted, "Where are we going?"

"Our dormitory for state visitors! Your seconds are already there!"

The dormitory on the eastern edge of Huru J'beij didn't much resemble the J'beij itself. It was faceted like an enormous piece of garnet, with tall rectangular windows resembling the panels in the Magistrate's command table. Following his host, Seth entered a foyer glassed about like an aquarium. He turned around to find that the sky was not discolored by the dormitory's tinted windows. He could see out without hindrance, but no prying Tropiard could see in. Nor could the wind rattle the immense panes visoring the front of the dormitory.

Anja, Trope's mercurial sun, hovered above the J'beij. A deepening purple spread over everything as it descended beyond the acropolis.

"Here," Seth said, removing the dairauddes and handing it to Magistrate Vrai. "I've been remiss in failing to give this to you before now. Once it belonged to Lady Turshebsel. Her chief advisor among all the aisautseb, Narthaimnar Chappouib, placed it in my keeping the day before we left Gla Taus as a gift to you and an emblem of our cooperation in the endeavor ahead." The phrasing was Pors's, but Douin had rehearsed Seth in its delivery a hundred times.

Magistrate Vrai accepted the dairauddes and turned it in his hands as if it were a flute and he an inexperienced musician.

"Is it true, then," he asked, "that the administrative head of Kier is perpetually sh'gosfi and that her shamans are exclusively male?"

"The priests are men," Seth replied, puzzled. "And Lady Turshebsel is of course a woman. Is that what your question means?"

The Magistrate, without answering, hefted the dairauddes. He took a sighting through it as if it were an abbreviated telescope. He inserted his finger in the wider end. He tapped it in his palm. He blew, to no purpose, across the smaller end. He plugged the wider end with the tip of his thumb and again blew across the smaller opening, this time producing an ear-splitting whistle. He shook the dairauddes like an old-fashioned thermometer. He twirled it gently on its chain, as if it were a winding tool. He pointed it at Seth.

"What is it?" he finally asked.

"A dairauddes, Magistrate. That's what the Kieri call it. A literal translation is—" Seth caught his breath. The Kieri had played a vicious trick on him. Or, if not the Kieri, then Chappouib and all the aisautseb. For an entire E-month he'd been carrying about with him, almost unquestioningly, a specimen of instrument that—in bloody orchestration with others like it—had slain his isosire. Was he buying his trip home in the coin of Kieri mockery?

"Yes?" the Magistrate urged him.

"A literal translation is demon killer, Magistrate Vrai." He was too confused to weep, but the impetus was there somewhere, biding its time. "It's a *spiritual* weapon, they say."

The Magistrate handed it back to Seth. "I'm sorry, Kahl Latimer, but the statutes of the Mwezahbe Legacy don't permit me to accept such a gift. The Magistrate of Trope never goes armed."

"Not to carry, then, sir; to keep as a memento among your other possessions. As I say, this is a spiritual weapon."

Seth looked despairingly across the tablerock at the J'beij. Trope's small, orchid-blue sun was balancing on the northern end of the building's long entablature. The sky around it seemed to be in a state of lush, organic rot. To return to Pors without having presented the dairauddes . . .

"But it's wounded you, this weapon, hasn't it?"

"Magistrate?" Seth asked.

"Never mind, Kahl Latimer. I can't accept it, not even as a memento to put in a museum case. Not only does the Legacy forbid me the possession of weapons, it likewise prohibits me from collecting or wearing the products of superstition or religious ritual." Vrai suddenly grasped the amulet hanging at his breast. "With one exception, that is, and by this we all acknowledge the ultimate mystery of origins."

Seth started to replace the dairauddes about his own neck.

The Magistrate's cool hand checked him. "No," he said. "Wear this in its place." Fumbling briefly at the chain, Vrai slipped the amulet over his head and placed it in Seth's free hand. Then, gesturing, he urged Seth to don it, which the young isohet did bemusedly.

—*Being men of one mind, we may safely share what's most important.*

Seth closed his eyes. He had registered the Magistrate's cerebration as a series of piquant, encephalic pin pricks—even though he knew full well that the brain has no nerve endings.

"Magistrate, what have you given me?"

"This ornament we call *dascra gosfi'mija*. It means treasure of the birth-parent. I wish you to wear mine. Perhaps its bestowal will atone in some small way for the insult your seconds are likely to perceive in my refusal of their Liege Mistress's spiritual weapon."

"I can't speak for their possible response, Magistrate."

"Of course you can't. In the meantime, wear this. I must have something from you in exchange—*not* the dairauddes—and you must agree to keep my gift with you at all times until your departure from Trope, when you must give it back into my keeping. Our exchange will betoken the bond between us during our mission to Palija Kadi. We are men of one mind."

Discomfited, Seth replied, "Magistrate, I don't know what you mean when you say that. I don't feel it as you seem to, and I believe you should know my confusion. What we have in common, I think, is a desire to settle our own private concerns through the Sh'gaidu. That's all."

—*I must have something in exchange*, the Magistrate cerebrated sharply, as if Seth hadn't even spoken.

"But I—"

"This will do, I think." The Magistrate stepped forward and with quick fingers unclasped still another chain at Seth's neck. Was he retrieving the amulet he'd just given? No, not that. Seth saw that clutched in Vrai's right hand were the collapsible eye coverings that Abel had told him to wear on Trope.

"But those are for the sun, Magistrate. I may require them tomorrow in the Sh'gaidu basin."

"If you do, we'll provide you with *anjajwedo*—slit-goggles, you might say—like our own. Yours I must have in exchange for the amulet." He put Seth's goggles around his neck.

The sky's orchid rot had quickened to a kind of overarching bruise. Deeply melancholy, this hurt stained the entire twilight landscape.

"I trust you, Kahl Latimer. I'm sensitive to emanations. I know you for a good man. Moreover, we have at least one thing else in common besides the Sh'gaidu."

Seth waited for clarification.

"We each wish to go home," the Magistrate cryptically obliged. "We each wish to go home."

SEVEN

The first-floor "room" in which Douin and Pors had been lodged was in reality an elevated platform with a pair of papery screens for walls. Another side was open to a corridor, and the fourth and final wall was glass: a prodigious dormitory window that the Kieri envoys had opaqued by some subtle interior fine tuning. Bronze in color, this window shimmered against Trope's mournful twilight.

Entering, Seth saw three sleeping pallets sunk like shallow graves into the carpeted platform. Pors and Douin sat in tulip chairs near the window, hunched over a small plastic gantry playing a Kieri counter game called *naugced.* It was comforting to see that they had retrieved their effects kits from the transcraft before coming to the dormitory; Seth's, too. He pulled off his clammy gloves and tossed them toward the only pallet not already littered with Kieri hair clasps, pumice-soap bundles, and ministerial caps.

This would be the first night since his boyhood in the Lausanne Paedoschol that he had slept in a room with someone other than Günter Latimer or his own isohet. How strange that his bedfellows should be Gla Tausians, jauddeb, *aliens.* A scent as of bitter cinnamon pervaded the area, and Seth knew this to be an intimate Kieri scent. Although Pors was smoking *fehtes,* a rare Feht Evashsted "tobacco" said to have strange effects on jauddeb metabolism, the smell in the room derived less from the burning cigarette than from the simple presence of Pors and Douin themselves.

They had turned their corner of this Tropish dormitory into a Kieri geffide.

Seth tossed the dairauddes into his pallet after his gloves, and Douin, who was awaiting Pors's next play, looked up.

"Master Seth!" he cried, rising.

Pors also looked up, and Seth was momentarily startled by the haggard-ness of the Point Marcher's face. It had an indrawn, cadaverous look that Seth couldn't attribute solely to fehtes and fatigue. But Pors returned his attention immediately to the naugced game, thus freeing Seth of the need to explain why the ebony demon killer was still in his possession.

He spoke first of his success: "Magistrate Vrai will accompany us tomor-row to the Sh'gaidu commune. He will intercede on our behalf with the Pledgechild—which, it seems, is the title of the Sh'gaidu leader."

"Excellent!" Douin exclaimed.

"I also met Vrai's administrative deputy, a Tropiard named Ehte Emah-pre. He says he's going, too."

"We also met Deputy Emahpre," Douin said. "He showed us a portion of the J'beij and a little of the tablerock. He has no very good opinion of the Sh'gaidu, I'm afraid."

"Ekthep ath agronomithz," Pors mumbled. "Which ith all we want them for." He ran a counter along one of the struts of the naugced gantry. Then he, too, rose.

Bewildered by Pors's appearance and unintelligibility, Seth confessed his only failure: "Magistrate Vrai refused Lady Turshebsel's gift. He said that the Mwezahbe Legacy prohibits him from having either weapons or religious artifacts. The dairauddes is both."

"Where is it?" Pors demanded.

Seth gestured toward his pallet. Pors, in turn, gestured brusquely at Dou-in, who walked with calm dignity to the sunken bed, knelt beside it, and picked up the spurned Kieri offering. It was with difficulty that Pors main-tained *his* composure, and when he next spoke, expanding his barrel chest to keep the words from spilling too quickly out, Seth realized what had caused the unsettling change in his looks and diction.

"Thith ith an inthult to uth," he began. "Thith ith . . . Mathta Dou-in, fetch him afta my thurrogathz! I won't continnoo like thith!" And Pors turned abruptly on his heel and faced the great bronze window.

"There's a lavalet at the end of the corridor," Douin told Seth, still kneel-ing. "He wants you to bring him his surrogates."

"His dentures?"

Douin merely nodded, embarrassed for the young isohet and chagrined that his Point Marcher had chosen this way to chastise Seth for a foreordained failure. Seth was amused, sorrier for Douin's discomfort than for the supposedly degrading task Pors had just set him. Never had he imagined that the Kieri had perfected orbiting vehicles before stumbling upon the necessary prophylactic measures to preserve an individual's natural teeth. Maybe someone had knocked Pors's out for him. Considering the Point Marcher's disposition, that seemed highly likely.

Seth left the sleeping area, walked down the corridor, and entered his first Tropish lavalet.

A transparent pedestal surmounted by a circular ceramic basin dominated the room. Against one wall was a wide marble shelf upon which stood three wingbacked lavatory chairs, stone strategically upholstered with a velvetlike fabric the same shade of plum as the Magistrate's carpet. Chromium pedals protruded from the base of each chair. Did male Tropiards stand or sit when they had to make water? The chairs seemed ill designed for the upright, face-on technique, nor were there any urinals or canted troughs to accommodate such an approach. Whatever your business, you apparently had to sit. Seth mounted the shelf and pushed a pedal with his foot. A blast of air rather than water cycloned in the hopper, creating an echo as if from the fathomless catacombs beneath Huru J'beij. That was all.

Satisfied that the contraption would neither devour nor emasculate him, Seth sat and relieved his bladder. Toilet training in the Lausanne Paedoschol all over again. He remembered that training only because one of the male warders had delighted in telling him what a troublesome case he had been. The bastard . . .

Water rather than air flowed through the pedestal of the wash basin. Seth used a half-melted bar of pumice-soap to scrub his hands, then shook them over the basin and wiped them lightly on his pantaloons because he saw no towels or air-blowing devices on the walls. Maybe Tropiards dripped dry.

Lord Pors's "surrogates"—which Seth had seen upon entering—hung by a thread of dental floss from a circular tray above the basin. Out of his mouth, they were, well, australopithecine. *Obscenely* australopithecine. At least to Seth's eye. The sort of thing that a fossil hunter—not a modern dental technician—would cast. But this was a homocentric prejudice that did him little credit. Really, what most disturbed him (Seth tried to tell himself) was having to tote the damn things back to Pors on a thread. He would have been no happier if the dentures had been designed for human use. But who, then, would? The task was just as demeaning as Pors wished it to be, although, it seemed to Seth, the Kieri lord lost as much face by exposing himself without his dentures as he saved by wreaking this petty and absurd punishment.

Carrying the teeth, Seth returned to Pors and Douin. Their naugced game was forgotten. Pors grabbed the surrogates from Seth, unwound the thread of floss, and stuck them firmly in his mouth. When he spoke, he was again intelligible:

"There's no excuse for his refusing the dairauddes! If he wished to insult us, he might just as well have pissed on our boots!"

"He didn't wish to insult us," Seth replied. "And the insult you propose may not be possible for Tropiards."

This made no impression on the Point Marcher. He stalked along the window, halted, and stared at Seth while ruefully shaking his head.

"It's senseless to worry about this," Douin told him. "We want to take the Sh'gaidu back to Gla Taus with us. The ultimate disposition of a ceramic blowgun is a simple irrelevancy."

"Not to the aisautseb!"

"The aisautseb aren't here."

"No, Master Douin, but *we* are. And by Chappouib's command we're their agents on Trope, as Master Seth is principally Lady Turshebsel's."

Seth asked, "Have either of you seen any female Tropiards? Any . . . women?"

Chappouib's Hawks of Conscience looked at Seth in surprise. Neither appeared to regard his question as meaningful; and, briefly, Pors and Douin were united again—in their annoyance at Seth's interruption.

"The lavalet facilities would suggest—" Douin began.

"Yes, they would," said Seth. "But were either of you introduced to a Tropiard who responded to a feminine pronoun? We bring jauddeb and human prejudices to our understanding of the lavalet facilities."

"This is their government complex," Pors snapped. "Their ruling hierarchy is masculine, as it is in Kier—with the exception of our Liege Mistress, may God protect her."

Douin put in, "Why do you ask, Master Seth?"

"I'm not sure, really. The Magistrate seemed pleased that I am an isohet: the male child of a single male birth-parent. *J'gosfi*, male sapient, was the term he used." Seth glanced toward the corridor behind him. "In the lavalet, though, it occurred to me that—except for height differences—everyone in the J'beij resembled the Magistrate. Do female sapients exist on Trope? That lavalet's not much evidence either way."

"We've seen nothing of Ardaja Huru or any of the other Tropish cities," Pors said. "Of course there are female sapients."

"I don't know," Seth demurred.

"It makes no difference!" Pors cried. "We don't wish to . . . to poke with them. We wish to put them in the Feht Evashsted as farmers." He strode to the naugced gantry and found the butt of his forgotten cigarette on one of its struts. One quick inhalation set the fehtes tobacco glowing again and the smell of bitter cinnamon drifting lazily toward Seth.

"Another possibility," Seth said, "is that female Tropiards may not interact with foreigners and offworlders."

Pors looked at Douin. "This is useless speculation. Nights on Trope are short, and we'd best take our rest." He inhaled deeply and expelled the pale blue smoke in a lacy, dissolving plume.

That was when Douin caught sight of the amulet hanging from Seth's neck. He approached to examine it.

"Every Tropiard wears one of these," he said, "much as devout Kieri wear their dairauddes. Where did you get this, Master Seth?"

"It was the Magistrate's."

"He gave it to you?"

"He insisted that I keep it until we've completed our mission to Palija Kadi, where the Sh'gaidu live."

"You should have refused to accept it," Pors said sourly.

"What is it?" Douin asked, still supporting it in his palm.

"A dascra gosfi'mija, or treasure of the birth-parent. He demanded that I give him my goggles in exchange."

"Was he dissatisfied with his own?" Pors asked, blowing out more smoke. "They all resemble jongleur-thieves, wearing those masklike goggles. Why would he want your pair?"

"In exchange," Seth said. "He had to have something in exchange."

"So long as it wasn't our dairauddes," Pors carped. But the amulet had begun to interest him, too, and he approached to grasp and heft it. "What *is* the birth-parent's treasure, Master Seth? The pouch feels as if it's laden with powder or fine sand. Do you know what it is?"

"No, Lord Pors. The Magistrate didn't say."

"Let's look, then."

Seth and Douin exchanged doubtful looks.

"Come, Master Seth. Remove it, please. It won't hurt to find out exactly what sort of treasure you're packing about for our host." Pors's garments reeked of fehtes—but his teeth were, or had been, clean.

"I'm afraid to do that," Seth said.

"Why?"

Seth told the Kieri about the Magistrate's ability to make messages flower in his mind. "I'm afraid he's also capable of reading my thoughts. He denied that he had this power, but if the Sh'gaidu possess it, as we've come to believe from the old Interstel reports, then why not Tropiards, too? What if . . . what if the Magistrate should *see* us opening his gift to me and examining its contents?"

Now Pors and Douin exchanged a glance. Their expressions, although full of meaning, were unreadable to Seth. A new uneasiness gripped his heart. He was among strangers.

Pors stubbed his cigarette in the palm of his hand, indifferent to the burn. Fehtes was supposed to offer the Kieri a degree of metabolic immunity to intense heat, but Seth had not known it could make a smoker unmindful of burns. The Point Marcher, understanding that Palija Kadi would be much warmer than Huru J'beij, was smoking in preparation for their journey there. The inhaled drug had numbed not only his anxiety about this trip but also his sensitivity to pain.

"Let me see the amulet," he said. "If the Magistrate gave it to you, he's also given you its contents . . . at least for the time being."

Seth relinquished the dascra gosfi'mija. Pors carried it to the ledge of smooth white stone traversing the dormitory's window. Seth and Douin followed. At the ledge Pors removed a tiny pin from the neck of the pouch and carefully laid the pin aside. Then he spread the lips of the amulet, shook it gently, and fanned a pattern of grayish-green dust across the ledge. Enough dust, thought Seth, to fill a pair of good-sized human thimbles. Little seemed extraordinary about the substance, but if Pors indulged a sudden whim and swept the stuff away merely to demonstrate his contempt of it, what would happen to them? Even a mere puff of breath would irrevocably scatter the substance. Seth, frightened, refused to breathe—but Pors turned to Douin with an exasperated shake of the head and gestured at the powder.

"Tropish gold?" he asked. "A rare mineral? A religious hallucinogen?"

"The Tropiards have no religion but reason," Douin said.

"Then what by the unholy Evashsteddan must it be?"

Averting his face, still half afraid to breathe, Seth said, "It *may* have religious significance. The Magistrate told me that by wearing the dascra gosfi'mija Tropiards acknowledge the ultimate mystery of origins."

"Dried semen?" Douin hazarded in complete seriousness.

"Wouldn't that qualify as a birth-parent's treasure?"

Pors made a noise of amused disgust. "Gosfi semen? Why not a powder of well-pestled gosfi ova?" He made the noise again. "Master Douin, your imagination indicts you for a morbid dreamer."

"I was simply attempting—" Douin began.

"We don't know what it is," Seth told the Kieri. "Nor do we have any way to analyze the substance. I'd feel much better if we returned it to the amulet. Suppose the Magistrate knows its quantity by weight. We may have all indicted ourselves not as dreamers but as losels and snoops. What footing do we gain by that?"

"None," Douin admitted. "You're right. You've gained us what footing we have by earning the Magistrate's trust, and we've imperiled that by strewing this substance about as if it were ground pumice."

"I would hardly call it strewn," said Pors testily, gesturing at the ledge. He took two small pieces of paper from his jacket, swept the substance onto one piece with the other, and carefully funneled the powder back into the amulet, which he then closed, pinned shut, and handed to Seth. "Wear your precious treasure, then. If this attire brings the Sh'gaidu to Gla Taus, it little matters to me what sort of foulness you wear around your neck."

Seth donned the amulet again. He watched as Lord Pors retrieved the dairauddes from his, Seth's, pallet and laid it reverently in the padded interior of a small leather case. Pors placed the case beside the pallet he had earlier claimed, and slumped back into his tulip chair.

"Do you wish to complete the naugced?" Douin asked him.

"Who leads in counters?"

"I do, my Lord."

"Then the naugced can go to Hell with Master Seth's isosire."

Seth, stung, glanced, indignantly at the Kieri lord. But before he could act upon his anger, Douin stepped forward and intercepted him. The Point Marcher, meanwhile, appeared completely unaware of the effect of his words. His posture betrayed his weariness. His mouth had fallen open, and his australopithecine dentures glittered in a film of saliva.

Thith ith an inthult, Seth thought at him mockingly, desperately coveting the Magistrate's ability to cerebrate.

Douin said, "The nights here are indeed short, Master Seth. We'd better get what sleep we can."

How could anyone sleep in those gravelike indentations on the floor? For that matter, how could he sleep in the same room with Pors and Douin? The contemplation of both prospects chilled Seth.

"I'll be back shortly," he told Clefrabbes Douin. "I need a few minutes alone."

Douin knelt and lifted something from his pallet. Approaching Seth, he said, "Here, you must be hungry. Take this with you. I'll leave the lights dimly glowing for your return."

Seth took the gift. Like a pear encased in a rind the color of Anja at sunset, it was a specimen of Tropish fruit. Holding it, Seth exited, strolled through the echoing darkness toward the dormitory's foyer, and, once there, bit into the fruit. Warm and juicy, tasting a bit like a Concord grape despite its size and texture, it appeased his hunger and somehow seemed to dissipate his wrath.

After he had finished the fruit and wiped his hands on his flanks, Seth studied the starscape. One of the stars was the *Dharmakaya*. Abel, his isohet, was inside it. Seth missed him.

EIGHT

In the morning, he was the first to open his eyes. He caught sight of a cloaked Tropiard studying his companions and him from the doorway. This alien, having ascertained that Seth was awake, slipped into the ill-secured chamber and knelt at his side with several small squeeze flasks and a bundle of fruit. Pors and Douin awakened after the Tropiard had entered.

"Drink," he urged in Vox, his goggles giving him the appearance of a thief. "You'll be departing for Palija Kadi in only a moment."

Seth accepted one of the squeeze flasks and drank. The liquid oozed into him, viscous and bittersweet, thirst- as well as hunger-slaking in spite of its honeylike consistency. He was reminded of milk and tart pineapple, smoothly blent.

Pors and Douin accepted the breakfast offerings of the kneeling Tropiard, too—undoubtedly one of the aliens who had met their transcraft yesterday afternoon—and their meal was quickly concluded. The Tropiard indicated that they should carry the fruit with them.

"What are they?" Seth asked.

"*Mwehanja,*" the messenger said, and it was impossible to miss his emphasis on the suffix.

They gathered their gear together and followed this tall, almost swash-buckling ghost out of the dormitory onto the tablerock. The shock of the cold air was as spirit-stiffening as it had been yesterday. How big and clean Trope seemed this morning, the sky like distilled water and the plains below the butte like an immense, brick-red apron. Ardaja Huru was huddled against the plateau's northern flank, invisible, and they walked past the rough-hewn buildings and the strange stone gazebos—which Seth supposed to be entrances to tubeways down to the city—as if they were the only living creatures on the planet.

A Tropish vehicle surmounted by a set of saucerlike wings waited on the circular terrace where they had landed the transcraft. It combined the appearance of an ancient cargo airplane with that of a modern helicraft, albeit one without rotors, and its skin shone silver-white. Two small figures stood near its nose, a bubblelike enclosure tinted, yes, a gleaming bronze; and using the figures to establish proportions, Seth judged the airship at least fourteen meters in length. It scarcely looked capable of flight. The Albatross, thought Seth. I'll call it The Albatross.

Pors was smoking fehtes again. The smoke trailed off behind him like an exhaust. He had spoken no more than three words since awakening, and he looked as fatigued as he had last night.

Deputy Emahpre, who had met and talked with all three offworlders, made the introductions. Magistrate Vrai welcomed Pors and Douin to Trope and offered a brief set speech in which he declared his world and Gla Taus "neighbors."

During these preliminaries, Emahpre stared fixedly at the amulet around Seth's neck. His gaze was persistent and incomprehensible. Although the goggles Tropiards wore made it hard to interpret their expressions, Seth feared that the little deputy's interest guaranteed his disapproval. You could read emanations without being psychic. Both Emahpre and Vrai were going to Palija Kadi, and neither was happy with the other's decision.

All five men boarded The Albatross. Emahpre went forward to take its helm, and a moment later Huru J'beij and Ardaja Huru were dropping away beneath Seth as the airship rose vertically. He had purposely come forward with the Deputy because the pilot's compartment offered such a splendid window on the landscape. He watched the portico and roof of the J'beij dwindle in size, the prairie expand, and blue-white streamers of sky creep into the peripheries of his vision. The Albatross was aloft, and moving. Its speed had increased to such an extent that the only cure for dizziness was more altitude. Emahpre considerately took them higher, and Seth turned his full attention to the feisty Tropiard.

Without looking at his human passenger, Emahpre said, "You're the only person since Vrai's assumption of the magistracy with whom he's shared his dascra. Did you know that?" Both the statement and the query felt like accusations.

"No," Seth said. "I didn't."

"You came by it terribly easily. When I met you in the J'beij yesterday afternoon, he hadn't yet given it to you, had he?"

"No, he hadn't."

"Vrai has made a terrible blunder, Kahl Latimer—an administrative, a cultural, and possibly even a spiritual blunder, even if my phrasing does smack of Sh'gaidu superstition."

"Is it your place to second-guess the Magistrate? Or to speak aloud to an offworlder the substance of such second-guessing?"

The Deputy's chin jerked toward Seth, but quickly swiveled back. "Yes, most definitely."

"And to voice your disagreements with him to others?"

Emahpre remained silent.

"I didn't ask him for the dascra," Seth said. "I told him that I didn't feel the same sense of union with him that he seemed to feel with me."

"Indeed?" Emahpre's voice was frankly incredulous.

"I don't even know what this is," Seth protested, covering the amulet with his palm. "I don't know what I'm—"

"If you were a Tropiard," Emahpre said, overriding him, "it would be a different matter. The bond would be mutual and absolute, whether you deserved the dascra or not. But you're a foreigner, an offworlder. It gives you an unjust advantage. You've become the manipulator of his peace of mind."

Seth said nothing.

The Deputy reiterated, "An unjust advantage."

"It's not one I wish to exploit. It's not one I asked for—Deputy Emahpre, what exactly has the Magistrate given me?"

"The treasure of the birth-parent," the Deputy replied curtly.

"The Magistrate told me that. He didn't tell me what that treasure is, though. I have no idea."

"*Jinalma.*"

"Sir?"

"I said jinalma, Kahl Latimer." The Deputy's head bobbed once. "Looking at you and your friends, looking at the moist places through which you perceive the world, I don't know how well you're likely to understand."

"I don't yet know what you're talking about."

"Would you disrobe before a being of another sapient species and stand before that being naked?"

"I did it on Gla Taus, Deputy Emahpre. The Kieri priests believe that the naked do not lie. Therefore, I stood naked before the Liege Mistress of that land and spoke to her from the absolute truthfulness of my heart." Seth still recalled, however, that his outer garments had been stripped from him before he could prevent that indignity.

"Naked before a"—the Voxian word arrived tardily—"*woman?*"

"Yes. It happened not altogether of my own free choice."

Seth could not understand how the conversation had moved in this direction. What was the Deputy trying to establish?

"This is a demeaning experience for you?" he asked.

"Only when it's compelled," Seth replied. "Any compelled action is demeaning, I think. Uncompelled nakedness holds no shame. Although my jacket and pants were taken without my consent, I removed the final garment, my breechclout. Momentarily, I must confess, I was very uncomfortable."

By this addition Seth felt that he was redeeming the half-truths that he had inadvertently spoken. He waited.

Ehte Emahpre turned his face to Seth and with a single slashing gesture of the hand and arm removed his slit-goggles. His eyes coruscated. They were olivine crystals set in a head of mottled beige stone. Despite the startling beauty of Emahpre's eyes, Seth helplessly recalled Pors's false teeth. Like them, these eyes had an unreal quality. Moreover, he should never have been granted this intimate glimpse of them. The solitary photograph he had found in the *Dharmakaya*'s tapes had not lied. Nor had it done justice to the reality.

"I am naked before you," Emahpre declared.

"But why? I didn't—"

"To explain to you the truth about the Magistrate's gift. Tell me what you now behold."

"Eyes. Eyes like fire." Involuntarily, he glanced away. Far below—a splintering of light from one of Trope's cities of the plains. Or maybe a jabbing afterimage thrown across his retinas by the Deputy's eyes. The planet, after all, was nothing but a barren, blood-brown stone.

"Our eyes are a living form of crystal, Kahl Latimer. The Magistrate's dascra—indeed, the dascra of any bereaved gosfi—contains the birth-parent's eyes. That's the treasure we speak of."

Seth looked disbelievingly from the amulet to Emahpre's face. Last night, Lord Pors had emptied onto the ledge of their dormitory room not a dicelike pair of eyes but a mysterious grayish-green grit. . . .

"Jinalma," Emahpre repeated. "Each amulet contains jinalma, Kahl Latimer. That's our word for the dust into which a Tropiard's eyes disintegrate within three or four days after his death. It's this substance that goes into the dascra, not the crystalline eyes themselves."

"And by this you acknowledge the mystery of ultimate origins?"

"Not really. We observe, under compulsion, the only Old Custom not forbidden Tropiards by the statutes of the Mwezahbe Legacy. Through our dascra we preserve a dramatic tie to our irrational past. I hardly believe that such a prescribed ritual gives any of us a deeper understanding of 'ultimate origins.' Instead, we glorify the strides we have made away from those origins." Emahpre reset his slit-goggles and snappishly averted his face.

"Why do you cover your eyes?"

"Why do you clothe your nakedness?"

"We don't, not always. When we do, it's for warmth and protection. Also, according to my isosire, since humans are bipedal creatures, we clothe ourselves to minimize the distractions of what would otherwise be a continuous genital display. Aren't those reasons that gosfi go clothed?"

"Essentially," Emahpre said.

"But that doesn't explain why you cover your eyes."

"Before Seitaba Mwezahbe established the Tropish state, Kahl Latimer, our eyes were thought to contain our souls. A gosfi's soul is his own, as a man's thoughts are, or ought to be, his own."

Seth was still not satisfied. "And do the eyes of a gosfi also have evolutionary import as a sexual signal?"

A birdlike twitch of the head. "Very astute, Kahl Latimer. Yes, you're correct, they do."

But the deputy no longer appeared anxious to discuss the matter. He shifted in his chair, traced his finger along a line of weird digital readouts on the pilot's console, and, so suddenly that Seth's stomach capsized, dropped The Albatross to a lower altitude. Even in a rational society, it seemed, you could still discover moodiness among the put-upon guardians of the state.

How odd. The eyes of gosfi—like the tails of peacocks, the manes of lions, and maybe even the breasts of human females—had evolved in part as sexual signals. Simultaneously, however, they were organs of higher perception and repositories of the gosfi soul. In order to preserve civilization, Ehte Emahpre seemed to be implying, a Tropiard's eyes had to be able to see without themselves being seen. He had uncovered for Seth to apprise him of the full meaning of the Magistrate's gift, yes—but the sexual connotations of this act were nullified by Seth's belonging to a sapient species with other origins and other procreational signals. Still, the Deputy was not pleased by what he had done, or had been forced to do, and the atmosphere in the pilot's bubble grew as chilly as it had been earlier that morning on the tablerock.

Keeping his own counsel, Seth saw that sharp-edged buttes and ridges had begun to push up out of the prairie to the far northeast. These gradually underwent severe metamorphoses, shaping themselves into hills. And behind these hills appeared hazy, nickle-red mountains, girdered and columned like no mountains he had seen before. They looked as if they had been carved from copper pyrite.

"And what did you give the Magistrate to complete the bond?" Emahpre suddenly asked. But he answered the question himself: "A pair of goggles, an Earthman's goggles. How appropriate."

"The Magistrate chose them himself," Seth said defensively.

Emahpre didn't look at him. "It won't be too much longer before we reach Palija Kadi. I'd like to have the pilot's bubble to myself until that time."

"Very well." Seth rose from his chair and made his way into the cabin where Vrai and the two Kieri had been engaged in desultory conversation for the past hour. The cabin now smelled of fehtes tobacco, of close confinement, and of a strange, pervasive nervousness.

The nation Trope, with its thirty-three camouflaged, clockwork cities, was not the only political entity on the planet Trope, but it dominated the entire southern hemisphere and lay a narrow ocean away from a vast continental mass partitioned by either local decree or various topographic barricades into countries. The people of the nation Trope had held themselves aloof from these feuding, primitive states for well over nine hundred years. They wanted no part of the northerners' warfare, resources, or unregenerate superstition. Trope, the nation, had come to its current level of technological achievement with only minimal help from its northern neighbors, whom they had long ago dubbed *Nuraju*, or the Mad Ones.

Now, despite the development of space travel and the discovery of other worlds with quasi-gosfid populations, the Tropiards held themselves aloof from Interstel and all its licensed trade companies. The habit of aloofness had become engrained. Further, who was to say that the agents and the constituency of Interstel did not represent an insidious, alien variety of the Nuraju? Technological achievement, the Tropiards reasoned, was not, by itself, proof against the viruses of barbarism and superstition.

Madness—*nuraj*—was almost a property of nature. To defeat it, one required not only full consciousness but the unflagging regulator of rationality. If such deliberate regulation seemed to counter or thwart the processes of nature, it did so only seemingly; otherwise, reason would never have been able to assert its preeminence in the first place. Indeed, once the evolution of consciousness had given the gosfi sufficient self-knowledge to recognize their emerging rationality, it was the natural duty of reason to establish its primacy.

Such was the philosophy of Seitaba Mwezahbe, founder of the Tropish state. Although the Mwezahbe Legacy did not demand the absolute annihilation of nuraj—pointing out, reasonably enough, that various forms of madness were profitable in their proper context—it did expressly discourage the cultivation of trance states, superstition, religious fervor, passive acceptance, sexual excess, and violence. The wearing of the dascra gosfi'mija looked back to pre-Mwezahbe days, primarily as a means of providing a nominal continuity with the past, but it also defined the limits of nuraj in the daily lives of obedient modern Tropiards.

That was why (Seth slowly gathered, talking with Magistrate Vrai as Deputy Emahpre piloted The Albatross) the Sh'gaidu were such an embarrassment to the state. Born Tropiards, they flouted the statutes of the Mwezahbe Legacy. Born Tropiards, they behaved no better than the Nuraju of that backward northern continent where stupidity, strife, and superstition were endemic. They had no excuse. They shamed their paisanos by their intransigence. They exploited the tolerance of Ulgraji Vrai, whose inclination was to recognize their gosfihood even in their flouting of the Legacy. Given his head, the Magistrate confessed, Deputy Emahpre would have solved the Sh'gaidu question decades ago, by wiping them out of Palija Kadi as unfeelingly as a soldier on bivouac might clean his dinner bowl with a crust of bread. Such a solution would have come easily for the state.

For centuries Trope, the nation, had possessed a well-equipped land- and sea-going force whose primary responsibilities were the surveillance of the many unpredictable barbarians to the north and the defense of their own country against Nuraju invaders. Periodic sea skirmishes with the crazier of the Mad Ones had kept the enemy at bay until the advent of such sophisticated Tropish weaponry that, today, the Nuraju seldom ventured more than a few kilometers from their coasts. For them and for their rational adversaries to the south, the world had been halved. What single-minded Tropiards had put asunder, the Nuraju had neither the technological capacity nor the insane bravado to struggle to unite. Hemisphere against hemisphere, like a spongy rubber ball sliced nearly but not altogether through. In such a case, the appearance of wholeness is a cruel deception.

In the decades since the Tropiards' discovery of Interstel, however, the armies of the state—substantially diminished in numbers—had remained in readiness as a planetary defense force.

Separated or not, all gosfi were siblings. The only way for Trope, the nation, to protect itself against incursions from beyond the Anja system was to assume the larger guardianship of Trope, the planet. But Interstel put out trade and cultural feelers rather than rude, acquisitive tentacles, thereby mollifying the suspicions of the Tropiards, and the result was regular sublimission contact between Trope and the various scattered representatives of Interstel. Trade and diplomatic alliances still hung fire, but Vox had been introduced to Tropiards in all Thirty-three Cities as an essential ingredient in their educations—for union with Interstel had seemed inevitable if not imminent. Meanwhile, several units of Trope's planetary defense force were assigned to bivouac around Palija Kadi, there to keep the Sh'gaidu—victims of a divine but dissident madness—under perpetual watch and guard.

Then, by a quirk of far-reaching simultaneity, the Latimer isohets had found themselves stranded on Gla Taus just as the Kieri Liege Mistress was deciding to take a new tack with the aisautseb, and just as the Magistrate of Trope was actively looking for a humane solution to the disposition of the Sh'gaidu. The taussanaur aboard the *Dharmakaya* had arranged a parley with Magistrate Vrai on Trope; and Seth, conscripted against both his understanding and his will, had come seven sublime light-years and many hundreds of mundane kilometers to tie together the strands of this intricate and mystifying web. As The Albatross descended toward the upland basin of the dissidents, Seth silently prayed that he might somehow succeed. For Abel's sake. For his own sake. And perhaps even for the sakes of the persecuted Sh'gaidu and the haunted Magistrate Vrai.

The interests of the Kieri, even though he admired Clefrabbes Douin and didn't really wish Porchaddos Pors ill, no longer seemed totally compelling to him. Gla Taus was a nightmare he wanted to forget.

"Magistrate, tell me about Seitaba Mwezahbe," Seth said. He and the others had been silent for a time, lost in private reveries, and his words made everyone in the passenger section start into grudging alertness.

"Mwezahbe was our first magistrate," Vrai responded. "He founded Trope, lifted it out of the wallow of our prehistory."

"A mythological figure?"

"Indeed not. The first true Tropiard. A multiselved genius. His legacy to us was civilization itself."

Alone with the Magistrate and the two Gla Tausian Hawks of Conscience, Seth sat in a white swivel chair in the belly of The Albatross. He watched as Vrai hefted himself from his own chair and took a purple fruit from a rope basket hanging in the center of the airship's fuselage. Pors was directly opposite the Magistrate, and Douin occupied a foldout bunk above Pors. Strange flowers hung in other baskets about The Albatross's interior, and light spilled in from a stipple-glass rectangle in the curved ceiling. Vrai, eating the mwehanja, returned to his place. Shifting dapples from the skylight played catch-as-catch-can on the bulkheads.

"How long ago was this?" Seth asked.

The Magistrate took a thoughtful bite of his fruit. After chewing for several seconds, he said, "A little more than nine hundred years, Kahl Latimer, although I'd best explain that although Trope makes its revolution around Anja in about 453 days, our day is only three fourths as long as a standard E-day. This means that our year is slightly less than a terrestrial year. Do you understand?"

Pors lit another cigarette into bittersweet pseudo-flame, his third since Seth had exited the pilot's bubble.

Distracted, Seth replied, "I understand."

"Can't we wait until we reach Palija Kadi?" Pors asked. He blew a puff of smoke and nodded deferentially at the Magistrate. "I intend no rudeness, Magistrate Vrai. It's simply that Master Douin and I like a few moments of undisturbed contemplation before undertaking an enterprise of this importance. Also, I'm beginning to feel the heat, even through the skins of our airship."

"Maybe if you—" Seth, who had been on the verge of advising the Point Marcher to stub out his cigarette, caught himself.

Vrai nodded politely at Pors, and the conversation, which seemed at least as vital to Seth as a few final moments of fehtes-blurred thought, was apparently dead. The Point Marcher had killed it.

—We record modern history from the first year of Seitaba Mwezahbe's magistracy. This, then, is the year 912.

Seth started again. To bypass the obstacle posed by Pors, the Magistrate had cerebrated this message. A windfall of microscopic seeds burying themselves in Seth's mind and instantly sprouting . . .

—I'm the sixth magistrate of our planet, Kahl Latimer, for we live what you might consider gratifyingly long lives. We do so without the biochemical assistance and the genetic tampering which we believe you must use to enjoy even a fraction of our longevity.

"But," Seth said, freshly dumbfounded, "but—"

Pors looked at him with irritation, and even Douin, propped on an elbow in his bunk, seemed confused by the tardiness of his bit-off objection. They had "heard" nothing of the Magistrate's message.

—Every Tropiard undergoes a series of evolutionary developments within his own person. These are preceded by biochemically induced events that we call auxiliary births. Their purpose is to offset our lack of prolificity as a species by ensuring that each individual effects in himself a process of 'natural selection' culminating in the emergency of his strongest and most viable personality. The ability to cerebrate seldom appears until after the fourth or fifth auxiliary birth.

"Except among the Sh'gaidu," Seth said aloud.

"Master Seth, you're talking to yourself," Clefrabbes Douin informed him gently. "Has the heat reached you, too?"

Flustered, Seth glanced apologetically at the Kieri in whose geffide he had lived for over a Gla Tausian year. "No, Master Douin, forgive me. A stray thought that escaped before I could stop it. Nothing more."

Douin nodded dubiously and lay back. Pors was smoking with his eyes closed, gauzy dragon wisps curling from his nostrils and half-parted lips. And the Magistrate was still gnawing at the purple-skinned fruit from the hanging basket. His concentration on the fruit was heroic, superhuman.

—The Sh'gaidu may indeed be exceptions to this rule. I confess this to you mind to mind.

This time Seth said nothing.

—*But you have just asked about Mwezahbe. He was a genius without benefit of auxiliary births. He midwifed the births of his own successive selves, in fact, without resorting to biomechanics. And just as Mwezahbe was many geniuses, each Tropiard is a series of progressively more enlightened consciousnesses in the same body. Unlike Mwezahbe, however, we must undergo the encephalic reorganization of the evo-steps, or our auxiliary births, in order to approach perfect rationality. The goal itself, of course, is never attained.*

Perfect rationality. The irrationality of this goal seemed transparent to Seth. Did the Tropiards wish to achieve godhood through these cryptomystical auxiliary births of theirs? Did they not see the contradiction inherent in the desire? There sat Magistrate Vrai, licking his fingers of the last bits of pulp from his sunfruit while transmitting verbal thought patterns to Seth; and, against the bizarre conjoining of these behaviors, he was telepathically prating of, dear God, perfect rationality.

—*Each individual possesses the capacity to become a multitude of individuals; the possible permutations of the mind are uncountable. In his lifetime a Tropiard may become as many as seven completely different people, concluding his evo-steps with a consciousness as far above his first as intellect is above instinct. Mwezahbe taught us how to prepare for and successfully pass through these biochemical auxiliary births. Having contributed what they could to the state, Kahl Latimer, our old selves die and fall away.*

Like snake skins, thought Seth.

The cerebrations continued: —*I've served as Magistrate of Trope for forty-three of our years. In my lifetime I've passed through five auxiliary births, each time working out my neonatal potential for the general good, as we all do. The dascra provides continuity not only with the distant past but from one life to the next.*

The Albatross was sinking, slowing. Seth could feel these changes in both his ear canals and his gut. A faint whine accompanied them, and the whine shimmied audibly through the hull of the airship. Pors's eyes were open again, and Douin swung his feet over the edge of the bunk, dropped to the floor beyond the Point Marcher, and took up a swivel chair. Seat harnesses were available, but Emahpre's piloting was so adroit they seemed unnecessary.

"May I ask the Magistrate a final question before we put down, Lord Pors?" Seth asked. "We're almost there, I think."

"Go ahead," Pors replied, stubbing his cigarette in his palm.

"How do Tropiards choose their magistrate?" Seth wanted to remark on how infrequently leadership in Trope changed hands, but to have done so would have alerted the Kieri to the fact that he had recently acquired information new to them. How, they would wonder, had he come by it?

This time Magistrate Vrai started. He looked at Seth as if his cerebrations had been betrayed. They had not, not by any means, but even the mask of his goggles didn't conceal the fact that his dark face had flushed a deeper shade of brown.

"How do Tropiards choose their magistrate?" Vrai repeated aloud.

Seth nodded, puzzled by the hesitation.

"Each magistrate selects his own successor," the Magistrate said, striving for forthrightness. "Only his decision matters."

"Why?"

"Because as the head of a nation based on the statutes of the Mwezahbe Legacy he is the gosfi embodiment of reason."

"Other Tropiards have no say in the selection?"

Vrai swiveled his chair so that he and Seth might take each other's measure with locked eyes. He seemed to feel that a gauntlet had been dropped. The mahogany flush in his face had not gone away.

"If I put to referendum the question of whether the sun is hot or cold, and if the populace overwhelmingly responds that it is cold, does this vote alter the basic truth of the matter?"

Seth was appalled by this tactic, one that his isosire would have ridiculed instructively. The Magistrate was trying to throw dust in his eyes: a blast of pseudo-Socratic jinalma. It didn't even graze the issue.

"Magistrate—" Seth started to protest.

"Come forward if you wish to see Palija Kadi from the air!" Ehte Emahpre shouted from the pilot's compartment. "Come forward, friends!"

BOOK THREE

NINE

Ulgraji Vrai led Seth and the two Kieri envoys forward to see what they could of the Sh'gaidu holdings. Kaleidoscopic patterns of light ran through the pilot's bubble, inducing Seth to lift the lightweight hood of his tunic against the glare—the Magistrate had his goggles. Pors, without invitation, sat down next to Emahpre while the others hunched forward to peer at the tilting landscape.

"I'm going to make a circle over the area so that you can see the surrounding cliffs as well as the basin," Emahpre said.

The Albatross, shuddering gently, banked to the right.

The Magistrate pointed. "Those are the permanent encampments of our surveillance force—there, along the cliff edges."

Seth and the others looked down. Small, dome-shaped structures resembling toadstools sprouted from the rocks. A number of squat land vehicles were parked in a dusty semicircle beside one of the toadstools. Farther along the cliff face, more craftily concealed, wallowed a camouflaged panel truck with its front end pointing toward the basin.

"What's that?"

The Magistrate had also been staring at the van. Seth's question seemed to jolt him from a reverie. "A van," he answered vaguely. "A troop-controller van, nothing extraordinary."

When The Albatross banked again, they saw the blindingly white figures of the soldiers themselves. Their chromium helmets flashed like silver platters. Perched on rocks, sitting in open truckbeds, strolling among the domes, they were terribly conspicuous from the air. The Sh'gaidu, Seth thought, must also be aware of them. What must it be like to live—minute to minute, hour to hour, day to day—with such clumsy prying? The state lacked even the grace of subtlety.

"Do they know we're coming?" Seth asked.

"Last night," the Magistrate replied, "I communicated with Commander Swodi of the surveillance force. He sent a soldier to the crofthouse to inform the Pledgechild of our visit. According to Swodi, she agreed to receive us."

Seth noted the pronoun. He asked, "Could she have refused?"

"Be civil," Douin rebuked him. "Remember where you are."

But the Tropiards had apparently heard no sarcasm in Seth's question, and Emahpre said, "She would have received us without notification. Now, however, she knows something's up. She will have spent her time since last night anticipating our motives and devising counterstratagems."

"Our motives aren't fungi, Deputy Emahpre," Vrai said. "They're not corrupt things that grow in the dark."

Emahpre addressed his passengers as if Vrai hadn't spoken: "I'm going to land on the roadway on the basin's northern end. Look for the crofthouse and the towers. The galleries are carved into the eastern cliff walls. You can also see the bridges linking the galleries to the basin's floor."

A road came out of the high rocks to the east and made a dusty, buckled ribbon through the formations grading into the lower, or northern, part of the Sh'gaidu holdings. Seth imagined that state vehicles would have no trouble getting down that road when it came time to evacuate the basin. Meanwhile, the bridges that Emahpre had mentioned were immense, coral-colored structures of astonishing intricacy; they made stairways from the eastern cliff face to the cultivated fields dominating the basin, and they crossed or intertwined at various heights like Möbius strips of stone. The galleries in the eastern cliff face were intricately balustraded with rock resembling twisted coral. From the air, the panorama was breathtaking.

Palija Kadi, the basin, raged with orchestrated color. Cleanly divided and terraced, the fields lapped almost to the tumbled rocks from which the walls of the basin arose. The crops undulating in these fields were mint green, cabbage red, Anja blue. They rippled under a wind whistling across them from the north and coursing them with graceful shadows.

The Albatross banked again.

Almost directly below the airship Seth saw terraces stepping upward in a wide semicircle to the huge wall enclosing the basin on the south. Unlike the other cliff faces, this wall was smooth rather than rugged, bone white rather than coral red. Emahpre brought The Albatross down a hundred meters or so and, after sweeping along inside the great southern wall, piloted them northward over the basin.

A tower jutted upward from each corner of Palija Kadi. The one in the southeast corner, rising from a field just below the southern terraces, pricked at The Albatross like a spear. Made of saplings bound together to form stilts, with a closed platform atop the stilts, the tower swayed like a lithe tree in the wind. A moment later the forward motion of the airship eclipsed it from view.

Hanging onto the back of Emahpre's metal chair, Seth glimpsed in the middle of the basin a vast, circular clearing. In the center of this clearing, a circular stone building thatched over with crimson reeds. Positioned at intervals about the building were lovely blue-green trees that reminded Seth of the cypresses in Lausanne. Descending crookedly to the building from the eastern cliff face, a prodigious rock bridge that extended so far into the basin as to halve its eastern hemisphere. When The Albatross flew over this bridge, the airship's bizarre shadow was thrown into one of the western fields bordering the circular clearing.

As they approached the roadway at the northern end of the basin, the stilt tower in the northeastern corner resolved itself out of the morning glare.

"What are the towers for?" Douin asked.

"Those are *kioba Najuma*," the Magistrate said. "The Holy One's lookouts. It's from these towers that the Sh'gaidu claim they'll see Duagahvi Gaidu returning from her odyssey through the continent of crazies to which she allegedly betook herself in search of converts. They believe she's still in the land of the Nuraju."

"But the towers don't clear the top of the basin," Douin pointed out.

"A matter of no concern to the Sh'gaidu," Emahpre said. "Nor is the fact that Gaidu herself disappeared nearly a century and three quarters ago, sixty-two years into the rule of Orisu Sfol, Magistrate Vrai's predecessor."

"Look!" cried Pors.

The Albatross began easing its ungainly bulk down toward the roadway, and clustered beneath the descending craft were small humanoid figures. Looking up, they nearly blinded the occupants of The Albatross with their gemlike eyes. Flashes of emerald, amber, and topaz detonated in their faces, each explosion pinwheeling brilliantly. Seth turned his head, but could still see, sidelong, small, naked figures running and dancing on the roadway.

Children. Sh'gaidu children.

They were the first children Seth had seen on Trope, the first gosfi to appear before him naked, and the first to come forth without eye coverings. No wonder the Deputy was outraged by these people: They had no shame.

As The Albatross settled lower and lower, the children prudently scattered. Then The Albatross was down. No one aboard had had to strap himself into a chair, and a side panel behind the pilot's bubble clicked back so suddenly that the heat of Palija Kadi roared in.

"We've indeed come to Hell," Pors whispered.

Nevertheless, he and the others exited. Anja hung low in the east, precarious above the galleries. The sky was a lavender parchment burning inward from its edges. The excitement of the naked children, the fever of their curiosity, trembled in the air. Resolute, the Magistrate gestured Seth, Douin, Pors, and Emahpre after him, then struck off through the gamboling children toward the Sh'gaidu crofthouse.

Seth found himself turning about to look at the ragtaggle group scrambling along with them. Several of the children seemed to be trying to make out his face inside the hood of his tunic. Their eyes had an acute monarchical fire.

Despite their nakedness, it wasn't easy to determine the sex of these children. They more nearly resembled females, for between their legs they had no conspicuous rope of flesh to identify them as males. Still, the external genital configuration was slightly more complicated than the soft, split mound by which Seth had long ago learned to recognize the parts of a young human female. There was this, but something else as well. A kind of dark fleshy button at the top of the cleft, like the head of a tiny animal indecisively peeping out. . . .

And none of the children, Seth noted with wonder, had navels. It seemed likely, though, that the gosfi umbilical cord might attach to the unborn child somewhere in the perineal region. No one had yet claimed, in any case, that gosfi—whether Tropiards or Sh'gaidu—sprang entire from their birth-parents' foreheads.

Was this what Ulgraji Vrai and Ehte Emahpre looked like under their jumpsuits? Seth refrained from asking. The lavalet equipment in the dormitory on the tablerock suggested that their morphology might well be similar to that of the Sh'gaidu children. This speculation gave rise in Seth to the private hypothesis that Tropiards and Sh'gaidu alike were . . . well, andro-gynes. Hermaphrodites. Yet—in Vox, at least—the Magistrate and Deputy Emahpre had consistently employed masculine pronouns for the citizenry of the state and feminine pronouns for the dissident Sh'gaidu. Why?

Meanwhile, the children bobbed and darted along beside their party of clothed interlopers.

Trailing his comrades, Seth watched Emahpre shake a jerky arm at the children, shoo them away, and threaten to cuff those who approached too near. Pors was similarly protective of his person, although less overt in his gestures of both warning and reproach.

"*Kwa tehdegu!*" Emahpre shouted. "*Kwa tehdegu!*"

For the most part, the children were unimpressed. They made mocking moues and performed temper-provoking dances, jigging along beside the newcomers on the narrow path leading to the crofthouse. On both sides of this path grew shoulder-high grains with ribbed stalks and enormous red-gold leaves.

Seth turned about and caught sight of a young Sh'gaidu as tall as Deputy Emahpre. She—yes, *she*—did not commit herself to the mindless revelry of the younger children. She followed along about ten meters behind Seth, maintaining a predetermined distance and a measured pace. Her skin, although a deep brown in color, had the unblemished texture of fine writing paper. Her eyes were a luminous tiger-eye green, hard and faceted. Seth found it difficult to look away from her. Her gaze ensnared. Worse—rut-driven even on a world where humans had no niche or claim—Seth registered an involuntary but torturous erotic stirring.

Idiot, he chastised himself. Miscegenetic goat.

But, helplessly, he kept glancing back at the young Sh'gaidu. Was there no cure for his libidinous feelings outside of their actual expression? The children romping about him had less substance than ghosts, for his whole attention now belonged to the creature pacing behind him, even if he found himself stumbling trying to keep his eyes on her. Ridiculous.

In Vox, the term for coitus between individuals of different sapient beings was *paragenation.* The prefix in this coinage meant "wrongly, incorrectly, unfavorably, harmfully."

All the connotations were bad.

What if you played a mental trick on yourself and insisted on thinking of this striking person as male? Seth asked himself. Would that remove your horns? If the Tropiards employ our Voxian pronouns arbitrarily, and it looks as if they do, then there's nothing to prevent you from alternating among pronouns at whim. Think of her as him. The objective reality of the situation won't be violated, will it?

Will it?

Seth glanced at the Sh'gaidu following them. *He* maintained a predetermined distance and a measured pace. *His* skin was a deep luminous brown. *His* skin had the unblemished texture of fine writing paper. *His* eyes were tiger-eye green. . . . Looking at *him*, though, Seth found it almost impossible to think of *him* as anything but *her.*

Besides, Seth's sexual orientation didn't preclude contact with males. Abel, his own isohet, had been his lover for four or five years. And what disturbed Seth about the carnal aspect of his relationship with Abel was not its homosexuality but its narcissism. Or, more honestly, his suspicion that Abel had introduced him early to their unique variety of autoeroticism because Abel's self-love was so great that it had to have an object outside itself. Or, then again, perhaps Abel had merely been seeking to possess their common isosire in his, Seth's, person. Günter Latimer had always held himself aloof from their "love play," tolerating it as a natural outgrowth of their isolation and their propinquity.

Seth halted on the pathway. It was dizzying to think about his own and Abel's possible motives—but, yes, there had been times that he had felt used by Abel, and times that his disgust after servicing his own and Abel's passion had turned him unaccountably surly and fractious. Where did the anger come from, where the guilt? In the Ommundi Paedoschol he had dallied with boys and girls alike, with seldom a hindrance and never a rebuke, and that had been a happier, more innocent time. . . .

"*Kwa tehdegu!*" the Deputy cried. But the children delighted in discomfiting him and didn't retreat any farther than necessary. The Magistrate, on the other hand, paid them no heed, just strode calmly forward, halting when a child danced into his path and continuing when the way was clear again. Douin followed the Magistrate's example, but Pors, sweating greasily, mopped his brow with a linen kerchief, which, each time his hand came away from his face, he shook in annoyance at the children. Seth was being left behind.

"I speak no Tropish," Seth told the young Sh'gaidu in Vox, amazed not only by the allure she held for him but also by his own foolishness in speaking to her. "I speak no Tropish but—"

"I speak Vox," she said. "My name is Lijadu."

Several meters still separated them, for she had halted when Seth had halted. Behind her, strange crops waved and heat shimmers danced on the ticking hull of The Albatross. Dumbfounded, Seth gaped.

"How do—" he began. "How do you happen to speak it?"

Farther up the pathway, Pors turned and hailed Seth: "Come on, envoy, let's get out of this sun! You delay us!"

"There'll be time to talk in the Sh'vaij," Lijadu said. "Our assembly place, I mean. What the Tropiards call our crofthouse."

"*Sh'vaij?*"

"Chapel of The Sisterhood—that's an approximation."

"Sh'gaidu, then, must mean The Sisterhood of Gaidu." Seth said.

"Unless, you're a Tropiard who is rigorously j'gosfi. In which case—almost *every* case outside Palija Kadi—it means something like The Bitches or The Harlots of Gaidu. Bitches is your word for … for a certain kind of female animal, isn't it? In any event, the terms of Vox are all approximations."

"Master Seth," Douin shouted, "please come on! The Pledgechild has arrived, and you're to speak with her on our behalf!"

Seth looked toward the crofthouse—the Sh'vaij—and saw that all the children had disappeared, probably into the fields. Approaching the Magistrate's group from the circular building, tottering down the path, came the Pledgechild. Slightly behind her, a less ancient adult kept pace. Although both were partially concealed from Seth's view by the clot of intervening bodies, he easily discerned that unlike Lijadu and the children, these Sh'gaidu were clothed.

They wore colorful sarilike garments. The old woman carried a staff. Their feet were bare, and their eyes, brilliant in the sunlight, were naked. Had they been dressed in jumpsuits and slit-goggles, however, it would have been impossible to distinguish them by gender from Vrai and Emahpre. In fact, the aged Pledgechild appeared to be the tallest figure on the path. Pronouns, and sexual distinctions, and all that went with them, seemed hopelessly muddled on Trope.

"I'd better get up there," Seth told Lijadu, as if the moment demanded a formal leavetaking.

"Go on," she said. Her voice was toneless.

When Seth arrived among the others, the Magistrate was making introductions. He and the Pledgechild knew each other by reputation, surely, and his public relationship with the Sh'gaidu was respectful if not friendly. Both Emahpre and Pors looked put out, the Deputy because of what the Sh'gaidu stood for, the Kieri because of the heat. Douin patiently endured.

"Welcome, Kahl Latimer," the Pledgechild said to Seth in excellent Vox. "Let me apologize for the unruliness of the children." She smiled. "Airships always excite and delight them."

Her eyes, Seth noted, were neither emerald, amber, nor topaz, but a deep black, like certain rare varieties of fire opal. Her skull was a faintly brown egg, as if long hours under Anja had leached the melanin from her skin. Her sari seemed to be dyed or printed with frondlike patterns of crimsons and even darker reds. The person behind her was similarly attired, but her skin was browner and her amber eyes were shot through with an unsettling milkiness. Only she of the two wore an amulet.

"This is Huspre," the Pledgechild said, indicating the milky-eyed woman with the dascra. "She's my right hand."

Huspre nodded, and Seth returned the nod.

"Her sojourn outside Palija Kadi occurred many years ago, for which reason she has only a limited command of Vox. Some of the young people taught me, you see, but Huspre is not quick with languages. I don't press her to learn. Here, in any case, there's little necessity—unless one must speak for the Sh'gaidu with outsiders who come on mysterious visits. I knew that might happen one day, and so it has." The Pledgechild's fingers were drumming on her staff: laughter. "Yes, I knew in my heart that one day we would be visited."

The Deputy nodded at Huspre. "She speaks the Ardaja dialect, doesn't she?"

"Yes, of course. But Huspre's not much of a talker even in our own tongue."

"Well, when she *does* talk," Emahpre said irritably, "either the Magistrate or I will be able to translate her words for our visitors. You needn't apologize for her lack of proficiency in Vox."

"Oh, I intended no apology," said the Pledgechild.

"May we go in?" the Magistrate asked, gesturing toward the Sh'vaij, which still lay eighty or ninety meters above. He was clearly trying to head off an unpleasantness between the Sh'gaidu leader and his own chief lieutenant. Pors looked grateful for the tactic Vrai had chosen.

"Indeed, indeed," the old woman said. "I would have waited for you there, but I feared the children were proving troublesome. Airships tickle them, as do the disembarked passengers of airships." She made a limp-wristed motion at the grain field to her right, and Seth saw several children squatting among the stalks, peering out with weird, mischievous faces. Two or three retreated at the Pledgechild's feeble gesture, but most held their ground. "They're oh so fond of airships," she informed her visitors again, then turned and limped unassisted toward the circular assembly building. Her staff, rather than Huspre, was her support.

Seth grabbed Douin's elbow and detained him. "That girl back there," he said, nodding at Lijadu, "speaks Vox."

Douin, obviously surprised, glanced at her. She had not moved. Her eyes glittered intimidatingly. "You're sure?"

"I spoke with her, Master Douin."

"She looks little more than a child."

"She told me that Sh'gaidu means The Sisterhood of Gaidu. The dissidents—everyone in Palija Kadi—are females. Girls and women, Master Douin."

"*Everyone?*" Douin was incredulous.

"So it seems. These are the female sapients Pors was certain existed on this world. Moreover, the Sh'gaidu are the only female sapients in Trope. Everyone else, every citizen of the Thirty-three Cities, is j'gosfi, male."

Douin pointed into the waving red-gold foliage of the monarchleaf. "But there are children here, several children. How—?" He broke off. "They're hermaphroditic," he declared with sudden insight. "Each gosfi has the reproductive apparatus of both the male and the female."

"The bodies of the children suggest as much."

"Ah," said Douin, taken aback by this discovery. "Ah."

"What will be the response of Lady Turshebsel and the aisautseb if we take back to Gla Taus three hundred Tropish women? How will they react to a tribe of female settlers in the Feht Evashsted?"

Douin covered his eyes and considered. "Master Seth?"

"Sir?"

"The answer, I think, is that the Tropiards—the gosfi—aren't properly either male or female. The Sh'gaidu *call* themselves female, but they're no different anatomically from the civil servants in the J'beij or the soldiers of the surveillance force. And vice versa, of course. I'm speaking solely of their physical makeup." He uncovered his eyes and peeked familiarly at Seth. "Do you see?"

Seth looked at Lijadu, who still had not moved. She was regarding Douin and him with such intense concentration that he felt uneasy. If reports about the telepathic abilities of the Sh'gaidu were true, perhaps she was actively tapping their minds or at least psychically amplifying their whispered conversation. No matter. *She* was lovely. *He* was lovely. *Lijadu* was lovely.

"Their physical makeup is of no consequence," Seth snapped, surprising himself.

"That's what I've just said," Douin replied. "Since it's of no consequence, neither Lady Turshebsel nor the aisautseb can object to the fact that we have returned to Gla Taus with three hundred gosfi. *Gosfi*, Master Seth; not men or women, but *gosfi*. Diplomacy is the art of the possible."

"Their *psychology* is of the utmost importance, though."

"We'd best go on, Master Seth. The others are entering the building. This accomplishes nothing." Douin gently disengaged himself from Seth's restraining hand and made to follow the Magistrate's party.

Seth caught his elbow again. "My isosire used to say that we are what we pretend to be."

"Yes?" Douin waited.

"The Sh'gaidu pretend to be female, the Tropiards male. Therefore, each *is* what it pretends. We'll be taking the members of a single culturally and psychologically determined sex back to Gla Taus with us, and we'll be taking females, only females." Seth's heart misgave him. The mission now struck him as a fiasco of grand proportions. Was this a misbegotten chivalry? Would he have objected to carting away three hundred self-proclaimed j'gosfi? Yes . . . no . . . he honestly didn't know.

"Master Seth, you're agonizing needlessly. On Trope, the terms male and female are virtually meaningless as jauddeb and humans understand them. The problem is as much linguistic as sexual, don't you see?"

"I don't know."

"In any case, the Sh'gaidu won't be compelled to do anything they don't wish to do. If they don't want to settle in the Feht Evashsted, why, then, we'll simply go home without them."

"And Abel and I? And the *Dharmakaya*?"

"Ah, Master Seth, that I can't say. I speak neither for Aisaut Chappouib nor for our beloved Liege Mistress." This time he succeeded in breaking Seth's grip and in escorting the young isohet towards the Sh'vaij.

The breeze blowing through the basin was fresh if not cool, and on the intricate coral-colored bridge looming ahead of them Seth saw a gaggle of children watching their progress. When he glanced back, Lijadu was gone. He and Douin attained the clearing of the crofthouse, an apron of well-swept, brick-red rock. Whisk patterns were visible in the clearing's fine gravel, but Douin, determined to get him inside the Sh'vaij, gave Seth no time to examine them.

"Wait a moment, strangers!" a voice cried. The language was Vox, and the voice—Seth already knew it—was Lijadu's.

He and Douin turned. Lijadu emerged from the right-hand field below the crofthouse and pointed around the building's curve to where the circular clearing joined the great stone bridge to the cliffs. Seth and Douin looked, but still could not see what Lijadu was trying to indicate.

"Here she comes," Lijadu called. "Little Omwhol wants you to see her flock. —Come, then, child."

A moment later, a very young Sh'gaidu came around the assembly building shooing eight or nine hissing beasties in front of her. To Seth, they resembled miniature dragons. They went on four legs and waved double sets of feather-scaled wings behind their small, beaked heads. Waddling and flapping, they hurried across the apron of the Sh'vaij and into the western fields. Omwhol, the child, caught one of them and carried it to Seth.

As she handed it to him, Lijadu stepped onto the apron and spoke: "They don't bite. They're *gocodre*. Take it. Omwhol was only recently given charge of them. She's quite pleased with herself."

Seth knelt and accepted the gocodre from the child. Captured, it didn't struggle. Transferred into his hands, it didn't try to fight free. Its skin was leathery, patterned copper and coral. What most amazed Seth about the creature was its eyes: They were tiny chrysoberyls. In the matter of physical optics, evolution on Trope had stuck to this tack and carried it through to creatures with intelligent self-awareness.

The animal flopped in Seth's hands, unexpectedly. He caught it. Omwhol's little fingers snapped in amusement. Douin stepped back.

"See," Lijadu said. "This one is j'gocodre, male. It had no choice in the matter. It hatched that way."

Seth released the beast, which scampered away after its broodmates.

Omwhol skipped off, too, unperturbed that her charges seemed to be getting beyond her tiny sphere of influence.

"We had no choice in the matter, either," said Seth, rising. "But we *weren't* hatched."

Lijadu regarded him peculiarly for vouchsafing this information. Then she entered the cool immensity of the Sh'vaij.

"Come with me," she said from inside the doorway. "The Pledgechild and the others have preceded us to her cell. I'll take you."

TEN

Even after he had thrown back his hood, it took a moment for Seth's eyes to adjust. Horizontal window slits ran about the interior of the Sh'vaij, just below its ceiling, but the building's thatched eaves blocked the passage of direct light. The place was dark and quiet. Gradually, however, both architectural and gosfi forms resolved themselves out of the dimness.

Directly opposite Seth, far across the nave, loomed an imposing, sloped wall. He recognized it immediately as a replica of the wall enclosing the basin on the south: bone white, slightly convex, smooth and blank. In the Sh'vaij, the wall served as a sacramental backdrop for what appeared to be a low altar set with unlit candles and fronted by a reed mat. Someone—an anonymous Sh'gaidu—lay supine on the mat, almost like an offering. Her stillness suggested death.

Carved wooden benches lined the walls of the assembly building. Upon these sat a number of adult Sh'gaidu, most of whom were clothed in colorful garments. They sat singly, apart from one another, either engaged in deep meditation (Seth decided) or else communing mind to mind. Their eyes were open—it seemed the gosfi had no eyelids, in any case—but the lack of fire in these organs bespoke a turning inward of the sense of vision: These people were scrutinizing their own souls. It then occurred to Seth that perhaps they were praying for the person who now lay before the replica of the basin's wall.

The Pledgechild, Magistrate Vrai, Deputy Emahpre, Lord Pors, and Huspre were nowhere to be seen.

Lijadu said, "The Pledgechild's rooms are behind Palija Dait, that wall you see there. You would say the Lesser Door. Palija Kadi, of course, means the Great Door."

"You regard that wall and your entire basin as *doors*?" Douin enquired.

The young Sh'gaidu found a blue-patterned garment on a bench to her left and fastened this serenely about her torso. "We regard them by the names they bear," she said. The pastel blue against her warm brown flesh in no way diminished Seth's desire. He cursed his desire, and she said, "Come pay your respects to my birth-parent Ifragsli, who died four days ago."

She set off toward the wall. Douin and Seth fell in behind, their boots scuffling obtrusively on the rock floor. At Palija Dait, Lijadu knelt beside the body of her birth-parent and swayed above it hypnotically.

The corpse was redolent of a faint perfume, like the bouquet of certain brandies. It was draped with a white cloth to the neck, and its face was concealed by a death mask of caked red clay. Most startling to Seth was the fact that the Sh'gaidu, using a moist, emerald-green pigment, had daubed eyes on the death mask. Subtly iridescent even in the gloom, these eyes looked challengingly real. Lijadu stopped swaying, leaned forward, and kissed each painted eye in turn. Then, nimbly, she rose.

"Ifragsli's *dascra'nol* ceremony is this evening. Each of you from Huru J'beij is invited to attend."

"This was your birth-parent?" Douin asked.

"My mother, you would say," Lijadu told Douin.

"She scarcely appears an old woman," the Kieri noted. "What brought about her death?"

"Thirty-seven days ago she fell ill, and swooned, and lay for many days in a coma that we were only rarely able to penetrate. The Pledgechild and I stayed with her until her death. Afterward, we prepared her for her last passage through Palija Kadi. She has only this morning come down from the kioba Najuma—the tower—to the southeast of the Sh'vaij. Now her final vision is ripe, and her eyes will soon crumble into dust. This evening's ceremony will reveal that vision."

"But the death itself?" Douin asked. "What caused it?"

"The Pledgechild, who is herself heirbarren, has told me that Ifragsli died of . . . anticipation."

"How does one die of anticipation?" Seth asked.

"I'm not sure," Lijadu said. "The Pledgechild says that self-aware creatures neither feed on time nor allow it to feed on them. We create time out of the vigor of our beings, she says, and were our spiritual vigor perfect, we would create time infinitely. Ifragsli was a woman of great character and vigor. Time flowed in her veins rather than blood, and it seemed her heart would sustain her forever. But thirty-seven days ago this changed. She grew anxious of the future and her anticipation of it poisoned the vigor by which she lived."

Seth felt for the dascra that Magistrate Vrai had given him. Although it was concealed inside his tunic, he could still place a hand on it. "Will Ifragsli's eyes now become your own?" he asked. "Will you wear her dascra gosfi'mija?"

"No, not I."

"But she was your birth-parent, wasn't she? Aren't you supposed to inherit her jinalma?"

"I have the Pledgechild's eyes."

This statement made no empirical sense to Seth. Lijadu's eyes were tiger green, pierced with spearlike yellow flaws, while the Pledgechild's eyes were an opalescent black. Then Seth understood that Lijadu had framed a metaphor.

"I'm the Pledgechild's heir," she said, confirming his reasoning. Her voice conveyed a quiet pride.

"But not the Pledgechild's offspring," Douin said. "How does that happen?"

"Ifragsli offered my life to the Pledgechild because she is heirbarren. The Pledgechild accepted me, and now I'm her child."

"And what of your birth-parent's jinalma?" Seth asked, pleased to be repeating this esoteric Tropish term because he knew Douin would not understand it. "Who will receive the dust of Ifragsli's eyes?"

"All of us," Lijadu said. "The dascra'nol will tell."

"All of you?"

"Because Ifragsli bequeathed me to the Pledgechild, it's now as if my birth-parent were among the heirbarren while she lived. The jinalma of the heirbarren—if they so will it—goes into the familistery urn, a closed amphora which the Pledgechild keeps in her rooms. Once a year the Sh'gaidu partake together of the jinalma of those who lost their heirs or who died without ever having given birth."

"How?" Seth asked. "How do you partake of this jinalma?"

"Here in the Sh'vaij, the familistery urn travels to each member of the sisterhood. As it passes, each rememberer—is that the word you would use?—puts her hand into the urn and touches a wet finger to the sacred dust. Then she does this." Lijadu sucked the tip of her finger, her eyes grown briefly cloudy. She was back, alert, as soon as she had dropped her hand.

Cannibalistic communion, Seth thought. He looked down at Ifragsli's corpse; the shroud and the death mask made him shudder, and the embalming fragrance was beginning to burn his nose. The bedaubed eyes haunted him. He realized that beneath the red clay of the death mask Ifragsli had no eyes at all. Either the Pledgechild or Lijadu had cut them out of her head in preparation for this ceremony called the dascra'nol.

"Master Douin, Master Seth, we're waiting for you." Porchaddos Pors stood at the right end of the wall, having just emerged from a nichelike doorway there. He was neither smoking nor wiping sweat from his brow, and the surprising coolness of the Sh'vaij had restored his spirits. He sounded only modestly put out with them for their tardiness. "The Pledgechild would like to ask us about our mission, I believe, and you had best not keep her waiting longer, Master Seth." Pors retreated into the tall, narrow passage.

"Go ahead, both of you, please," Lijadu said. "I'll follow shortly." She knelt again beside her birth-parent's corpse. "Go on, Kahl Latimer."

Seth and Douin entered a tiny, wedge-shaped room lined from floor to ceiling with shelves. The shelves, in turn, were lined with countless clay urns, of all shapes and sizes, so that the room nearly drowned them in a smell at once clumsy and delicate—as of damp cement and wet tea leaves. Seth caught Douin's elbow again.

"She called me Kahl Latimer, Master Douin."

"Which, along with the Tropish honorific, happens to be your name."

"I never told her my name. And when the Magistrate introduced me to the Pledgechild, Lijadu wasn't close enough to hear."

"Lord Pors has just called you by name."

"He called me Master Seth. He didn't call me by my surname."

"Well, what do you think it means?"

"It means she either picked my name from my head or learned it by way of telepathic cerebrations from the Pledgechild."

Douin was cold-bloodedly matter-of-fact: "What do you think we should do about it, then?"

"I don't know," Seth admitted.

"Neither do I." Douin led him toward a door standing slightly ajar. "So let's just join the others."

The Pledgechild's audience room was cramped but well lit. A large, rectangular window faced out on the terraces rising to the base of Palija Kadi, the Great Wall. The Magistrate, Deputy Emahpre, and Pors sat together on a wooden bench against the wall facing this window—looking very much like naughty schoolboys dragged in for disciplining. The Pledgechild faced her visitors in a backless wooden chair resembling an elevated footstool. She sat to the right of the window, near a small amphora stand, her hands toying with an odd, carefully carved Y-shaped stick.

A scepter? A divining rod? A wand? It didn't appear to be any of these things, really, for at the end of each prong was a kind of circular clip bespeaking a practical if arcane purpose for the instrument. Seeing Douin and Seth enter, the Pledgechild gestured them to a second bench with her Y-shaped toy, and they obeyed as if she were Lady Turshebsel herself.

"I was telling your friends," the old woman began, aspirating her words, "that it's unfortunate your journey to the basin has coincided with the removal of a dead sister from one of the Holy One's lookouts. We're preparing for her dascra'nol ceremony. We can conduct no talks involving the welfare of the community until we've seen tomorrow through this sister's eyes and laid her respectfully to earth."

Emahpre was outraged, and only as tactful as his indignation would permit him to be: "Commander Swodi sent a soldier to you last night to inform you of our coming. You might have conveyed this message to the soldier, who would have reported to Swodi, and so on to the Magistrate. It would have been easy for us to delay our visit to the basin for a day."

"Ah," said the old woman. She raised her Y-shaped scepter and looked through its circular clips at the Deputy, as if through a lorgnette. "But you would have been suspicious of my motives. You would have wondered what I was plotting. Is it so bad you arrived early?"

"The Magistrate's time is valuable," Emahpre retorted.

The Pledgechild lowered her stick. "It may also be valuable for you to witness the dascra'nol. Gaidu once told me that there's no such thing as a coincidence. And last night I dreamed of her . . . again."

Seth now understood why the Pledgechild wore no dascra: She was the rightful heir of the departed messiah, but that messiah had disappeared without a trace nearly a century and three quarters ago. Therefore, the Pledgechild had had no way to recover the Holy One's eyes and commit their jinalma to the obligatory amulet. Lijadu wore no amulet because her birth-parent had only recently died, and because Ifragsli had in any case bequeathed her to the heirbarren and still living Pledgechild. If you paid attention, it wasn't impossible to dope out these people's relationships.

From nowhere Huspre appeared before Douin and Seth to give them each a bowl of water. A Sh'gaidu much younger than Huspre came through a door in the other side of the Pledgechild's reception cell and presented Magistrate Vrai, Lord Pors, and Deputy Emahpre with similar gifts. She had balanced all three glazed bowls so deftly that not a drop was spilled. Both Huspre and the newcomer wore dascra, Seth noted, but they had tucked the amulets inside their loose garments to keep from trailing them in the water bowls.

Emahpre was the last to be served by the newcomer. As she was backing away from him, the Deputy swore viciously in Tropish and thrust his bowl away from him so that it fell to the floor and shattered. Water splashed his boots, and shards skipped across the floor in every direction.

"*Gosfithuri!*" he cried, looking to Vrai. "*Gosfithuri!*"

Pors and the Magistrate stood, by necessity, and Seth found himself on his feet with everyone else. Only the Pledgechild remained seated, apparently unperturbed by what seemed to Seth a wholly gratuitous outburst. The Deputy gestured at the woman who had just attempted to serve him and repeated a third and fourth time the same urgent word. The young Sh'gaidu accused by this term merely stared at Emahpre, her dignity not only intact but radiant.

Meanwhile, the Pledgechild, Vrai, and Emahpre engaged in a discussion in their own tongue. While they were talking, Lijadu entered the cell through the door by which the young Sh'gaidu had also entered, and Seth's eyes went to her like smoke seeking an upward passage. Lijadu, Huspre, and the woman at the center of this mysterious brouhaha knelt to pick up the pieces of the broken bowl.

Unmindful of his status as envoy and guest, Seth put down his own bowl and commenced to help them.

Emahpre's voice grew louder, almost abusive, and finally the Magistrate overrode him with such authority that, briefly, no one else seemed capable of speech. The only sound was the clicking of earthenware shards as Seth and the others dropped them into a bowl that Lijadu held. Seth kept his head down. They were almost finished cleaning up, but he was not yet ready to confront the enigma of the prevailing situation. Then the Deputy pivoted and strode past the Pledgechild, heading for the musty little pantry bordering her reception cell.

"*Emahpre!*" Magistrate Vrai barked. "*Emahpre, asul tehdegu!*"

But the Deputy didn't return, and they all heard his boots ringing on the stones of the Sh'vaij as he departed.

The Pledgechild waved her Y-shaped dowel as if blessing the ensuing silence. "J'gosfi nuraju," she said eloquently, and even Seth understood her: They had all just witnessed the departure of a crazy man.

"Please accept my apology for the behavior of Deputy Emahpre," the Magistrate said, returning to Vox. He was trembling.

The Pledgechild graciously inclined her head—but Seth, rising from the floor with Lijadu and the others, saw that against the taut material stretched over the old woman's knobby knee her fingers were drumming helplessly. It made him want to laugh, too.

Half appalled by his own boldness, he asked, "What does *gosfithuri* mean?" He looked at the person who had suffered Emahpre's verbal abuse. She was as unruffled as the Pledgechild.

"Pregnant," Lijadu said. "It means pregnant. Before the turn of the year, Tantai will bear a child."

Seth looked again at Tantai. Her stomach was indeed swollen inside her simple garment. Gosfithuri. Heavy with life. Tantai and Huspre, after securing the Pledgechild's permission, exited the cell. Lijadu remained.

Still shaken by Emahpre's unexpected mutiny, Magistrate Vrai averted his face and strolled a few steps inside.

Seth asked him, "Did Deputy Emahpre leave because of Tantai's being . . . gosfithuri?"

"Master Seth, this is none of our affair," Lord Pors cautioned him.

But the Pledgechild said, "Oh, the Deputy was indeed offended. Good Tropiards regard the gosfithuri among them as either criminals or bearers of a contagious disease."

Vrai turned about. "Our visitors need no sociological treatise, Pledgechild. They've come to you with a proposal of considerable importance."

"During the gestation of a child," the old woman continued, undeterred, still addressing Seth, "the body insists on a sh'gosfi orientation. Pregnancy is therefore either a willful crime or an unfortunately contracted disease. Although the state has been making babies in bottles for almost two centuries, Kahl Latimer, crimes or accidents still occasionally happen. The criminal, or the afflicted one, is sequestered away from her fellows until she is delivered of her child. Once delivered, he is rehabilitated, cured. The child is invariably j'gosfi, of course. In this way the keepers of the Mwezahbe Legacy perpetuate their code of reason."

"We have compassion for the gosfithuri among us!" Magistrate Vrai said. "We set them apart to protect them. We don't subject them to the indignity and danger of serving those who are well." Then, as if ashamed of his passion and his phraseology, he sat down and stared at the floor. Nearly inaudibly he emended his final words: "Of serving those, that is, who are not themselves vessels of new life."

"So, yes, Deputy Emahpre left because Tantai is pregnant," the Pledgechild reiterated for Seth's benefit. "On Trope, reasonable persons are offended by pregnancy. It represents an alternative that has recently been denied them by law."

Lifting his head, Magistrate Vrai said: "Pledgechild, I believe you summoned the Sh'gaidu called Tantai for the purpose of discomfiting us. Hoping to precipitate a scene that would humiliate us before our visitors, you had Tantai rather than Huspre serve my deputy and me."

"One doesn't always get what one hopes for."

"Then you admit your deceitfulness in this?"

The old woman gestured with her Y-shaped scepter. "Tantai and Huspre attend to me under ordinary conditions, Magistrate, and because Tantai is gosfithuri is no reason to deny her the joy of that service. I admit only that I give you no special dispensation for your prejudices, particularly if I must do so at Tantai's expense. Judge my motives as you choose. If Tantai's ripening beautifully with child has offended your testy compatriot, I little care."

The Hawks of Conscience were as uneasy as Seth. The old woman had pushed the Magistrate into a corner. How could he escape it without demeaning himself in his own eyes or sabotaging their mission with a sharp rebuttal?

Then Lijadu said, "The Deputy's anger will cool. This evening he and our other visitors will attend Ifragsli's dascra'nol. In the morning there'll be time for proposals and discussions."

The Magistrate regarded her with steep surprise. Although she had spoken before in his presence, only now had he realized that she had an idiomatic command of Vox. She might just as well have shown him a talent for water-walking.

"In the meantime," Lijadu said, "I would ask the Pledgechild to entertain us with a recitation of her dream vision. This vision, Magistrate Vrai, which the Pledgechild often dreams, details a meeting between Seitaba Mwezahbe,

First Magistrate of Trope, and Duagahvi Gaidu, the Holy One who led her outcast people to Palija Kadi."

The Magistrate looked from Lijadu to the Pledgechild. "The lives of Mwezahbe and Gaidu at no point coincided," he said.

"From the perspective of dream," the Pledgechild said, "all lives are coincident, and not accidentally so, either."

"Please relate your vision, then," Lijadu said. "You dreamed it again last night, didn't you?"

"I did," the old woman said.

The Magistrate said, "I must tell you, Pledgechild, that if your arbitrary vision establishes the First Magistrate as a straw man for Gaidu's convenient shredding, you will estrange us further. It will do you no good to tell it, or us any good to hear it. I won't have our time wasted. We came here with a proposal whose significance—"

"But we can't discuss that proposal yet," Lijadu interrupted. "I've asked the Pledgechild to relate her vision, Magistrate, because it may *improve* your temper."

"Improve my temper?" Clearly, the Magistrate didn't like the implications of Lijadu's phrasing.

"Gaidu scarcely speaks," Lijadu said. "Mwezahbe carries the entire debate, if it's to be called that. In many ways, the dream vision offers every Sh'gaidu a challenging test of her faith and every Tropiard a defense of the Legacy by which he lives."

"Then why should the Pledgechild wish to recite it?" Vrai asked. "Why abet the enemy and perplex the faithful?"

"I'm bound by the *Path of Duagahvi Gaidu* to recite my dreams," the old woman replied. "Their content doesn't matter. I receive and report, and if the substance of my vision seems a threat to our beliefs, I must speak that which threatens and disturbs. This was my pledge to Gaidu before she left us for the Nuraju."

Magistrate Vrai turned to Seth. "What do you say, my bond-partner? If you don't wish to hear, we'll retreat to our airship until it's time for the dascra'nol."

"I'd be pleased to hear the Pledgechild." Despite the old woman's intimidating gaze, Seth knew that he'd answered not from queasiness or fear but from a genuine curiosity about the workings of her mind and of the society of her sh'gosfi-by-choice disciples.

ELEVEN

Seth was permitted to sit down beside the Magistrate, while Pors and Douin settled on another bench with their water bowls. Huspre left the cell, and Lijadu propped herself on the window ledge to the left of the Pledgechild's amphora stand. The old woman laid her scepter in her lap and cleared her throat.

The sound was startlingly masculine. No matter. Seth already knew that he could not distinguish the voices of Tropiards as "male" or "female." Each individual had a voice uniquely his or her own. To Seth's ear, Deputy Emahpre had the high-pitched but musical voice of a woman. Lijadu, on the other hand, spoke with a pleasing adolescent huskiness.

"I call my dream vision—or, rather, it demands to be called—'The Messiah Who Came Too Late,'" the Pledgechild said. "Last night was the third time I've dreamed it this year, and it's always the same."

And she began:

> A light comes on inside my mind. Seitaba Mwezahbe and our Holy One stand together on a lofty glass scaffold in the building that Tropiards call the J'beij. The light in my mind goes out. When it comes back on, I see the messiah and the magistrate standing in each other's company atop the wall we know as Palija Kadi. For the remainder of my dream, these places alternate so rapidly that only the figures of Mwezahbe and Gaidu themselves have any real outline.

Time doesn't exist for them. Gaidu has not gone back to the era of the First Magistrate, nor has he come forward to the advent of the Holy One. Instead, they have met at a flickering intersection of their intellects and souls.

When Mwezahbe speaks, however, he attempts to define the moment in terms of measured and identifiable units. It's as if I'm dreaming a vision that Mwezahbe has dreamed before me.

"Welcome, Gaidu, to the year 223," he says. "This is the last year of my life, three and a half centuries before your own birth. It's only in this way we'll ever be able to talk, for very shortly in your own lifetime you'll disappear from your people and suffer a violent death.

"Each of us has striven to alter and improve the lot of our followers, I as maker and lawgiver, you as apostate. Many of those who come after me will wish to kill you. One will undoubtedly succeed. Still, I don't wish to punish you for your apostasy by threatening you with a death that you won't believe in. What sort of punishment is that? Instead, your punishment must consist of a single, soul-destroying revelation.

"You see, my late-arriving adversary, your life hasn't been your own."

Gaidu does not respond. She stands before the First Magistrate in a state of silent receptiveness, attempting to read the multifaceted personality behind his concealing goggles. She herself is naked.

"You were a statistical probability," Mwezahbe continues. "All my life I've encountered resistance to my Legacy, minor insurrections that failed out of sheer, short-circuited *wrongness*. But I knew that one day a few would rebel because, touched to the heart with an ancient sh'gosfi madness that we've labored, first, to mute and, finally, to forbid, they would elevate superstition over science, and mysticism over the probing empirical mind. The Tropish state being what it is, Gaidu, I knew that any future rebellion would evolve as a movement more religious than political, and that a madwoman would become for the apostates a new focal point of authority. I've known all along that you would come, and that your advent would cast you in the role of a savior."

But our savior answers Seitaba Mwezahbe nothing.

"The domination of the sh'gosfi—as a people rather than as an essential aberration of the light—will be cramped and short-lived," the First Magistrate declares. "It has no future. It evolved in the first place only out of a failure of full self-awareness, and its purpose was to provide the necessary contrast by which we could come to recognize and pursue the path of an aggressive, thoroughgoing rationality. I'm the embodiment of that recognition and that pursuit. It was for me to codify the way to both, and I did so, much to your disadvantage, long before you arrived on the scene to challenge my success.

"Holy One, the simplest and most decisive truth about your advent is that it will be inopportune. You will have come too late to undo the good that my reign inaugurates and gives enduring passage."

Gaidu's eyes bejewel the darkness of my dream, but still she keeps her peace, letting Mwezahbe accuse and chastise.

"Gosfi of reason—j'gosfi, by very definition—function beyond the limits of worship, Holy One. They cry out for ideas to respect, for rulers who will capture not only their imaginations but their intellects. Therefore, they have subordinated themselves to my Legacy, which has freed them from the irrational fears and the animal longings of their baser selves. In being bound to reason, Gaidu, there is no slavery and no despair.

"But the beginnings of *your* ministry, over four centuries hence, will dazzle and enslave only those who have failed to assimilate the statutes of the Legacy. From the state you'll siphon off only those still backward enough to demand a focus of veneration rather than a fount of inspiration. You will have gained the souls of harlots, perverts, and madwomen, the very ones too feeble to abide by the truths that commit their souls into their own keeping. These are the ones who will be looking for a Great Mother to save them from themselves, the sh'gocodre of legend who hides her crippled broodlings under the monumental tents of her double wings. For your own purposes, then, you will have come too late. Can't you recognize your failure, Gaidu?"

Although the eyes of the Holy One gleam, she doesn't speak.

"As one who would provide an alternative authority by ensnaring gosfi souls, you've timed things badly.

"Perhaps, however, you could argue that you will perform miracles to bring about your Sh'gaidu Millennium. But we have created a society in which the miraculous is looked upon with all the grand and mighty suspicion of the intellect. Even that which briefly appears worthy of the mind's dread has explanation, and derives from this fact a mystery of its own. It becomes even more miraculous for having an empirical basis.

"If an unsolvable riddle exists, it may well be death, or entropy, or the spirit's waste. But we deny that you unriddle these final conundrums. You shroud them in the rags of superstition and answer them with riddles of your own.

"How, then, can you disclose to any gosfi a metaphysics more incisive and transcendent than the state's? Our miracles, grounded in a method quantifiable and exact, are so much more certain than yours. And because we have deprived you of the weapon of miracle, Gaidu, you've presented yourself to the Tropiards of the Thirty-three Cities too late to make use of it."

Now I thrash in my sleep, angry for my Holy One and desirous of rebuking her inquisitor for his rudeness. A light goes on and off in my brain. Now I'm on a scaffold in the J'beij, now on the edge of Palija Kadi overlooking the laser-singed fields of the basin. I see the ruin that's to come, and I wish to wake up. But Gaidu holds me in my dream. With the violence of a rape, she opens me to the relentless arguments of First Magistrate Mwezahbe.

"Why don't you answer me?" he asks. "Do you believe yourself the spirit-of-mystery made flesh? Do you mean to imply by your silence that you must work through mystery to attain your ends? *Mystery.* Is this the metaphysical cloister in which you take refuge? Well, it won't do, Gaidu. It won't do. Even you must realize the inadequacy of your stratagem.

"Mystery made flesh! The mystery of your birthing—if mystery you insist upon—lies in the fact that insentience may somehow generate life, that the organic may somehow derive from the inorganic, that flesh may contain spirit. But you're not unique in being the product of such a wondrous quickening. Not by any means. What feeling, fiery creature doesn't illustrate and embody the same mystery, Holy One?

"Answer me! Open your soul to me! How are you, Gaidu, more miraculous—in essence, not simply in degree—than the smallest mite that hatches, gluts itself on blood, and dies? Answer me!"

At this point, I'm in torment. I begin to fear that Mwezahbe has pushed our savior to the extremity of self-doubt. But she remains serene. She grants my dreaming self a brief glimpse into the calmness of her heart. Otherwise, she knows, I would rage out of my sleep like a j'gosfi warrior dutifully fulfilling the madnesses of reason.

Mwezahbe resumes his inquisition: "We both know that your coming coincides with a time not truly vulnerable to your message. Who's to blame for that? You know as well as I, and this knowledge, by itself, is partial punishment for your apostasy, Holy One. However, there's more, and I intend to reveal to you that which must condemn the worthiness of your ministry and so inflict upon your soul a punishment suitable to your betrayal.

"My Legacy has sought to provide for the weak, the mind-crippled, and the pathologically sh'gosfi, either by curing them or by offering them an outlet for their weaknesses. One such outlet will be your Sh'gaidu community of misfits and mystics.

"Therefore, on a modest if misleadingly successful scale, the experiment at Palija Kadi will survive for some time. But eventually you'll find yourselves outdistanced by the programmed evolution of a million Tropiards working through

their minds and auxiliary births toward a transcendental gosfi
condition. When we attain to this condition, Holy One, your
people will have perished. The Sh'gaidu will have disappeared
from the face of the planet.

"Holy One, you came too late.

"Had you come earlier, before my own lifetime, nothing
I could have done would have erased your image. The nation would be wholly sh'gosfi or divided against itself in the
self-destructive polarity of desperate males and unmerciful
madwomen. Probably the former—for I would not have yet
appeared to lift all Trope out of ignorance and superstition.
Your own view would have prevailed, and sh'gosfi nationwide
would have bravely resisted the imposition of my upstart authority. Martyrs by the thousands would have arisen to die for
your holy illusions.

"And I, Seitaba Mwezahbe, would be the Second Messiah. A second messiah is an anomaly, Holy One. She is either
Nuraju or charlatan. She has no official status and only the
adherents she deserves. Her Elect are a pitiful and deluded
group, and that's why she has them. In fact, it may be that
she needs her Elect far more desperately than they need her.
Though they're too weak to live entirely by their own wills,
a few will gain the strength to desert her. Others will deny
reality their whole lives, and these few sad specimens of gosfihood she will exploit, their needs feeding hers and hers theirs
in a melancholy symbiosis.

"Meanwhile, the religion of her rebellion has become a
cauldron wherein the disenchanted, the deranged, and the
desolate are boiled away. The real substance of the state remains behind, purified.

"And those who are boiled off, Gaidu, what of them?
What do you care for them beyond their usefulness as psychic grist? Can you even answer? If so, try. Answer one who's
granted freedom *and* dignity to his people—for I've done that
by administering to their worldly needs, giving them fathom-
able mysteries, and vanquishing their terror of the dark. All
this I did from the challenge of doing it, and from love, and

from a secret but not unnatural desire to be known forever as a powerful benefactor.

"But what of *your* motives, Holy One? What are they? Are they too dark to voice? Speak, I command you!"

Gaidu torments me in my sleep by refusing to respond to these provocations. I would answer for her, sing her praises, but my tongue is a hibernating animal in my mouth, no more able to awake than I.

"You came too late," the First Magistrate says. "The source of your strength lies in a vast pettiness yearning toward the honor that three million Tropiards give me alone. If not, speak. Give me your thoughts, or vanish into time like the phantom you are."

Here the Pledgechild stopped. She lifted her Y-shaped scepter, studied it, and put it back in her lap. Everyone in her reception cell waited for her to go on.

"Is that all, Pledgechild?" Porchaddos Pors asked. "Does the vision have an ending? Does your messiah answer Mwezahbe anything?"

The old woman looked up. "You may judge for yourself, Kahl Pors. My dream vision always concludes in the same way."

"Tell it," Lijadu urged from the windowsill.

"Never fear, my darling Lijadu." The Pledgechild pointed her stick at Seth and Magistrate Vrai, one prong to each. "It's at this point that Gaidu replies, you see, and although she doesn't attack Mwezahbe verbally or disparage Tropish ideals, her behavior would strike a good Tropiard—a successor to the First Magistrate—as unseemly. I spell this out explicitly before I proceed."

"Do you want my permission to finish?" the Magistrate asked.

"Oh, no," the old woman said. "I must finish every recitation, as Lijadu, despite her unnecessary urgings, well knows. But if you don't wish to hear it, Magistrate, you may join Emahpre in your airship."

Vrai hesitated only a moment. "I will stay."

"Yes," the Pledgechild said. "My vision ended last night as it always does."

With a nervousness I can feel, Mwezahbe waits for Gaidu to rebut his attack. The Holy One senses the First Magistrate's fear that he has not woven tight some threadbare place in his argument. But, strangely, she also senses that Mwezahbe longs for the rebuttal he fears.

At length she turns toward the First Magistrate and spreads wide her arms. In the next instant—there in the J'beij, here on our wall's summit—she steps into the body of Seitaba Mwezahbe. She joins with the dream flesh of her inquisitor. For a moment, the two are a unity, drinking starlight through the same fiery eyes and sharing a pulse that reverberates in time with my own. Together, they are whole and seamless.

So is the world.

But Mwezahbe shakes his head, discomfited by the surrender of his self. When he can stand it no longer, he backs away from Gaidu's all-encompassing embrace, thereby denying his nuclear union with her. I can read his feelings. Exhilaration diluted with shame. Against his will, he has been immersed in sh'gosfi consciousness, and although the immersion has not deprived him of his self, he feels disoriented and shamefully aflame.

"Return to your time," he commands our Holy One. "Soon, in our own eras, you and I will die, nor do I believe that we'll meet again. That which created us has little use for dialectics. Farewell, sibling and fleshsharer."

Gaidu touches the First Magistrate with her mind, tilting her head so that the stars may evict her from my vision. A nimbus seizes her, light winks in her veins, and she is gone. Mwezahbe, too, crumbles, and all that remains in my vision is a glittering panorama of Palija Kadi: cliffs, fields, bridges, Sh'gaidu communicants. Our crops rage with fire. The roar of their burning climbs through the night like the cries of a million tortured spirits.

No one moved. Seth could hear the roaring of the fires. Outside, however, through the window, only the wind-stirred Sh'gaidu crops. Lijadu's tigerish green eyes captured his. Her stare unsettled him. How could you interpret the meaning of such a stony, inhuman appraisal? Guiltily, he looked away.

The Pledgechild rescued Seth with a question: "Does the ending of my dream vision displease you, too, Kahl Latimer?"

"Displease me?" Seth shook his head. "No, Pledgechild. In many ways, Gaidu's response to Seitaba Mwezahbe is more poetic than his lengthy inquisition."

"That poetry displeases Magistrate Vrai," she said. "It and the merging of j'gosfi and sh'gosfi in a'union whose significance is not simply sexual."

Vrai said, "If Gaidu triumphs in your vision, Pledgechild, she does so because your sleeping self controls the dream's direction. That's self-evident."

"Is it?"

"The vision has an aesthetic rightness, from the Sh'gaidu perspective—but it doesn't reflect reality, and the flames at the end are history rather than prophecy."

"In which instance it *does* reflect reality," the Pledgechild said. "In its other parts it symbolizes rather than reflects the real. Do you expect consistency of a dream?"

"Dreaming is a sh'gosfi enterprise, Pledgechild."

"You never dream?"

The Magistrate shifted in his seat. "Of course. Dreams are a natural outlet for the irrational, a failsafe against madness."

Lijadu continued to study Seth. Her interest made his earlobes burn, but it also quelled the ardor that had earlier tormented him.

The Pledgechild also swung her attention from the Magistrate to Seth. "Do you love anyone, Kahl Latimer?"

"Love anyone?" Everyone in the room seemed to be regarding him.

"I ask because love is an emotion—a fixation, if you like—that often has no rational source. Sometimes we love as helplessly as we dream. Do you, then, love anyone, Kahl Latimer?"

"My isosire," Seth said after a moment, glancing at Pors. "My birth-parent. And my isohet, my older sibling, Abel." Would this admission convict him in the Sh'gaidu's glittering eyes as a narcissist? Did they know what isosire and isohet meant? Would his heart love for Abel absolve him of the charge of narcissism? After all, he did finally love someone outside of Seth Latimer, even if this love object happened to be his genetic twin. Abel was a person, as was he.

"Is this a rational love?" the Pledgechild asked.

"Stop," the Magistrate said. "Kahl Latimer is a guest on Trope and a guest here in Palija Kadi."

"It's all right," Seth said. "I don't mind her questions."

"Well, then?" The Pledgechild waited.

"I would suppose that pure reason would rule out love as a human, or a gosfi, or a jauddeb, possibility. Instinct at least preserves the possibility. I don't believe I'm a full-fledged devotee of either system."

"You define the Sh'gaidu 'system' in terms of instinct?" the old woman asked.

"Maybe as a ritualization of it, Pledgechild."

"Then how would you define the Magistrate's 'system'?" The last word emerged from her lips like something contaminated.

Seth glanced at Vrai. "Maybe as an attempt at instinct modification," he said.

"Not as a negation of instinct?"

"That wouldn't be possible, would it?"

The Pledgechild began to rise from her backless chair. Lijadu, springing from her place on the windowsill, hurried to help her. Everyone else rose out of deference to the Sh'gaidu leader, who, freeing herself from Lijadu's hand, put her scepter down and tottered the few remaining steps from her chair to Seth's. Her almost predatory black eyes approached. Her thin arms opened. A moment later he was captive in their embrace, rigid under the baffled gazes of the Magistrate, Pors, and Douin. The Pledgechild held him for at least a minute, released him, and shuffled unassisted into the room opposite the pottery-storage niche. For a time, no one spoke or tried to sit again.

"Why did she do that?" Douin finally asked Seth.

"I don't know." Seth shook his head. Lijadu was still watching him, her eyes as indecipherable as alien runes.

Pors said, "Her embracing Master Seth concerns me far less, Magistrate Vrai, than her leaving. We've made no substantial progress, and the better part of the afternoon lies ahead."

"Forgive her," Lijadu said. "Her recitation has sapped her strength. She must rest. This evening's dascra'nol ceremony will also be fatiguing for her."

"What would you have us do now?" the Magistrate asked.

Huspre reentered the reception cell, with her milky eyes and her mismatched facial features.

"Remain here if you like," Lijadu said. "Huspre will bring food. Or you may tour the basin with me and eat later, or return to your airship on the roadway."

"I don't care to tour the basin," Pors declared.

"Then we'll eat something," the Magistrate said.

Lijadu spoke to Huspre in Tropish, and Huspre retreated into the Pledgechild's adjoining room, only to come back a moment later laden with baskets of bread and fresh uncooked vegetables. Huspre refilled everyone's water bowls from the amphora on the stand next to the Pledgechild's chair. Then, with Lijadu's help, she distributed the bread and vegetable stalks into another set of bowls. Tantai, the pregnant Sh'gaidu, was conspicuous by her absence.

"I'd like to see the basin," Seth said, anxious to escape the others. "If I could take a piece of bread with me, I'd need nothing else."

"Very well," Lijadu said. "I'll show you."

"Kahl Latimer," the Magistrate blurted. Seth turned towards him. "Do you require your goggles against the sun?" He touched the chain by which they hung inside the bodice of the jumpsuit.

"No, I'll be fine." But Seth wondered if the Magistrate's concern for his eyes was actually a warning to protect the dascra that lay inside his own tunic.

Pors said, "Master Seth, where will we meet again?" Both Pors and Douin seemed apprehensive about his departure.

"I'll bring him back to the Sh'vaij," Lijadu said.

The Magistrate said, "We'll either be here, Kahl Latimer, or in the airship with Deputy Emahpre."

Seth ached to be outside. Except for a few short walks in the open air, he had been confined to walled and roofed-in places for nearly two months: Douin's geffide, the *Dharmakaya*, and, if only briefly, the J'beij and the crofthouse here on Trope. Anja was an alien sun, true, but, desiring its blessing, he relished the prospect of sweating from its conjectural heat rather than from a craven anxiety.

Lijadu beckoned him out of the Pledgechild's cell.

TWELVE

It was almost noon. Seth beheld everything as if by a magnesium flare. Anja hung overhead like a pinwheel running alternately blue and white, and the whole basin had the magnified clarity of a rock garden beneath a still mountain spring.

Lijadu and Seth walked toward the Great Wall, climbing terraces that stepped upward to its base. Occasionally, Lijadu paused to bend down a stalk and examine the fruit at its tip. Seth nibbled a Sh'gaidu breadstick that he had brought with him from the Pledgechild's cell, deciding gradually that he liked the taste.

In the fields labored other Sh'gaidu, adults with wooden or stone implements to chop out weeds or to ready the ground for new plantings. Seth detected their presence by the stabbing glints of sunlight from their eyes as they turned among the stalks. The heat did not worry him, but the brightness did. Should he raise his hood for protection? On so warm a day, that seemed silly. Lijadu, in her abbreviated sari, was practically naked. Whenever she moved, her limbs flashed brown: she was an uncanny brightness herself, and Seth had no desire to shield his eyes from her.

"I can't translate the names of all the plants," Lijadu said. "They're specific to Trope, as the plants of your world are specific to it—but a few we call by descriptive names that allow rough translation." She gripped the stalk of a shoulder-high plant and showed Seth the deep-green cluster at its head. "This we call emerald-eye, *lijadu*. I'm not named for the plant, however, or it for me. We share our name because of the suitability of the metaphor to us both." She let the stalk go and set off again toward the blinding white wall whose bulk dwarfed them both.

Over Seth's shoulder, the Sh'vaij was far away. The cypresslike trees around it rippled like small blue flames.

Ahead, hedges of amber, lilac, and crimson encircled the base of the wall, mounting toward it inexorably. Lijadu picked her way through this vegetation with a skill born of familiarity and practice. Seth was hard put to keep up, but fixed his eyes on the Sh'gaidu's supple legs so that admiration and desire soon neutralized his windedness. Finally, at the wall, Lijadu reached out her hands and touched the warm white rock. Seth aped her stance, palms flat and head thrown back.

"Palija Kadi," Lijadu said. "The Great Wall. A portion of the buried heart of the planet. It was here before the Tropish state, long before the protogosfi who first lived in the galleries." She nodded at the balustraded cliff face in which the Sh'gaidu apparently had their individual dwellings.

Perhaps because of an assisting wind, Seth thought he could hear vast machines whirring in the hidden chambers in the eastern wall. A kind of roar.

"Who were these protogosfi?" Seth asked.

Lijadu dropped her hands and faced him. "Ancestors of the people of Trope, but the state refuses to think on our origins here in Palija Kadi."

"Surely the state has explored gosfi prehistory, Lijadu."

"Excavations? Archaeology? Is that what you mean?"

"I suppose it is, yes."

"To a limited extent the state has engaged in these things, on the grounds that to ignore the past is senseless. But for most Tropiards, including especially their own First Magistrate, prehistory is *was*. Mwezahbe said that the state must look forward rather than back. The purpose of each Tropiard and of the technocracy to which he belongs is to comprehend the significance of their *becoming*. They believe that this becoming defines them."

Seth tried a pun in Vox: "It's the defining that becomes you."

"No, Kahl Latimer, it's the *being* that interests us, essence rather than process. We revere the protogosfi for what they were. The state ignores them because what they were is anterior to the evolutionary path that all good Tropiards follow toward a doubtful transcendence. They don't care to think much on that from which they've arisen."

"Why?" Lijadu's knowledge, sophistication, and aplomb astonished and daunted Seth. He hardly expected them from a member of a dissident, mystagogic commune. That she and her tribe would agree to leave this place for a world light-years away began to seem more and more unlikely.

"Because like humans and jauddeb, every species of protogosfi to live on Trope had two distinct sexes. None were—as all modern gosfi are—hermaphroditic."

"Is that why Trope continues to hold itself aloof from Interstel?"

"Because humanity still has two sexes? Probably. I don't know everything about the rational aversions of the present magistrate."

"He seems a decent person."

"Much better than the last one. I'm so grateful I never knew Orisu Sfol."

"But these protogosfi, Lijadu—how do the Sh'gaidu know about them?"

She nodded at the eastern cliff. "We live where they did, or where several bands of the most successful protogosfids lived. Tropiards refer collectively to our apartments in the rock as the galleries, but their true name—which even the protogosfi who lived here may have spoken, Kahl Latimer—is Yaji Tropei, Earth Womb. They prepared these mansions for us millions of years ago, and died becoming us. Their earliest descendants survived and prospered through androgyny, but the technocracy succeeding this culture a mere nine hundred years ago arose on the suppression of the sh'gosfi impulse in every one of its *sons*." Lijadu used the Vox for "self-aware male offspring" with what struck Seth as tactful moral neutrality. "Yaji Tropei is a painstaking feat of engineering, Kahl Latimer, and you'll have a chance to see it before you leave. We find it satisfying that our protogosfid ancestors built these galleries many millennia before the First Magistrate codified the statutes of the Mwezahbe Legacy."

Lijadu led Seth along the base of the great wall and then down a series of stone-braced steps to a terrace where a regiment of stunted-looking bushes grew. Their leaves were acid green and palmate. They smelled keenly of an unnamable spice. Lijadu stalked along this tier, found a plant to her liking, and knelt beside it. After glancing cryptically at Seth, she took the plant's central stalk between her fingers and pushed the clustering leaves aside. Revealed halfway down the stalk was a tumorlike pod not quite the size of her fist. Lijadu snapped this pod from the plant, cupped it in her hands with an affecting gentleness. She extended the pod to Seth, signaling with her chin that he should accept her gift and cradle it in his hands. He did so.

A moment later she said, "Return it, Kahl Latimer."

Seth returned the strange seed pod.

Now Lijadu peeled back the long hard petals of the iridescent green exoskin. Working carefully, she reduced the pod to a miniature chalice, in which there grew a round blue ball. Weblike filaments anchored the ball in the chalice, but Lijadu cut these by scooping her finger around the pod's open interior. Then she let the casing drop and closed her fist around the ball.

"This we call the heartseed, Kahl Latimer. Do you know it?"

"No."

"Then watch." Lijadu undid her fist and held her palm out before her. The ball trembled as if something inside it were struggling to break out. "The heartseed grows for everyone on Trope, the sane and the mad alike."

As in time-lapse photography, the heartseed ballooned on Lijadu's hand. In less than a minute it had become a cerulean-blue spheroid, the size of an ancient ecclesiastical censer and almost as aromatic. But it had no more substance than a soap bubble. Seth reached to touch it and felt only a resilient silkiness.

"Of all the plants in Palija Kadi," Lijadu said, "only this is not for food. Not for food, but for beauty."

Like the mwehanja Seth had eaten in the Tropish dormitory and again aboard The Albatross, the heartseed resembled the sun.

Lijadu stood, lifted her cupped hands to the sky, and pulled them down to free the sphere. It dipped on the wind and spun away above the colorful stairstep terraces towards the Sh'vaij. It blurred with the noon's brilliance, lifting on a thermal and pirouetting away into infinity. Seth squinted after it into the stinging light.

"Care to see the kioba Najuma from which my birth-parent kept watch after her death?" Lijadu pointed to the tower below them to their right.

When Seth nodded, Lijadu led him along the same terrace to another series of stone-braced steps descending to the north. Seth could see the boxed-in lookout at the top of the tower, surprised to find it still a little *below* them. But Lijadu danced easily down the steps to the base of the tower, and Seth, no longer winded, followed.

From the tower's platform dangled a rope. Lijadu braced it for Seth so that he could shinny up it and through the floor into the lookout. Then, so gracefully that the rope hardly danced despite being unbraced by anyone on the ground, Lijadu climbed up after him. From the kioba, Seth and Lijadu surveyed the quilt patterns of the fields and terraces beneath them. Neither spoke, but Seth moved from side to side to experience each new view in turn.

The curious roaring he had heard from Yaji Tropei—the galleries—seemed to have stopped. Looking that way, he saw members of the Sh'gaidu sect moving behind the cliff's coral balustrades and pacing back and forth along the twisted stone bridges connecting the galleries to the fields. Palija Kadi was alive.

In the center of the lookout ran a pole from ceiling to floor. Pensively, Lijadu gripped this and spoke:

"These are places of vision. We bring our dead to them and bind them to the pole-trees, as my own birth-parent Ifragsli was bound here four nights ago. From here the dead look out on their lives and recall Duagahvi Gaidu. They remain three days. Before their eyes crumble into jinalma, the dead are cut down and their eyes taken out in preparation for the ceremony we call dascra'nol."

"And, from these lookouts, the dead will see your Holy One returning from her sojourn among the northern gosfi?"

"Not with hard, living eyes, Kahl Latimer, but with the essence giving those eyes life. The Sh'gaidu believe the dead need a period of solitude in which their final visions may ripen."

"And what of these final visions you speak of?"

"This evening you'll see." Lijadu stared out across the fields.

Although she no longer faced him, Seth began to feel that his mind was as clear to her as a glass bell. Hadn't she called him by his isosire's surname even though she'd had no chance to hear his name spoken? Was she even now communing with the Pledgechild or other members of the Sh'gaidu scattered about the basin. Vrai had said that a telepathic community—where reading as well as sending is commonplace—would be a community of either wholly paranoiac or wholly indistinguishable personalities.

That condition didn't seem to obtain in Palija Kadi. From what he had seen so far, Seth judged the Pledgechild, Lijadu, Huspre, Tantai, and the little girl Omwhol as complete persons; suspicion was not a conspicuous character trait in any of them. Were they, though, suspicious of the mission that had brought two high-ranking Tropiards and a trio of motley offworlders to their basin? A guilt without an identifiable correlative began to well in Seth.

"Lijadu."

She turned to him.

"Lijadu, Magistrate Vrai speaks to me mind to mind. Can you do that, too?"

—*We can.*

He accepted the admission, or the avowal, as if it had been voiced—even though Lijadu had been mutely staring at him for a long, disconcerting moment. He was neither surprised nor frightened.

"Do your capabilities extend beyond simple transmission?" he asked. "Can you read as well as send?"

"Kahl Latimer, you are now uneasy. Would a straightforward answer banish your uneasiness or simply replace it with a gnawing fear?"

"You've answered my question, haven't you?"

"Yes, but not straightforwardly." Lijadu drummed the fingers of one hand against her other bare shoulder. "And do you fear me?"

Seth considered this. "No, but—"

"You don't know why the Magistrate is capable of sending but not of reading?"

Nodding, Seth acknowledged Lijadu's insight.

"Sending is an intellectual ability, lineal in nature and active in origin. A Tropiard has little difficulty mastering the rudiments of sending because the Mwezahbe Legacy valorizes the very qualities that make the act possible."

"Whereas reading—"

"Reading is intuitive, diffuse rather than lineal. It requires receptiveness rather than self-assertion. Our Holy One and her Pledgechild have taught us to esteem the sort of awareness that makes this capability as natural as breathing. Nor do we experience their capabilities solely in verbal terms. We also read emotional states."

"What do you read in me?"

"Anxiety," said Lijadu, touching his face. "A fierce desire to succeed balanced against a fiercer one to please everyone whom you inwardly validate as a person; hence, Kahl Latimer, your anxiousness."

"I don't understand."

"I understand that you don't." She dropped her hand. On the roadway below the Sh'vaij, with all the other naked children, Lijadu had seemed a child. Now, however, she radiated the wisdom and confidence of a goddess. How had she gained her knowledge not only of Palija Kadi but of the greater world beyond it?

A flight of cranelike reptiles passed over the basin, trailing their thin legs behind them like powder-blue streamers.

When they had gone, Lijadu said, "Upon attaining twenty harvests, each Sh'gaidu must embark on a sojourn to one of the Thirty-three Cities. In the year Tropiards called 908, I journeyed to the city of Ebsu Ebsa. In the guise of a j'gosfi who had still not had his first auxiliary birth, I stayed among the citizens of Ebsu Ebsa for three complete turns of the sun. Having seen the world the Magistrate rules, I know firsthand its virtues and its shortcomings. I returned to Palija Kadi grateful that the state allows our community to exist. If it did not exist, I would find a way to die."

"You're older than I am," Seth said incredulously.

"I'm twenty-three of Trope's years—but our years are shorter than yours."

"I'm twenty-one, Earth reckoning."

"Then, by an absolute measure, you're *my* elder, Kahl Latimer."

Odd: To learn that Lijadu was younger than he, yet possessed of adult knowledge and confidence, seemed a slap at his own intellectual and moral progress. Moreover, on Trope, Lijadu was still a preadolescent. Chagrin blossomed in Seth, reddening his cheeks. He also wondered how Lijadu had emerged from her years in a Tropish city still a devout Sh'gaidu, if no longer a total innocent.

Tactfully, Lijadu recited her story: "Not long after the disappearance of our Holy One, the Pledgechild established the ritual of a three-year sojourn among the j'gosfi. She stipulated that only fledglings well past the most impressionable period of their growth were eligible to go. The reason for these sojourns was not only to expose the young Sh'gaidu to an alien way of life, but to give her a chance to search among our enemies for the departed Holy One."

"I thought she'd gone to the barbarian northern continent looking for converts."

"That idea is a part of Sh'gaidu lore, but we've also always felt it likely that the state had taken her captive and confined her in one of the Thirty-three Cities. The hope of her captors would have been that the fellowship here at Palija Kadi would have fallen apart for want of leadership."

"Wouldn't you know if she were still alive?" Seth asked. "Wouldn't you receive her cerebrations, and she yours?"

"If she weren't injured somehow, yes. But perhaps the j'gosfi subjected her to an auxiliary birth and so destroyed the personality by which we knew her."

"Couldn't you read the Magistrate or Deputy Emahpre to find out?"

"Tropiards are hard to read, Kahl Latimer. They live close to the surface of their skins. It's hard for us to go deeper into their inner lives than they go themselves. And yet, yes, we could learn important things while Magistrate Vrai and his deputy are here."

These words seemed to imply something ominous. He turned away and asked, "Isn't leaving the basin dangerous for a young Sh'gaidu? Doesn't the state know of these three-year sojourns in its cities?" Light winked above the western cliff face, a reminder of the perpetual presence of state troops.

"The state has known about them all along. But it does nothing to discourage our pilgrims; it feels it can only benefit by our presence in the cities."

"How?"

"Occasionally, a young Sh'gaidu surrenders to the workaday glitter of Tropish life. Bodily comfort prevails over spiritual rigor. The state finds this rewarding."

"What does your Pledgechild believe?"

"That one day the defector will see, with fiery clarity, the error of her choice. Besides, these defections are rare. Most of us come home, and we come home wiser than we left."

Lijadu told what it had been like to learn the Sh'gaidu were not the only people on Trope possessed of a savior. The citizens of Ebsu Ebsa revered Seitaba Mwezahbe as the communards of the basin revered Duagahvi Gaidu. Moreover, years were counted not from Gaidu's birth but from Mwezahbe's creation of the office of magistrate. Lijadu had not known that before. She had assumed that time passed unregistered, except in the minds of such eminences as the Pledgechild and her counselors. Most miraculous of all, the Pledgechild had actually known the Holy One. No one alive in the city, however, had ever seen Seitaba Mwezahbe in person. He was many, many years dead.

Still, for the duration of her sojourn in the clockwork city of Ebsu Ebsa, where Lijadu had earned her way taking the memory transcriptions and compiling the evo-step genealogies of j'gosfi preparing to undergo auxiliary birth, the knowledge that Gaidu was not the center of the universe for everyone had gnawed at her heart. She had suffered excruciating agonies of the soul. It had seemed to her that the universe resolved itself into one great polarity: Mwezahbe versus Gaidu. With which savior did one cast her lot? Although the weight of time and numbers lay with the Tropiard's First Magistrate, Lijadu had felt the emptiness in the hearts of Ebsu Ebsa's people, the abysses yawning beneath their unreasoning obedience to the Legacy.

On the other hand, what if Gaidu, whose devotees numbered today in the meager hundreds, had been nothing but a biochemical aberration of the j'gosfi norm, or the product of an abortive auxiliary birth? Or just a frail soul who had fallen into the grip of a galvanizing nuraj? Throughout the whole of her stay in Ebsu Ebsa, Lijadu had agonized over these questions.

More than once she had nearly compromised her identity, already well known to the city's leaders, by hectoring complacent Tropiards about their dull j'gosfihood, by proselytizing them with mock-sardonic references to the glories of witchery. She had done these unwise things as if for their faintly illicit humor, as a high-placed Tropiard might indulge a weakness for scatology with his friends. Consequently, she was always relieved when her targets drummed their fingers in glee instead of calling her down for a pervert or an apostate. In truth, doubtful of Gaidu's origins and mystagogic authenticity, Lijadu had envied these bland reasonable souls their certitude. They never suffered from insomnia. For them the Holy One was a joke, and Palija Kadi an insane asylum. The Sh'gaidu, meanwhile, were the freaks, cripples, and madwomen who worshiped the joke and inhabited the asylum. Wasn't it grand that the state had a reservation for these sad people? Well-adjusted j'gosfi had no need to associate with their like.

The kioba groaned as a breeze gusted across the basin. Seth felt himself swaying with the lookout. "How did you resolve your crisis?"

"Toward the end of my sojourn in Ebsu Ebsa, I had a dream vision."

"Like the Pledgechild's?"

"Not very, no. The similarity lies only in the fact that our Holy One figures in both. But in mine, Duagahvi Gaidu appears at midday atop the central transport wheel in Ebsu Ebsa and turns her naked eyes on every person in the streets. Seeing her, the eyes of unbelieving Tropiards melt behind their goggles and stream through the stone canals and gutters in a shiny flow of lava. Gaidu descends from the transport wheel and walks at the head of this scorching flood. With her staff, she directs this river of melted crystal out of the city and across the wasteland prairie called Chaelu Sro.

"The blind follow our Holy One, Kahl Latimer. Although for nearly three years, I have doubted Gaidu, my eyes have not melted from my face. I am not one of those who stumble blindly in her wake. Free to discard my j'gosfi eye coverings, I run beside the stricken ones until I'm nearly abreast of the divine madwoman directing the flood. The flood seethes with greens and interthreading filaments of ruby. It coils across the barren Sro, responding to the least motion of the Holy One's body—as if endowed with a vision too powerful for its many contributors' disbelief.

"Helpless, the citizens of Ebsu Ebsa grope along the banks of the stream until new tributaries of lava converge from every horizon. Then the first-stricken are joined by the blind from every other Tropish city. Gaidu skips ecstatically at the head of these various streams, knitting them together with rhythmic jabs of her staff and graceful sweeps of her tattered cloak. I alone am a sighted witness to these events. Everyone else moves by touch-and-turn, turn-and-touch. And now it's my lot to feel pity for the very ones who have for three years enraged and perplexed me.

"At last Gaidu leads all these converging rivers of crystal to the summit of Palija Kadi. Halting here, she commands the tide and the groping Tropiards to ebb away from the precipice. As far as I can see, there are eyeless people among the molten streams knotted in dazzling patterns across the Chaelu Sro.

"Gaidu summons me. Bending at my side, she creates new eyes from the matter everywhere visible, hands these scalding organs to me, and bids me distribute them to those penitent Tropiards who come forward to have their vision restored. Anja is low in the western sky, but it doesn't set. Even as the Holy One shapes her millionth pair of eyes from the receding rivers of crystal, Anja hangs on the horizon. I take the hot, hard eyes from Gaidu's hands and push them into the sockets of the blind. All that lingering twilight, the Tropiards come to us. And when the plains of Chaelu Sro are again nothing but dust and red rock, I find that even our penitents have deserted us. I'm alone with the woman whom I have doubted, prayed to, reviled, and prayed to again.

"'Where are the people whose vision I've helped you restore?' I ask her.

"'You are they,' Duagahvi Gaidu responds. 'Only in the labors of faith does faith evolve. The vision we've restored, Lijadu, is your own.'"

Lijadu fell silent. Moved, Seth studied her profile and tried to find in his own experience an apocalyptic vision comparable to the young Sh'gaidu's. But all that winked against the screens of his memory was a blood-stained, halting film of his naked isosire going up the side of the Kieri Obelisk. . . .

"Your vision was sufficient to allay your doubts?" Seth asked.

"Yes," Lijadu said. "Because Gaidu sent it to me. I knew that her spirit lived even if her body had died, and I understood that one day even j'gosfi Tropiards would share in our fiery sh'gosfi vision. And so it was easy for me to return to Palija Kadi."

For you, perhaps, Seth thought. A dream, after all, was merely a dream, whereas his memory of Günter Latimer's death had had its birth in a lurid reality. How balance that cold fact against a mere vision in which the High Priestess of the Sh'gaidu had restored the sight of the blind? Persecution could come from many quarters; ideologies were its most nutritious fuel.

"What made my reimmersion in my faith possible," Lijadu went on, "was the realization that the polarity I'd made myself see in Ebsu Ebsa—that between our Holy One and the First Magistrate—was *not* a polarity. J'gosfi and sh'gosfi are orientations toward the truth, Kahl Latimer, not embodiments or absolute negations of it. A sh'gosfi need not forfeit her identity if she learns to analyze her visions, nor a j'gosfi surrender his rational orientation if he begins to perceive the world through Sh'gaidu eyes of fire. What I learned to hate in Tropiards was the blindness that leads them to deny the existence of a choice. That's why I gladly came home."

"To be sh'gosfi. Otherwise you couldn't live in Palija Kadi. It seems you must be what *you* are, sh'gosfi, just as Tropiards must be what *they* are, j'gosfi."

Lijadu turned on Seth with eyes coruscating. "We affirm our belief in free choice by being what we are! If we were j'gosfi, what kind of statement would we be making with our lives? That only one orientation towards the truth is possible! Does your own biologically determined j'gosfihood blind you to the situation on Trope?"

Seth gripped the pole-tree to which Ifragsli had been bound. "I don't know. I think of you as a woman, and—"

"That's inaccurate. This artificial language gets in our way."

"I think of you as a woman," Seth repeated, "and the idea of an exclusively female community seems . . . unnatural to me."

"What of an exclusively male community?"

Seth hesitated. "That, too," he said.

"But because of your biologically determined maleness, less so? Is that correct?" Lijadu gave him no quarter. "What would a female representative of your species have felt? Of course, the state would never have let such a person come. Thus you and your colleagues are here rather than the Kieri Liege Mistress and her sh'gosfid retainers."

Seth said nothing. What Lijadu had told him was undoubtedly true. Meanwhile, for Tropiards and offworlders alike, Vox distorted and traduced the reality of gosfi sexuality.

"We'd best go down," Lijadu said. She pointed into the northwestern corner of the basin, where a party of Sh'gaidu laborers was working its way through a square of trellises supporting eellike, purplish vines.

They spent the remainder of the afternoon touring the arbors, terraces, vegetable gardens, and grain fields of Palija Kadi.

BOOK FOUR

THIRTEEN

As Anja set, the sky hemorrhaged. Dark blood trembled behind the tissue of dim stars overarching the basin.

"It's nearly time for the dascra'nol," Lijadu told Seth.

They made their way down from a ledge above the Sh'gaidu vineyards, where Seth had examined the workings of a gravity-powered irrigation system. Indeed, there were water channels throughout the basin, cunningly laid out and braced. An evening breeze kicked up. Around the Sh'vaij, the branches of the stately cypresses lifted together like ragged black fans.

Other Sh'gaidu converged on the building. From the fields, from the irrigation terraces above the basin, from the stupendous bridges climbing to the shadow-riven eastern cliff face. And up the same path by which Seth's party had reached the crofthouse earlier that day there now traipsed five tiny figures: Porchaddos Pors, Clefrabbes Douin, Magistrate Vrai, and Deputy Emahpre, all preceded by the Pledgechild's right hand, Huspre. At this bloody twilight moment, visible to Seth from only the waist up, they each wore aureoles of dust upon their heads and shoulders, and so resembled medieval friars slumming toward a grubby canonization.

Palija Kadi, thought Seth, was a hotbed of dubious saints.

Everyone foregathered on the apron of rock in front of the Sh'vaij, hosts, guests, young and old. The children, this evening, wore lightweight dalmatics with embroidered sleeves and hems, but, like the adults, they were still barefoot. The adults wore the garments they had worked in. No one paused to eat, or drink, or chat. Seth wanted to confer with Douin, to tell him about the heartseed, Lijadu's dream vision, and all the pragmatic wonders of Sh'gaidu agriculture, but he could not get close enough to do anything but nod in greeting.

In a supple, almost choreographed procession, the Sh'gaidu herded their children into the Sh'vaij ahead of them. One by one, people filed through the doorway. As his own turn to enter approached, Seth could see that the building's interior was lit by ceramic lanterns set in a ring on the curving walls. Shaped to resemble heartseeds, these lanterns emitted a pungent incense, like roses and charcoal. Lijadu was behind Seth, and bringing up the rear were Huspre, the Tropiards, and the Kieri.

Inside, Seth whispered, "Where's the Pledgechild?"

"In her cell," Lijadu said. "She'll appear when everyone's passed the corpse and done Ifragsli silent homage."

The procession circled along the right-hand wall toward Palija Dait and Lijadu's dead birth-parent. Although several children tried to walk along the benches lining this wall, adults pulled them down and enforced a mature propriety. At last Seth and Lijadu passed Ifragsli, her bedaubed death mask eerie in the shifting glow of the heartseed lanterns, and Huspre separated from her charges and disappeared into the Pledgechild's rooms behind the Lesser Wall.

Soon, Seth found himself seated on a bench against the left-hand wall, Deputy Emahpre on one side and Lord Pors on the other. Lijadu had knelt in front of him. All the other Sh'gaidu sat on benches or cross-legged on the stony floor. In the Sh'vaij's center was a vast open area waiting for a performer to occupy it. Seth began to understand what it meant to "die of anticipation."

He felt coursing through his blood an atonal humming, as if all three hundred Sh'gaidu had interthreaded their private celebrations of mourning and benediction into one resonating chord: a silent hallelujah.

The Pledgechild stepped from her cell. Her patterned sari scarcely concealed her nakedness, her black eyes glittered, and before her, draped with a fluttering cloth, she bore her Y-shaped scepter. Huspre followed the old woman, solicitous but unobtrusive, as if fearful that her mistress might stumble. She carried a lantern of strange design. At Ifragsli's corpse the Pledgechild halted and inclined her head in prayer. Then she turned and proceeded to the center of the Sh'vaij, the Chapel of The Sisterhood. There she lifted her covered scepter like a crucifix, turned in a circle, and offered the blessing of this instrument to everyone in attendance. Heads bowed as she languidly swept the circle of the Sh'vaij. Huspre, still holding her lantern, stared at the floor.

Seth leaned forward, gripped Lijadu's shoulders, and whispered, "What's the Pledgechild doing?"

Deputy Emahpre pulled Seth back. "That's a *saisei* she's holding. It's an ancient instrument, as old as the species, nearly, and if you watch you'll learn all there is to know about it." He offered this information as if it were abhorrent to him, released Seth, and rolled his head resignedly against the cold stone wall.

Lijadu glanced behind her, but did not confirm or deny the Deputy's words.

Lowering the Y-shaped scepter, the saisei, the Pledgechild spoke aloud in a musical Tropish dialect. Seth could distinguish no individual words or even any of the spaces between them. If conducted entirely in this dialect, the ceremony would remain impenetrable to him.

Then, in Vox, the Pledgechild said, "I wish to welcome five visitors to the dascra'nol of Ifragsli. For this brief hour, they hold their hopes in abeyance to partake with us of the final vision of the birth-parent of my heir." The Pledgechild lifted the saisei again, spoke in oddly syncopated Tropish, and knelt in the middle of the Sh'vaij. Huspre hurried to assist her. In the flickering darkness, three hundred pairs of gemlike eyes were fixed on the Pledgechild. Painstakingly, the old woman screwed the saisei into a hole in the floor. Squatting, one hand under her frail body, Palija Dait directly before her, she spoke in Tropish again.

Emahpre, lantern light reflecting from his slit-goggles, leaned toward Seth. "She says she intends to conduct the rest of the ceremony in the language of her visitors, that the Sh'gaidu will receive cerebrations more powerful than words, and that the message of Ifragsli's living eyes will be as meaningful for us, her visitors, as for the assembled sisterhood."

"How does she know that?"

"She doesn't, Kahl Latimer. It's all gibberish."

Lijadu shot the Deputy a stinkeye. He flinched and stared into the darkening fields. Erect and noncommittal, the Magistrate sat to Emahpre's right.

"Lijadu," the Pledgechild intoned, "step between the body of your birth-parent and her living eyes, that she may see you."

Lijadu stalked across the Sh'vaij, stopped before Ifragsli's corpse, and halted. The Pledgechild responded by drawing the cloth off the saisei's prongs and handing this cloth to Huspre. Mounted in the circular wooded clips of the instrument were the dead Sh'gaidu's eyes, flashing now with mysterious emerald luster.

"Lijadu," the Pledgechild said, "you must let the spirit of your birth-parent enter you. Answer me as the spirit of Ifragsli dictates. You are no longer yourself but rather she from whose womb you derived your life. Do you understand?"

"Yes, Pledgechild." Lijadu's eyes locked with the disembodied eyes in the saisei.

"Who are you?" the Pledgechild asked ritually.

"*Ifragsli,*" Lijadu answered, transfixed. Although she spoke aloud, her lips scarcely moved and her voice was not her own.

"To whom do you bequeath the immortal dust of your dust?"

"*I stand among the heirbarren, Pledgechild.*"

"How so, if your fleshchild stands in your place?"

"*I've surrendered her to our people.*"

"Willingly?"

"*Yes, Pledgechild.*"

"To what end?"

"*That she may inherit the dascra gosfi'mija of her catechist.*"

"Heirbarren though you may be, Ifragsli, you are fruitful of soul. Whom do you designate to receive the jinalma of your living eyes?"

"*All of you, and none.*"

Crouching before the saisei, her old, mottled head cocked to one side, the Pledgechild asked, "How may you make your bequeathment to both none and all?" This question seemed an improvisation, so tardily did it follow Lijadu's—or Ifragsli's—final response.

"*Time has run from my veins, and I can no longer say.*"

"How did time slip from you, Ifragsli?"

"*I ceased to create it, and so died.*"

"But in your flesh only."

"*In my flesh only,*" Ifragsli agreed through her fleshchild's lips.

"Why did you cease to create it, departed one?"

"*My heart filled with the surplus I made, and the surplus gave me visions that I could not bear.*"

"And these visions caused your death?"

"*Not the visions, but the time in excess of our present: the future made me die, for I could not grow into it.*"

"What of your three days in the Holy One's lookout?"

"*Dead, I searched for Duagahvi Gaidu.*"

"And?"

"*I could not find her, Pledgechild.*"

For the first time that evening the Sh'gaidu reacted to the exchange between their Pledgechild and Ifragsli's proxy: Bodies moved, and garments rustled. The Pledgechild improvised: "The Holy One failed to appear to you in your place of vision?"

"*Yes, Pledgechild, she did.*"

"Weren't you, then, purged of the evil visions that uncreated you in your surfeited heart?"

"*I don't know, Pledgechild.*" Formerly rigid, Lijadu began to sway; her upper body, as if in mourning for the birth-parent she had become, swung dolorously from side to side.

"Ifragsli!" the Pledgechild cried.

Lijadu ceased swaying. "*I don't know, Pledgechild,*" she repeated in what was apparently her dead birth-parent's voice. "*Perhaps my eyes will tell.*"

"Have we permission to read them, Ifragsli?"

"*Please, before they crumble into dust.*"

"We thank you for your permission, Ifragsli, and for your child."

"*Lijadu belongs to the people of Palija Kadi. I can't withhold her. She belongs to Palija Kadi and to the islands of our exile.*"

Tilting back her mottled head and peering sidelong at her heir, the old woman again let the catechism lapse. Although Seth had no way of knowing what was traditional and what extraordinary, nothing about this ritual seemed to go as planned. The Sh'gaidu, reading the emotional content of Lijadu's words, even if she framed them in Vox, shifted restively. The flickering of the heartseed lanterns embodied and shadowed forth their apprehensions.

"The islands of our exile?" the Pledgechild asked.

"*Please, Pledgechild,*" Lijadu said, swaying again. "*Read my eyes and free me of my vision.*"

The old woman waved her left arm. "You're of the dead, Ifragsli," she declared. "Go where the dead go while we read your eyes."

Obedient, Lijadu—or the spirit of Ifragsli inhabiting her—stopped her worrisome swaying and stepped away. Someone near the left-hand door to the Pledgechild's room drew her out of Seth's sight. Lord Pors, Seth noted, was conferring in whispers with Douin, who sat immediately to Pors's left.

They were using Kieri, and he couldn't follow their conversation.

Still squatting, the old woman fiddled with the clips supporting Ifragsli's eyes. A moment later Huspre, bearing the odd-looking heartseed lantern with which she had entered, knelt beside the Pledgechild to assist with these adjustments. What magic were they brewing? None, it seemed. The entire pageant had degenerated into a dumbshow of mundane tinkering.

Then the old woman said, "Let the light of the heartseed shine through Ifragsli's eyes that we may know her final vision."

Huspre, having crept around the Pledgechild to position the lantern, canted its bowl so that it yawned upward at the prongs of the saisei and the naked white slope of the wall beyond. She pulled a ceramic plate from the lantern.

A spreading beam of light shone forth from the bowl, projecting an immense, druidic rune onto the wall, a sort of Y. The Pledgechild's face, touched by the beam, was that of a gargoyle. As she continued to adjust the clips, her hands and arms made shadow pictures on the wall. Huspre moved the lantern mouth so that the rune on Palija Dait disappeared.

"The wonder," Emahpre told Seth sotto voce, "is that they continue to believe this hocus-pocus means anything."

"But what are they doing?"

"Attempting to externalize, there on the wall, what they persist in regarding as the deceased's 'final vision.'"

"The last thing Ifragsli saw?"

"Not the last physical thing, no," Emahpre replied, leaning toward Seth. "That would be too easy. The Sh'gaidu believe that during the deceased's three days in the kioba she constructs in her eyes a prophetic pattern that must be read and interpreted by the Pledgechild. This pattern is her final vision, and the community must share in it."

"The Sh'gaidu originated this practice?"

"Indeed not. In the days before Seitaba Mwezahbe, every nomadic gosfi band had its shaman, who cast and then construed the altered crystalline structure of the eyes of the dead. It's a wretched, powermongering hocus-pocus designed to confer status on the interpreter, and that's all it is."

"How do you know?" Seth asked. He looked from the Deputy to the wall: Watery colors—ill-resolved jades and melting blues—had begun to glide across its face as Huspre fiddled with the lantern.

The Deputy gripped Seth's knee with pincerlike fingers. "Because Mwezahbe in his earliest assault on superstition demonstrated that the so-called upheaval in the gosfi soul—which is supposed to create the prophetic pattern—is nothing but a stabbing chemical change."

"But couldn't the chemical change be the means of—"

"Don't play the fool!" Emahpre said, still sotto voce. "The chemical change is a natural result of death. It shatters the eyes' molecular structure, creating murky blooms and interthreadings that charlatans like that one" —he nodded at the Pledgechild— "can pretend to read. Hocus-pocus, Kahl Latimer, disreputable hocus-pocus!"

"Enough, Deputy Emahpre," the Magistrate whispered. "Tonight we're in their house. Hold your tongue and watch."

No pattern had yet emerged from the swimming colors; only fluid motion, a weird primeval sea, roiled in the radiance refracted through the dead Sh'gaidu's eyes.

"Ifragsli!" the Pledgechild shouted.

Seth glanced to his left, past Pors and Douin and a host of silent Sh'gaidu to the place where Lijadu had disappeared.

"Ifragsli!"

Lijadu, rising from her place, answered in the same unfamiliar voice she had used earlier: "*Yes, Pledgechild.*"

"Is this the state of your soul, Ifragsli? I cannot read a moving pattern. Tell us what swims in torment here."

"*Chaos struggling toward a definition, Pledgechild.*"

"Is it, then, your final vision?"

"*No, Pledgechild: That chaos has a shape.*"

"Reveal it, Ifragsli."

Lijadu swayed in sympathy with the undulant patterns on the wall. "*I will. . . . I will. . . . But first return my fleshchild to herself and consign me prayerfully into the keeping of our Holy One.*"

"Very well. Depart, Ifragsli."

One of Lijadu's sisters rose and caught her—for at the Pledgechild's command she had nearly collapsed to the floor. Ifragsli had departed her.

The Pledgechild, still crouching, slid her arms into the incandescence of the lantern, turned the disembodied eyes in their clips. The colors on the wall revolved in great, slow wheels, melting into blue-green lava and languid ambiguity. A pattern began to take shape. Facet lines imposed a terrible geometry on the churning verdigris. Before the Sh'gaidu and their visitors a huge, organic mural grew. A pair of distorted arms reached out of the congealing emerald seas toward the ceiling. A thrown-back head lifted to the night a scream all too easily imagined. These images froze on the wall, lingered on it like a stain. Below them was the body of Lijadu's birth-parent, emptied, apparently, of her final watchtower fears. Deputy Emahpre rose to his feet.

"Tell us what this vision means!" he challenged the Pledgechild. "Read it for us!"

Three hundred pairs of eyes revolved toward the Deputy, and Ulgraji Vrai sprang to his feet to rebuke the deputy administrator. To Seth, it seemed a tiresome reenactment of his outburst over the pregnancy of Tantai.

Huspre helped the old woman up. Looking with clear annoyance at Emahpre, the Pledgechild accepted from her attendant the cloth that had earlier covered the saisei and dropped it over the mouth of the heartseed lantern. The projected image remained on the wall, however, muted in color but as starkly etched.

Shaking off the Magistrate's hand, the Deputy repeated, "Read it for us, harlot! Tell us its mystic meaning!"

The Magistrate, his mouth twisting, resorted to Tropish to rebuke his deputy. How truly alien and unreal he looked in his anger.

"The dascra'nol is over," the Pledgechild said in Vox, half lifting one thin arm to silence her visitors. "Ifragsli's final vision interprets itself. That which she dreamt in her soul is manifest."

"That?" Emahpre demanded, nodding at the wall. "What can that hideous mess possibly mean?"

Gripping Emahpre by the shoulders, the Magistrate sat him down. Seth could feel his face reddening, an unfocused embarrassment spreading through him. The Sh'gaidu and their uncomprehending children were watching; and Emahpre, in his singleminded allegiance to reason, had unreasonably insulted them in their own house. By what standards of humanity, of gosfihood, was this intense little man sane?

Huspre slipped a ceramic shutter into the heartseed lantern, and the grief-stricken figure on the wall disappeared. Then, letting her eyes roam over the faces of her bereaved but resolute people, the Pledgechild turned in a halting arc. The nods of agreement or acquiescence of the Sh'gaidu told Seth that she was addressing them with cerebrations. A moment later, they began to file out of the Sh'vaij, the children as solemn and orderly as their elders. Soon only Lijadu, the Pledgechild, Huspre, and the Magistrate's party of five remained in the assembly building. Ifragsli, whose corpse still lay beneath the wall, no longer counted: her spirit had flown.

In much the way that she had approached him that morning in her reception cell, the Pledgechild neared Seth. He shrank from her, looking to the Kieri for moral support or even outright rescue. But Pors was in a state of repressed hysteria, evidenced by the way his hands gripped his tunic and his heavy jaw jutted, and Douin hung back as if afflicted with an attack of timidity or conscience.

"How do you interpret what you saw here, Kahl Latimer?" the Pledgechild asked.

"He doesn't pretend to be a shaman," Emahpre interrupted.

The Magistrate, who had been censoriously hovering over him, sat down to stare out the open door at the night.

"I little care," the Pledgechild told Emahpre.

She then turned to the two Kieri. "Or you, Kahl Pors. Or you, Kahl Douin. How should I read what Ifragsli's altered eyes have vouchsafed us?"

"This is out of our province," Pors replied.

"You're not religious men? I had thought you were religious men."

Pors and Douin stared at the Pledgechild blankly.

Lijadu approached from the left-hand side of Palija Dait. "How many days were you in transit from Gla Taus to Trope?" she asked.

Pors told her.

"Your departure from your home world coincides with the beginning of my birth-parent's illness and your arrival here with the reading of her final vision."

The Magistrate looked up. "You don't contend the two sets of events have a causal relationship, do you?"

When no one replied, Pors said, "Is *this* the time to discuss our reasons for coming to you, Pledgechild? If so, Kahl Latimer's prepared to set out clearly and explicitly the terms our government has authorized him to convey. It's our belief that both Tropiards and Sh'gaidu will find—"

"This *isn't* the time," the Pledgechild said. "Nor do I see why Kahl Latimer must speak for the Kieri government."

Douin responded: "The *Dharmakaya*—the vessel by which we journeyed to Trope—belongs to the Ommundi Trade Company, which he represents."

"Then he's a go-between rather than a principal."

"Yes, Pledgechild, but he and his isohet have experience that may well ensure a just arrangement for both sides."

"This one," said the Pledgechild, indicating Seth, "has very little experience of anything but her own heart—*his* own heart, I should say. But state governments don't ordinarily single out such persons for emissarial duties."

"If you'd talk with him," Douin urged, "you'd see that he's—"

"This isn't the time," the Pledgechild reiterated with annoyance. Huspre, having gathered up the paraphernalia that had revealed Ifragsli's final vision, was retreating into the rooms behind Palija Dait.

Without grasping why, Seth felt caught out and exposed by the resultant silence. He gestured toward the wall.

"What will you do with Ifragsli's body?"

Lijadu said, "She'll be cut into pieces and fed to our crops."

"Of course," Emahpre said.

"Her dead self will nourish living beauty," Lijadu rejoined. "Is cremation a kinder or more reasonable method of disposing of the dead?"

Seth recalled the Kieri myth of Jaud and Aisaut. Villages had sprung up from the severed fingers of Conscience, an entire civilization from his hands. But that civilization was seven light-years across the empty riddle of The Sublime. . . .

"And her eyes go into the Sh'gaidu familistery urn," the Pledgechild said.

Seth noticed how drained and frail the old woman looked. Her mottled head threatened to topple from her shoulders. If she refused to open talks, she refused because her weariness would allow her no more physical sacrifices. Huspre stepped behind the Pledgechild and slipped an arm around her waist.

"No more tonight," the old woman said. "We'll talk in the morning, here in the Sh'vaij. What sleeping arrangements will we make?"

"I'll take Kahl Latimer into the galleries," Lijadu said. "Huspre can escort the Magistrate's party to resting places here in the Sh'vaij after she's seen you to your own cot, Pledgechild."

The Magistrate said, "We'll return to our airship for the night." He stood. "Kahl Latimer will accompany us."

"This afternoon," Lijadu said, "I showed him everything in Palija Kadi but the galleries. Let him come with me now. No harm will befall him."

"I don't *anticipate* any harm befalling him."

Almost slyly, it seemed to Seth, the Pledgechild asked, "Is there any reason why he must spend the night in your company?"

"He's a guest of the state," Magistrate Vrai replied.

"And for this evening you're all guests of the Sh'gaidu," the Pledgechild pointed out. "Let Kahl Latimer decide where he wishes to sleep."

Pors whispered something in Kieri to Douin, and Douin addressed the Magistrate: "We don't object to his going with the young Sh'gaidu, sir."

"Do *you* object?" the old woman asked the Magistrate.

Driven to intimacy before friends and foes alike, Vrai took Seth's wrist and pulled him aside. Even though his strength was at least that of the Tropiard's, Seth let himself be pulled.

"We're bond-partners, Kahl Latimer," the Magistrate whispered. "I know you for a good person, and I don't command you anything. I don't forbid you anything. Yaji Tropei's an ancient protogosfi fastness with distasteful connotations for us. It represents what we were, not what we are. Neither my deputy nor I wish to cross back over a bridge that Mwezahbe directed us over a long time ago. Do as you wish. You can't betray me by being true to yourself."

"What's Kahl Latimer's decision?" the Pledgechild demanded.

Seth stepped away from the Magistrate and surveyed the faces of the "imperfect isohets" into whose daunting company he had fallen. In how many different ways he was the odd soul out.

"I'll go with Lijadu," he heard himself announce.

FOURTEEN

Outside: millions of stars. One moved slowly across the sky, and Seth's first thought was that it was the *Dharmakaya*. He imagined Abel sitting in the light-tripper's library listening to Bach's *Selig ist der Mann* and working out a complicated hand of solitaire. Why hadn't Abel come, too?

Despite Lijadu and all the others, Seth regarded his human isolation on the surface of Trope as a variety of solitaire. You played the game out alone. If you cheated—that is, if you pretended you had a supportive group of well-wishers and backers—well, as odd as the notion might seem, perhaps such a fantasy would help you beat the game. Gazing into Trope's pewter-on-ebony sky, Seth pretended that Abel was the focal point of just such a group.

The cypresses around the Sh'vaij lashed restlessly in the grit-casting wind. The crops beyond them murmured and ticked as if each gust were a fusillade from the soldiers bivouacked on the high perimeters of the basin.

Lijadu led Seth around the apron of the Sh'vaij toward the wide stone bridges climbing giddily to the eastern cliffs. Torches burned along these rugged spans, but their flames were whipped and tattered by the wind. The scene had a fairy-tale grandeur, a fairy-tale insubstantiality and imperma-nence. But it was real, and Seth's knowledge that Lijadu and he must mount and cross its central bridge led him to imagine their bodies flung to disaster by a sudden nudging gust.

"Kahl Latimer," Lijadu said, looking at him sidelong near the base of the central span. "Let me see something."

After a glimpse at the looming bridge, he turned to her. "What?"

She put her hands on his shoulders. "The tiny black eyes inside your outer eyes are widening. The blue's being eaten away from the inside out."

Seth laughed, startling Lijadu away from him. He gained her back by drumming his fingers on his chest to translate into gosfi terms the meaning of his laughter.

"Then you're not ill—your eyes aren't . . . misbehaving?"

"No. I'm well enough. I think."

They hiked together up the first long, swooping incline, barricades of dark red stone glinting in the buffeted torchlight, the wind's warmth a benediction. The jagged, coral arc of another span passed over their heads, like a streamer of petrified dust, the roaring of the wind inordinately loud.

Then Seth realized that a portion of this roaring was emanating from the galleries. He'd heard this sound earlier in the kioba and had taken it, briefly, for the intransigent droning of machines. Four pairs of eyes flashed in the darkness ahead of them, and a moment later four naked children came hurtling past Lijadu and Seth on a narrow span near the summit.

"When do they sleep?" Seth asked.

"When they tire of play. Or when the adults around them see that they're running on spent energies."

At the top—and the terminus—of the central bridge, Lijadu led Seth to the left along a gallery running north and south like a wide natural stratum in the rock. Here the roaring of Yaji Tropei was deafening. Heartseed lanterns placed about the honeycombed interior provided an almost phosphorescent illumination. By this light, Seth could see wavering curtains of water pouring through the cliff, dividing it into rooms. How far back into the mountain these chambers went, he could not tell—but the silvery veils falling continuously from ceiling crevices to narrow gutters in the floor, then cascading through deeper rock to irrigation conduits below the galleries, dazzled the eyes and buzzed in his ears.

"Is it always like this?" Seth shouted.

Lijadu spoke mind to mind: —*There's a reservoir in the mountains north of Palija Kadi, and our irrigation system operates through the force of gravity. There are times when we let the waters fall.*

Having to shout while Lijadu simply eased her messages into his mind struck Seth as an injustice, but a fascinating one. "You can turn it off, this system?" he cried.

—*Easily. The walls shimmering here exist only intermittently. The Sh'gaidu aren't altogether ignorant of engineering and technology.*

"The noise!" Seth shouted. "It . . . it hurts!"

—*It won't plague you long. We shut off the flow at night—but in the evening, with the lantern glow playing on the curtains, isn't it beautiful, Kahl Latimer?*

"Indeed!" Inward from the gallery, Seth saw Sh'gaidu shadows outlined against the veils. Yaji Tropei teemed with shadow beings, some of whom emerged from behind their waterwalls, to study him as intently as he scrutinized their fastness. Spray misted outward from the caverns.

"The protogosfi used this irrigation system?"

—*Oh, no,* Lijadu cerebrated. —*This was the result of nearly sixty years of labor, made possible by the many channels already present in the cliffs, the technical ingenuity of the Pledgechild, and Sh'gaidu courage. Yaji Tropei claimed several lives toward the end, giving us to know that we had done all she would permit. The bones of our dead lie deep in her body, as sacrifices to her patience.*

At the north end of the gallery, Lijadu took Seth into the cliff and halted him at a niche holding a large, slate-grey statue. Seated on an ottoman of rock, this naked figure had been worn smooth by people passing by it on their way to and from the fields. Even now a young Sh'gaidu, only slightly older than Lijadu, had paused to drape her arm over the statue's shoulder in confession and prayer. The statue's eye sockets contained no eyes. In the shadows beyond it, dozens of Sh'gaidu waited to embrace or commune mind to mind with the stone figure.

—*This is Duagahvi Gaidu,* Lijadu cerebrated. —*We come to her with our prayers, our love, and our fears.*

"Who?" Seth made chiseling motions with his hands.

—*One of the first of the Palija Kadi communards made this image, working many days to achieve what you see. She spent her daylight hours laboring in the fields or crawling through Yaji Tropei to open irrigation conduits.*

Seth drew Lijadu to him and spoke directly into her ear: "What have they come for tonight? Are they praying, or confessing, or speaking their fears?"

"Most are frightened." This time Lijadu also spoke aloud, using their proximity to good advantage.

"Of what?"

"Of my birth-parent's final vision. The Pledgechild said that it interpreted itself, but no one here is certain of its meaning."

"I don't find the meaning of Ifragsli's vision in what I saw on the wall,

Lijadu. In that, I suppose, I am like Deputy Emahpre."

"And in little else, thankfully. But we may find its meaning in the Pledge-child's reticence."

"What meaning, then?"

"An evil, Kahl Latimer. The Pledgechild didn't wish to interpret Ifragsli's vision for fear of frightening us."

"But she's frightened you by not interpreting it?"

"Yes."

"An error on her part."

"She's mortal, Kahl Latimer. Nor did she like to be prodded to her reading by Emahpre." Lijadu separated from Seth and strode past the long curving file of Sh'gaidu waiting to commune with the statue.

—*Come*, she cerebrated from beside a curtain of water.

Then, astonishingly fleet, she leaped through it, her image an evanescent pattern in the torrents of that swaying wall. Like a ship sliding into The Sublime, she had more or less disappeared.

—*Come*, she beckoned again, invisible.

The roaring of the waters and that of his blood virtually indistinguishable, Seth followed. Mist prickled his face and hands. When he leaped the wide gutter beneath the ever-falling veil of the wall, his heart leaped inside him, too; and the iciness of the water plunging down his back and running from his brow woke him immediately to the beauty of the farther chamber.

Taking his hand, Lijadu led him through a corridor whose left-hand wall was rock plaster and whose right-hand wall was water. An arabesque red and tan fresco dominated the plaster wall, depicting fish, gocodre, birdlike creatures, strange four-legged landgoers, and a variety of hominid, or protogosfid, figures arrayed in cryptic community. The scene was not altogether idyllic. The farther along this fresco Seth went, the more vivid and disconcerting were the figures portrayed.

Gocodre ate gosfi, gosfi dismembered birds, and disembodied eyes, pressed into the plaster in pigments of metallic blue or green, surveyed the carnage from lofty or well-hidden vantage points: cliff ledges or caves.

This fresco, a virtual mural, looked ancient to Seth. Its surface was cracked in many places, or blistered. Parts of the underlying rock had long ago crumbled and broken away. The Sh'gaidu had clearly spent a good deal of time and effort restoring the fresco, replastering, freshening the faded colors, maybe even improvising detail where the many indifferent millennia had erased it.

"How old?" Seth shouted.

—We don't know. But older than any other paintings discovered on our world. Gosfi have lived here perhaps since the beginning.

Sh'gaidu of every age passed them in the corridor. One adolescent, naked and amber-eyed, carried a silver-furred creature whose eyes almost exactly matched her own, in both size and color.

They continued inward, until—without warning—the roar of the falling water became a single stupendous crash, followed by a series of wet pistol shots echoing back and forth. Afterward, a thunderous whooshing and a delicate runneling away into the lower depths of Yaji Tropei. The waterwalls had vanished, but the ceilings continued to drip and a blurry dampness hung in the air.

Other rock walls—wide portals cut in their faces and earth-colored frescoes daubed upon them—glistened in the lantern sheen. Seth could look from one chamber into the next, and so on, almost forever. Against the painted walls were sleeping pallets, urns, stone hampers, benches, woven baskets, and a variety of simple housekeeping items. On many of the pallets, Sh'gaidu lay, alone or paired, their eyes brilliant signal fires. No one here wore slit-goggles, but the community had not disintegrated because of the relentless provocation of so many uncovered eyes. No one here was property, Seth told himself; everyone was a person, and, as several sh'gosfi muffled their lanterns and shadows began spilling through the abutting rooms, Seth walked and watched.

"Where are we going?" he asked Lijadu.

"To my sleeping place—only a little farther."

"Many portals, but no doors."

"Doors make no sense among us," Lijadu said. "Palija Kadi and Palija Dait are the only doors we require."

At last they entered a cove where a lamp still fitfully burned. Lijadu pointed Seth to a ledge at the foot of the widest wall, upon which an erotic fresco blazed, and handed him two small bowls. One she filled with dark meal from a stone hamper, the other with water from a pretty urn. After serving herself, she climbed atop the hamper and ate. When Seth had eaten, he handed his bowls to her and gestured for more. He felt, as she replenished them, that she saw his hunger—his show of animal rapacity—as something extraordinary if not reprehensible. But he was famished, and he ate until the ache inside him had dwindled to a faint throb, the ebbing of his exhilaration and the resurgent pulse of his anxiety. What strange place had he come to?

"Are you finished?" Lijadu asked. He nodded.

She removed her garment and used it to wipe the moisture from her limbs and flanks. Her dark body glistened, a configuration of planes, triangles, lines, and functional curves implying health and vigor rather than any distinct sexual identity. Above Seth, the fresco. He leaned out to look at it: two gosfi entwined about each other in an excruciating coital ballet. The partners' eyes were visible, nearly twice life-size, at least in proportion to the figures themselves. Lijadu, meanwhile, laid her short sari aside and crossed the chamber to douse the heartseed lantern.

"There's only one sleeping pallet," Seth said.

"Unless you object, we'll share it."

This news, casually proffered, startled him. Still, he'd hoped for it. *Paragenation.* Intensifying his confusion was the ambiguity of their relationship. Lijadu was the Pledgechild's heir, ostensibly a female, and nothing in her earlier behavior had suggested anything more intimate than the desire to be a good host. With the exception, perhaps, of her eagerness to bring him into Yaji Tropei . . .

"Share it?" he said.

"For comfort. For warmth. For sleep." A thin blue glow seeped into Lijadu's cove from another part of the Sh'gaidu hive, and her body was defined by the highlights shifting on her limbs and by the wan jade fires in her eyes. "I can get another pallet if you wish me to."

Seth heard a Günter Latimer pragmatism escaping his lips: "I don't know whether I'll be able to sleep."

"Then let me fetch another pallet." Lijadu turned as if to get it.

"We could *try* it this way."

Lijadu returned and sank to her knees before him to smooth the pallet with her hands. Then she folded back the coverlet and arranged herself so that half the sleeping area remained for Seth. When he did not move to join her, she said, "You're not yet tired enough to sleep?"

"I'm taking off my boots." Seth took off his boots. He spent two minutes on each one, undoing every plastic catch. Then he aligned the boots on the ledge and wiped their toes with his sleeve.

"Remove your tunic," Lijadu said. "It's damp. You won't be comfortable wearing it to sleep in."

It wasn't cold in the galleries. The suggestion seemed sensible. Seth took off his tunic, rolled it into a bundle, and, damp or no, placed it at the head of his side of Lijadu's pallet for a pillow.

"And your leg coverings, if your customs permit."

"For sleeping? Yes, it's permissible. Besides, they're damp, too, and a bit grimy from hiking through the basin." He began, tentatively, to remove his leg coverings. "I don't like to sleep in my clothes if they're grimy. Sometimes I do, of course, but not often. It depends on circumstances. In Master Douin's geffide—his house in Feln—it was customary to wear a special sleeping garment. I didn't always conform, however." Lijadu stared at him as his words spilled out. "The term in Vox is pajamas. It's taken directly from an ancient language called Persian, I believe—an ancient *Earth* language. My isohet Abel—my sibling, my brother—has a brown pair with yellow polka dots. They're made of synthetic silk. But we don't consider pajamas a necessity. Some people never wear—"

"You're wearing a dascra," Lijadu observed.

Naked but for the Magistrate's amulet, Seth hurried to lie at full length beside Lijadu, to take most of his body out of the range of her vision. Gooseflesh stippled his flesh. Cued by embarrassment, his member maintained a decorous profile. He had never slept with an alien before. Douin and Pors, he recalled with belated gratitude, had kept to their own pallets last night.

"Whose dascra gosfi'mija do you have, Kahl Latimer?"

"Magistrate Vrai's."

"I saw in the Sh'vaij that he wasn't wearing one. Instead he had an additional pair of eye coverings."

Shivering, Seth said, "I gave him the goggles in exchange for his amulet."

"He suggested the trade?"

"He did, completely unbidden."

"Why?"

"I'm not sure. He seems to think we're . . . well, j'gosfi of one mind. He wants our mission to Palija Kadi to succeed."

Lijadu's breath had the sweet fragrance of the pasty grain they had shared—but her eyes seemed to belong to a smart predatory insect: They scared him. The dark had dehumanized Lijadu. Her supple body could have been made of chitin or calcium. "What, exactly, is your mission?"

"We've come to offer the Sh'gaidu a territory on Gla Taus richer than your basin here on Trope. If this offer pleases you, we'll transport your entire community there and free you forever from the persecution of the state."

"And the state from the conscience-pricking of the Sh'gaidu?"

"I should not have spoken," Seth said. "The Pledgechild said we'd negotiate in the morning, and I've broached this matter too soon."

"Have you heard of auxiliary births, Kahl Latimer? We spoke of them briefly this afternoon, but do you know what they are?"

"The Magistrate told me something. They're a means of promoting evolutionary diversity among a long-lived but unprolific species."

"*Social* diversity, perhaps. Acquired characteristics are no more inheritable on Trope than elsewhere."

"But the effects on gosfi society are the effects of a much larger gene pool, aren't they? Isn't that why Trope has outpaced the nations to the north?"

Lijadu placed a chilly hand on his flank. "You're wearing the dascra of a j'gosfi who, for evolution's sake, has gone through perhaps five auxiliary births. But from one rebirth to the next there's no continuity. The old self dies, but the new self doesn't even possess the soul of the old one. Everything about the person is different."

"Better, the Magistrate says."

"*Different*, Kahl Latimer. Wearing the dascra of a person who's not the person originally born out of the birth-parent is an evil.

"An evil?"

"The Magistrate, Deputy Emahpre—all Tropiards—have renounced their souls."

"Perhaps they have several souls in succession, one for each personality." Seth indulged this speculation for its outrageousness. He was tired, desperately tired. If none of his asinine erotic fantasies were going to come true, he wanted to table all talk and sleep. Or at least try to.

"Among the Tropiards of the Thirty-three Cities the wearing of the dascra no longer has real meaning," Lijadu said. "You know that. And you know what the dascra contains, too, don't you?"

"Jinalma."

"The eyes of our birth-parents. We treasure them for the final visions they give us before disintegrating. But the final visions of j'gosfi who have gone through auxiliary births are nearly worthless."

"Why?"

"After so many different selves succeed one another, the final vision can belong only to the last one and only partly to it. The j'gosfi sacrifices part of himself each time he's altered."

Altered: Seth thought of the castration of domestic animals.

"One must live her whole life with a single consciousness, Kahl Latimer. She must change, but remember the changes. A person is a tower forever in the act of being built. The Mwezahbe Legacy destroys the tower by dividing it into segments, as if it were so many stacked stools. Such a person never knows the soul."

"The Magistrate claims that the personality born from the Tropiard's final auxiliary birth is the best personality he may possess. It's a unified self: the *ultimate* unified self."

"It's a garment that hides the skin beneath. Tropiards bundle themselves in such garments, Kahl Latimer."

"Don't they remember anything of their past selves?"

"In Ebsu Ebsa I did the sort of work that permits them to 'remember.' Tropiards know their earlier lives only through evo-step genealogies, which I reviewed and indited for the most influential among them. Still, if j'gosfi do have knowledge of their early selves, it's second-hand. They learn about these selves as if studying the biographies of dead historical personages."

"Maybe that's appropriate."

"Entirely. There's no sense of underlying union, though. There's distance from the essential self."

"Doesn't distance provide perspective?"

"In the context of the essential person, Kahl Latimer, distance is estrangement. Tropiards don't know who they are."

"Perhaps I don't know who *I* am," Seth said. "I'm j'gosfi by genetic dictate: a perfect replica of my dead isosire, whom I never understood, and a perfect twin of my isohet Abel, who has sent me to your Pledgechild when he might have come himself." As best he could, Seth detailed his specific origins.

"Whose soul do I have?" he then demanded of Lijadu. "Or did Günter Latimer die with the only soul granted by the Creator to his own DNA? If that's so, Abel and I are as soulless as any poor, damned Tropiard you scold for losing himself at his state-ordained auxiliary births! Abel and I are shadows of our isosire, and neither of us has a soul!" He had not shouted, but pain had pushed his voice toward an alarming falsetto.

Lijadu touched his forehead and smoothed his hair back. —*You're a person,* she cerebrated. —*Persons have souls.*

"Unless they're Tropiards," Seth whispered. "Then, in your eyes, they become nonpersons, forfeiters of their gosfihood."

"Not so," she, too, whispered.

"But you've already said as much," he accused.

"I said only that many Tropiards never truly know their souls—not that they're soulless. They dilute their essence by auxiliary births, but they remain persons. To be j'gosfi on our world, Kahl Latimer, is to be self-estranged. I pity self-estranged persons their lack of wholeness."

"Do you pity me?" Anger had purged him of his tentativeness; her touch seemed a deliberate goad. He put a hand to the small of Lijadu's back and found in his willful erection a means of declaring his identity. It scraped the cleft between her legs and slid glancingly up her lower belly, lubricating its way like a snail.

—*Stop!* Lijadu cerebrated.

But the pain of this imperative was brief, if piercing, and Seth tried to drop his hips for another angry thrust. She would know he had a soul even if he had to plant its seed in her as she had planted her cerebrations in his brain. Her body was a puzzle, though. It opened and then closed. And Lijadu, resolute, had begun to exert a willful counterforce against him. She was strong. Before he could salvage any of the momentum of his initial assault, she was astraddle his buttocks. His left arm was bent across his back. She deployed so much leverage against it that he feared it would break. His identity, smothered beneath him, deflated.

"Would you allow me to enter you without consent?" Lijadu asked.

Sweat stinging his eyes, he grimly replied, "You couldn't. You can't."

"I could. I could do so now. I won't, though. Even Tropiards loathe such tactics, Kahl Latimer. They inhibit rather than induce *kemmai*."

Fear, anger, shame. Seth did not know what she was talking about. He had run a gauntlet of unpleasant emotional states, and now all he could do was lie on his belly beneath Lijadu and hope for absolution. She had pinioned him as Abel had often done, and what usually came next was acceptable or degrading according to his frame of mind. The shame of a prodigal angel filled him. He had not actually plotted his assault on Lijadu, and that he should now lie utterly at her mercy had a justice about it that was also cruel. Seth wept. What was she talking about? He had no idea why he had tried to rape her. In heart and body, he hurt. The hurt intensified, and he wept.

"In kemmai we become lovers, Kahl Latimer, and only genuine affection and mutual longing create acceptable conditions."

"You invited me here," Seth said, staring into blue darkness. "You bid me remove my clothes."

"I'm sorry." She declined to release him. "Among the Sh'gaidu—even among the general run of decent Tropiards of less than administrative rank—such behaviors pass for simple hospitality. More may occur if guest and host modulate into kemmai together. Conscious orientations of life style—j'gosfi, sh'gosfi—mean absolutely nothing in such circumstances. Often I've passed in and out of both states during a single kemmai, altering with the alterations of my partner. Exchange and reciprocity are everything during these sweet arousals."

Seth heard her from oceans away. His hurt—his shame—occupied the forefront of his attention: Frenziedly, he conjured ways to release and drain it off. "You've entered my mind unbidden," he told her. "That's a trespass as violent as anything I've done. It's a rape and a trespass."

Letting his arm go, Lijadu eased down to her place on the pallet. Seth turned to his left side and again confronted the smoky jade of the Sh'gaidu's eyes.

"You consider it a violation?" she asked.

"Yes, of course. We all do."

"You didn't object before. You object now because I've rebuked you for your unseemly behavior?"

"Yes," Seth admitted.

"I won't do it again," Lijadu said. "No more cerebrations, even if the roaring of the waterwalls keeps you from hearing my voice."

They lay facing each other in the dark. The shame in Seth had not yet subsided. He had found these people's cerebrations more fascinating than obtrusive or painful, and yet he had just extracted from Lijadu a promise never to send such pleasant messages to him again. Was this a clever vengeance for his self-inflicted shame? Maybe so: a clever vengeance upon himself.

"Let's sleep," Lijadu said. "Let's hold each other and sleep." She draped an arm over his shoulder and with her other hand touched the amulet lying between them on the pallet: Magistrate Vrai's dascra.

Seth glanced down. "I don't know whether I can. I'm overwrought. You can hear my heart pounding."

Her hand roamed from the amulet to his chest. There it opened and spread out as it had that afternoon against Palija Kadi, the Great Wall. How long ago that seemed, a thousand transcended selves ago.

"If we hold each other, we'll sleep."

Lijadu and Seth held each other. Her startling, faceted eyes brushed his face, her body moved chastely against his, and sleep spiraled up to Seth's brain from the depths of a weariness he had tried to deny. Several portals away, a heartseed lantern bobbed in the blue darkness like a channel buoy. Seth's dreams ranged unceasingly up and down these waters. Eventually his dreams began to trouble him.

Nightmares of nitrogen narcosis, they came both surreal and suffocating, and Seth awoke from them in befuddled self-defense.

FIFTEEN

Lijadu was gone. As soon as Seth realized that she'd left him, he rolled his head side to side, trying to orient. Darkness blanketed him, more heavily than before.

"Lijadu!" he called. "*Lijadu!*" He rebuked himself for shouting: Did he wish to wake the children, the elderly, everyone?

His fingers felt his naked chest. Where the Magistrate's dascra should have been, in the hollow between his breastplates, nothing! His hand moved involuntarily to his throat, groping about for the chain that had held the amulet.

That, too, was gone. Lijadu had betrayed him, and in allowing her to accomplish that betrayal, he had betrayed the Magistrate.

"*Lijadu!*" He could not believe in her treachery even though the evidence seemed damning. "*Lijadu!*"

Instantly, the din of crashing waters filled Yaji Tropei. The caverns boomed with noise. A freshet of cool air swept through the chambers, a light spray circulating on its back. Seth rose on the twisted pallet, put his hands to his ears, and opened his mouth as if to scream. It was impossible—so misted was his flesh—to know if he'd been sweating in his sleep or if spray from the waterwalls had glazed him in bursts. No matter. His blood firehosed through him, his heart pumping hot gouts.

"*Lijadu!*"

He could scarcely hear himself. He *couldn't* hear himself. Falling to his knees, Seth shook out his overtunic. The Magistrate's dascra had not been hidden in it. Maybe, though, Lijadu had hidden the amulet somewhere close by. Seth pulled his damp tunic over his head, stepped into his pants, and hopped about getting his feet into his boot linings. His boot catches still undone, he ransacked the urns, baskets, and ewers arranged at seeming random about the open-ended cell. He found nothing but tools, trinkets, grain, cloth, and earthenware bowls. Desperate, he even uncapped the heartseed lantern to peer into its ceramic bowl.

What would this theft mean to Magistrate Vrai? What did it mean to Lijadu and her people? Would she have taken the dascra if he had not revealed to her the gist of the Kieri proposal? Or if he'd kept in check the stirrings of his own sexuality? Or if he'd somehow induced kemmai in her by a gentle human chivalry? Or could he shed his guilt by attributing the theft to Ifragsli's haunting final vision?

Did the placing of blame finally matter? Yes. He had betrayed the Magistrate of Trope by permitting his own betrayal at the hands of a young sh'gosfi whose loyalties were all to her persecuted people.

Seth had to find and recover the amulet.

He stumbled out of Lijadu's cell into the next one, which was vacant, and from that cell to a third chamber. Here, bending above a Sh'gaidu whose topaz eyes had lit his way inward, he shouted, "*Lijadu!*" The Sh'gaidu's eyes seemed to cloud, and he knew he would get nothing from this terrified person but an autistic silence, perfect and gemlike. He stumbled on, attempting to retrace the route by which Lijadu and he had first attained her cell.

Veils of water danced where none had danced before, and every cell, every portal, was like every other. Frescoes might differ, their stylized figures killing, or cooking, or copulating in distinctive ways; even the waterwalls defining certain vast hollows in the rock might vary, swaying with colorful movements all their own—but the overall pattern of the hive was unreadable. Seth kept breaking in upon the same contingents of huddled Sh'gaidu, who either spoke no Vox or would not speak it to him.

"Show me the way out!" he cried. Maybe they could not hear him. He was an intruder, afflicted with the impenetrable nuraj of Tropiards. Instead of triggering their compassion, he terrified them. Or maybe Lijadu had told them not to help them. She had promised not to cerebrate to him again, and, even if these bemused Sh'gaidu could cast their mental messages in Vox, none would do so. Their sole concession to his presence was lighting more heartseed lanterns—until all of Yaji Tropei flickered with radiance and the noise of the waterwalls built in increments with the light.

Seth stepped into a room where many gocodre stirred: tiny dragons on ledges, stone benches, everywhere. Several waddled in a thin sluiceway parallel to the chamber's rear wall. Omwhol, the child, sat up and stared groggily after Seth as he blundered into yet another chamber.

This room, wider and higher, sheltered a bevy of silver-furred animals like the one Seth had seen earlier that evening. They bore approximately the same relation to Trope's gosfi inhabitants as monkeys did to human beings. Resting on pallets, huddled in family groups, standing partially erect, they evinced more curiosity than fear when Seth broke in upon them. All that Seth noted about them was that the species clearly possessed both males and females.

He retreated through the gocodre den, exited by another portal, and emerged in an immense cavern where a lone Sh'gaidu appeared to be waiting for him. Standing before a veil of water, she beckoned him toward her with her left arm: a brusque, raking motion. This person was Huspre. Seth knew her by her milky eyes and the odd misalignment of her facial features.

"Lijadu stole the Magistrate's dascra!" he shouted.

Huspre stared at him blankly, with no desire to comprehend. Then she repeated her beckoning motion, turned, and strolled almost casually toward a farther portal. Seth followed. In less than five minutes she had led him along the mural near Yaji Tropei's entrance, past the nook in which stood the statue of Duagahvi Gaidu, and on to the balustraded balcony overlooking Palija Kadi, the basin.

"Friends below," Huspre said in stammering Vox, pointing to the Sh'vaij. Her words were just audible over the booming waters. Stars twinkled in the southern sky, but above the cliffs to the north reared several tall cancers of clouds, metastasizing in the darkness. The torches that had been alight along the bridges looping downward from Yaji Tropei no longer flared, and the Sh'vaij was a round smudge at the center of an indistinct abyss. Huspre set off undaunted toward that smudge.

Clefrabbes Douin awaited Seth on the assembly hall's apron. His ministerial cap was missing, and, in the wan starlight, his face was sallow and bloated-looking. Huspre left them together.

"What are you doing here?" Seth demanded of the Kieri envoy.

"Lord Pors and I received pallets in the Sh'vaij. Not long ago, the Pledgechild woke me and said I ought to come out here to intercept you on your return from the cliffs. That was all she'd say."

"And Lord Pors?"

"I left him to his sleep. After the Magistrate and Deputy Emahpre returned to the airship, Lord Pors disclosed the major features of our proposal—not to negotiate them, he said, but to give the Pledgechild a chance to think about them before morning. That may have been a costly misjudgment, considering the old woman's negative state of mind."

"I told Lijadu, too," Seth admitted.

"How did she react?"

"She seemed to believe the removal of the Sh'gaidu to Gla Taus would amount to a coup for the state."

Douin uttered a mild Kieri curse. Abruptly, he looked up. "And what are *you* doing here? Why was I roused?"

"Lijadu stole the Magistrate's dascra from me as we—as I—slept. I awoke and plunged through the galleries after her."

"To no avail?" Douin took Seth's shoulders and peered into his face. The lashing of the cypresses was both distracting and cold-blooded in its persistence. The flailing of a nearby tree was reflected in Douin's near-human pupils.

"To no avail. Huspre rescued me. The Pledgechild knows of the theft, I'm certain. Perhaps she commanded it."

"What advantage do they hope to gain?"

"Our embarrassment, yours and mine. They hope to discredit us with Magistrate Vrai and the entire Tropish state."

Douin shook his head. "If they didn't care for our proposal, they merely had to say so. This theft, well, it's *senseless*."

"Not to the Sh'gaidu, Master Douin. Not to them, obviously."

"Your carelessness discredits us," the Kieri said. "How could you let that child deceive you?"

"She's not a child. She's nearly as old as I. In some ways she's older."

"Everything's falling apart," Douin said serenely. "I'm almost grateful."

"You were never going to return the *Dharmakaya* to us, were you?"

"Certainly we were. I didn't mean to imply that I was grateful our failure would deprive you and Abel of your ship."

"Then for what are you grateful?" Seth cried, stepping away from the man in whose geffide he had lived. "What's going on, Master Douin? Why am

I here, rather than Abel? What will become of these people?" He gestured grandiloquently, poignantly, at the basin.

"Go down to the roadway and tell the Magistrate what's happened," Douin said. "I'll see that Lord Pors knows, and perhaps, with some cooperation from the Pledgechild, we can undertake a search for your Sh'gaidu sleeping partner."

Seth bridled. "Don't tell the Point Marcher!" As soon as the words were out, he regretted them.

"Master Seth, go to Magistrate Vrai. Tell him the truth. Don't wait till morning."

"Come with me. Help me."

But Douin strolled back into the Sh'vaij.

The cypresses, meantime, had ceased to toss their manes, and the alien corn still made unsettling ticking noises.

A few minutes later, approaching The Albatross on its landing terrace, Seth fixed his eyes on the pilot's bubble. No light shone in the craft.

Abel, he thought, why aren't you here in my place? Why can't I commune with you as isohets are supposed to do?

His task set, he pounded on the airship door. A dull light came on in the pilot's bubble, like a filament in a coated bulb. Emahpre appeared behind this bronze coating, a player behind a transparent screen. He motioned with his hands as if they were delicate, ivory-strutted fans. Be quiet, his gestures meant.

Seth stopped pounding. Then the side panel slid back, and he climbed into The Albatross's confessional gloom. The Deputy helped him aboard. A small heartseed globe rested in one of the baskets suspended beneath the ship's skylight. Although a faint blue sheen encircled this globe, the ambient dark was scarcely affected. The lamp appeared to draw rather than scatter illumination.

"Didn't your accommodations in the galleries suit you?" Emahpre whispered.

Seth's courage failed him. "Nightmares," he said.

Then the Magistrate let himself down from a bunk on the airship's opposite bulkhead. With a sleeping cape falling from his shoulders in voluted disarray, he stood in shadows.

"You know you're welcome here, Kahl Latimer."

"Of course he is," Emahpre agreed. "But you'd best go back to sleep, Magistrate. The morning's a few hours away."

But Vrai said, "Now that you've seen these people, what do you think of them, Kahl Latimer?"

"I don't believe they're insane, stricken with nuraj." Seth glanced at the Deputy, who apparently believed they were.

"Do you think they're dangerous?"

Seth considered. If Lijadu had betrayed him, would the Pledgechild think to order some more devastating betrayal?

"I don't know, Magistrate."

"They're not in the least a peril to the state," Vrai said, moving aside and sitting in a swivel chair. He rotated it to peer into The Albatross's aft section.

"They undermine the authority of the Mwezahbe Legacy," Emahpre said.

The Magistrate ignored this. "One of my main duties, Kahl Latimer, is determining what constitutes reasonable action under extraordinary circumstances."

"It's reasonable to preserve those institutions predicated on reason," Emahpre said, "and to uproot those that are not." He pointed Seth to a chair and ensconced himself hurriedly in another.

"'Uproot'?" The Magistrate swiveled to face them. "An invidious euphemism, Deputy."

"A problem doesn't cease to exist because one ceases to consider it a problem."

"Very often, Deputy Emahpre, it does."

Seth's hand went to his chest. Would informing the Magistrate of Lijadu's theft of the amulet alter his feelings toward the Sh'gaidu? Thus mocked and affronted, would Vrai, too, take an implacable stand against them? Seth glanced at the Deputy. He was startled to find that Emahpre had witnessed his involuntary fumbling at his chest and throat. Dear God, he had revealed his secret to Emahpre even before breaking the news to the Magistrate. Now the Deputy watched him with such rigid intentness that Seth feared to speak. His mouth opened. Emahpre, out of the seeing of Magistrate Vrai, shook his head in warning.

Didn't either of these rational Tropiards care to know why he'd left Yaji Tropei in the middle of the night? Emahpre had asked, but Seth had offered up a lie—or, at best, a partial truth—and the Magistrate had subjected him to a pair of polite, if nonessential, questions. In truth, Vrai had been catechizing himself.

Obsessively, he continued: "My deputy thinks he's the only Tropiard who understands the Sh'gaidu. But I know something about them, too. You see—" He swiveled away, peered into the darkness aft. "You see, I'm capable of empathy even with rebels, pariahs, discards. I have to be. I am the guilty conscience of my nation."

"These people are sh'gosfi by choice, Magistrate! Harlots and mystagogues! By choice!"

But Vrai said only, "Let's think again of sleep. Prepare a bunk for Kahl Latimer."

"Tell Kahl Latimer your decision, Magistrate. He may not be able to sleep."

"What decision?" Seth asked, taken by the conflict between these Tropiards but too intimidated by Emahpre to confess his sin.

Still facing aft, the Magistrate said, "Because we're bond-partners, I trust you'll understand and accept my decision. It's not one I arrived at easily."

"Only quickly," Emahpre said.

"That's simply not so. My reasons have historical antecedents. What we saw in the Sh'vaij this evening played a part, of course, but really just to tip me toward the only possible decision among all my seeming options."

"Tell him," Emahpre urged.

The Magistrate swiveled toward Seth. Tropiards slept masked, apparently. Vrai's face suggested that of an aristocratic bandit.

"I've decided that we must let the Sh'gaidu be."

Seth lay in a berth opposite the Magistrate's. Deputy Emahpre slept, or pretended to sleep, in the bunk below his commander's. A half hour or more had passed. All that Seth knew for certain about this finite eternity was that the Deputy had spent it trying to gauge how soundly Magistrate Vrai was sleeping.

At last the little Tropiard eased out of his bunk, crossed the cabin, and tapped Seth on the brow.

"Come into the pilot's bubble," he whispered.

Haggard and fearful, Seth swung his feet over the edge of his berth and dropped lightly to the floor. After ducking into the pilot's compartment, he slid into a frame chair before the instrument console.

"Where's the Magistrate's dascra, Latimer?"

Seth, noting that the Deputy had dispensed with the usual honorific, told Emahpre what had happened in the cliffs. His inquisitor stared through the dome of the pilot's bubble at the weird stars and the thunderhead growing in the northern sky. As if silently commiserating with his superior, the Deputy fingered his own amulet, now and again rubbing the amber stone decorating its pouch. When Seth had finished his story, Emahpre remained silent a long time.

"Latimer, you've given me a lever," he at last said.

"A lever?"

"Your crass negligence can be made to appear nothing but Sh'gaidu deceit."

Seth hissed in return: "I had no reason to suspect this theft would happen!"

"The Magistrate warned you. Then you slept with the Pledgechild's heir without seeing to the safety of his dascra. If not negligence, what do you call such irresponsible flouting of a trust?"

Seth averted his gaze. "It's past recall. Recriminations are pointless. We need to recover the amulet. And I must tell Magistrate Vrai what's happened."

"Let him sleep." The Deputy gripped Seth's wrist. "My intention *is* to recover the amulet. I'll do so by refusing to overlook this provocation."

"*How* will you do that?"

Deputy Emahpre released Seth's wrist and touched the lighted console before him. The viridescent glow of the panel X-rayed his hand. Seth could see the bones of each finger strung like elongated bamboo beads. Then the fingers played lightly across a series of communication keys, and Emahpre's alien visage took on an almost ghoulish aspect as he leaned forward to speak into The Albatross's batonlike mike. There then ensued a rapid, static-free exchange in Tropish with a disembodied voice that Seth had never heard before.

"What was that about?" he asked afterward.

"Using the Magistrate's code, I've called Commander Swodi of the surveillance force. I informed him of the theft and ordered him to dispatch a convoy of evacuation vehicles to the roadway before sunrise. Support troops, too."

"That contravenes the Magistrate's decision," Seth said, perplexed.

"I'm seeing to it that you and the Kieri envoys return to Gla Taus with exactly what you came for."

"You've committed treason, Deputy."

When Seth tried to climb out of his chair again, Emahpre's cerebration twisted through his brain like a fruit-corer: —*Sit down, Latimer.*

Seth sat down. Aloud, the Deputy said, "The recovery of Magistrate Vrai's amulet hardly constitutes a treason."

"You stole his personal code, deployed a portion of the surveillance force, and authorized an invasion of Palija Kadi. That's treason, Deputy Emahpre." Bracing against the inevitable, Seth lurched sidelong to get free of his chair.

—*Sit down!*

The command countered Seth's own animating will. Awkwardly, he sat again.

"This is an internal state matter outside the province of you and your friends, Latimer. But by acting in Trope's best interest, I'll help you fulfill your mission. All you need do is renounce all Tropish executive, political, and military concerns. Any other posture is illicit intervention. Even Interstel recognizes the truth of what I've said and forbids such meddlesome arrogance."

Seth whispered, "You're committing treason against Magistrate Vrai."

"*For* Magistrate Vrai, Latimer. I love both the Mwezahbe Legacy and Magistrate Vrai enough to commit such 'treasons' endlessly on their behalf."

Down the southern sky above The Albatross, a meteor plummeted, tracing its path like a crisply burning fuse, fiery against the indigo of the night. Seth's heart plummeted with it. For a moment it seemed that the *Dharmakaya* had fallen from its orbit. Abel, he silently cried, save yourself. But the meteor was only a meteor, not a light-tripper skipping to its death; and Seth was hurled back into his unwilling complicity with Deputy Emahpre.

Cheerily, the Deputy said, "It may please you, Latimer, how this works out. Why don't you withhold judgment until you see?"

Eventually, exhausted, Seth slept where he sat.

BOOK FIVE

BOOK FIVE

SIXTEEN

Dawn broke gray. Sixteen trucks descended out of the rocks west of Palija Kadi, floating down its dusty roadway in single file. They were clumsy-looking vehicles. Their high sideboards supporting rounded, plastiglas roofs, these trucks rolled on heavy rubber tires as tall as an adult Tropiard. The whine the trucks made seemed little more than the droning of an auroral breeze, and the helmeted Tropiards in their lofty cabs looked like mannequins or marionettes.

Emahpre espied the convoy coming and woke Seth up. "It's time to recover what you lost, Kahl Latimer. Come."

Seth rose groggily and followed the Deputy into the airship's passenger compartment. Rolled tightly in his sleeping cape, Magistrate Vrai resembled a creature undergoing an arcane metamorphosis. He was dead to the two intruders from the pilot's bubble, dead to the baleful susurrus of the morning.

"Go on," Emahpre said, scarcely bothering to whisper. "Wake him and confess your negligence."

It seemed a pointless and cruel suggestion. Seth glanced guiltily at the sleeping Tropiard and decided to let him lie. Maybe Douin or Pors had found the missing amulet. Maybe the Pledgechild, having recovered it from Lijadu, was even now awaiting his arrival in the Sh'vaij to restore it to him, and to explain the significance of the apparent theft. Maybe the fey Lijadu herself intended to hand it over. If any of these speculations approached the truth, why worry the Magistrate with a premature and therefore needless confession?

Emahpre, drumming the fingers of one hand against his thigh, opened the ship's side panel and gestured Seth through it ahead of him.

The trucks in the convoy had lined up sixteen abreast behind The Alba-tross, their noses pointing upbasin toward the Sh'vaij. At the driver's window of the only vehicle whose nose protruded a hood's length beyond all the others, Deputy Emahpre conferred with the officer in the cab. Seth took this opportunity to walk between two of the trucks, examining their construction and marveling at the indecipherable hieroglyphs painted on their doors.

Behind the parked trucks, however, he came face to face with a group of Tropish soldiers who had spilled from the enclosed carriers into the light. They stared blankly at Seth, each one masked. They wore small chromium helmets, single-piece garments of white, and broad black belts from which several pieces of complicated metal equipment hung. Two or three soldiers held long, tubelike implements before them; corrugated hoses ran from the tubes to gleaming, plastic canisters on their belts. Virtually all these warrior j'gosfi had laser rifles slung across their backs.

"Kahl Latimer!" the Deputy called.

Seth backpedaled away from the soldiers until he had at last turned about and confronted Emahpre. "What are *they* for?" he asked.

"The necessary." The Deputy nodded at the officer in the point truck. "Captain Yithuju will see to the comfort of the Magistrate. When he awakes, the captain will tell him what's occurred and where we've gone. I'm not aban-doning the Magistrate, Latimer. My loyalty is still his."

"Why don't *we* tell him, then?"

"Follow your conscience. I'm going to the Sh'vaij, however." He hurried up the path through the rich Sh'gaidu crops, knees and elbows pumping. Seth fell in behind him, demoralized by his grogginess and the weather.

The thunderheads that had formed above the basin during the night had toppled to the south, flattening out across all the visible sky. They had become something decidedly odd. Giving off a mother-of-pearl sheen, they resembled clusters of depending human breasts. Palija Kadi was a shadow beneath their matriarchal heaviness.

It was going to rain.

Almost as if he had been there all night, Douin awaited Seth and Deputy Emahpre on the assembly building's apron.

"Something's going on in there," he said, indicating the Sh'vaij. "The Pledgechild and several of the Sh'gaidu elders—"

"Midwives," Emahpre said. "They call esteemed older communards by a title that translates 'midwives.'" The term plainly disgusted him.

"Very well, then. The Pledgechild and several . . . midwives . . . have gathered in the old woman's cell," Douin said. "They know your trucks are on the roadway. The rest of the Sh'gaidu are still in the galleries. The old woman says they'll remain there until this business is settled."

"Where's Lord Pors?" the Deputy asked.

"He went out in search of Lijadu. He's convinced she abandoned the galleries for the fields. He wants to check each of the kioba in turn, beginning with the one where Lijadu's birth-parent kept her three-day vigil."

"You told him of the theft?" Seth asked Douin.

"Of course. Did you tell the Magistrate, Master Seth?"

"I encouraged him not to," Deputy Emahpre said, surprising Seth by the readiness with which he excused, before the Kieri, Seth's failure of will. "But did the Sh'gaidu allow Lord Pors to traipse unmolested into the fields? Didn't they try to prevent him from going?"

"No," Douin replied. "Our freedom hasn't been restricted in the least. In fact, the Sh'gaidu haven't paid much attention to us this morning."

Inside the assembly building, Seth's party came upon the Pledgechild, Huspre, and three midwives kneeling at the altar before Palija Dait. Ifragsli's corpse was gone, and only a single heartseed lantern burned. With help from Huspre and a midwife, the Pledgechild stood to receive those who had interrupted her meditations.

"Where's your heir?" Emahpre demanded.

"I don't intend to tell you," the old woman said.

"She stole from Kahl Latimer the Magistrate's dascra—last night, when she took him into the galleries."

"We don't deny that, Deputy. But Lijadu's reasons are her own."

"Her motives—her goals!—derive from you!"

The old woman said nothing. Seth shifted from foot to foot, while Douin kept his head bowed, as if to downplay his existence among these argumentative people by a self-effacing silence.

Deputy Emahpre made a slashing hand motion. "The Sh'gaidu have been a wart on the nose of the state for over two hundred years! What can't be healed must be cut away! Your heir has at long last forced us to essay that surgery!"

"And you are the knife?"

"I am the knife," the Deputy declared.

"Where's Ulgraji Vrai, Deputy?"

"This morning I act in his stead, Pledgechild. My hands are his."

"Then you're to blame for the trucks in the basin—also for the foolhardy soldiers scarring the face of Palija Kadi with their ropes."

Emahpre stalked off several paces. "The trucks, yes. The other, however, means nothing to me. Foolhardy soldiers? Ropes? If you're seeking to deflect me from the recovery of Magistrate Vrai's dascra, you'd—"

"Go outside!" The old woman flapped her hand at the Deputy. "Go look at the Great Wall! See for yourself the nuraj you're perpetrating!"

The Deputy scornfully beckoned Douin and Seth to accompany him and trotted toward the door. "I'll be back," he told the Pledgechild. "Whatever you're talking about, I'll be back to conclude this business."

Seth and Douin bewilderedly dogging his heels, he exited the Sh'vaij. Then, outside, the three of them ran along the building's apron until they had reached a vantage from which the Great Wall was visible.

Above the stair-step terraces ascending to Palija Kadi, upon the wall's awesome bone-white face, ten or twelve figures emulated the gravity-defying antics of ballooning spiders. They rappelled down the wall on ropes no more substantial-seeming than threads of spiders' silk.

"What are they doing?" Douin asked, nearly winded.

Bitterly, Emahpre said, "I intend to find out."

He surged toward the terraces, scrambling away from Seth and Douin like a puppet being lifted a full body's length at a time. At the base of the terraces, he halted, and his companions caught up. Meanwhile, four or five of the rappelling soldiers had reached the bottom of the wall. Several more began to leapfrog down its face from the summit. Two of those already down were snapping pods off heartseed plants, scooping out the balls inside the fruits, and releasing these spheres on the wind. A number of these effervesced up the face of Palija Kadi like pale blue champagne bubbles. Emahpre swore in Tropish. In counterpoint, thunder mumbled in the bizarre cloud cover. The Deputy bounded up the stair steps to the wall on a grim steeplechase.

Before Seth could pursue him, Douin intervened. "Don't, Master Seth. Even he doesn't know what he's going to do when he gets up there. Look to the east." He pointed toward the kioba in which Lijadu had told Seth of her sojourn in the Tropish city of Ebsu Ebsa. "Let's see if Lord Pors is there."

"We'll have to climb toward the wall," Seth told Douin, "and cut across to the left from one of the terraces." If they tried to go directly to the lookout, uninterrupted stands of monarchleaf and silverbriar would impede their progress.

They climbed. More state soldiers dropped lightly down the wall, leaping out and sliding along their taut double ropes. Emahpre had disappeared on a higher terrace, and neither Seth nor Douin tried to spot him. They struck southward along a tier of slender bushes loaded with mottled brown-and-yellow legumes.

"Look!" Douin cried. He nodded at the kioba, which was below them now. Two naked Sh'gaidu were digging in the loose earth beneath the tower's lookout. "What do you suppose they're doing?"

"Maybe they're burying a part of Lijadu's birth-parent." Douin had no chance to debate this proposition with Seth because Lord Pors appeared in the lookout and hailed them with a wave and a shout.

"I've found the Pledgechild's heir!" he called. "Hurry, Master Douin! Hurry, Master Seth! She's here, the deceitful slut!"

Startled, the two Sh'gaidu beneath the tower looked up. One rose from her crouch and began climbing the rope hanging from the platform. The other turned her topaz eyes on Seth and Douin.

"I've found her!" Pors shouted again, unaware of his peril.

"Look to the rope beneath you!" Douin cried in warning. "Look to the rope, Lord Pors!" An anxious noise escaped his lungs, and he ran for the steps descending toward the kioba.

A low booming of thunder sounded.

An instant later, Lord Pors screamed. He was pulled away from the lookout's southern wall. His screaming grew more bloodcurdling, modulated into a banshee wail, and ceased. As Douin and Seth reached the stone-braced steps leading downward, Pors's body came hurtling out of the tower. It completed only half a somersault before striking the ground.

The Sh'gaidu who had knifed Pors came shinnying down one of the stilts of the tower—for she had pulled the rope onto the platform after her and left it there. Her accomplice on the ground hurried to Pors's body and crouched beside it with her back to Seth and Douin.

Douin crumpled to his knees. Crucified with grief or incredulity, he threw out his arms and called out his compatriot's private Kieri name. Seth tried to raise him. Both Sh'gaidu were huddled over Pors now, and two wayward heartseed globes bobbed down the basin toward them. Raindrops pattered among the leaves and pocked the dust.

"Master Douin, you can't stay here!" Seth cried. "It's going to pour!"

Meanwhile, Pors's murderers rose from the body and scampered away toward the Sh'vaij. At last Douin looked up. Seth, numbed by what he'd witnessed, helped the other man up. Then, the deluge threatening, they descended the stone-braced steps. Once down, Seth knelt over the corpse of the Kieri noble.

"Dear God," he said, "what have they done to him?"

Douin replied, "They've cut out his eyes, as if he were Sh'gaidu."

"I'm sorry." Seth tried to compute the degree of his own culpability in Pors's death and mutilation. "Master Douin, I'm sorry."

"Go into the tower," Douin said tonelessly. "He said he'd found the Pledgechild's heir."

Seth stumbled away from Lord Pors's face, with its ragged, empty eye sockets and its knocked-askew dentures. He climbed hand-over-hand up the kioba's strut. The entire structure swayed. When Seth reached the underside of its platform, he locked his knees about the strut, reached for the opening in the floor, and swung out over the ground. He hung for a moment in free space and then did a strenuous pushup into the tower. His fingers had begun to bleed. "Lijadu!" he called.

She did not respond. She appeared to be bound to the lookout's central pole, as Ifragsli had been before her. But when Seth approached and looked at Lijadu's hands, he found that she was not tied at all. She was leaning against the pole as if in empathy with her dismembered birth-parent. Seth jerked her around and prepared to revile her for her duplicitous treatment of him, for standing by complacently while Lord Pors was knifed, tossed overboard, and then mutilated.

But Lijadu's features were bruised, her eyes shot through with crystalline clouds. She was elsewhere, if anywhere. Was this a self-induced spiritual trance or a catalepsy meant to thwart his questioning of her?

Seth turned her face from side to side. "Lijadu, Lijadu," he intoned. "What have you done with the Magistrate's dascra?" Clearly she didn't have it. She was naked this morning; no amulet hung from her neck. Nor did it seem likely that she had hidden it in the kioba. The only other artifact in the lookout was the rope the Sh'gaidu had pulled up after her. Retrieving it from the corner, Seth considered what to do. He had to get Lijadu down and back to the Sh'vaij. He fashioned a harness, slipped it about her, and eased her through the opening in the platform, paying out more rope and bracing himself against her weight. Douin received Lijadu and undid the makeshift harness.

"She doesn't have it," Seth called.

Glancing over his shoulder, he saw that the Great Wall was streaked with blowing rain. The drops spatted more heavily now. Fewer soldiers rappelled down the wall, and no one had thrown a new set of ropes over the summit. Maybe the Deputy had made his displeasure known. Several of the Tropiards were running purposefully through the basin toward the Sh'vaij.

Seth tied his rope to the pole in the kioba and slid down it to the ground. Yesterday, he recalled, Lijadu had braced it for him. . . .

Douin was waiting for Seth with Lord Pors thrown over his shoulder like a sack. He nodded at Lijadu, now lying on her side in the dust. The foliage on the terraces above them crackled insanely in the quickening rain.

"Pick up the Pledgechild's heir as I have Lord Pors."

Seth knelt, struggled, and hoisted Lijadu onto his shoulders. "She's been beaten," he said. "Lord Pors beat her, Master Douin."

"For your sake," Douin said bitterly. "To recover the dascra."

"In that he failed miserably," Seth said.

Douin did not reply, but trudged northward through the lashing vegetation toward the Sh'vaij. Seth trudged in his footsteps. Rain spilled in torrents, battering the crops and running underfoot in muddy floods.

Thirty or forty state soldiers—a few of whom may have rappelled down Palija Kadi—huddled in front of the assembly building. Drenched and dispirited, they made no attempt to enter. But as if they had some vague notion who Seth and Douin were, they cleared a narrow corridor to the door. The eaves of the Sh'vaij were the color of running blood.

"I'm not going in!" Douin shouted.

"But why not?"

"I'm taking Lord Pors to the airship!"

"You'll wake the Magistrate!"

"If the rain hasn't already done that, Master Seth!" Lugging the dead Point Marcher, Douin set off down the muddy path to the roadway.

Seth glanced at the uniformed Tropiards huddled in the rain, swung about, and carried Lijadu into the Sh'vaij. It was instantly quieter, but another noise—an internal noise—assaulted Seth, for the Sh'gaidu were mind-keening together: a dissonant, angry, melancholy music; a choiring of cloistered but interwoven minds. He was "hearing" it. The sounds ran through his aching blood and pulsed in his heart: cerebrations from Yaji Tropei, the galleries, and the mournful Sh'gaidu.

In the short time since Seth, Douin, and Emahpre had rushed out of the Sh'vaij to check the unauthorized rappelling on the Great Wall, several more midwives had joined their sisters in front of Palija Dait. They sat in a semicircular ring facing outward, each in a modified lotus position. Seth estimated fifteen elders altogether, all ritually naked, as if in protest of the state's heavy-handed maneuvers. Also, a number of younger adults occupied the wooden benches all about the great room. The Pledgechild wasn't among these people, and it was she whom Seth most wanted to see.

Near collapse, he staggered into the open nave of the Sh'vaij. Two communards with muddy feet and ankles sprang from the room's shadowy edges. They took Lijadu from his shoulders, as gracefully as drawing a scarf from his tunic pocket, and he was surprised to find himself dripping but unburdened before the midwives. As Lijadu's rescuers bore her into the left-hand chamber behind Palija Dait, their wet bodies and muddy feet registered in Seth's mind as telltale indictments and he pointed a shaking hand after them in accusation.

"They killed Lord Pors!" he cried. "Those two killed an official representative of Lady Turshebsel, Liege Mistress of Kier!"

This accusation impressed no one, but, echoing in the Sh'vaij, it sounded within Seth like his own feeble mind cry. "I want to talk to the Pledgechild!" he insisted. No one answered, and he started toward the door through which Pors's assassins had just disappeared.

"Latimer!"

He turned. Deputy Emahpre was coming into the Sh'vaij with a tall, lean Tropiard in boots and siege helmet. Dripping rain water, the newcomers stamped their feet and picked gingerly at their sodden clothes.

"This is Commander Swodi," the Deputy said. "He thought the acrobatics on the Great Wall a fine way to get his troops down from the basin's rim."

Swodi was plainly discomfited by Emahpre's remarks. He looked chastened and annoyed at once. He undoubtedly had only a little Vox.

"An exercise in agility, adaptability, equipment use," the Deputy said, berating the commander in a language that insulted him simply by being alien. "So realistic was the exercise, one rappeller fell and died." He then shouted out the crofthouse door at the men in the rain. A moment later four Tropish soldiers entered, carrying rain-beaded laser rifles and glancing about the interior of the Sh'vaij as if it were Seitaba Mwezahbe's tomb and they awestruck tourists.

Seth spoke up loudly: "Lord Pors is dead, too. Master Douin and I found Lijadu in the tower, but without the dascra."

Deputy Emahpre stalked across the nave, stood almost on tiptoe before Seth, and, his head drawn back like that of a cobra preparing to strike a hovering assailant, hissed, "Explain!"

As Seth explained, the two Sh'gaidu who had taken Lijadu from Seth reemerged from the Pledgechild's cells and moved along the wall to a bench. Their bodies were dry now, wiped clean of mud.

Emahpre interrupted Seth's story: "You let your friend carry Lord Pors's body to our airship?"

"Was that wrong?"

"No, not wrong." The Deputy strutted about Sethe, muttering unintelligibly. Then he halted and said, "When the Magistrate learns what's happened here, when he sees the corpse of the Kieri envoy, he'll return to his senses. He'll see the need for harsh measures against these people."

"Lord Pors had beaten the Pledgechild's heir," Seth said. "He'd—"

"Would you recognize the murderers?" the Deputy demanded.

"They're here in the Sh'vaij." Seth nodded toward the eastern wall. But at least a dozen Sh'gaidu sat on benches against this wall, three or four with topaz eyes, and Seth could no longer say who was who.

Emahpre whirled and spoke in Tropish to the soldiers who had just entered. The four of them strode to the eastern wall, yanked a pair of Sh'gaidu to their feet, and then bullied them across the nave and out into the rain. Four more Tropish dragoons entered to replace those who had left.

"You may have arrested the wrong ones," Seth said.

"They'll do."

"Do for what? What's going to happen to them?" He was amazed that none of the midwives or communards along the wall had offered the soldiers any resistance. Their encephalic choiring had grown more baleful—he had a headache, a severe migraine in his frontal lobes—but that was the extent of their opposition to the state's strong-arm tactics. Seth wasn't sure that the Tropiards were even aware of these people's dissonant mind cries.

Emahpre spoke to the soldiers who had just entered. He gestured

abruptly, raised his voice to a shout, and, when Commander Swodi responded, shook his head. Swodi, militarily rigid, pivoted and strolled into the rain.

The Deputy looked at Seth. "I told him to join the other sufferers. What
right does he have to stand beneath a roof after sending his troops over Palija
Kadi, after causing a soldier's death?"

"Not all the sufferers in this basin are standing in the rain."

"Maybe they should be," Emahpre countered.

The Pledgechild came through the tall niche to the left of Palija Dait and
halted near the ring of Sh'gaidu midwives. Her eyes glittered like those of a
bird or a mouse: a small, brave creature in the clutches of something bigger
than itself. She had shed her garment and in her shriveled nudity had the
vulnerability of a newborn.

"Do you believe you've evened accounts, Deputy Emahpre?" she asked.

"Two of your people for the Kieri envoy?"

"A weighted ratio."

"Not when those two are the envoy's murderers, slut. Not when your heir
has stolen the treasure of my superior."

Seth stepped toward the old woman. "Pledgechild, I beg you to have
Lijadu return the amulet, that I may give it to Magistrate Vrai before departing Trope."

"Please don't beg me to do what I can't, Kahl Latimer."

"Things have gone beyond the Magistrate's—maybe even the Deputy's—control, Pledgechild. If you don't return the amulet, it's likely—"

"It's likely *you'll* suffer," the Deputy said.

The old woman's eyes flashed at the little Tropiard. "Suffering unites us.
We come to unavoidable suffering—to your crass j'gosfi persecution—just
as we came into our lives." She lifted her arms so that their loose skin hung
like wattles. "Look upon this body, Deputy Emahpre, and tell me you don't
recognize yourself in it."

He averted his eyes. "All I care to look upon, slut, is Magistrate Vrai's
dascra. Return it or suffer the consequences."

Hearing a commotion at the Sh'vaij's entrance, Seth turned. A pair of
apparitions glided in from the rain: Clefrabbes Douin and Magistrate Vrai.
The Magistrate had not removed his sleeping cape. So drenched was his
garment that it clung to him like a sleek, black placenta. Douin led the be-
mused-looking Vrai toward the Pledgechild and her two anxious petitioners,
Emahpre and Seth.

"Outside," the Magistrate said, speaking to his deputy but sweeping his arm at the door, "outside, a pair of Sh'gaidu lie garroted. Why?"

"They were Lord Pors's assassins, Magistrate."

"But they were not!" the Pledgechild said. "Your soldiers have indiscriminately subjected two of my people to a blind retribution!"

"The community must share in the guilt of the envoy's death," Emahpre rejoined. "Whether the two persons who have just died actually killed him is irrelevant. We don't intend to sort and particularize the guilt."

Ignoring this exchange, the Magistrate approached Seth and put his hands on the young isohet's shoulders. "Master Douin says the young Sh'gaidu stole my dascra from you. Then, last night, you failed to tell me."

"I wouldn't let him," Emahpre said. "You weren't yet prepared to find your trust in these people shattered."

"Is learning of the theft *along with* Lord Pors's murder a revelation any less disruptive of my serenity?"

Emahpre pressed his own attack: "The treasure of your birth-parent, Magistrate Vrai, is the treasure of every Tropiard of the Thirty-three Cities. It must be recovered. We all owe allegiance to the final vision of your birth-parent because you're the embodiment of its dictates. Figuratively, Magistrate, your amulet contains the jinalma of Seitaba Mwezahbe."

"Figuratively," Vrai admitted. He glanced at the Pledgechild. His whole manner bespoke doubt and hesitancy.

"Magistrate," Emahpre said, "you've gone as far as anyone may go to credit the Sh'gaidu with generous, pacific souls. They've betrayed your magnanimity by stealing your dascra from Kahl Latimer and slaying a guest of the state simply for seeking to recover it."

"For brutally assaulting my heir," the old woman said.

Emahpre bore on: "Let me redeem their betrayal of Kahl Latimer's faith in them, Magistrate. Let me proceed with our recovery operations. Let me redeem their flouting of your generosity."

Vrai turned to the Pledgechild. "You know where my dascra is?"

Her eyes glittering fiercely, she said nothing.

"She knows!" Emahpre insisted.

"Return it, Pledgechild. You know I haven't deserved this. Since assuming this office my goal has been to achieve justice for the Sh'gaidu as well as for the Tropiards." Vrai began to fumble with the slit-goggles that Seth had given him.

"I'm unable to do what you ask," the Pledgechild said.

Besodden in his sleeping cape, the Magistrate stared bleakly at the old woman. Then he turned to Deputy Emahpre.

"Do what you must," he told that j'gosfi. "Do what you must."

SEVENTEEN

Chaos followed. Given his head, Emahpre rigorously prosecuted the search for the dascra.

First, he asked Magistrate Vrai to examine the amulets of the midwives sitting before Palija Dait in their prayer ring. Vrai docilely fulfilled this task while a pair of rifle-carrying dragoons circled inside the Sh'vaij collecting the amulets of the younger communards. When it was found that none of these amulets belonged to the Magistrate, they were redistributed to their rightful owners. Seth helped with the redistribution. The Sh'gaidu knew their own "treasure" as animals know their own cubs or fledglings, and the process took less time than Seth would have imagined. Afterward, the Pledgechild took up a position on the floor with the other midwives, and Magistrate Vrai, exhausted by this search and dispirited by its outcome, retired to the Pledge-child's rooms behind the Lesser Wall.

Seth and Douin accompanied the Magistrate to a nook where the two Kieri envoys had spent the previous night. On their way in, they saw Lijadu, either sleeping or unconscious, lying on a pallet in the Pledgechild's private cell. Seth wanted to ask her what was happening, plead with her to yield the secret of the amulet's whereabouts—but Douin gestured him on, and he and the Kieri man-of-letters removed the Magistrate's sleeping cape and settled him onto a bench surrounded by shelves burdened with a dismaying number of earthenware urns.

As soon as he was safely down, soldiers began marching through these rooms carrying clay vessels, wooden bowls, and ceramic amphorae, anything that might contain or conceal the Magistrate's dascra. The soldiers dripped rainwater wherever they walked. When two paused beside the Magistrate's bench to indicate that they wished to search the pottery on the shelves around him, he shooed them away, his words ringing with disdain and invective.

"It probably ought to be searched," Seth noted, leaning over him.

"Master Douin will do that for me," Vrai said, returning to his bench. He moved as if he had received a physical wound, and Seth wondered if the loss of the dascra had somehow actually deprived him of both courage and will. "You don't mind, do you, Master Douin?"

"No, Magistrate."

"What do you want me to do?" Seth asked.

"Watch my deputy. See what he's doing. I can't empower you to inter-vene, but I want you to . . . to *watch* him."

"He's behaving like a tyrant."

"At my behest, Kahl Latimer, to do what must be done."

Seth made a moue of bewilderment at Douin, and returned to the nave of the Sh'vaij, purposely not looking into Lijadu's cell as he passed it.

At the door, Deputy Emahpre shouted orders into the rain. Seth joined him, and a unit of Tropish soldiers, armed with canisters and corrugated tubes, disappeared around a corner of the Sh'vaij on its way to the bridges of Yaji Tropei. Heedless of the rain, Seth dashed outside and half around the assembly hall to watch the soldiers depart.

Close-order drill in a thunderstorm confounded the whole ragged lot. One glanced back toward Seth, revealing a mask atop his obligatory goggles. This mask appeared to be made of black plastic: it hooded the nostrils as well as the eyes, giving its wearer the look of a serious, upright raccoon. Seth had an unsettling glimpse of the soldier's face. Then he ran back to the crofthouse door.

"What are they going to do?" he cried, pointing after the soldiers.

"The necessary!" It was absurdly comical the way Emahpre refused to leave the shelter of the hall. Seth ducked beneath the eaves and shook water on him like a spaniel emerging from a lake. "Get back, Latimer! Watch what you're doing!"

"That was a gas mask, wasn't it?"

"They're carrying gas masks, gas dispensers, laser rifles, garrotes. If the amulet isn't returned soon, they'll flush the Sh'gaidu from the cliffs."

"Is Commander Swodi in charge?"

"He's *with* them."

"And you can trust him to behave . . . rationally?"

The Deputy pivoted and crossed the assembly hall to the Pledgechild and the ring of praying midwives. Four dragoons, held back from Swodi's siege force, followed him at a distance. Seth watched, weary of trekking back and forth and no longer eager to stand conspicuously in the old woman's field of vision. Complementary kinds of nuraj seemed to afflict both the Pledgechild and Magistrate Vrai. The mental choiring of the Sh'gaidu continued, in a bleak minor key that made the incessant rain seem, by contrast, joyous and invigorating. Pacing and gesticulating, Emahpre raged at the Pledgechild in their own tongue. She replied curtly or not at all, and the Deputy urged a pair of dragoons to lift one of the midwives to her feet. Still elsewhere, she rose unsteadily. The soldiers then escorted her past Seth into the basin.

As Seth looked on in disbelief, a slender Tropiard removed a self-constricting metal garrote from his belt, fitted it about the midwife's neck, and let it strangle her on her feet. Then the executioner and his companion dragged the Sh'gaidu's body into the stalks of monarchleaf west of the path to the roadway. Another stray pair of feet stuck out into the path from the field farther down: one of Lord Pors's "assassins." Where was the other?

When the drenched soldiers reentered the Sh'vaij, the whole episode dissolved in Seth's imagination as if a nightmare from which he had fled by an exit marked Objective Reality. Except that he had not escaped. The episode instantly reconstituted itself in his mind, and he knew that he had seen the real.

"Deputy Emahpre!" Seth cried. "You can't do this!"

But the Deputy had no time for Seth's offworlder's scruples. He harangued the Pledgechild and the remaining Sh'gaidu elders, ordered a second pair of dragoons to lay hands on a midwife, and stepped aside so that they could prod her through the Sh'vaij and into the rain. This was Huspre, who stepped as docilely to her doom as had the other three Sh'gaidu. Even the Pledgechild raised no protest on her behalf.

Without thinking Seth interposed himself between door and dragoons. "Deputy!" he cried. "Three deaths are sufficient! These people will passively resist you until not one of them remains! You won't recover the dascra thus!"

"Out of their way, Latimer!"

"Emahpre, be reasonable!"

"You can't confront irrationality with reason, Latimer! Get out of their way! If the Sh'gaidu want us to exterminate them, so be it!"

Seth levered a kick at the soldier to Huspre's left, striking him in the genitalia. This sent the Tropiard sprawling on the stony floor, screaming his pain and surprise. His laser rifle bounced free, and the tools on his belt jingled and sang like temple bells. In retaliation, the other dragoon swung his rifle butt at Seth's belly. Seth avoided the blow, took a breath, and shouted his dismay when the follow-through caught him under the chin and knocked him into the wall. Huspre, formerly as logy as if she had been drugged, used the occasion to dart into the rain.

The dragoon who had struck Seth swung his rifle about to laser the fleeing midwife. Dazed, Seth watched Huspre zigzag down the path toward the roadway and a pencil of light burst from the soldier's rifle, like a ruby filament sizzling through the rain in vengeful pursuit. Huspre evaded it. She leaped into a battered stand of monarchleaf and vanished. As the dragoon readied to fire again, Seth kicked the rifle out of his hands and clubbed him on the back of his head. The Tropiard pitched out the door onto his weapon. Seth jumped over his sprawled body to see if Huspre had survived and where exactly she had headed.

But even the Deputy seemed to recognize the idiocy of standing on legalities now. Screaming orders at his fallen dragoons, he ran through the Sh'vaij and reached its door before the first man whom Seth had laid out could get back on his feet. This time the Deputy did not hesitate to brave the rain. His nose tick-tocking as he scanned the blurred landscape, he darted past Seth to the top of the pathway, but Huspre was still nowhere to be seen.

"Where is she, Latimer?" the Deputy yelled. "Did she head for the galleries?"

"Why would she do that? They're already teeming with state soldiers."

Somewhat recovered but holding no clear grudge against Seth, the two dragoons stumbled from the Sh'vaij with their belts straightened and their rifles canted across their chests. Seth was still leery of them. As Emahpre signaled them to begin the search for Huspre, Seth sidled away along the outer wall of the assembly hall, Magistrate Vrai's dascra momentarily forgotten.

"Come with us, Latimer!" Emahpre cried.

Reluctantly, Seth obeyed. The Deputy, realizing that Seth did not mean to tell him anything about Huspre's likely whereabouts, asked no questions but kept Seth beside him like a dog at heel. Meanwhile, the dragoons separated to east and west and moved down-basin through the crops. Occasionally one or the other threw a laser bolt into a sodden thicket to see if anything jumped. Seth was glad that nothing did. For twenty minutes, they combed the area north of the Sh'vaij, but without result.

"Futile! Useless!" Emahpre angrily indicted Seth for their failure. "Back to the assembly building!" he called to the dragoons, and swung about on the flooding pathway. When he slipped in the mud and nearly fell, he loftily permitted Seth to save him. Seth, for his part, had to resist the temptation to throw Emahpre back down, rip his slit-goggles from his eyes, and hold his face in the muck until he choked. All that prevented Seth was his knowledge that he would be shot and left to rot on a world that he had not made and had no desire to belong to. Trope was worse than Gla Taus, and the Gla Tausians—the Kieri—had martyred his isosire in a way that still haunted him and that ate at poor Abel Latimer's dreams like a chronic and ultimately fatal disease. Here, however, genocide loomed.

And Earth?

Earth was an unfulfilled promise. Interstel determined its policies, but Ommundi owned its soul. . . .

A dragoon shouted something from the depths of his lungs. His counterpart took up the cry, and when Emahpre and Seth looked around to find the source of the soldiers' excitement, they saw The Albatross—the airship in which the Magistrate's party had flown from Huru J'beij—lifting off the roadway. Rising above a stand of monarchleaf on the basin's northern edge, it hovered in the thinning rain like the ghost of its real self. Its bronze pilot's bubble was a grotesque eye. It seemed that The Albatross would falter and plunge to the ground—but it steadied, tilted heavily, and swept toward the Sh'vaij with rapidly increasing speed. As it passed overhead, Emahpre, Seth, and the two soldiers involuntarily ducked. Seth feared that Huspre—assuredly it was she at the controls—would perform a spectacular kamikaze maneuver into the Sh'vaij. If her people were going to die, she must have decided, let their midwives die in a symbolic conflagration together. . . . But The Albatross lifted, as if on an updraft, and yawed toward the Great Wall. Although Huspre had probably never flown before, she had managed to get the craft airborne. Now she goaded it upward through the rain to higher altitudes. Emahpre, Seth, and the soldiers chased The Albatross as far as possible, sprinting along the western margin of the Sh'vaij, past the disheveled cypresses, to the hall's southern end. Here—winded, soaked through, and incredulous—they halted.

Because she had not suicided into the Sh'vaij, Seth had expected to see Huspre sailing off over the wall to some ill-defined utopia of self-fulfillment and freedom. What Emahpre and the soldiers had expected was unknown to Seth, but what they all actually saw appalled them.

The Albatross struck the Great Wall three quarters of the way from its summit. Although the ship made a doomed effort to keep going, it was now a shell. Scattering odd pieces of equipment, it slid down the wall in a slow-motion parody of disaster, collided with the highest terrace, and toppled sidelong down the next several tiers before coming to rest in a bed of clotted vegetation.

"Lord Pors's body is in the wreckage!" Seth shouted.

The Deputy resorted to his own language.

"What?"

"Unrequited kemmai to Lord Pors!"

This impromptu curse was so silly that Seth laughed mirthlessly. "Very good! But you must recover his body and see if Huspre still lives."

Ignoring Seth, Emahpre sent a dragoon up the terrace levels to the fallen airship, and another to Yaji Tropei to recruit reinforcements for the search through its wreckage. This second soldier would also fetch two of his comrades back to the Sh'vaij so that Emahpre could continue his harassment of the Sh'gaidu midwives. These plans, along with a warning that he would brook no more interference, the Deputy spelled out for Seth on their way back to the assembly building.

"The loss of the airship is as much your doing as was the loss of the Magistrate's dascra," Emahpre said. "I won't let this go on."

"Pledgechild, this is the familistery urn of the Sh'gaidu," the Deputy said a few minutes later, holding the huge black vessel for all those seated before Palija Dait to see. "Am I not correct?"

Seth stood helpless before Emahpre's singlemindedness. A soldier had found the urn in the Pledgechild's private rooms and given it into the Deputy's hands as soon as Seth and he had returned from pursuing Huspre. Several other soldiers lined up behind Emahpre as he confronted the Pledgechild.

"This *is* your familistery urn, isn't it?" he asked again.

The Pledgechild regarded him contemptuously. "Why would I admit such a thing to you if it were?"

"Then I assume that it is indeed the familistery urn."

"Or why would I correct you if you were wrong?"

Emahpre looked at Seth, hefted the urn as if for his benefit, and turned back to the Pledgechild and the midwives. "Unless you return the Magistrate's dascra, this vessel becomes property of the state."

"Even if you take it, Deputy, you won't truly own it."

"And neither do you own the dascra of the Magistrate of Trope, even though you've stolen it!"

"It belongs to us as well as to the people of the Thirty-three Cities."

"You long ago forfeited your interest in it, Pledgechild."

"Our interest in it is greater now than at any time since our Holy One departed Palija Kadi."

"Return it, slut!"

"Not even to save ourselves—for we wouldn't be saved at all. Do what you think you must, j'gosfi pervert. Whatever you do, you will do through the combined wills of Seitaba Mwezahbe and Duagahvi Gaidu."

"The combined wills!" Emahpre said. "What Sh'gaidu vomit are you attempting to serve up to us now?"

The Pledgechild spat two words—"*Smai donj!*"—and clasped her hands.

Outraged, Emahpre lifted the urn to shoulder height, thrust it out, and dropped it. It shattered, kicking out a cloud of glittering green dust. Shards whirled across the floor in every direction.

"*Smai donj!*" the Pledgechild said more vehemently.

But Emahpre was playing to Seth. "For however long Magistrate Vrai continues to suffer the absence of his birthright, we will periodically escort one of your midwives into the rain. Do you understand?"

"*Smai donj!*"

"It's time for one to go now, Pledgechild." Emahpre said, and a pair of soldiers neared the midwives and lifted to her feet a woman to the Pledgechild's right. Swinging their victim about, the dragoons walked her past Seth tauntingly.

He could not intervene. An anonymous martyrdom on Trope would mean nothing to any of these people. He could die for himself, for the sake of his own integrity—but right now that seemed an overheroic and downright fatuous course. It was premature. He waved bitterly at the Deputy, lowered his head, and stalked toward the rooms behind Palija Dait.

"Where are you going, Latimer?"

"To join the Magistrate and Master Douin behind the wall, for I don't intend to watch this."

"You have my personal invitation to remain."

"*Smai donj!*" Seth said, disdainful of his own bravado. On the edge of fury, he beheld the frail midwife stagger into the rain between her executioners.

As Emahpre, mock-scandalized by Seth's Tropish curse, drummed the fingers of his hands against his breast bone, Seth marched into the first claustrophobic room behind Palija Dait. Here, leaning against a wall, he expelled a tense breath. His heart thudded. But something inside him was different. With a start, he realized that the telepathic choiring of the Sh'gaidu in the galleries had ceased. What remained was the droning of the midwives and those few adult Sh'gaidu who occupied the benches in the nave: a sensation like music drifting into audibility from a long way off.

When Seth looked up, Lijadu stood before him. She had come into the room as soundlessly as snow.

"They're killing my sisters, Kahl Latimer."

"Your people killed Lord Pors."

They locked eyes. Facing her, trying to brave the accusation of her bruises and her pitiless gaze, Seth wrestled with his torment. Lijadu had wronged him by her theft of the dascra, which act had precipitated the chaotic events of last night and this morning. Wasn't she at least as responsible as he for everything that had happened? The whole, crazy tapestry of provocation, reprisal, counter-reprisal, and systematic slaughter was senseless. It got crazier and more tangled as it unraveled, and Seth could not see the point. Not of any of it.

"Damn it, Lijadu, why did you do it?"

"They've gassed the Sh'gaidu in the galleries. They've put them out of their minds on their feet."

"*Why did you do it?*" he insisted.

"I took what was ours, Kahl Latimer. Nothing more."

"It's only symbolically yours! Surely, you don't claim sole ownership of the birth treasure of the Tropish Magistrate. Surely, you must have known Emahpre would use the theft to justify this horror."

"They're killing my people."

"Exactly. It's maddening, Lijadu. Everything about this is maddening."

"Get the Magistrate, Kahl Latimer. Have him stop it." Like a wraith, she vanished beyond him into the Sh'vaij: Emahpre's slaughterhouse.

When Seth arrived in the tiny room where the Magistrate had sequestered himself, he found Clefrabbes Douin in a chair asleep and the ruler of
Trope staring at the ceiling with uncovered eyes. His goggles hung limply
from his left hand, which dangled off the side of the bench like a dead man's.
His eyes were pale diamonds.

"Magistrate," Seth said.

Douin awoke, and the Magistrate tilted his head to see who had spoken.
Then, slowly, he sat up, making no effort to cover his eyes.

"Have you abdicated to Emahpre entirely?" Seth challenged him.

"You see me naked, Kahl Latimer. This is who I am. I'm helpless to be
anything but what I am."

"Despite all the vested authority of the state? Despite a half dozen auxiliary births? I thought you could be anything you wished."

"The Pledgechild's heir has stolen my identity."

"Emahpre is *killing* people, Magistrate."

Douin, who had found his ministerial cap, put it on his head, picked up
an effects kit that Seth recognized as Lord Pors's, and struggled to his feet.
Clutching the kit under his arm, he went to the Magistrate and raised him as
if lifting a statue to an unsteady pedestal. It amazed Seth how tractable Vrai
had become. Maybe Lijadu had in fact stolen his identity—in a gut-deep,
psychological way that defied understanding.

"We're going out there," Douin said. "This is our fault, Lord Pors's and
my own, and we must stop the killing."

"I'm bereft of power," Vrai protested—but, with Seth's assistance,
Douin headed him out the door and through the suite of cells toward the
Sh'vaij. At every step, the Magistrate chanted his powerlessness, his absence
of identity.

Upon entering the building's nave, they saw Lijadu against the left-hand
wall, just ahead of them, staring into a pair of laser rifles. The dragoons who
had drawn down on her stood several meters away, near Deputy Emahpre,
who had sent another midwife into the rain since Seth's departure and who
continued to conduct this impromptu pogrom like a maestro afire with self-
importance.

"She's confessed she has the amulet," the Deputy said. "See—it's in her
hand."

Lijadu held the dascra aloft, the dascra for which her people had already
suffered several deaths and the ignominy of gassing in Yaji Tropei.

"She insists she'll scatter its jinalma if we approach her," Emahpre went on, affecting a calm he clearly did not feel. Then he caught sight of Vrai's naked face and cried, "Magistrate—!"

Vrai shrugged off Douin's and Seth's supporting arms and approached Lijadu, his hand extended. "That's mine," he said. "Return it to me, and you have my word that no representative of the state—no j'gosfi—will ever set foot in Palija Kadi again. Do you understand?"

Although initially mesmerized by the Magistrate's naked gaze, Lijadu shook off this paralysis, stepped toward the ring of midwives, and with a graceful, underhand motion pitched the amulet to the Pledgechild. It landed in her lap, and every set of eyes and rifle barrel in the Sh'vaij swiveled toward her. She lifted the dascra in cupped hands, cherishing its weight and feel. The Magistrate moved uncertainly toward her, interposing himself between the prayer ring and the state's armed dragoons

"I'm too old to travel to another world," the Pledgechild said, glancing sidelong at Douin and Seth. "But perhaps the Sh'gaidu younger than I will find the Holy One there, in her spirit if not her flesh. Perhaps we were foolish to try to recover what we could of her in this world, since we are few and our strength is in our souls and not our arms."

"Pledgechild—" the Magistrate said.

Emahpre shouted something curt and high-pitched in Tropish.

"I've been too long without the solace of my birth-parent's eyes," the Pledgechild said, and she broke the Magistrate's amulet against her chest. Then she pulled the pouch along the inside of her left arm, switched hands, and pulled it along the slack flesh of her right arm. Indeed, she ground jinalma into her body, summoning the plush crimson of her blood: crimson.

We are all imperfect isohets of the same perfect progenitor. . . .

"I'm both the reader and the reading of Ifragsli's final vision," the old woman said. The empty amulet had fallen into her lap. She lifted her arms to the ceiling and let the blood flow down.

Horrified, the Deputy, the Magistrate, and all the state's soldiers watched. Lijadu, meanwhile, crossed to the Pledgechild, knelt before her, and laid her head on one of the bleeding woman's gnarled knees.

"I here appoint Lijadu as my successor, Kahl Latimer," the Pledgechild said. "In the islands of our exile, she will lead the Sh'gaidu to communion with our Holy One and so redeem us even on that strange world."

Lijadu argued briefly with the Pledgechild in the Sh'gaidu dialect. Otherwise, she appeared in total control of herself, as if she had foreseen all that had happened since her return to the nave of the Sh'vaij.

Somewhat recovered, Vrai stumbled forward and knelt beside Lijadu. Seth and Douin hurried to him and tried to lift him to his feet. He would have none of it, though, and shook himself free. He put his face directly before that of the dying old woman, whom Lijadu was now struggling to support. Meanwhile, the Pledgechild's mottled head lolled toward one shoulder as if broken at the neck.

The Magistrate whispered, "Dear slut, you've deprived both of us of our heritage. My amulet contained the jinalma of your Holy One."

"I know," the Pledgechild wheezed, her eyes incongruously asparkle. "Hence the theft and hence my dying here in Palija Kadi: home. Home, Ulgraji Vrai."

"How could you know?" the Magistrate asked. "How?"

The midwives around the Pledgechild cleared a space and Lijadu eased her dying benefactor to the floor. As the Magistrate, Seth, and Douin looked on, Emahpre directed his soldiers to escort the midwives to the trucks waiting to evacuate them and their sisters out of the basin.

"No more deaths!" Seth shouted at the Deputy.

"You don't want damaged goods, do you, Latimer? You don't want your capital depleted."

"Emahpre—"

"No worry of that now. Our search is over. The responsibility for the debacle is all yours." The Deputy, too, left the Sh'vaij, apparently to assist with truck assignments and loading. The rain had begun to abate, but the gloom in the building gave no sign of departing with it. Seth stood isolated and defeated.

"Our Holy One has come home," the prostrate Pledgechild said, the fire going out of her eyes. "She's come home. . . ."

It took her a while to die, but the exact moment of her death identified itself when the last faint droning of the Sh'gaidu mind cries ceased and a terrible stillness fell over the world.

Later, a pair of dragoons carried the Pledgechild's body to a waiting truck and laid it in a preservation cylinder for transport to Ebsu Ebsa, the nearest of the Thirty-three Cities, and eventually off-planet with her people.

Neither Seth nor Clefrabbes Douin had anything to do with this business, for they'd gone into the fields to join Deputy Emahpre and several other soldiers in examining the wreckage of The Albatross for the corpses of Huspre and Lord Pors.

In the remorseless drizzle that had supplanted the rain, this party worked for over an hour and a half without success. Huspre's body was extracted from the caved-in pilot's bubble, but no one found any sign that Porchaddos Pors had also been aboard until a bewildered dragoon turned up the Point Marcher's surrogates—his false teeth—on the topmost terrace.

But what had happened to the body? Had it been flung into another dimension? Or diced into so many pieces that no one could find them all? This was a great mystery. Perhaps Huspre had done something sinister to Lord Pors's corpse before boosting The Albatross aloft. . . .

"I must return to Feln with only a name for the body," Douin said despairingly. "The Point Marcher is lost."

Emahpre assured Douin that his soldiers would keep searching. He explained that since Huspre had destroyed their transportation back to the tablerock, they must ride to Ebsu Ebsa in a truck, like the Sh'gaidu evacuees, and transfer from there to an airship suitable for the return trip to Ardaja Huru. This would be an inconvenience, but perhaps not a horrible discomfort. Later, the state would have the Sh'gaidu lifted into orbit aboard a series of shuttles. The *Dharmakaya* would take the evacuees and convey them through The Sublime to their promised land on the southern coast of Kier.

"They don't want to go," Seth said.

"Their wishes are now immaterial," Emahpre said. "Even the Pledgechild, before she killed herself, saw fit to anoint her heir with the burden of leadership on Gla Taus. That, Latimer, was because she knew the Sh'gaidu would be leaving Trope."

Sick of the Deputy, the drizzle, and his own complicity in this affair, Seth was about to protest when Douin said:

"Did you hear the Magistrate tell the old woman that his amulet had contained the jinalma of Gaidu?"

"I heard." But the Deputy did not like the subject. He wiped his wet forehead with a wet sleeve and kept hiking down-basin with his typical angry jauntiness.

"Why would he tell her that?" Douin asked. "Was it to intensify the Pledgechild's problematical guilt for ordering the dascra stolen?"

Emahpre halted and faced Douin. "What the Magistrate said was non-sense, a forgivable lapse. He could not accept that his birth treasure was forever lost to him. He tried to project the loss onto the Pledgechild. It was all a fabrication, a fabrication he was helpless to avoid."

"And the Pledgechild trumped him with a fabrication of her own?" Douin asked. "Is that it?"

"I suppose so. When Gaidu vanished, the Magistrate—who was not then Ulgraji Vrai but a j'gosfi named Ulvri in his fifth evo-step—carried the dascra of his natural birth-parent. That's one aspect of a Tropiard's life that never alters through all the various watersheds of his personal evolution." Emahpre set off again, forcing Seth and Douin to keep up with his herky-jerky pace.

Breathlessly, Seth asked, "Was the dascra really the Magistrate's? Could Lijadu have substituted another for it?"

"If it wasn't his," Emahpre said, halting again, "the damage is nevertheless done. We'll never recover the real one."

"Indeed not," Douin said. "It's much smaller than a man's body."

"We'd better get to the trucks," the Deputy answered.

When they reached the northern apron of the Sh'vaij, Seth saw several dragoons bracketing a group of Sh'gaidu children. The children's bodies were coated with a film dreadfully similar to mucus, a film summoned in self-protective response to the gas that the Tropiards had used in the galleries. With their rifle butts and gas-dispenser tubes, the soldiers jostled their young captives down the roadway to the trucks. Groggy and docile, they slipped and staggered, but neither cried out nor tried to escape. They would recover quite soon, Emahpre assured his guests; the effects of the gas were purposely short-lived.

On the roadway itself, Lijadu stood between two dragoons several trucks away. Her eyes seemed to stream in the unremitting drizzle; they had a beaded, mutated look, like melting chrysoberyl. Before Seth could catch her attention, however, she was shoved out of sight—on her way, undoubtedly, to a truckbed apparently reserved for children and other latecomers.

EIGHTEEN

"This one's ours," Emahpre said. "Let's board."

The driver was Captain Yithuju, who had led the trucks down into the basin early that morning. Emahpre took a moment to rebuke the captain for failing to secure The Albatross and for letting Huspre sneak aboard, take its controls, and lift the airship off the roadway right in front of his nose. This dressing-down was dramatic but brief, and the Deputy returned to Seth and Douin in a viler mood than any he had manifested since coming back from the wreckage.

His eyes still uncovered, Magistrate Vrai was already in a truck, his back against its port gunwale. As a concession to the eminence of this group of evacuees, Yithuju had covered the truckbed with a clean, white, spongy mat. As Seth, Douin, and Emahpre climbed aboard, pausing to clean their boots on a tailgate scraper, the Magistrate turned his eyes toward them but said nothing. Seth believed he was replaying the Pledgechild's death and mourning the loss of his dascra.

Although Seth had expected the convoy to get moving quickly, none of the trucks budged. This delay—as Tropish soldiers scoured the galleries for stragglers and those few wretched Sh'gaidu holding out against the inevitable—lengthened toward twilight. It was dark before Yithuju fired their truck's engine to life and urged the vehicle up the muddy gradient out of Palija Kadi. Theirs was the lead truck, though, and Seth stood at its tailgate to watch the basin drop away and the headlights of all the trailing vehicles bob fuzzily in the mist. He hardly regretted leaving this place, but would have been happier if he had never come at all.

After a time, his companions all sleeping, Seth lay down, too. Despite the truck's jouncing and its huge tires' sluthering, he fell asleep, exhausted by everything that had happened and vaguely hungry. In his delirium, Abel came whistling across his mind like something made of blown glass, its surfaces reflecting many distorted images of Günter Latimer. When this Abelesque bauble had shattered against the glassy wall of Seth's dreaming, there arose from the shards a dust of fireflies, as thick and mobile as gnats. Seth tried to brush them away.

—*Kahl Latimer, wake up.*

He awoke to find the Magistrate sitting beside him, his hard naked eyes like match flames.

"It's time to conclude our bond-sharing, Kahl Latimer." The Magistrate dangled something over his chest before dropping it. Seth's hand crept up his body to claim this item: a pair of goggles.

"I'm returning them," the Magistrate said. "We've concluded this enterprise, but our bond will never be severed. Had I another amulet to put into your keeping, I would readily do so. One failure doesn't disgrace you in my eyes, Kahl Latimer. I would bond with you again."

"Even if your dascra held the eyes of Gaidu?"

The Magistrate refused to wince. "Especially then," he said.

"What would Ulvri, a simple j'gosfi in his fifth lifetime, be doing with the eyes of the Sh'gaidu Holy One?"

Magistrate Vrai drew back a little, but at last said, "I'm still Ulvri, Kahl Latimer, even today."

"How?"

"I've undergone only four auxiliary births. Since long before the disappearance of Gaidu, I have been one continuous personality, a Tropiard defying the Mwezahbe Legacy even as I struggled to uphold it."

"Were you once a Sh'gaidu?" Seth asked, unable to make sense of what he was being told.

"No, no. You jump ahead of me."

"Then why should you have ever possessed the jinalma of Gaidu?"

"Before I was Ulvri, Kahl Latimer, in my first incarnation, I repudiated the vision of my birth-parent and cast his jinalma into the winds screaming across the prairie we call Chaelu Sro."

"But why?"

"Because on a trek between Ebsu Ebsa and Ardaja Huru, my birth-par-

ent betrayed the Mwezahbe Legacy by taking up with a band of nomads—
sh'gosfi, perverts, thieves—people at odds with the progressive policies of the
state. These outlanders have always been with us, Kahl Latimer, traveling together in the vacancies among the great cities, usually in groups of from four
to twelve people. Gaidu drew on some of these pariahs for her first converts.
My birth-parent lived too long ago to become a follower. Instead he allied
himself with a small but active band known for chicanery and violence, and
so abstracted himself from my life. I never saw him again."

"But you acquired his jinalma when he died?"

"The private records say that I was preparing for my first auxiliary birth
when the dascra was delivered to me. My birth-parent had entrusted it to a
fellow outcast, who risked capture to enter the dormitory of my horticultural
workers' brotherhood in Ardaja Huru. I awoke to find the amulet about my
neck and a long letter atop a work console near my door. I tore up the letter
after reading it, then delayed my auxiliary birth long enough to go into the
wastelands of Chaelu Sro to repudiate my birthright. The records say I cast
away the dust of my birth-parent's eyes."

"And you wore no amulet at all into your second lifetime?"

"I did as all Tropiards who have lost their treasure do, Kahl Latimer. I
wore an amulet filled with sand."

"Until you acquired the eyes of Gaidu?"

In the truckbed, the Magistrate leaned close to Seth and told the strange
story of his meeting with the sh'gosfi messiah, the self-proclaimed redeemer
of all Tropiards, dead now for 172 years:

> I was a soldier with the previous magistrate, Orisu Sfol,
> whom I came to know quite well indeed. He instituted a po-
> grom against the Sh'gaidu. I wasn't a common soldier, you
> understand, but a troop controller with a vehicle of my own
> and a compelling responsibility.
>
> On a night I have never been able to forget, from a van-
> tage high on the western rim of Palija Kadi, Ulvri—the self
> I haven't yet shed—directed an operation designed to harass
> the people of the unlawful sisterhood. It resembled what
> happened today in the basin except that it was deadlier. The
> mission of Orisu Sfol's dragoons that night was to slaughter
> at least three quarters of Palija Kadi's inhabitants, including

Gaidu herself if that were possible.

The Fifth Magistrate understood true intimidation. Those dissidents who remained alive would give up their fanaticism and return to the state; potential converts to Gaidu in the Thirty-three Cities would be dissuaded from falling from grace. And to some extent Magistrate Sfol's ruthless variety of intimidation had results: fear of reprisal, along with the Holy One's disappearance, worked to chill the fervor of the original Sh'gaidu and to discourage the defection of any impressionable Tropiards.

Ulvri, from his communications vehicle, directed one portion of the state's assault on the basin. He relayed an order to a lieutenant on the northern roadway and watched a single line of three hundred dragoons fan out across the basin floor firing their laser weapons and running the fleeing sh'gosfi to ground. There was nothing subtle or sneaky about this assault. The state meant business, and it met its objectives with the utmost efficiency.

His own role in the slaughter fulfilled early, Ulvri left his van and climbed to the edge of the western wall to watch the final sweep of the dragoons. Crop fires and laser bursts illuminated Palija Kadi. Although Ulvri could not see the dead, already he could smell them: an acrid stench rising to his nostrils and seeming to sear even his eyes. The operation had been a success. The rumor of this cruelty would perhaps avert the need for a follow-up.

As he stood on the basin rim, his feet straddling a crevice that deepened below him, Ulvri heard small stones snicking and sliding away in deceitful avalanche—deceitful because the sound betrayed someone climbing up from the basin's floor through the crevice. Ulvri was fascinated. As if amplified by the natural rock funnel, the noise of the sliding stones muted the roaring of the crop fires into mere background hiss.

The fugitive's ascent deserved admiration. Having wedged herself into the crevice, she used the pressure of her hands and arms to squeeze slowly upward through the funnel. When she finally reached a slope where she could crawl, she scrambled on her hands and knees, dislodging pebbles behind her but advancing steadily nonetheless.

Ulvri stepped back to wait. At last the fugitive emerged, and her nakedness identified her as Sh'gaidu. Wearing just a greatcoat of shadows, she crept forward a few steps and then stood upright as if the starless darkness would protect her from discovery. Ulvri leaped out at her and beat her cruelly before she could plead for mercy or lift an arm to deflect the assault. Then Ulvri bent the fugitive over a slab of rock and gripped her face to see what she looked like.

The biting, sky-blue eyes were enough to tell the troop controller who she was: Duagahvi Gaidu herself. Duty dictated that Ulvri must set sentiment aside and kill her.

"What will you do with my eyes after you've killed me?"

Ulvri reared back, startled. "Cast them into the planet's deepest gorge and lose them forever."

"That would be a senseless waste of power."

"Don't try to bribe me from my purpose."

"I tempt no thinking being from its duty—but once I'm dead, my eyes are yours. Don't spill them into the wind."

"How are they mine?"

"You have no dascra. You reside in neither the past nor the future, but only in the now. Since you must kill me, I beg you: Take my eyes and wear them."

Ulvri had no answer. He was dumbfounded. To wear Gaidu's eyes would be an unspeakable offense against the Legacy of Seitaba Mwezahbe.

"Tell me your name," the Holy One asked, still bent beneath his hands, and he told her. "Ulvri, if you become my heir, if you accept my eyes, one day you will be more. You will be the benefactor of all Tropiards, the docile and the defiant alike. You will rule the Thirty-three Cities."

"Nuraju!" Ulvri cursed her. To end her life beneath the starless sky, all he need do was tighten his fingers about her neck and squeeze.

"Yes, kill me," she urged. "But keep my eyes and submit to no more auxiliary births. When Magistrate Sfol comes to die,

tell him of your deed so that you may be preferred. Give him
the proof of my jinalma, of my bones—but tell him that he
may not announce my death in the Thirty-three Cities. If he
does, the Sh'gaidu will claim my resurrection and evangelism
will begin again. Let everyone think me abroad in the world,
and my people will wait—wait patiently—growing in power
and in their dependency on one another."

"If I wore your dascra, I would be Sh'gaidu myself."

"No, Ulvri. You must be Tropiard. It's fitting that I should
have a j'gosfi heir, hostile in his appointed post but friendly
in his inmost self. Thus the Sh'gaidu, who will always be few,
may come to fulfill themselves on Trope."

"And I will be Magistrate after Orisu Sfol?"

"For having killed me. For having preserved the secret of
my death. For being who you are."

"One isn't preferred to the magistracy of Trope for a single deed, even that of slaying Duagahvi Gaidu!"

"In the years following this one, you will grow in wisdom,
heart, and purpose. Your rise to the magistracy will have its
basis in a body of achievement totally apart from the murder
you must commit. Only you and Orisu Sfol will know of this
murder."

"How can you possibly guarantee this?" Ulvri cried.

"I will work for you in death, as will my people, infusing
you with wisdom, heart, and purpose. . . ."

"Enough!" Terrified by these speculations, Ulvri tight-
ened his hands about Gaidu's neck, slammed a knee into her
belly, and bent her backward over the rock. Crimson spilled
from her nostrils, and the Holy One, still youthful in her appearance, lay dead.

Ulvri considered what to do. Deeply agitated, he went
to his van, found a flat-bladed knife in a compartment beneath the driver's seat, and returned to the body to cut away
its eyes. Although his hands trembled, he removed the eyes
cleanly, emptied the sand from his dascra, and replaced it with
the Holy One's two eerily perfect eyes, there to bulge gro-
tesquely until they disintegrated. Lost in the lofty dark, he felt

like a vivisectionist as well as a murderer. The person he had killed was in some ineffable, threatening way still alive. He had started back toward his van when a faint cerebral tingling halted him between steps.

—*My body, Ulvri. Don't leave my naked body the prey of your soldiers.*

Ulvri, willing each step, went back to the body, lifted it to his shoulders, and carried it along the basin rim. When he had found a funnel in the cliff similar to the one Gaidu had climbed, he dropped her into it and nearly toppled headlong after her as she plunged into the dark.

Who would find the corpse in this place? Only Ulvri, no one else. One day he would reveal the site to Orisu Sfol and would be believed. He would bring the bones up, the bones would be studied by Tropiards ignorant of what they studied, and he would be formally preferred for killing the Holy One and for withholding from the world the fact of her death. In the years between the murder and the secret revelation, he would grow in moral stature just as Gaidu had predicted, developing a character fit for the needs of the position he would one day assume. Eventually everything would happen just as the Holy One had said.

Ulvri became Ulgraji Vrai, Sixth Magistrate of Trope, without renouncing his former self or the understanding of that self acquired after the Holy One's death. He did not fully understand the process by which he had reached this pinnacle, but he hoped that one day he could bring about a spiritual reconciliation of his people akin to the private one that had taken place in his heart. When he became magistrate, he halted the persecution of the Sh'gaidu pursued so vindictively by Orisu Sfol, a well-meaning butcher, and waited. Although he feared that because of the Mwezahbe Legacy few real Tropiards would ever subordinate themselves to the "illogical," he hoped that a more rigorous and humane logic would one day prevail.

Officers and advisors—Ehte Emahpre among them—pressed for a policy of watchfulness, along with discreet applications of force. Vrai accepted surveillance as reasonable, but resisted using force for as long as he was able. The power of the magistracy is not unlimited, he had learned, and under intense pressure even moral force may erode. He began to fear that he was no longer strong enough for the task that Gaidu, a dreamer and mage, had said he would carry out with honor. Sometimes it seemed that love and tolerance were at odds with the priorities of his office, and that he must either abdicate or enforce a minority tyranny that would finally drive him from power.

Then came overtures from Kieri officials aboard an Ommundi ship in orbit about Gla Taus, and Vrai began to believe that if reconciliation were impossible, the voluntary emigration of the Sh'gaidu to another world might offer a lasting solution. He rejoiced. Upon learning that two men from Earth had agreed to help, his hopes soared. There was something fatefully compelling about aid from so far away, particularly since for decades Trope had allowed only limited contact with the agents of Interstel.

As the *Dharmakaya* traversed The Sublime, Vrai cultivated the conviction that the human being destined to speak for the Kieri must be someone with goals and motivations like his own. A native of neither Gla Taus nor Trope, he would view the situation on each planet with a keen and impartial eye. The Magistrate's first interview with this person confirmed him in his initial opinion. By a rare but fortunate string of events, Seth Latimer had arrived on Trope, and a new era had arrived with him.

The Magistrate fell silent. A less fortunate string of events had destroyed his belief in this apocryphal "new era," and even if the Sh'gaidu ended up seven light-years away, Trope would go on as hidebound and as enmired as before—in the name of Mwezahbe, Reason, and Holy Technocracy, the sacred trinity by which it had lived for over nine hundred years.

Seth whispered, "Magistrate, you can reverse what happened today. Simply send the Sh'gaidu back to the basin."

"Emahpre had Palija Kadi destroyed the moment this convoy was safely clear of the cliffs."

"Destroyed?"

"The reservoir above the basin was undammed, explosives were planted in Yaji Tropei, and what was not blown apart, Kahl Latimer, lies under at least fifty meters of water. Tonight Palija Kadi is a lake."

"Then relocate the Sh'gaidu somewhere else!"

"Yes, Kahl Latimer. On Gla Taus. They deserve the benefit of what you propose, and I bequeath the Pledgechild's people into your care. Do you understand me? They're your responsibility and your charge."

"Magistrate—"

"The Pledgechild knew for years that Gaidu was dead—but she continued to have visions presaging the Holy One's return. I think, Kahl Latimer, that you are Gaidu, returned from death at this crucial time."

"That's nonsense!" Seth hissed, trying to keep his voice low.

"Your eyes, albeit different in kind, have the same brisk blue as did Gaidu's."

"Abel and I undertook this mission only to regain our ship."

"None of us knows precisely who we are, Kahl Latimer. That's as true for the Sh'gaidu as for Tropiards, as true for you as for me."

"You're talking like the Pledgechild or Lijadu."

"In my own way, I am one of them. Tonight, in fact, I declare myself sh'gosfi. I repudiate both my office and the state."

"Declare yourself sh'gosfi?"

But the Magistrate rose from the mat, stumbled past Seth to the tailgate, and stared into the darkness. Seth followed. They were still in mountainous country, not yet having descended to the prairie known as Chaelu Sro, and the vehicle trailing theirs had fallen a quarter of a kilometer behind. They could see its headlights, along with those of two or three other trucks, burning fiercely in a declivity far below them. The remaining convoy vehicles were eclipsed by the rocky terrain through which the switchbacking road climbed. Despite the whine of the truck's engine and the continual jouncing, Emahpre and Douin slept on.

"Farewell," Magistrate Vrai said. She eased herself over the tailgate to stand on the truck's step-like rear bumper. Her eyes coruscated almost merrily.

"What're you doing?" Seth asked her, stunned.

"Defecting to the outlanders. What the Sh'gaidu represented must be kept alive here. Although they go with you to a better place, I will range about this nation like their righteous walking ghost."

"Then be their ghost from a position of power!"

"That's impossible. I was too hemmed in by the magistracy's restrictions and limitations, and today I disgraced myself by a spiritual failure. Nothing like that will ever befall me again. Tonight, I'm free."

Seth pointed at Emahpre. "What do I tell him? How do I explain your absence?"

"Pretend to be asleep. Explain nothing."

At the top of a steep grade, the Tropiard called Ulvri leaped free of the truck. Seth watched her roll several meters down the slope, a tumbling shadow. Then, in stark silhouette, limned by the trailing headlights, she scrambled into an outcropping of rocks at roadside. When the lead truck crested this grade and headed down the opposite slope toward Chaelu Sro, a portion of Seth's life departed with that surprising sh'gosfi convert. He would never see her again.

Much later, dawn seeping up and the sixteen-vehicle convoy strung out single-file across the vast tabula rasa of the prairie, Seth was still standing at the tailgate. Deputy Emahpre awoke, stirred, looked about, and sprang to his feet. Bracing himself with one hand against the truckbed's wall, he made his way to Seth.

"Where's Magistrate Vrai?" he asked in his most piercing falsetto. "Where's the Magistrate?"

"Gone," Seth said. "She's long gone, Emahpre."

That evening Clefrabbes Douin and Seth shared a dormitory room on Huru J'beij where they had slept two nights ago. This time only two gravelike indentations for pallets deformed the carpeted floor's platform, and the smell of fehtes tobacco, at once acrid and sweet, was only a memory.

They had arrived by airship from Ebsu Ebsa late that afternoon, and already a Tropish shuttlecraft holding a fourth of the Sh'gaidu dissidents had been dispatched from the tablerock toward the orbiting *Dharmakaya*. Another shuttle would leave in the morning, and by tomorrow evening two additional shuttles would complete the transfer of Lijadu's people from Trope to the Ommundi light-tripper. Once all the Sh'gaidu were aboard, Deputy

Emahpre—in his capacity as interim magistrate—would let Seth and Douin pilot their transcraft back to the light-tripper's underslung hangar; and the history of the Sh'gaidu on Trope would be a chronicle written entirely in the past tense.

Douin was sitting in the chair from which he'd directed his last game of naugced against Lord Pors. Barefoot and shirtless, Seth paced the perimeter of the arbitrarily delimited room, anxious to be off-planet and on his way home. The ache in his breast derived from the utter impossibility of his second desire: Magistrate Vrai, before leaping into the dark, had given him a charge to fulfill.

"I must confess something." Douin's words fell like pebbles fretting the surface of a pond.

Seth kept pacing.

"Lady Turshebsel and the Kieri government—specifically, Lord Pors and I—were reluctant to engage the Magistrate in face-to-face negotiations."

At this, Seth halted and stared at Douin.

"We needed an innocent, Master Seth, someone who could present our case with conviction because he believed in it implicitly and therefore felt no need for subterfuge or dissembling."

"What are you talking about?"

"We lied to you, Master Seth. The Sh'gaidu won't be given a fertile piece of property in the Feht Evashsted. We told this same lie to Narthaimnar Chappouib knowing that the aisautseb would reject the plan upon which Lady Turshebsel, Lord Pors, and I had secretly agreed."

"Then where will they go?" A sad indignation arose in Seth, as if his conscience had reactivated in a tiny homunculus somewhere near his heart.

"An arid group of islands in the Evashsteddan called the Fire Chain, where they'll labor under Ommundi supervision to exploit those islands' animal and plant resources for the pioneers in the Obsidian Wastes and also for themselves. Much of the Feht Evashsted is wasteland. Its volcanic topsoil is tainted by a chemical indigenous to the subterranean geology there, and we've no cheap way to remove it. Even Chappouib doesn't know this. That's why we couldn't tell either Chappouib or the Magistrate our true plans. Chappouib would have objected for religious reasons stemming from antiquated superstition, the Magistrate for reasons of conscience."

"Are reasons of conscience antiquated, too, Master Douin?"

Douin stared out the window at the massive red-brown J'beij, far across the tablerock. "From the beginning, I've believed that we'd be doing the Sh'gaidu a service by getting them off Trope."

"Then why in God's name did you need someone to lie for you?"

"To make it work. Nonetheless, I'm ashamed that it's worked out as it has, that we had to gull you in order to pull off a larger deception."

Seth approached Douin. "Did Abel know about this, too?"

"From the beginning," Douin said.

Turning, Seth hurled the sunfruit in his hand through one of the paper partitions dividing their room from the emptiness of the dormitory beyond. "My own isohet! The flesh to which I'm twin!"

"He wished to regain the *Dharmakaya* and take you home, Master Seth. He saw no other way. Nor did we, for our purposes."

Seth stood dazed by the outrage he ought to be mining from his hurt. It lay somewhere beyond him, this vein of outrage, but he ached too badly to break through to its coal-black gleam. He looked at Douin. "There's an aisautseb aboard our light-tripper. How will you transfer three hundred Sh'gaidu to the Fire Chain without his knowing and reporting the fact to Chappouib?"

"One of the taussanaur aboard will help him have an accident before we reach Gla Taus. Chappouib will simply be told that our mission failed."

"I would never have believed that you'd sanction murder, Master Douin."

"The tyranny of the aisautseb moves me to it. For too long their ritual obfuscation of simple truths and their bloodthirsty commitment to bogus mysteries have betrayed the Kieri into superstition. Lady Turshebsel is a beacon out of that darkness, and my belief in her prompted me to otherwise uncharacteristic deeds. I make no apologies."

"Except to me," Seth said.

"For implicating you, Master Seth, in a scheme that's gone awry: The Sh'gaidu are victims twice over, and so perhaps are you."

"Ulvri—Magistrate Vrai—bequeathed the Sh'gaidu into my care, Master Douin. Spare us further victimization. Let me fulfill this charge."

"And remain on Gla Taus?"

Seth waved one hand distractedly. "For a time," he said. "I swear, Master Douin, it seems I'm under a painful obligation. . . ."

*

We are all imperfect isohets of the same perfect progenitor.

Lying awake in the dark, half encoffined by his pallet, Seth silently cursed Abel for betraying him. He wished Abel in Hell, his testicles enshrined in hardened clay, his body strapped to a rotating spit, flayed alive by lovely Kieri women, and consigned to suffocating vacuum. None of these horrors conveyed the vehemence or the confusion of his hate, however, and at last Seth wished for Abel the ultimate curse at his disposal: a death like Günter Latimer's.

—*Seth, don't do this to me!*

The words sounded in him as clearly as if they had been spoken. They came along with a corollary of Abel's emotional pain and a vague sensation that seemed to Seth an analogue of his isohet's rising nausea. For the first time in their lives, though separated by great distance, Abel and he were yoked through the manifold links of their common biological heritage. It had finally happened: They were attuned.

—Abel, you used me like a whore.

—*We needed someone free of any motivational taint,* Abel replied faintly, still recoiling from Seth's curses. —*Someone who believed in the righteousness of what he was doing.*

—Taint? Seth cerebrated. —Then you see the taint in your own soul? You know your own guilt?

—*We've no world of our own, not where we are now. I wanted to get us home. . . .*

—You knew the Sh'gaidu were to be transshipped not to the coast of Kier but to a group of islands in the Evashsteddan?

—*I knew.*

—Then picture the Kieri Obelisk in Feln again, Abel, and see yourself going up it like a trussed pig!

—*Seth, have pity. . . .*

A wave of hysteria—pain, bewilderment, nausea—swept through Seth, a comber of such undulant weight that, to divert its course, he had to address Abel in his mind, say No to his isohet's image, and utterly break contact.

Seth awoke again in a room on the tablerock of an alien world. Bathed in clammy sweat, he arose and paced about until Anja was a half circle of radiant blue on Trope's northwestern horizon.

EPILOGUE

At a point nearly equidistant between Trope and Gla Taus, where the closest suns were mere fiery dots, Seth Latimer and Clefrabbes Douin pushed away from an airlock on the *Dharmakaya*'s conning module, fired their backpack rockets, and floated out into interstellar space. Between them, they hoisted a spacesuit just like the ones they wore—except that it was empty.

This unscheduled stop, which had required the *Dharmakaya* to emerge from The Sublime fourteen E-days after leaving Trope, was Seth's doing. The empty suit between Douin and him represented the dead Porchaddos Pors. Seth had insisted that the slain Kieri noble be given an impromptu but decorous "burial" in space, a funeral ceremony to commemorate his efforts to bridge the light-years between two distinctive and dissimilar worlds. Nothing anyone aboard the *Dharmakaya* could say to Seth—whether to cite the astrogational problems such a stop would cause, or to say that Pors would have rejected a funeral in space, or to scold Seth for trying to mitigate his guilt in the matter of Pors's death—*nothing* would dissuade him from this goal. It was as if only the lineaments of ritual could exorcise for Seth the trauma of recent events. Hence, no one held out against him too insistently, for no one wanted an avenging madman loose in their light-tripper the last fourteen days of their voyage.

Looking "down" at the conning module and the stark, trailing superstructure from which hung the passenger and cargo nacelles of the ship, Seth felt isolated and lost. Much had happened since departing Trope. Most of it had either enraged or perplexed him. The beadlike lights winking along

Dharmakaya's skeleton seemed to him more illusory than the flashes of clair-voyant doubt that plagued his sleep. Even aboard the great ship, he was isolated and lost.

Two days out from Trope, the young aisautseb aboard had been found dead in his cabin's lavalet, his head plunged into the hopper of the chemtoilet. The cause of death was inhalation of the solvents used to decompose and deodorize waste matter. Although Seth knew that one of the taussanaur had murdered the young priest, he found it hard to credit that Douin had sanctioned the act. Douin, whom Seth had lived and worked with, was an exemplar of good behavior, a writer, the head of an enviable geffide. How could he have shown his loyalty to Lady Turshebsel by authorizing an orbital guard to hold the face of that poor aisautseb in a chemtoilet? Now the priest's body lay in a preservation cylinder in a cargo module. This same module held the corpses of the Pledgechild and thirteen Sh'gaidu dissidents who had died from the effects of gassing, close confinement, and brusque transshipments into orbit from Huru J'beij.

To Seth, the empty spacesuit represented all these unfortunate people, too: priest, Sh'gaidu, and Lord Pors alike. They all deserved commemoration. Once, their lives had meant something to others. That they should all go to the special territories beyond death without eulogy or remembrance struck him as vile. The truth, as Seth understood, was that this funeral for Lord Pors, the aisautseb, and the fourteen Sh'gaidu was also a funeral for a piece of himself. That was why he had insisted on what still seemed to both Abel and Douin a time-consuming travesty.

Seth and Douin fired their backpack rockets again. By its unresisting arms they pulled their tenantless companion along, out into the tenantless wilderness of night. Amazing, the silence and the ebony cold . . .

No longer did Seth share a cabin with Abel. He had taken up the farthest aft cubicle in the passenger nacelle where Douin lived and where the Kieri priest had met his mocking end. This change of quarters, considered objectively, had done little to separate Seth from his isohet, for the ability to commune with Abel through cerebrations had come from Trope to the *Dharmakaya* with Seth. He could tap into his isohet's emotional and mental state whenever he wished; and Abel, although less adept at initiating such contact, was now possessed of a like skill. They had intimacy without proximity. What they no longer had, however, was sexual intimacy. In that context, Abel had always been the initiator, and for Seth it had meant submerging himself in the grander image of his isohet's desire. No more. That was over. He would never find the whole of his identity in Abel; and, if nothing else, the fiasco of their expedition to Trope had given him the freedom to mark out his own boundaries as a moral agent. Perplexedly, he was still trying to stake these boundaries out. They were, he had learned, far more nebulous and far less arbitrary than those of death.

In the meantime, he had forgiven Abel his trespasses.

Douin grew alarmed at the distance between them and the dreamily floating bulk of the light-tripper. Mere specks in the universe's obsidian fish-bowl, they had traveled nearly half a kilometer from the *Dharmakaya*.

"Master Seth," Douin said, his voice hollow-sounding in the earphones of Seth's helmet. "Master Seth, let's finish this."

"Let me take Lord Pors a bit farther out," Seth replied, peering through two sets of faceplates at Douin's features. "Far enough out to send him to his death privately—to commit him to the infinite suns." He had come out here expressly to put distance between himself and the hovering Ommundi ship, and he could not understand Douin's reluctance to proceed.

"Lord Pors was my kinsman," the Kieri said. "I'll take him out."

The empty helmet of the empty suit gaped at Douin, who, before Seth could protest, fired his backpack rockets and whirled the suit away with him in a slow-motion waltz. Tilting his clumsy helmet back, Seth watched the two figures dwindle "above" him, faceplate to faceplate like dancers in a ball-room of shiny black marble.

Meanwhile, he hung virtually nowhere, dream-suspended. In one direc-tion, the *Dharmakaya* maintained a gaudy hauteur; in another, Douin and the suit climbed into the night's vertigo-inducing recesses. Elsewhere, only the star-dusted void.

"Master Douin," Seth said. "Master Douin." But a dead light inside his helmet indicated that Douin had switched his suit radio off. He undoubtedly maintained at least listening contact with the light-tripper's conning mod-ule, but Seth's umbilical to Douin had been cut. Why? Did Abel and Douin intend to murder *him*, too?

Alone, Seth recalled boarding the *Dharmakaya* fourteen days ago to find the Sh'gaidu cramped together in an aft cargo nacelle with only poor life-support facilities: four chemtoilets for 274 people, water from a condensa-tion tray beneath the ceiling of the nacelle, once-a-day food calls at twelve automatic dispensers in the port bulkhead, and a sadly inadequate supply of bedding. About all you could say for the accommodations was that the air was good and no one harassed or intruded upon the Sh'gaidu.

After checking on them that first evening back aboardship, Seth had purposely avoided setting foot in their squalid barracoon. Ulvri—Magistrate Vrai—had bequeathed the Sh'gaidu into his keeping, yes, but he would not exert himself on their behalf until they made planetfall and established a permanent colony in that cindery group of islands called the Fire Chain. For now, though, he had to come to terms with the custodial duties awaiting him and the odd chain of events that had foisted these duties on him. Earth was Paradise Lost. In the hardship of honor, he had given himself to Gla Taus, and, dear God, he deserved a reprieve from the burdens of that commitment. Reasoning thus, he stayed away from the compartment where the Sh'gaidu dwelt.

Lijadu had been amid that crowd the first and only time that Seth had gone back there. He hadn't seen her. Or, if he *had*, he hadn't recognized her among the naked and gem-eyed scores confined in the nacelle. They had stared at him as if he were Ehte Emahpre, Seth had thought, or some other tight-assed agent of the Tropish state, and he had hurried off without trying to find the one pair of crystalline, tiger-green eyes that would have identified their owner as Lijadu. What would he have said to her?

Seth had no idea.

Abel and Douin had seen to the most pressing needs of the Sh'gaidu, without ever suggesting that any come into the main passenger compartments. The only change of accommodations they had supervised was the shifting of the thirteen dead Sh'gaidu to the compartment where the Pledgechild and the murdered Kieri priest lay. Later, they had let one of the midwives visit this compartment to cut away the eyes of the corpses, in accordance with Tropish custom. Abel had also regularly provided medical treatment since the first fatality, but the *Dharmakaya* was not equipped to handle so many living passengers in its cargo bays. Seth felt sure that three or four more Sh'gaidu would die before they reached Gla Taus. Inside his helmet, he grimaced and opened his eyes on the surreal and painful blankness of space.

"Seth, how are you doing?"

The voice was Abel's, coming to him from the conning module through a faint rush of static. It disoriented Seth.

"Fine," he fuzzily replied.

"What're you doing? Are you about finished?"

"Douin's waltzing the empty suit away. They're almost as far from me as I am from the ship. I seem to be something for Douin to mark distances by. Yes, we're almost finished."

"Want me to pipe you some music?"

"Abel," Seth said, "I don't care."

"Okay. Hang on and I'll do it."

There was a scratching in Seth's earphones, an audible retreat, and a moment later "Ode to Joy" from Beethoven's *Ninth* poured into his helmet from the conning module. Although Seth spoke Abel's name admonitorily, the music overrode him, climbing on exultant strains. Looking about, Seth realized that he could no longer find Douin or the empty suit; that, in fact, he had managed to lose even his fix on the *Dharmakaya*. All that remained as reality supports were Beethoven's music and the illimitable night.

"Abel!"

To glide out of his vertigo, Seth fired his backpack rockets. He moved, but did so in a drowning pool of haloed stars. What were Abel and Douin trying to do to him? Then he spotted Douin. The Kieri envoy was alone, hanging motionless some distance away. Seth headed for him, and as his rockets' pale flames propelled him toward Douin's suited figure, the music in Seth's earphones died. He shot a glance "downward," but instead of the *Dharmakaya* saw only the depthful obsidian of space. His orienting focal point was the unmoving Douin, who hung "above" him like a nameless god's pathetic trophy. Why didn't he fire his rockets and drift back to Seth? If Seth had thought, he would have known. But in striving to reach the one thing in the cosmos that seemed familiar, Seth did not think; he glided passively toward solace and companionship. No voices spoke to set him right. He had only his own imperfect knowledge for guidance.

And so Seth came face to face with the tenantless suit that Douin had waltzed into this place and then deserted. Bemused, Seth stared into the helmet. He saw himself in the warp of the faceplate, a hundred colors dancing in the glass. Then he saw something else: He had forgotten to screw the suit's corrugated gloves into its sleeves. As a result, he could look into one of the suit's bent arms, right into the blackness of its nonexistent occupant. Inside his own suit, Seth shuddered.

As if dredging some prehistoric era of his own consciousness, he remembered the myth about the jongleur-thief Jaud that he'd read in Master Douin's geffide, from one of Master Douin's books, and how Jaud had confronted his own handless image in the final wall of the Obsidian Wastes. Somehow, Seth realized, this was the same thing, this confrontation.

He could not move. He could not draw away from the empty spacesuit's aura of accusation and reproach, not even when voices began to call to him in his earphones. At any moment, he feared, the creature before him would throw out its arms and embrace him as the aged Pledgechild had done in her cell in Palija Kadi.

Not until the real Clefrabbes Douin appeared from out of nowhere, touched his sleeve, and tugged him away from the suit did Seth begin to grasp what had happened. Then his perspective returned. He found the fragile lights of their ship blinking in the dark, and he yielded as Douin, who had sanctioned murder, guided him through the unmappable void to the haven of the *Dharmakaya*.

Through the ritual of a mock-funeral, he had sought to make himself whole, and if no one else understood the mystery or the mechanics of such a feat, Seth no longer cared. Let them mock him.

Later that "evening," Seth recommended that many of the Sh'gaidu be allowed to take up quarters in the forward passenger rooms. There were forty-two unoccupied cabins in the two adjacent passenger nacelles, and if they put three dissident sisters in each available cabin, they could almost halve the number of Sh'gaidu now crowded in the bay of the aft cargo nacelle.

It was criminal that they had not already made such an arrangement, and if Abel and Douin resisted his suggestion, Seth vowed to delay their reentry into The Sublime by plying K/R Caranicas with dodecaphonic messages of moral outrage that would seduce the triune to mutiny against them, too. Caranicas would strand them all in normal space until they submitted to Seth's superior humanitarian view.

To prove that he meant what he said, Seth took up the microphone from the astrogational console and regaled Caranicas with the details of his plan. The computer translated his words into a weird electronic toodling; and soon, after the triune had spun about on its gyroscopic track to face Douin, Abel, and Seth, a reply was coded through the communications unit:

"*We'll remain here until the transfer is complete.*"

Seth headed for the aft cargo section. When he presented himself to the occupants of the nacelle, which stank now with the natural effluvia of living bodies pent together for long stretches, he strolled through them until he found Lijadu caring for an elderly sister near the starboard bulkhead, not far from a segment of the clear condensation tray cutting across the ceiling.

Lijadu looked at him without accusation. He explained why he'd come, what they could do, and how a change of quarters could be carried out. He would leave to Lijadu and the Sh'gaidu the issue of who would come forward and who would remain aft. No matter who went and who stayed (Seth promised), Abel, Master Douin, the taussanaur, and he would do their best to clean up and refit the cargo nacelle.

"Tantai should have a forward cabin," Lijadu said. She stood, hailed a sister in a group of onlooking Sh'gaidu, and waited until Tantai had threaded her way through the others. Seth remembered the woman. Along with Huspre, she had waited on Magistrate Vrai's party in the Sh'vaij. Deputy Emahpre had indignantly run her off.

"*Gosfithuri,*" Seth said.

"*Gosfithuri,*" Tantai and Lijadu both agreed.

Even the midwife lying on a soiled blanket under the condensation tray drummed her fingers on her breast bone, and this word circled the cargo nacelle like the refrain of a carol.

Three hours later, they completed the passenger transfer, and the *Dharmakaya* again effortlessly treaded The Sublime.

AFTERWORD

First Novel, Seventh Novel

In February 1975, Ballantine Books published my first novel. A paperback, it bore the rococo title *A Funeral for the Eyes of Fire*. My seventh novel, published in 1980, was also called *A Funeral for the Eyes of Fire*, except that, of course, it wasn't. This may take some explaining.

In 1975, my career as a science fiction writer was about five years old, and I had already published stories ornately dubbed "On the Street of the Serpents," "The Windows in Dante's Hell," "The White Otters of Childhood," and "Death and Designation Among the Asadi." One of the reasons that I liked science fiction, in fact, was that Harlan Ellison, Samuel R. Delany, Roger Zelazny, and even J. G. Ballard—icons in the late 1960s/early 1970s—often used titles of a nakedly poetic stamp; and my own love of language put me immediately in tune with the field they represented.

Ellison, for instance, had published "'Repent, Harlequin!' Said the Ticktockman," "I Have No Mouth and I Must Scream," "The Beast That Shouted Love at the Heart of the World," "Shattered Like a Glass Goblin." Delany had written "We, In Some Strange Power's Employ, Move on a Rigorous Line" and—wow!—"Time Considered as a Helix of Semi-Precious Stones." Zelazny had by then offered up "A Rose for Ecclesiastes," "The Doors of His Face, the Lamps of His Mouth," and ". . . And Call Me Conrad," while J. G. Ballard had given us "The Thousand Dreams of Stellavista," "The Gioconda of the Twilight Noon," "You: Coma: Marilyn Monroe," and, a miracle of evocativeness, "The Cloud Sculptors of Coral D."

A new writer, I felt, could not hope to walk among these word-drunk visionaries without jousting with them. So my early stories usually arose less from a fascinating scientific concept, or a nifty metaphysical notion, or a dazzling plot twist than from a lovely phrase, a would-be title. And if a story did not grow from an exotic concatenation of syllables, I labored to find the concatenation *afterwards,* for I had the titles of Ellison, Delany, Zelazny, and Ballard—plus those of an earlier influence, Ray Bradbury, he of "Dark They Were, and Golden-eyed," "A Medicine for Melancholy," "All Summer in a Day," and *Something Wicked This Way Comes*—to live up to.

I no doubt went overboard.

Anyone who still has a copy of the first, and only, Ballantine edition of *A Funeral for the Eyes of Fire*—a text I don't want reprinted, ever—will see that the novel consists of a prologue, an epilogue, and fifteen intervening chapters, and that I gave every chapter not one, but two, titles. My tenth chapter, for instance, appears on the contents page as "**PERFIDY**: Out of Our Several Sleeps We Ascend." Other chapters include "**BEDFELLOWS**: A Seduction Rich and Strange," "**COVENANT**: Derringer and Dascra," and, most convolute of all, "**USURPATION**: Two Meteors, Prodigal of Light." Today, I read these titles with incredulity and embarrassment, but also—forgive me—with a rush of excitement and exhilaration. The words, even those in clunky combinations, still sing (at least for me, albeit with some Dylanesque wheezing), and I recall again the youthful energy and idealism, the naive poetic fervor, with which I tackled the scary, and heady, task of writing my first novel.

As a result, I still feel affection for the original version of *A Funeral for the Eyes of Fire,* its callow narrator, and a few of the baroque images and metaphors with which I salted the text. But I also recognize the fumble-fingeredness and immaturity of that initial version. I recognized them soon after my novel appeared to a mostly unimpressed, if not rabidly indifferent, American public.

Not soon enough, I'll admit in this aside, to keep me from lifting a line from Archibald MacLeish's "You, Andrew Marvell" and calling my second novel, and first hardcover, *And Strange at Ecbatan the Trees*—a title that Donald A. Wollheim at DAW Books, publisher of its mass-market edition, could not envision on the cover of an SF adventure in a whirl rack in a bus station in Mokena, Illinois, or a grungy five-and-dime in Pueblo, Colorado. And so *Ecbatan*, as a paperback, became *Beneath the Shattered Moons*, with a nod to Edgar Rice Burroughs and a silent raspberry for the jilted MacLeish.

You may now wonder if I wrote an entire novel on the dubious foundation of a preconceived title. No, I didn't. If I had any literary forerunner in mind during the writing of *Funeral*, it was Ursula K. Le Guin's award-winning Ace Science Fiction Special, *The Left Hand of Darkness* (1968).

As I have noted elsewhere, I may owe my career as a science-fiction writer to this novel. I read it when I was consciously trying to indoctrinate myself into the best that science fiction offered: Arthur C. Clarke, Theodore Sturgeon, Walter M. Miller, Jr., and all the profane radical New Wavers then cropping up in Damon Knight's *Orbit* series, Ellison's *Dangerous Visions*, and an occasional Judith Merril anthology such as *SF 12* and *England Swings SF* (UK title *The Space-Time Journal*).

Even among this glut of invigorating stuff, *The Left Hand of Darkness* stood out. I realized that Le Guin's novel demonstrated, unequivocally, that SF provided a legitimate vehicle for adroit speculation about both technology and the human condition. Therefore, and because Le Guin writes like a seraph, I admired her novel hugely . . . but I still wasn't ready to start one of my own. In fact, I was several months away from placing my first story, "Piñon Fall," with Ejler Jakobsson at *Galaxy*. I had some heavy lifting to do, a writerly apprenticeship to fulfill.

I subscribed to *Fantasy & Science Fiction* and *Galaxy*. I bought new paperbacks off the racks of the Hallmark gift shop near the May D&F department store in Colorado Springs, notably the Ace Science Fiction Specials edited by Terry Carr. (At this Hallmark shop, I found *The Left Hand of Darkness*, Alexei Panshin's *Rite of Passage*, Zelazny's *Isle of the Dead*, Keith Roberts's *Pavane*, Joanna Russ's *And Chaos Died*, Michael Moorcock's *The Black Corridor*, R. A. Lafferty's *Fourth Mansions*, Bob Shaw's *The Palace of Eternity*, and many other fascinating titles.)

From the dusty bins of second-hand emporia in Colorado Springs or Denver, I salvaged used or out-of-print sf classics. I began to write "imaginative" tales of my own. Along with Klaus Krause, my English-department officemate at the Air Force Academy Prep School, I attended meetings of the Denver Area Science Fiction Association, all held in the basement of a branch bank several blocks from downtown.

One noteworthy evening, Harlan Ellison himself showed up—late, of course—in the company of a club officer. He read from a copy of his story "One Life, Furnished in Early Poverty," soon to appear in *Orbit 8*. He held up the cover proof of his Avon story collection *The Beast That Shouted Love at the Heart of the World* (1969). He signed autographs for those of us who had brought copies of his books. (The young Ed Bryant, whom I met that night, was a DASFA member on hand for Ellison's visit, and Bryant, the dog, had already *sold* some stories of his own.)

In asking for a signature for my well-fingered copy of *Paingod*, I got Ellison's back up by inquiring if he had ever written a novel. With audible annoyance, he let me know that he'd done several—four, if memory serves. I was delighted as well as abashed to have yanked his chain, for although I still haven't read a full-length novel by Ellison (who later told my wife, Jeri, that my "marmoset eyes" made me an untrustworthy companion), I left that unforgettable meeting, knowing that even a short-story writer, including a *natural* one like the Harlequin, may have the ability to go long as well as short. Although that lesson did not sink in on our drive back to Colorado Springs, or even in the following three years, it registered on *some* level, and one day I would surely have need of it.

A love of arresting, multiword titles.

Ursula Le Guin's novel about a planet called Winter and its population of alien but *human* androgynes.

A self-directed crash course in contemporary science fiction.

And a meeting at which an energetic short-story writer told me that, yeah, he'd written a novel, several, and why didn't I wake up and smell the java?

These are the foundations of my first novel, *A Funeral for the Eyes of Fire* ... or, at least, some of them.

As noted earlier, my first sale was to *Galaxy*. That occurred in the spring of 1970, and "Piñon Fall" appeared in the Oct.-Nov. issue. I then placed several pieces with Edward L. Ferman, editor of *Fantasy & Science Fiction*: "Darktree, Darktide," "A Tapestry of Little Murders," "Spacemen and Gypsies." I sold a novelette in my Urban Nucleus series, "If a Flower Could Eclipse," to Jakobsson at *Worlds of Fantasy*, and a second UrNu story, "The Windows in Dante's Hell" to Damon Knight at *Orbit*. These stories were SF, horror, fantasy, or hybrid mongrels of these forms.

My sixth or seventh sale proved my most important, although I did not understand that until later. Best known for his *Star Trek* script "The Trouble With Tribbles," David Gerrold was editing original paperback anthologies for Ballantine (*Protostars*) and Dell (*Generation*). In the spring of 1972, he was assembling a second Ballantine anthology, presumably the beginning of a series, *Science Fiction Emphasis*.

To David, I sent my first novella, a work pushing seventy pages, a projection of myself as a character into a future Spain in which the dying Franco has had his brain transplanted into the body of a healthy Nordic; meanwhile, the artist Picasso, reconciled to the old generalissimo and kept alive by mechanical means, returns to Spain to take part in its first free elections in decades. This story was "On the Street of the Serpents." After I mailed it off, David replied with a letter noting that it was exactly the sort for which he'd inaugurated *SF Emphasis*. He wanted—hallelujah!—to buy it.

Eventually, Betty Ballantine of Ballantine Books read "On the Street of the Serpents." The cofounder of that trail-blazing paperback house liked it, too—enough, at least, to ask David to ask me if I had a novel in the works or if I could at least show her a proposal for one. She would look with favor on almost anything I sent her. This news flattered me, but I was a lieutenant in the Air Force, a rank beginner with only a few sales to my credit, and I had pushed my limits to write one coherent story of seventy pages. How could I do a hundred, much less three hundred, without my prose degenerating into jargon and my story into surreal argle-bargle?

Actually, I was *afraid* to write a novel. But an image began to haunt me, a striking mental picture of a humanoid alien with gemstones for eyes, a vestigial scar for a mouth, and a skin structure permitting it to absorb nutrients through the palms of its hands. But I had no story, only this outré concept. I fiddled with it. I scratched out notes on the blotter of my desk at the Prep School. Either before drifting to sleep at night or while driving to work in the morning, I tried to figure out some of the likely metabolic consequences of my alien's unlikely anatomy.

During all this futzing about, I wrote a novelette deploying representatives of my imaginary species. In it, I called them *Doukhobors* after a sect of Russian Christians who advocated loyalty to one's own spiritual light and the rejection of all external authority. My models were the modern Canadian Doukhobors, immigrants from Russia, who, as recently as the 1950s, had stripped naked and marched in groups to protest what they saw as official, and godless, discrimination against their faith. I set my story on another planet, in an island chain virtually identical in topography and ecology to the Galapagos Islands off the coast of Ecuador, and I called this novelette—forgive me—"A Far Galapagos, an Inward Heart." I then afforded every editor in the field a chance to reject my earnest mishmash. All of them did, but Ted White at Sol Cohen's *Amazing* and *Fantastic* did offer me the consolation of encouragement.

So I filed the abortion away, shoving its inchoate conceits into mental limbo, fearing them too pulpish and grotesque for credible fulfillment and doubting my ability to devise a story that would redeem them. I also doubted my ability to expand "A Far Galapagos, an Inward Heart" to a strong end 85,000 words from its opening sentence. I had a deep-seated novel-writing phobia. Meanwhile, I wrote two other stories; each grew to approximately the length of my *SF Emphasis* sale: "The White Otters of Childhood" and "Death and Designation among the Asadi." These novellas landed on the final Nebula ballot for 1973. Also, I secured a position as an instructor of freshman English at the University of Georgia, left the service, and returned to Athens with Jeri and our infant son, Jamie. There, I finished the last sections of "Death and Designation" and the stories "Allegiances," "Cathadonian Odyssey," "Rogue Tomato," "Blooded on Arachne," "The Samurai and the Willows," "In Rubble, Pleading," my first draft of "The House of Compassionate Sharers," and a Vietnam War story, "The Tigers of Hysteria Feed Only on Themselves." I began to believe, sort of, that I could write a novel.

Here, my memory gets fuzzy. As Joseph Brodsky puts it in his memoir *Less Than One*, "As failures go, attempting to recall the past is like trying to grasp the meaning of existence. Both make one feel like a baby clutching at a basketball: one's palms keep sliding off." I pulled out my old notes about the aliens with gems for eyes and my scruffy copy of "A Far Galapagos," etc., and, at David Gerrold's urging, wrote the first three or four chapters of the book that mutated into *A Funeral for the Eyes of Fire*. I sent these chapters, again at David's urging, to Ballantine Books (which, at that point, still had not published the anthology for which he had acquired "On the Street of the Serpents"), and Betty Ballantine liked them well enough to ask for more.

In June of 1973, then, I signed my first contract for a novel; my delivery date was September 15, 1973, but I probably overshot it: Jeri delivered our daughter, Stephanie, before I delivered my novel. When I did get the book in to Betty and her assistant, Judy-Lynn del Rey (née Benjamin), they agreed that reading it was like watching a colorful alien pageant "through a waterfall." Revisions seemed called for.

In either late 1973 or early 1974, Betty Ballantine flew down to Athens from New York to talk with me about the novel. Jeri and I put her up in our drafty rented house on Virginia Avenue. For one long weekend, with a welcome break for a catfish or barbecue dinner at an outlying eatery known as the Swamp Guinea, we pored over the manuscript. Betty explained why Gunnar Balduin could not—*should* not—be the cynical backstabber that I'd made him and how to remove the verbal waterfall veiling the novel's events.

After reviewing my book chapter by chapter in New York, Betty wrote one or more typed pages detailing the problems with each one. I kept these pages with me when she left Athens and did my damnedest to comply with her instructions to turn *Funeral* into an interplanetary thriller with a strong anthropological dimension and a pervasive aura of neo-Shakespearean tragedy. In fact, almost from the first, I had seen my novel as an Elizabethan drama in tie-dyed pulp clothing.

About a year after Betty's visit, after we Bishops had moved to a Victorian house in Pine Mountain, Georgia, the novel appeared. Square on its paperback's cover stood a gem-eyed alien, nude but visible from only the waist up. The faceted green jewels of its eyes gave it the look of a humanoid BEM, or bug-eyed monster, and the "vestigial scar" replacing its evolutionarily obsolete mouth curved upward in a dismaying grin-cum-smirk. Also, Gene Szafran, the artist, had depicted this alien as pink-skinned as any card-carrying Caucasian. The sky above this naked humanoid creature was a somewhat darker pink. Behind the smirking creature, a V of plant-lined terraces balanced on its shoulders like out-of-focus wings.

I didn't hate the cover, but I knew that in this gaudy guise—a package altogether suited to the product—*A Funeral for the Eyes of Fire* would never bump *Portrait of the Artist as a Young Man* or *Sons and Lovers* from any university's course syllabi or recommended reading lists. To me, the paperback looked like the sort that a teenage boy would thumb through under his bed-covers with a flashlight.

I was at once proud and chagrined.

Where did I get my title? The Ballantine edition of *Funeral* contained four epigrams, the first from *The Making of a Counter Culture* by Theodore Roszak: "The Shaman, then, is one who knows that there is more to be seen of reality than the waking eye sees. Besides our eyes of flesh, there are eyes of fire that burn through the ordinariness of the world and perceive the wonders and terrors beyond." The quotation is from Chapter VIII, "Eyes of Flesh, Eyes of Fire." In an Author's Note to my reworked novel, published by Pocket Books as *Eyes of Fire* early in 1980, I termed Roszak's chapter "a trenchant essay on the conflict between the world views of the shaman and the technocrat."

The other three epigrams in the 1975 Ballantine edition come from *On Aggression* by Konrad Lorenz, Vittorio Lanternari's *The Religions of the Oppressed*, and *African Genesis* by Robert Ardrey. All throw light on my novel's major themes, but I booted them out of the front matter of *Eyes of Fire* because they, like my chapter titles, now struck me as overexplicit or pretentious. Even so, the one from Lanternari may warrant repeating, for my reading of *The Religions of the Oppressed*, along with that of Le Guin's *The Left Hand of Darkness*, prompted the line of thought underlying the moral dilemma in both versions of the book:

"In the final analysis, all the endogenous messianic movements, regardless of their cultural level, are impelled by their nature to escape from society and from the world in order to establish a society beyond history, beyond reality, and beyond the necessity of fighting to bring about change and improvement."

In the Ballantine edition of *Funeral*, this messianic movement comprised the intuitive Ouemartsee, resistors of the technocratic Tropemen who rule the planet at large. In *Eyes of Fire,* these sectarians are the Sh'gaidu, a group of introspective, feminine, and mystical beings in contrast to the extrovert, masculine, and literal-minded rationalists who rule the continent Trope from Ardaja Huru, their capital. In short, although *Eyes of Fire* was a wholesale *reimagining* of my first novel, with new names, settings, characters, and complexity, it retained the thematic thrusts suggested by the discarded epigrams.

But did the presence of these epigrams in the Ballantine original prove helpful to anyone? Did anyone care?

A Funeral for the Eyes of Fire sold poorly. It received six recommendations over the Nebula year, but did not make the final ballot. Attention in both the general press and the review columns of SF specialty magazines was at best spotty; notices that did see print were, generally, either mixed or noncommittally descriptive. Or so I remember the bulk of them today.

One review did make made a lasting impact. It appeared in the Books column of the August 1975 issue of *F&SF*. In this column, Alexei and Cory Panshin called *Funeral* "the most impressive first novel so far seen in the Seventies" and its author "one of the new and still rare breed of [sf] writer attempting to produce art without rejecting the pulp vigor that is science fiction's continuing strength. If the cover blurbs of his book are to be believed, *A Funeral for the Eyes of Fire* is just so much pulp trash. But the blurbs are a lie. Bishop is attempting to use undiluted science fiction to present a tragic action of Shakespearean dimension, a disintegrating situation comparable in its mindless destructiveness and pain to our conduct of the Vietnamese war."

The Panshins followed this praise with a plot summary and then a rigorous catalogue of the novel's failures and their likely causes: 1) The book's basic situation was a "set-up"—because, wishing to write tragedy, I had designed this situation to facilitate my goal. 2) The first-person narrator existed "without knowledge, sincerity, history, or personal characteristics." He was a "cypher whose eloquence and special vision are not his own, but Bishop's," for I had chosen the "safety and ease of first-person narrative" when I could have elected to view my protagonist "from the outside."

The Panshins' second point struck a telling chord. I *did* find first-person narration more natural and easier than third, and I feared the work I had done at Betty Ballantine's request to make my protagonist seem less a villain than a dupe had turned him into, yes, a cypher. I began hoping that I could revise the book. After all, Arthur C. Clarke had turned *Against the Fall of Night* into *The City and the Stars*, hadn't he? At least one precedent existed.

Precedent be damned. As an upstart SF writer struggling with Jeri's help to stay out of debt and raise our two children, I could not afford the luxury of revising old work. The only royalty checks I had seen thus far had stemmed from the reprinting of my short fiction in best-of-the-year anthologies, and if I wanted to make a living, I had to do new work at novel length. And so I produced *And Strange at Ecbatan the Trees* (1976), *Stolen Faces* (1977), *A Little Knowledge* (1977), and a series of stories—the Urban Nucleus sequence—that I had planned, almost from the beginning, to yoke together in a noveloid "fix-up," as Bradbury had assembled *The Martian Chronicles*, James Blish *The Seedling Stars*, and Clifford D. Simak *City*. The resultant book was *Catacomb Years* (1979), followed that same year by *Transfigurations*, and suddenly I had come to the end of a fairly sustained run and had no clear idea of what to do next.

My editor at Berkley/Putnam had been David Hartwell. When Buz Wyeth at Harper & Row declined *A Little Knowledge*, David had accepted it; he later stood behind me on the projects that became *Catacomb Years* and *Transfigurations*. But, in 1978, David left Berkley/Putnam to edit the SF program at Pocket Books, and I had to complete *Transfigurations* without his input or help. Finished, I was at an impasse. Hartwell—as he had done before and as he did many times later—came to my rescue. Although *Funeral* still had not recouped its $2,500 advance from Ballantine, David offered me twice that sum to pull an Arthur C. Clarke. Rewrite *A Funeral for the Eyes of Fire* just as you've wanted to, he said. Go on, he urged: Get to it.

I responded with incredulity, gratitude, and hard work.

I'd learned a lot over the past four years, and Pocket Books, at Hartwell's behest, would pay me to put that savvy to work doing something I would have jumped to do for free—if, that is, paying utility bills and keeping milk in the fridge had not loomed as major priorities.

During the late winter and the spring of 1979, I thoroughly revised *Funeral* and turned in the result before the first of June. Gunnar Balduin became Seth Latimer. The planet Glaparcus was now Gla Taus. The Ouemartsee were now the Sh'gaidu. My first-person narration had metamorphosed into third-person. And when my revision hit the bookstores, its Pocket Books paperback boasted two maps, a list of characters, and a division into books meant to reflect the five-act structure of an Elizabethan play. But its cover bore the same painting that had marked the Ballantine edition . . . except that Pocket Books had reversed it, getting it *right* for the first time. Also, the emerald eyes of the Ballantine alien had become yellow chrysoberyls. Again, only a slim chance that Norman Mailer, Gore Vidal, or Susan Sontag would expatiate about my novel in the *New York Review of Books*.

Well, so what? It *was* a reprint, wasn't it?

No. No, it wasn't. It was a top-to-bottom revision of a paperback space opera that had sold, like, seventy-four copies on its initial go-round. Besides, we had dropped that upsetting word *funeral* from the title, amputating it to the brief—albeit, to my mind, derivative and undistinguished—*Eyes of Fire*.

Why had we done that?

It would have been foolish to release the novel under its first title, David Hartwell had said, because a few potential purchasers—*eight*, I thought— would mistakenly assume they had already read our new version. Contrariwise, it would have been unfair to release our novel under a *totally* fresh title—my choice had been *The Isohet*—because a few who put out cash for the Pocket Books version would think they'd paid for an alternate-universe text of the old Ballantine edition. In the first case, David said with off-putting logic, we'd cheat ourselves; in the second, our readers. *Eyes of Fire* as a title, then, was our middle course between the self-destructive white lie of *A Funeral for the Eyes of Fire* and the wrath-provoking deceit of *The Isohet*.

Arrrggggh, thought I.

In 1981, Pocket Books reprinted *Eyes of Fire*, the Authorized Version. This time the novel had a bright blue jacket, and the Szafran cover painting had shrunk to a detail of the alien's face the size of an extra-large postage stamp. (Maybe, by downplaying the creature's nudity, Pocket hoped to attract demographic groups in addition to randy teens with flashlights.) Still, it would be a lie, and more than a white one, to hint that my novel ever threatened to become a best seller. It didn't, and it remained out of print for a good while until a new edition appeared in England in 1989. (I wrote the first version of this afterword in June 1988.) And when Jim Goddard of Kerosina approached me about doing a limited-edition hardcover, we briefly considered calling it *The Isohet*. But I still liked *A Funeral for the Eyes of Fire*, and when, in a letter to Ian Watson, I alluded to our drift toward *The Isohet*, he replied frankly, zapping that title's "unapproachability" and raising another troubling question:

"I, um, don't care for it much, if you don't mind my saying. Also, I think it's a bit unfair on one's fans & buyers to possibly confuse them thus. Okay, well, many people will buy it as a first world hardcover, a collector's item, so they won't worry, but suppose I was an innocent Bishop-fan who heard of a new title and I laid out the bread on getting it from a foreign land to find that I had already read it, I'd be peeved. Don't feel so cold shouldery about ... FUNERAL FOR THE EYES OF FIRE. It was pretty good." He ended self-effacingly, "However, however, not my business; shut up, Watson."

But it was his business, for he and I are comrades, even if an intervening ocean has kept us from meeting face to face. Also, Ian's candor made me realize that the only suitable title for a new edition of my first novel—or, rather, of this re-revised version of the first one, which became the seventh—is, well, *A Funeral for the Eyes of Fire.* After all, from my youthful love of Bradbury to my mature appreciation of Ballard, bravura titles and bardic language played a big role in hooking me into SF writing, and it would have been a sad *self-*deceit to rebaptize the novel that solidified my early commitment to sf with a title as cold and lacking in referents as *The Isohet.*

So I didn't.

As for the heart of this novel, the meaning of the story that grew grudgingly from a single haunting visual image, I have nothing else to say. The novel—in what I now consider its most likely final text—requires each reader to reach a private accommodation with its characters, events, and meanings. May your journey to that end prove gratifying.

— Revised December 2014
Pine Mountain, Georgia

ABOUT THE AUTHOR

Michael Bishop is the author of the Nebula Award-winning novel *No Enemy But Time*, the Mythopoeic Fantasy Award-winning novel *Unicorn Mountain*, the Shirley Jackson Award-winning short story, "The Pile" (based on notes left behind on his late son Jamie's computer), and several other novels and story collections, including *The Door Gunner and Other Perilous Flights of Fancy: A Retrospective*, edited by Michael H. Hutchins. He also writes poetry and criticism, and has edited the acclaimed anthologies *Light Years and Dark*, three volumes of the annual Nebula Awards collections, and, more recently, *A Cross of Centuries: Twenty-Five Imaginative Tales About the Christ*, and, with Steven Utley, *Passing for Human*. Soon to appear is his novel for young persons, *Joel-Brock the Brave and the Valorous Smalls*, dedicated to the Bishops' exemplary grandchildren, Annabel English Loftin and Joel Bridger Loftin. Michael Bishop lives in Pine Mountain, Georgia, with his wife, Jeri, a retired elementary school counselor who is now an avid gardener and yoga practitioner. They share their house, Bluestone Homestead, with far too many books.

REDISCOVER
Michael Bishop

What if a living specimen of Homo habilis appeared in the pecan grove of a female artist living in Georgia? What if she reached out to her ex-husband, a restaurant owner in the small town of Beulah Fork, to help her establish the creature's precise identity? A rare combination of science fiction, noir mystery, and comedy of manners, *Ancient of Days* will involve and challenge you as have few other novels.

In 1943, at the height of World War II, the Highbridge Hellbenders of the the class-C Chattahoochee Valley League deep in Georgia acquire a 17-year-old shortstop from Oklahoma named Danny Boles. Jumbo Hank Clerval, a mysterious giant, and the mute Danny Boles strike up an improbable friendship that culminates in a host of haunting discoveries in both the simmering South and the wind-swept Aleutian Islands. Hailed by critics as a contender for the Great American Novel laurel, *Brittle Innings* evokes a bygone era of worldwide conflict and homeland unity.

from **Michael Bishop**
Nebula Award-winning author

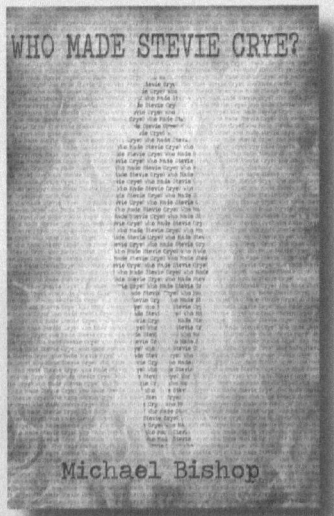

WHO MADE STEVIE CRYE?

Michael Bishop

While skinny-dipping in a pool polluted with radioactive waste, Xavier Thaxton, arts editor at a major Southern daily, is afflicted with superpowers all his own and becomes that which he most scorns. A radiation-induced ailment, the Philistine Syndrome, forces him to assume the persona of comic-book hero Count Geiger to allay its career- and indeed life-threatening symptoms. This novel of intellectual heft and self-spoofing kitsch is a take on superheroes like no other: a rollicking foray into high and low culture that mines the vicissitudes and tragedies of everyday life for serious belly laughs and bona fide heartbreak.

Mary Stevenson Crye, a recently widowed young mother known as Stevie depends on a balky PDE Exceleriter for her free-lance writing. Then the PDE Exceleriter goes noisily on the fritz, and so many other things begin to go wrong as a result, including her machine's insistence on typing segments of her everyday life as she either lives or hallucinates it. A novel of the American south, an alternately tender and scathing parody of twentieth-century horror novels, and an involving account of one woman's battle to maintain her sanity.

COUNT GEIGER'S BLUES

MICHAEL BISHOP

from **Fairwood Press**
& Kudzu Planet Productions

www.fairwoodpress.com

OTHER TITLES FROM FAIRWOOD PRESS

Cracking the Sky
by Brenda Cooper
trade paper: $17.99
ISBN: 978-1-933846-50-7

The Best of Electric Velocipede
edited by John Klima
trade paper: $17.99
ISBN: 978-1-933846-47-7

Are You There
by Jack Skillingstead
trade paper: $17.99
ISBN: 978-1-933846-45-3

The Court of Lies
by Mark Teppo
trade paper: $17.99
ISBN: 978-1-933846-44-6

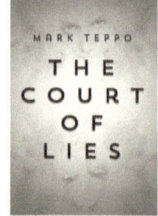

If Angels Fight
by Richard Bowes
trade paper: $16.99
ISBN: 978-1-933846-40-8

Bravado's House of Blues
by J.A. Pitts
trade paper: $15.99
ISBN: 978-1-933846-41-5

A Cup of Normal
by Devon Monk
trade paper: $16.99
ISBN: 978-0-9820730-9-4

The Terrorists of Irustan
by Louise Marley
trade paper: $16.99

Pandora's Gun
by James Van Pelt
trade paper: 14.99
ISBN: 978-1-933846-53-8

Unpossible
by Daryl Gregory
trade paper: $16.99
ISBN: 978-1-933846-30-9

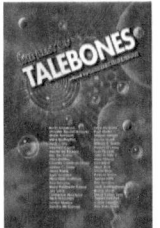

Dragon Virus
by Laura Anne Gilman
limited hardcover: $25
ISBN: 978-1-933846-25-5

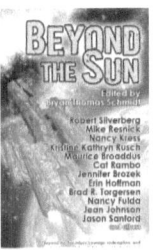

Beyond the Sun
edited by Bryan Thomas Schmidt
trade paper: $17.99
ISBN: 978-1-933846-38-5

The Best of Talebones
edited by Patrick Swenson
trade paper: $18.99
ISBN: 978-1-933846-24-8

*Flying in the Heart of the
Lafayette Escadrille*
by James Van Pelt
trade paper: $17.99
ISBN: 978-1-933846-34-7

Branegate
by James C. Glass
trade paper $17.99
ISBN: 978-1-933846-33-0

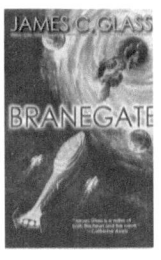

Permeable Borders
by Nina Kiriki Hoffman
trade paper: $16.99
ISBN: 978-1-933846-32-3
ISBN: 978-1-933846-37-8

www.fairwoodpress.com
21528 104th Street Court East;
Bonney Lake, WA   98391

www.ingramcontent.com/pod-product-compliance
Lightning Source LLC
Chambersburg PA
CBHW031212260626
47169CB00007B/2035